Dear Reader,

I'm delighted to welcome you to a very special Bestselling Author Collection for 2024! In celebration of Harlequin's 75 years in publishing, this collection features fan-favorite stories from some of our readers' most cherished authors. Each book also includes a free full-length story by an exciting writer from one of our current programs.

Our company has grown and changed since its inception 75 years ago. Today, Harlequin publishes more than 100 titles a month in 30 countries and 15 languages, with stories for a diverse readership across a range of genres and formats, including hardcover, trade paperback, mass-market paperback, ebook and audiobook.

But our commitment to you, our romance reader, remains the same: in every Harlequin romance, a guaranteed happily-ever-after!

Thank you for coming on this journey with us. And happy reading as we embark on the next 75 years of bringing joy to readers around the world!

Dianne Moggy

Vice-President, Editorial

Harlequin

New York Times and *USA TODAY* bestselling author **B.J. Daniels** lives in Montana with her husband, Parker, and three springer spaniels. When not writing, she quilts, boats and plays tennis. Contact her at bjdaniels.com, or on Facebook or Twitter @bjdanielsauthor.

Nicole Helm grew up with her nose in a book and the dream of one day becoming a writer. Luckily, after a few failed career choices, she gets to follow that dream—writing down-to-earth contemporary romance and romantic suspense. From farmers to cowboys, Midwest to the West, Nicole writes stories about people finding themselves and finding love in the process. She lives in Missouri with her husband and two sons and dreams of someday owning a barn.

A TEXAS BRAND OF JUSTICE

NEW YORK TIMES BESTSELLING AUTHOR
B.J. DANIELS

Previously published as *The Agent's Secret Child*

Harlequin

BESTSELLING AUTHOR COLLECTION

 **Harlequin®**
BESTSELLING
AUTHOR
COLLECTION

Recycling programs
for this product may
not exist in your area.

ISBN-13: 978-1-335-00884-8

A Texas Brand of Justice
First published as The Agent's Secret Child in 2000.
This edition published in 2024.
Copyright © 2000 by Harlequin Enterprises ULC

Stone Cold Undercover Agent
First published in 2017.
This edition published in 2024.
Copyright © 2017 by Nicole Helm

 Harlequin Enterprises ULC
22 Adelaide St. West, 41st Floor
Toronto, Ontario M5H 4E3, Canada
www.Harlequin.com

Printed in U.S.A.

CONTENTS

A TEXAS BRAND OF JUSTICE   7
B.J. Daniels

STONE COLD UNDERCOVER AGENT   217
Nicole Helm

A TEXAS BRAND
OF JUSTICE

B.J. Daniels

This book is dedicated to my aunt,
Lenore Collmorgen Bateman (1912–1999).
I never think of Texas without thinking of her.
Some of my fondest memories are of her making
pancakes over a Coleman, joking and laughing.
She was a great cook and one of the strong women
in my life I have tried to emulate.

Prologue

She smelled smoke. Just moments before, she'd been helping her daughter Elena look for her lost doll. Now she stopped, alarmed. Her hand went to the small scars at her temple, memory of the fire and the pain sending panic racing through her. Why would Julio build a fire on such a hot spring day in Mexico?

Then she heard the raised voices below her in the kitchen and the heavy, unfamiliar tread on the stairs.

The feeling came in a rush. Strong, sure, knowing, like only one she'd ever felt before. And yet she trusted this one. Whoever was coming up the stairs intended to harm her and her five-year-old daughter.

Fear paralyzed her as she realized she and Elena were trapped on the second floor. The only way out was the stairs the man now climbed. Her husband had barred the windows and he had the only key. She'd often wondered: what if there was another house fire and Julio wasn't home?

But Julio always left someone to watch over them when he was gone.

The lumbering footsteps reached the second-floor landing. She shot her daughter a silent warning as she scooped the child into her arms and hurried to the attic stairs at the back of the house.

Her heart lunged in her chest as she moved through the hot cluttered attic, frantically searching for a place to hide. She found the only space large enough for the two of them in a dark corner behind an old bureau where the roof pitched out over the eave and a pile of old lumber formed a small partition.

She could hear the men ransacking the house, their voices raised in angry Spanish she couldn't make out.

When she heard the plodding tread on the attic stairs, she'd motioned to Elena to keep silent but the child's wide-eyed look told her that she understood their danger, just as she always had.

The man was in the attic now, moving slowly, carefully. The other men called to him, their feet thumping on the steps as they hurried up to him.

"Where is Isabella and the child?" one of the men demanded in Spanish. He had a quick, nervous voice like the brightly colored hummingbirds flickering in the bougainvillea outside the window.

"I don't know," a deeper voice answered. "Montenegro must have gotten them out before we arrived."

"Damn Julio. Find the money. Tear the place apart if you have to, but find the money."

"What if he gave it to her?" one of them asked, only to be answered with a curse.

As the men searched the house, she hugged her daughter tightly, determined to protect her child as she had since Elena's birth, feeling as defenseless and trapped as she always had.

The men eventually searched the attic, including the bureau drawers, while she'd held her breath and prayed they wouldn't find her and Elena crouched in the darkness and dust.

She took hope when she sensed the men were losing momentum, their movements less frantic but no less angry and frustrated.

"He wouldn't hide it in the house," one of the men snapped in Spanish. "He was too smart for that. So why are we wasting our time? He gave it to the woman and kid to hide somewhere for him."

"Shut up!" the nervous one growled. "Keep searching." But he said it as he tromped back down the stairs and soon the others followed.

She waited until she thought they'd left before she crept from the hiding place and stole with her daughter down one floor to her bedroom. With a chilling calm that frightened her more than the men had, she packed a bag with a few belongings.

She started at a noise behind her. Click, click, click. Someone was still downstairs, she thought, glancing at the phone beside her bed. It was making that faint clicking sound as the extension downstairs was being dialed.

With that same cold calm, she carefully picked up the extension. Two voices. One coarse as sand. The other nervous and quick and now familiar.

"I want my money, Ramon," the coarse one snarled.

"The woman must have taken it and the child with her."

"Find them. Make them tell you where Julio hid the money he stole from me. Then bring them and the money to me. *Comprende?*"

"*Si,* Señor Calderone, I understand." The man named Ramon promised on his dead mother's grave.

She hung up the phone and finished packing. Since the day she'd awakened in the hospital after the house fire to find Julio beside her bed, she'd suspected her husband was involved with drug lord Tomaso Calderone.

She'd awakened in pain. From her injuries and the surgeries. From the confusion in her mind.

But it was awakening to find herself pregnant that made her close her eyes and ears to Julio's dealings, thinking only of her baby, her sweet precious daughter. Julio had never shown any interest in either of them, leaving her alone to cook and clean and raise the child he wanted nothing to do with.

Once she got some of her strength back physically and Elena was old enough to travel, she'd tried to leave her marriage. But Julio had caught her and brought her back, warning her that she and Elena could never leave. They were his and he would rather see them both dead than ever let them go.

She had looked into Julio Montenegro's eyes and known then that he felt nothing for her or Elena, something she had long suspected. She and Elena were his prisoners for reasons she could not understand. But for Elena's sake, she'd never tried to escape again.

Instead, without realizing it, she'd been biding her time, waiting. She hadn't known what she'd been waiting for. Until today.

With the bag in one hand and Elena's small hand in the other, she crept down the stairs as soon as the lower floor grew silent again.

Julio lay sprawled on the white tile floor of the kitchen in a pool of blood, his eyes blank, his body lifeless.

Shielding Elena from the sight, Isabella moved to him, her gaze not on his face, but on the knife sticking out of his chest.

With a cold, calculating detachment she hadn't known she possessed, she grasped the knife handle in both hands, and pulled it from her husband's chest. Then she calmly wiped the knife clean on his shirt and slipped the slim blade into her bag.

She looked down at his face for a moment, wishing she felt something. Then, like a sleepwalker, she knelt and searched his pockets, lifting him enough to remove the small wad of pesos his business associates had obviously passed up as too trivial to bother with from his hip pocket.

It wasn't much money. Not nearly enough to get her and Elena out of Mexico, let alone to some place safe in the States. But was there any place safe from Calderone and his men?

She started to rise, then noticed that when she'd lifted Julio, she'd also lifted the edge of the rug under him. The corner of a manila envelope was now visible beneath the rug.

With that same chilling calm, she raised Julio enough

to free the parcel from beneath him and the rug. She stared at the large envelope, then the fire he'd built in the stove. Had he been planning to burn the envelope? Why else would he have built a fire in a room already unbearably hot?

She looked again at the envelope. She knew it didn't contain the missing money. It was too lightweight, too thin, to hold the amount of money she feared Julio had stolen. But maybe it had information about where he'd hidden the drug money. Why else would he try to burn it just before he'd been killed, if not to protect his ill-gotten gains?

She grasped the hope. If she had the location of the stolen money, then maybe she could buy her freedom and her daughter's from Calderone.

As she lifted the parcel to look inside, something fell out and tinkled to the tiles. The tiny object rolled to a stop and as she stopped to pick it up, she saw that it was a silver heart-shaped locket. It had no chain and the silver was tarnished and scratched, making it hard at first to read the name engraved on it.

Abby.

She stared at the locket. Should that name mean something to her? Was it one of her husband's mistresses? One of her lost relatives?

She pried the two halves open and stared down at a man's photo inside, her fingers trembling. Not Julio. Not any man she'd ever seen before. She felt Elena beside her and tried to shield her from the body on the floor, but saw that her daughter was more interested in the locket—and the photo inside.

"Papacito," Elena whispered, eyes wide as she stared down at the photo of the stranger.

"No, my little bright angel," she said softly, sick inside. For the first time, she let herself hate Julio. She'd never wanted him as a husband, but he could have been a father to Elena, who desperately needed a father's love.

Instead their daughter preferred to believe a total stranger in a small black-and-white photograph was her father rather than Julio Montenegro, the unfeeling man who'd given her life.

A car backfired outside, making her jump. Hurriedly, she shoved the locket back into the envelope with the official-looking papers. Like the weapon she'd taken from Julio's chest, she put the parcel into her bag. As she turned to leave, she saw her daughter's lost rag doll and, wondering absently how it had gotten there, she scooped it up from the floor, took her daughter's small hand, and ran.

Jake Cantrell stood back, sipping his beer, watching the wedding reception as if through binoculars. The Smoking Barrel Ranch had taken on a sound and feel and level of gaiety that seemed surreal, as if it had an alternate personality—one he didn't recognize.

He hadn't been brought here for this and right now, he just wanted it to be over. Not that he wasn't happy for Brady and Grace...now Catherine. He was. He just didn't believe in happy-ever-after anymore. Mostly, he told himself, he was just anxious to get back to work.

But that was a lie. All day he'd felt an uneasiness he couldn't shake. Like when he felt someone following him or waiting for him in a dark alley. The feeling hummed like a low-pitched vibration inside him, making him anxious and irritable and wary.

Mitchell had called a meeting later tonight. Jake wanted a new assignment, something that would take him away from the ranch for a while. Away from everything. Work kept him sane—relatively sane. It was also the only thing that kept him from dwelling on the past.

He felt eyes on him. Not just watching him. But staring at him. He shifted his gaze and saw Penny Archer across the room, standing with her back to the library door she'd just closed behind her. Earlier he'd noticed when she'd gotten a beep on the priority line. Noticing was something he was good at. That and finding people who didn't want to be found.

It had to have been a business call. That was the only kind that would make the administrative assistant leave the wedding reception and the boisterous crowd, and disappear into the library. From there the hidden elevator would take her to the basement and the secret office of Texas Confidential. The true heart of the ranch. Its aberrant split personality.

Now he met Penny's intent gaze and felt a jolt. She was as tough as they came. It took a lot to upset her. And right now, she was visibly upset.

He made his way across the room, knowing it had been the priority call that had upset her. Just as he knew the call had to do with him.

"What?" he asked, never one to mince words.

She motioned for him to follow and led him away from the crowd and the noise of the party, outside to a corner of the porch. In the distance, mesquite stood dark-limbed against the horizon, shadows piled cool and deep beneath them. The land beyond was as vast and open as the night sky.

"I just got the strangest call," she said the moment they were alone and out of earshot of the others. Her gaze came up to his. "It was from a little girl. A child. No more than three or four. She spoke Spanish and—" Penny's voice broke. "She was crying. She sounded really scared, Jake."

"What did she want?" he asked, wondering what this could possibly have to do with him.

"She said her mommy was in trouble and needed help. She asked for her daddy." Penny seemed to hesitate. "Her daddy Jake."

He felt a chill even as a warm Texas wind whispered through the May night. He shook his head. A mistake. A wrong number. An odd coincidence.

"Jake, she called through your old FBI contact number."

He stared, his heart now a sledgehammer. Only three people in the world had ever known that number and two of them were dead. "What did she say? Exactly." Not that he had to add that. Penny could remember conversations verbatim. That was part of her charm—and the reason the thirty-four-year-old was Mitchell Forbes's right-hand woman.

She repeated the Spanish words. "Then I heard a woman's voice in the background. The woman cried, *'No, chica suena.'* Then the line went dead. Of course, I put a trace on the call immediately. It came from a small motel on the other side of the Mexican border."

Chica suena. The light in the trees seemed to shift. Lighter to darker. The porch under him no longer felt solid, became a swampland of deadly potholes. His world, the fragile one he'd made for himself here, spun on the edge of out of control. Just as it had six years ago. Before Mitchell had saved him.

From far off, he heard Penny ask, "Jake, are you all right? Jake?"

Chica suena. He hadn't heard the unusual Spanish endearment in years. Six long years. Nor was it one he'd ever heard before he'd met Abby Diaz. It was something her grandmother had called her. It meant "my little dream girl." And it suited Abby.

Abby Diaz had been everything to him. The woman he was to marry. His FBI partner. His most trusted friend.

His *chica suena.*

He bounded off the porch, his long legs carrying him away from the party and the faint sound of music and laughter. Away from the pain and anger and memory of the death of his dreams of love ever after. Away. But he knew, gut-deep, that running wouldn't help. It never had.

Someone had found out about him and Abby. Had found out their most intimate secret. Daddy Jake. *Chica suena.* Someone wanted him running scared again. And they'd succeeded.

Chapter 1

Isabella Montenegro lay on the bed, her body drenched in sweat, fear choking off her breath. Dark shadows shifted in the shabby motel room, one image refusing to fade—the image of her husband, Julio, sprawled in a pool of blood on the kitchen floor. But it was the knife sticking out of his chest, rather than his blank eyes, that she saw so clearly.

She shuddered, watching herself pull the knife from his chest. She watched it in her mind's eye, watched the unfeeling woman wipe the blade clean on his shirt, then slip the weapon into her bag.

She closed her eyes. Who was that unfeeling woman? Or had she always been this cold, this uncaring?

Yes, she thought, unable to recall the other feeling, the only other strong, sure, knowing one she'd ever had, one she hadn't trusted. A feeling that she'd known earth-shaking passion.

A lie, she thought. She'd never known passion. Not with Julio, who'd never been a husband to her. Not with anyone. She couldn't even call up the feeling.

She closed her eyes to the horrible image of her moving his body to retrieve the envelope. But the image danced in the darkness behind her eyelids, taunting her. What kind of woman was she?

She opened her eyes and snapped on the lamp beside her bed, chasing the shadows from the cramped room and illuminating the tiny body sleeping next to her.

Elena was curled in a fetal position, her small, warm back against her mother's side, her dark hair hiding her face.

She had done it for Elena, she told herself now as she sat up, careful not to wake her daughter. Everything she'd done, she'd done for Elena.

Only now they were running for their lives. Scared, with no one to turn to and nowhere to go. Her sleepless hours filled her with nightmares. Not of the men chasing her and her daughter, but of the memory of the emotionless woman who'd pulled the knife from her husband's chest, then calmly picked up her daughter's doll and left without looking back.

What had she planned to do with the knife? Surely not use it as a weapon. What had she been thinking? And where did she think the two of them would go? What would they do?

She glanced at the envelope beside her on the nightstand, still upset and confused by what she'd found inside it. Nothing about the drug money Julio had stolen from Calderone. Nothing to help her.

She picked up the envelope. It still had some of Julio's blood dried into one corner. She felt nothing. Not a twinge at the sight of the blood, nor anything for the cold distant man who'd been her husband. What kind of woman was she? she wondered again. How could she feel nothing for the man who'd given her Elena?

She opened the envelope as if the contents might explode, slipping the papers out onto her lap, quietly, cautiously, not wanting to wake Elena, still stunned by what she'd found.

A passport and Texas driver's license tumbled out, the accusing eyes staring up at her from the photo on the license. The woman's name, it read, was Abby Diaz. Abby, like the name engraved on the silver heart-shaped locket. Abby Diaz, an FBI agent.

But what made Isabella's fingers tremble and her heart pound was that the woman looked like her.

She reached up to touch her face, running her fingers along the tiny scars left from her surgery. What had she looked like before the fire? She couldn't remember. Worse, why did she suspect she'd been made to look like this Abby Diaz?

She didn't want to think about that. Nor about the other papers she'd found in the envelope. She looked down at her daughter. Elena still had the locket clutched in her fist.

The sight tugged at Isabella's heart and concerned her more than she wanted to admit. Her daughter had cried until she'd been given the locket to hold. The battered heart-shaped silver locket with a stranger's face inside it.

Then Isabella had awakened to find Elena on the phone and the envelope's contents on the floor beside her, the silver locket open and empty, the photo in Elena's small hand.

"Why did you call the number inside the envelope?" Isabella had demanded after she'd hurriedly hung up.

She didn't ask how the little girl had realized it was a phone number or how she'd known to make a call. Elena had taught herself to read at three. She was smart. Too smart, Julio used to say. Gifted. Precocious. Frightening even to Isabella sometimes. Her grandmother would have called Elena an Old Soul.

Elena had shown her the phone number and explained it was like ones Julio had called in the States. Isabella wondered who Julio had called.

"But why would you call *this* number?" she'd asked, growing more afraid for her daughter.

Elena had handed her the tiny photograph of the stranger from the locket. On the back was printed: "Love, Jake." When Elena had found the name Jake Cantrell in the envelope with a telephone number, she'd called it.

"Daddy will help us," Elena had declared stubbornly.

"*Julio* was your father," she'd said, "and he cannot help us."

Elena's lower lip had begun to tremble. Tears welled in the child's eyes. "Daddy Jake will help us, though." She'd cried inconsolably until Isabella had put the picture back into the locket and given it to the child to hold again.

What disturbed her most was that Elena was convinced Jake Cantrell was her father. Why was that? Had Julio planted this seed? The same way the hospital surgeons might have been told to make Isabella look like another woman? A former FBI agent named Abby Diaz?

She felt sick now as she watched her daughter sleep. Elena expected some stranger to come and save them from Calderone's men.

But what the child didn't know was that if Jake Cantrell found them, it wouldn't be to save them. In the envelope, Isabella had found evidence that former FBI agent Jake Cantrell had set up his partner Abby Diaz to die in a drug raid six years ago. What scared her was that she looked enough like this woman that he might think she *was* Abby Diaz.

Isabella now feared that Elena's call for help had only given away their location and set an even more dangerous man after them.

Chapter 2

Everything from the wedding reception had been cleared away by the time Jake returned. The ranch house felt cool and dark and blessedly normal again. He regretted that he hadn't got to tell Brady goodbye before he took off on his honeymoon, but he knew Brady would understand.

He could hear Rosa and Slim in the kitchen, Slim trying to flatter the short, round, good-natured cook, but Rosa resisting the crusty old ranch hand's charm to the clatter of dishes and Mexican music on the radio.

He breathed it in, wishing he could get back some of the tranquillity he'd found over the last five years here at the Smoking Barrel. Usually riding his horse Majesty under the vast Texas sky brought him some peace. But not tonight.

He couldn't get the call off his mind. Still, he felt a

little better after his long ride and regretted snapping at Penny earlier when she'd followed him down to the stables. She'd only been concerned, but he'd wanted to be alone. He'd felt like a powder keg ready to blow and needed to feel the wind in his face and a good fast horse beneath him.

Hat in hand, he now tapped lightly at Penny's door, hoping to catch her before she went down to the meeting.

She opened her door and looked surprised, the air around her sweet with the scent of perfume, her hair pulled up into a style he'd never seen on her before and a hairbrush in her hand. No, not surprised. Embarrassed to be caught primping. He wondered if the carefully applied makeup and new hairdo had something to do with the date he'd heard discussed over coffee this morning in the kitchen.

"These are for you," he said, drawing the fistful of wildflowers he'd picked from behind his back. They seemed too small a gesture, but her eyes lit at the sight of them and her face softened as she gazed up at him.

"You didn't have to do this," she said, too much understanding in her voice.

The last thing he wanted was sympathy right now. He wanted even less to discuss the call.

"I'm just sorry I barked at you in the stables before," he said, turning away quickly.

Before she could reply, he walked away. Downstairs, he took the hidden elevator to the basement, to find the three men already waiting for him. He realized Penny wouldn't be joining them. Cody and Rafe were discussing the recent cattle-rustling and new evidence that someone had been camping on the ranch. For once, the young and cocky Rafael Alvarez wasn't clowning around, but then Penny wasn't here. Half Spanish, half Irish, Rafe had a way with women and he loved to tease Penny mercilessly.

Cody Gannon, a former rodeo bronc rider and the youngest of the bunch, was insisting what should be done about the rustling. Mitchell Forbes seemed only to listen at the head of the table.

Wondering why a meeting had been called, especially without Penny present, Jake took his place, his gaze on Mitchell. The older man didn't look sixty-five, not even with his head of white hair. The ex-Texas Ranger and Vietnam vet owned the Smoking Barrel, a pretty impressive spread, even by Texas standards. On the surface, the widower seemed exactly what he was, a wealthy rancher.

Few people knew that the ranch was headquarters for Mitchell's ragtag group of misfits known as the Texas Confidentials—an offshoot of the Federal Department of Public Safety. The confidentials were secret agents who handled cases that required a bit more sensitivity and stealth. When they weren't on assignment, they worked the huge ranch just like the cowboys they were.

Jake knew he'd been handpicked for the job by Mitchell. He'd just never understood why. But he was grateful. Not only had Mitchell given him something to do that mattered, he'd given him a home and a family.

"I think that covers it." Mitchell's deep voice pulled Jake back from his thoughts. "We'll step up security and see what happens."

Jake realized he hadn't been paying attention. Cody and Rafe got to their feet to leave, arguing over whose turn it was to ride lookout tonight. Jake started to rise, but Mitchell motioned for him to wait.

Once they were alone, Mitchell studied the tip of his cigar, taking his time to light it with an elaborate silver lighter, then he turned the lighter in his hand. Over and over, as if he didn't know quite how to begin. That wasn't like Mitchell.

Nor was he supposed to be smoking. Maddie would throw a fit if she knew. Maddie Wells, a neighboring rancher, was in love with Mitchell. His health was one of the things they squabbled about. That, and why Mitchell hadn't gotten around to popping the question.

For Mitchell to be smoking again— Jake watched him through a haze of cigar smoke, his earlier anxiety growing with each passing moment.

"Penny told me about the call from the little girl," Mitchell said at last.

Jake felt a wave of annoyance. Nothing that happened on the ranch escaped Mitchell's attention. Penny saw to that. "It was just a prank call. Penny shouldn't have worried you with it."

Mitchell studied him, the lighter suddenly motionless. "Jake, I got a call from Frank Jordan, over at the FBI. I believe you worked for him when you were with the Bureau."

Jake nodded warily.

"Julio Montenegro, a high-ranking distributor for Tomaso Calderone, has been killed. His wife and child are missing, along with a very large amount of Calderone's drug money. The FBI wants us to find the woman and child before Calderone's men do. Frank asked for you."

Jake stared at his boss in disbelief. For the last six

years he'd wanted nothing more than to nail Calderone, but it had been Mitchell who refused to give him any assignment that had anything to do with the drug lord.

"Excuse me?" he said now, getting to his feet. "You're giving *me* this assignment? After all the years of telling me to forget what happened, to forget Calderone?"

Mitchell started to speak but Jake cut him off.

"Now, just because Frank asks, you're going to let me go after the wife and child of Calderone's top Mexican distributor? Would you like to tell me just what the hell is *really* going on?" he demanded, angry and not sure exactly why. Maybe because he didn't want to dig up the past again. Not now. Not when he'd finally accepted what Mitchell had for years been trying to convince him of. Getting Calderone wouldn't bring Abby back.

"Sit down, Jake," Mitchell said quietly. He puffed on his cigar for a moment. Tension stretched as taut as a hangman's noose between them.

Slowly, Jake sat back down. "Dammit, Mitchell, why now?"

"Jake, I've always told you that personal vendettas have no place in this business. That hasn't changed."

"If you think I can go into this and not be part of taking down Calderone—"

"This isn't *about* Calderone," Mitchell snapped. "This woman, Julio Montenegro's wife… Frank has reason to believe she might be Abby Diaz."

The words dropped into the quiet room like boulders. He was too stunned to breathe, let alone speak.

"Abby is dead," he whispered at last. He ought to know. He'd been one of the six-member FBI team that had gone into that building on a routine investigation, not knowing Tomaso Calderone was waiting for them. They'd walked into the trap and Abby had died in the explosion and fire that followed, along with two other FBI agents.

Mitchell took a puff on his cigar and continued as if Jake hadn't spoken. "Julio Montenegro recently contacted the FBI with a deal. He said he had proof that Abby Diaz was alive. He had rescued her from the fire that night. She was burned, but survived."

"No." Jake shook his head adamantly. "I saw her body after the fire."

"You saw *a* body. What if the charred remains found after the explosion weren't Abby's? Julio claims the body was that of woman who worked for him. Three bodies were found in that fire. We just assumed the female was Abby."

"Abby, Buster McNorton and Dell Harper," Jake said, more to himself, than Mitchell. He could never forget.

"As we understand it, Julio kept Abby under wraps, hiding her as his wife in the small town where he lived in Mexico, until he was ready to make a deal. That deal was a trade. The FBI would help him get citizenship and into a witness-protection program in the States in exchange for FBI agent Abby Diaz."

"Why would he keep her *six* years?"

"Maybe he needed time to build himself a nest egg," Mitchell suggested. "He must have gotten greedy, though, and finally got caught."

He shook his head. "This woman can't possibly be Abby."

"Jake, if there is any chance that Abby might still be alive, you owe it to yourself to find out. Frank has already ordered that the body in Abby Diaz's grave be exhumed for identification."

He swore, pulling off his Stetson to rake a hand through this hair. "Dammit, Mitchell, I don't want this. I don't want Abby dug up. I don't want—" Cold fury filled him. "I don't want to relive Abby's death all over again. Nor do I want to do Frank's bidding for him. This feels like a trap. Or something Frank dreamed up to advance his career."

Mitchell puffed on the cigar for a moment, studying him. "They knew about the two of you."

Jake's gaze jerked up. He didn't have to ask who knew.

"They've always known."

Jake wanted to laugh. He and Abby had thought they were being so discreet. Hell, they were FBI agents, trained in deception. But it seemed they hadn't fooled anyone. Especially the people they worked for.

"Because of the affair you had—"

"It was a hell of a lot more than an affair," Jake snapped.

"—Frank wants you on this case. As her former FBI partner and lover, you are the one person who'll know whether or not this Isabella Montenegro is Abby Diaz or an imposter."

"Of course she's an imposter. I can tell you that without even seeing her."

"Jake, we have confirmation that Isabella Montenegro *was* burned in a fire and had to have plastic surgery. She's the right size, about the right age—"

"Come on, Mitchell. You aren't buying into this, are

you? Someone wants me to think Abby is alive, that this is my…kid."

He'd actually believed that no one had known about Abby's pregnancy. But obviously someone had. And now they were trying to use it against him.

"It explains the fake phone call from the little girl. Don't you think if Abby were alive she'd have gotten in touch with me?"

His boss worried the lighter in his hand like a stone for a moment before he spoke. "Abby might have defected."

"Bull," Jake growled, getting to his feet again. "You didn't know her. You don't know what we had together. We were getting married. Dammit, Mitchell, we were going to have a baby." The words were out before he could call them back.

Mitchell nodded and frowned. "That's what I was afraid of. Jake, this child with Isabella Montenegro, she's about five years old and—"

"No, dammit. If Abby *was* alive, she'd have contacted me," he said adamantly. "Especially if she'd given birth to our baby."

"She might have reason to believe you betrayed her," Mitchell said, the words seeming to come hard to him.

Jake looked at the man, speechless.

"Abby might believe you set her up to die in that explosion," his boss said. "She might have been given some sort of evidence—"

"No!" Jake cried. "She'd have never taken the word of a man like Calderone."

"What if the evidence came from the FBI?"

Jake stared at him. "What are you saying?"

"Part of the deal with Julio was proof not only that Isabella Montenegro was Abby, but that she'd been the target the night of the explosion. Julio said he knew who'd tried to kill her and why. According to Frank, that evidence points to you."

"You don't really believe—"

"It doesn't matter what I believe," Mitchell said, cutting him off. "The point is, this woman might believe that you're a killer. A man who set up his partner and lover six years ago to die. That could explain why, if she *is* Abby, she didn't contact you."

"That's crazy," Jake said. Abby was the target? It didn't make any sense. Two other agents had died that night as well and another was injured. "Why? Why would someone want to kill Abby?"

Mitchell squinted through the cigar smoke. "Maybe only Abby knows that."

He shook his head. "Wait a minute. If Frank really believes that I was the one who set up Abby, then why would he want me on this case?"

"Frank doesn't believe you had anything to do with Abby Diaz's death. Or alleged death. You're the obvious person to send. Like I said, you, of all people, will know if this woman is Abby."

Mitchell slid a sheet of paper across the desk.

Jake watched him, his mouth suddenly dry.

"This is the faxed photo Julio sent Frank," Mitchell said. "It's the Montenegro child and her mother. I think you'd better take a look, Jake."

The black and white copy of the photograph was blurry, the resolution poor and the paper even worse.

But Jake felt his heart lurch, his breath catching in his throat, the pain sharp and bright, blinding.

He stared down at the woman. Frank was right. Isabella Montenegro looked enough like Abby Diaz to make him ache. But that was the point, wasn't it? To make him hurt. To make him doubt himself. To make him desperately want to believe Abby was alive.

But *was* it possible? Could this woman really be Abby? Or an imposter, designed to draw him back into something he'd spent six years trying to forget?

He shifted his gaze from the woman to the child in the photograph. His pulse pounded just at the sight of the little girl. He felt his eyes burn, his heart slamming against his ribs. Oh, God, could it be possible? He couldn't take his eyes from the child's face. There was something about her. So small, so sweet. And so scared. He could see it in her expression.

He crumpled the sheet of paper in his fist and closed his eyes, his throat tight, the pain unbearable. He told himself she wasn't his daughter, but she was someone's, and damned if he'd let whoever was behind this use an innocent child to get to him.

But he knew he was lying to himself. As much as he fought it, he wanted it to be true. He wanted Abby to be alive. He wanted their lost child more than he wanted life itself. And knew he wouldn't rest until he found out the truth. He just feared he was walking into a trap, one that even if it didn't get him killed, would destroy him.

"I'll understand if you don't want this case," Mitchell said softly.

Jake did laugh then. He opened his eyes and looked across the table at his boss, his friend, the man who'd saved him from his obsession to destroy Calderone, from his need to destroy himself. "You know damned well you couldn't keep me off this case now."

"Then you think there is a chance this woman is Abby?"

Jake shook his head, his words belying the battle going on inside him. "Abby is dead. The woman is an imposter. So is the kid. And I'll prove it."

Mitchell let out a long sigh. "I thought you might feel that way." He regarded Jake for a long moment, his gaze sad, worried. Then he continued as if this was just another assignment. "One of Calderone's henchmen is already on her trail. Ramon Hernandez."

Jake knew of Ramon. A crazy, ferret-faced man with a thirst for blood. Calderone's kind of man.

"Frank is hoping you can find her before Ramon does and keep her alive until you can turn her over to the FBI back in the States," Mitchell said.

Jake only nodded. He wasn't worried about finding Isabella Montenegro. After all, finding people was his specialty.

What worried him was what he'd do *when* he found her. He'd thought he'd buried the past, but one look at the woman in the photo brought it all back. He swore a silent oath. If this woman was part of a ploy to make him believe Abby Diaz was still alive, she would rue the day she ever laid eyes on him.

And if she was Abby?

He wouldn't let himself think about that now. He had to get to her and the kid before Calderone's men did.

Chapter 3

Isabella Montenegro cracked the curtains to peer out into the dirt street. This time of the morning the plaza was still empty, the sun barely peeking through the adobe buildings. A dog barked in the distance. Coyotes howled, the sound echoing from the hills surrounding the small Mexican town.

She closed the curtain and glanced back at Elena sitting, half-asleep, on the edge of the bed. Her daughter looked as worried as Isabella felt. They both knew that Calderone's men were out there and they couldn't keep evading them much longer.

So why keep running? Why not just give up now? They couldn't possibly get away from Calderone, one of the most powerful, influential men in Mexico. Not a woman and a child with very little money, no defenses—

Other than the knife she'd taken from Julio's chest, she reminded herself.

She shuddered at the thought. What *had* she been thinking?

And now she had not only Calderone and his men after her but possibly Jake Cantrell and the FBI.

That all-too-familiar feeling of defenselessness threatened to paralyze her. She ached from it and the fear. Not for herself but Elena. She had to protect her daughter. But how?

She had no idea. Yesterday, she'd felt as if she'd been on automatic pilot. Not thinking. Just moving. She hadn't taken Julio's car. Too conspicuous. Instead she'd stopped the first bus she'd seen and boarded, having no idea where she was headed. Did it matter?

The bus had been going northwest, along the U.S. border. She realized that she was headed for the States and that was where she wanted to go. She wasn't sure how she'd get the two of them across the border, but she knew that once they were across, it might be the one place she could escape Tomaso Calderone.

She and Elena wouldn't last long in Mexico. Not with Calderone's connections. She tried not to think past getting to the border, because she feared they'd never get that far.

Right now Ramon and the rest were probably outside waiting for her to open the door of the motel room knowing they had her trapped. No reason not to wait and take her peacefully. Quietly. Calderone would prefer that they not cause a commotion if possible. Not that anyone would help a strange woman and her child. Especially if told she had run away from her husband.

From her responsibilities. Isn't that what had happened the last time?

But what could she do?

She looked around the motel room. It was small, with a makeshift kitchenette complete with cockroaches and beat-up cookware. She opened the cupboards, searching for something, she had no idea what. Just something to buy them a little time. Enough time to escape again. To be free just a little longer.

Finding Isabella Montenegro and her daughter had been child's play for Jake. Penny had traced the call from the kid to a rundown Mexican motel southeast of Del Rio, Texas. He figured she'd head for the States and try to cross the border at Piedras Negras, since that was the direction she was headed and it was closer than Ciudad Acuna across from Del Rio.

But he also knew that Calderone's men would figure the same thing. That's why he decided following Ramon Hernandez and his pack of *javelinas* would be the easiest, fastest way to get to Montenegro and the kid.

That was how he'd found himself in a tiny Mexican town about seventy miles from the border, watching Ramon's men wait for the sun to come up and Isabella and Elena Montenegro to come out of a dilapidated motel.

The narrow, one-story strip of five motel rooms faced the square and the church. Jake spotted two of Ramon's men hiding behind the rock wall of the church, another behind the motel. The men didn't look too concerned. It seemed pretty obvious that Isabella and her daughter would be coming out at some point and the men would be waiting.

A desert-dust-colored van was parked behind the church, the driver dozing. Ramon was down the street at the cantina having breakfast.

Jake had taken a room in the aging hotel. His window looked out over the square. He had a view of the church, the motel and the cantina. At this distance, he'd be able to take out Ramon's men easily—and Ramon as well, if it came to that. Then, by way of the balcony and fire escape directly outside his hotel-room window, he could grab the woman and kid.

He preferred not to kill Ramon and his men if possible but no matter what he did, he knew Calderone would hear about it and set an army of men after him. He just hoped to get out of Mexico before they caught up to him. But he wasn't going without the woman and kid.

Like Ramon's men, he waited without much concern. He'd checked out the small town and had convinced himself he hadn't walked into a trap. If it'd been a trap, Ramon's men would be wired with a bad case of the jitters, looking around anxiously, worried about the former FBI agent.

Instead, they seemed half-asleep and bored. They probably were. How hard could it be to catch a woman and a little kid?

He looked over the desert-hued adobe buildings, the sun grazing the tile rooftops, wondering if his instincts were trustworthy when it came to Calderone. He didn't want to end up like Daniel Austin, the Texas Confidential agent who was missing and presumed dead. Daniel probably hadn't thought he was walking into a trap, either. Nor had Abby.

Jake was thinking how Abby Diaz would have been

too smart though to get caught in a motel like the one below his window. Nor would she have slept in this late with killers after her. The sun crested, bathing the dusty little town in gold.

He was thinking how Isabella Montenegro might have been made to look like Abby, but she couldn't be made to think like her, when suddenly, the pace picked up.

No more sleepy little Mexican town. No dozing, waiting for something to happen. In a matter of seconds, the motel-room doors began to fly open followed by loud curses as patrons stumbled out into the square.

Jake stared down at the commotion. Smoke rolled out of the doors of the rooms as if the entire motel was on fire.

He let out a curse, staring in disbelief as he came fully awake himself. Four of the five motel-room doors stood open, smoke pouring out. Couples stood in skimpy clothing or nothing at all, coughing and cursing, several of the men trying to hide their faces.

The motel was a brothel!

The noisy excitement brought onlookers from the cantina and the church and the motel office. Ramon Hernandez was one of the people who rushed out into the square. And the man he'd had watching the back of the motel ran around to see what was happening, as well.

Instantly, Jake saw that he had two big problems. Ramon's men had blended in with the small crowd gathering outside the motel. Shooting into this bunch was out of the question. So was getting to Isabella

Montenegro and the kid without having to confront Ramon and his men. The odds had suddenly changed.

The second problem was that Isabella and Elena Montenegro weren't among the guests who'd tumbled out of the rooms. In fact, only the one motel-room door was still closed and he could see smoke curling from around its edges.

Where there is smoke there's—

He swore again and dove for the balcony and fire escape. Either Isabella and the kid were still in the motel room, dying of smoke inhalation or—

He rounded the back corner of the motel in time to see a woman and a small child scurrying down the alley, their heads draped with wet bath towels like veils, smoke trailing after them.

As he passed the small open bathroom window that the pair had just come out of, he realized he hadn't given the woman enough credit. He shook his head as he took off after her. Who *was* this woman?

Isabella had found the flammable kitchen cleaner under the sink. Her gaze had leapt to the bathroom window, then to the metal grate in the ceiling. Standing on the night table with a kitchen knife, she'd been able to pry the grate open. Sure enough, it was an air vent and she suspected it ran the length of the motel. At least she hoped so.

She climbed down and, taking the assortment of threadbare towels from the bathroom, she soaked all but the two largest and thickest with the cheap cleaning fluid. From beside the two-burner gas stove, she'd taken the box of matches and a candle she'd found next to the stove.

"I'm going to need your help," she'd said to her daughter.

Elena had nodded solemnly and looked up at the open metal grate as if she already knew what her mother needed her to do.

Jake found the discarded wet towels still reeking of smoke a few blocks from the motel.

But just when he was starting to think Isabella might not be as dumb as he'd first thought, she disappointed him. She made a serious mistake. She tried to flag down a bus.

Didn't she realize Ramon's men would stop and search the bus as soon as they realized she wasn't in the motel room? Apparently not. Either that, or the bus was the best plan she could come up with on short notice.

He wondered how she'd gotten this far as he watched her from a distance, debating what to do. He didn't have to debate long.

The roar of an engine preceded the dust-colored van he'd seen parked behind the church earlier. One of Ramon's men was driving, another riding shotgun. Jake guessed the others were in the back. He wondered where Ramon was.

He looked back at the bus and the two figures running to catch up with the slowing vehicle. Dust churned up under the wheels, the tiny sun-soaked particles sparkling against the desolate background.

Jake swore as the van careened around the corner,

headed straight for him and the bus. Isabella Montenegro and the kid had just run out of luck.

He lifted the rifle from under the serape he wore and, taking careful aim, squeezed off a shot. Boom. The right front tire blew. The van began to rock and reel out of control. One of the men hurled himself out the passenger side of the van just before it hit a low rock wall with a resounding crash. Steam billowed up from the badly crumpled front end and the engine died with a final groan.

Jake turned. The bus had stopped, the door open. But Isabella and the child were no longer next to it. Had she foolishly gotten in, thinking there was safety in numbers? Surely not.

Off to his right, he caught a glimpse of movement and saw a woman running with a child in her arms. He had to give the woman her due. She could move flat-out when she had to.

He ducked into an alley. He'd cut her off and get her to hell out of this town before she got herself and the kid killed. Or worse, got him killed as well.

Isabella rounded a corner at a run, the sound of the gunshots and the crash still ringing in her ears, and skidded to a stop at the sight of the man blocking the alley.

He stood in the middle of the narrow alleyway, boots apart, arms at his side, just yards from her. He wore a serape. She could make out enough of the short-barreled rifle's shape under the thick woven cloth to know he was armed. She knew he was dangerous because she recognized him.

He wore a hat pulled down low. It shaded his face, as did the sunless alley. But she didn't need to see his face clearly to know who he was.

Right now, he looked like one of those gunfighter heroes from an old spaghetti western. But she didn't fool herself that this man was any kind of hero.

From the instant she saw him, it happened within seconds. She stopped running and shot a look over her shoulder. She could hear curses and running footfalls and knew Calderone's men were close behind her.

She hugged Elena to her and swung her gaze back to the man blocking the alley. FBI agent Jake Cantrell.

He hadn't moved, but he looked like he could in an instant. And would. She heard Calderone's men, close now. Any moment they'd come around the corner of the building but suddenly they seemed less dangerous than the man facing her.

She started to turn and run back toward Calderone's men, but didn't get two strides before strong fingers closed over her arm and jerked her and Elena into a recessed doorway.

"Don't make a sound," Jake Cantrell warned as he flattened them against the wall with his body.

She could feel the solid steel of the rifle barrel pressed against one breast, the business end tucked up under her chin, cold and deadly. *"Silencio,"* she whispered to Elena.

She couldn't see Jake's face because of the way he had her pinned to the wall with his body and his weapon. But she could feel the coarse fabric of the serape against her cheek and the stark incongruity of the cold rifle barrel and the warmth where his body pressed against hers. She could also smell him. Dust. Sweat. Cedar. Soap. And an undentifiable dangerous male scent that filled her senses like an admonition.

The running footfalls stopped at the mouth of the alley. She could hear just enough of the hurried discussion among Calderone's men to know that they were desperate to find her and Elena. Ramon was furious, and if they came back without the woman and child—

Jake lifted her chin a little with the end of the rifle barrel.

Her fear made enough room for a pulse of anger. Why did he feel he had to threaten her further? Wasn't holding her at gunpoint sufficient? Holding her against a rough rock wall with his body *and* his weapon?

But she concealed the anger quickly, just as she'd learned to do with Julio.

Calderone's men moved on, running again, the sound of their retreat finally drowned out by the pounding of her heart and the terror and repressed rage thrumming through her bloodstream.

Jake Cantrell had them now. From the frying pan into the fire. Calderone's men had frightened her, but nothing like this cold, calculating man. A man who'd betrayed his partner. His country. A man who had no mercy. No honor.

The anger tried to surface again, but she held it at bay. How wonderful it would have been to let it out. Like releasing a wild beast that had been caged too long. To finally not feel defenseless.

He leaned back a little as if to listen, his body easing off hers and Elena's, but the rifle barrel still against her throat, his body still hard and unyielding.

She let her gaze rise to his face, getting her first good look at him.

She let out a gasp, feeling as if she'd been struck. It was the same visage as the one in the locket. But it wasn't his face that turned her blood to ice water, leaving her shocked and scared to her very bones.

It was his eyes.

He shifted his gaze to hers. Her heart thundered in her ears and her mouth went dry as she looked into the deep green depths of Jake Cantrell's eyes. The most unusual green she'd ever seen. But not unfamiliar. Dear God, no.

Chapter 4

Jake felt her gaze and looked down into the woman's face. Shock ricocheted through him. Stunned, he stared at her, his heart flopping like a fish inside his chest.

In the faxed photo, she'd resembled Abby Diaz enough to make him hurt. But now, he could clearly see the dissimilarities. The not-so-subtle differences. Differences that should have quickly convinced him the woman wasn't Abby Diaz.

Yet when he looked into her dark eyes he felt a jolt that shocked him to his soul. Something intimately familiar. Abby. My God, she *was* alive.

Her name came to his lips, his arms ached to hold her to him while his heart surged with joy. For just an instant, Abby Diaz was alive again and standing before him. And for that instant, he was fooled.

Then he saw something he should have seen immediately. She stared back at him with a cold blankness. She didn't know him!

He searched her gaze. Nothing. No reaction. No lover's affirmation. Nothing but fear.

He groaned inwardly. He hadn't realized how badly he'd wanted her to be Abby. Or how much it hurt that she wasn't. He'd even thought he saw something in this woman, felt something.

Slowly, he touched his fingers to her face, the lump in his throat making it impossible to speak. He jerked back, the tiny shock of electricity startling him. What a fool he was. It was nothing more than dry-wind static, something common in his part of Texas. But for just an instant, he'd thought it was something more.

He quickly brushed her long, dark, luxurious hair back from her cheek—and saw the tiny tell-tale scars. How much more proof did he need that she wasn't Abby?

And yet he gazed deep into her dark eyes again. Still hoping. But he saw nothing, no intimate connection. No hint of the woman he'd known. He could see now that she lacked Abby's fire. That irresistible aura of excitement that made the air around her crackle. That made his body ache and his skin feverish for her touch.

He'd been wrong. This woman wasn't Abby Diaz.

Still she held just enough resemblance to Abby to make him ache. Whoever was behind this had picked the perfect woman for the deception. She was about Abby's height. Five-four. And she had that same slight build. The same womanly curves.

But her face was different in ways he couldn't quite

define. She had the same wide, exotic dark eyes, the high cheekbones, the full, bow-shaped, sensuous mouth. The surgeons had done an incredible job, but they hadn't been able to make her look like his Abby. Not entirely.

He shook his head and flashed her a bitter smile. "If I didn't know better, I might think you really were Abby Diaz."

"I am Isabella Montenegro."

Her voice lacked Abby's spirit and fire and yet he thought he heard Abby in it. Her gaze met his for only an instant, then the dark lashes quickly dropped, the movement submissive, yielding. Nothing like Abby.

He yearned to see Abby's passion flare in those eyes. Anger. Defiance. Pride. Desire. All the things that were missing from this woman. Mostly he ached to see the passion that had smoldered in the depths of Abby's dark eyes. Passion that could ignite in an instant and set his loins on fire with just a glare.

When the woman lifted her gaze again, it held no spark. Only surrender. He felt a wave of regret. Of guilt, all over again, for his loss.

"What do you want with us?" she asked in a small, meek voice.

He shifted his gaze to the child. A curtain of thick black hair hid her face as she ducked her head shyly into her mother's shoulder. If this woman really was her mother.

"Come on," he said, motioning with the rifle before taking the woman's arm again. "I'm getting you out of here." He'd expected her to at least ask where he was taking her, but she didn't. She came without even a second's resistance. Without even a word of argument or question. Nothing like Abby.

He smiled bitterly again. She might resemble Abby, but she damned sure didn't act like her. Abby had always given him a run for his money. God, how he missed her. He felt sorry for this woman. She was out of her league.

He spotted Calderone's men about to search a passing motor home and quickly ushered Isabella and Elena in the other direction, back toward the vehicle he had waiting. The little girl ran along side her mother, her hand in the woman's. Neither turned to look back, to see if he was still there. They were obviously used to following orders. It made him wonder who they were and how their lives had reached this point.

He walked with the rifle in his hands but hidden under the serape, expecting an ambush, planning for it, almost welcoming it. A release for the anger building like a time bomb inside him. Who had cooked up this charade? Why? Not that it mattered. He swore to himself: he'd find out who was behind it and make them regret it.

The nondescript club-cab Ford pickup was parked on the far edge of town. It had a small camper shell on the back, a sliding window between the two, the opening large enough to crawl through, Mexican plates on the bumpers and a handmade sign on the side that read Umberto's Produce with a Nuevo Laredo phone number. The kind of pickup that would get little notice in this part of Mexico.

He'd thrown a mattress in the back, a blanket and a cooler with food and water, along with several large boxes of produce that hid everything else.

The woman stopped only long enough to pick up the little girl and the worn rag doll she'd dropped. Behind them, Jake heard gunfire and voices raised in anger. He kept moving, the woman in front of him, the child in her arms.

When they finally reached the truck, he put down the tailgate, moved the produce and motioned for the two to get in. For the first time, he noticed how exhausted the woman looked. The child had fallen asleep in her arms and Isabella looked as if only determination kept her standing. He figured she hadn't gotten much more sleep last night than he had.

Was it possible she was only a pawn in this?

He slipped the rifle into the built-in sling inside his serape and reached for the little girl.

The woman stepped back, hugging the napping child to her. Their gazes met and he saw her distrust, her fear. She didn't want to hand over the girl.

But she would. He saw that in her eyes as well. Because she knew she had no other choice. And she was a woman who accepted that.

He took Elena from her, keeping his eye on the woman. But he didn't have to worry about her making a run for it. Or trying anything. Even if it had been her nature to do something daring, he had the feeling that she wouldn't have done anything that jeopardized the girl's life. Nor would she leave the child behind, even to save herself.

Maybe Elena really *was* her daughter.

He laid the sleeping little girl on the mattress, her arm locked around her doll. Her hair fell away from her face. He'd been struck by the adorable innocence of her face in the fax photo, but in person, she was even more striking. She had a face like an angel. He'd never seen a more beautiful child.

The dark lashes fluttered against skin lighter than her mother's. Suddenly the eyes flashed open. He jerked back in shock. They were green. A deep, dark, emerald green. So like his own.

If Abby had lived— If their child had been a little girl— If she'd gotten her father's green eyes and her mother's coloring— Then she might have looked exactly like Elena Montenegro.

The pain was unbearable. The doubts were worse. Isn't this what the person behind this horrible deception had hoped for? That he'd be beguiled by this woman and her child? That he'd question whether she was Abby? Whether this beautiful little girl could be his? Or worse, wish it were so?

Anger swept over him. A grass fire of fury. Quick and deadly, all-encompassing.

"Get in," he ordered the woman, his mood explosive. It was all he could do not to grab her and shake the truth out of her. But the frightened look in her eyes stopped him.

She hurriedly climbed into the back of the pickup with the child, keeping her head down, her eyes averted from his.

He slid the boxes of produce over to hide the two of them from view through the narrow camper-shell window, then slammed the tailgate, closed the top, and stood for a moment, fighting for control. But his body shook like an oak in a gale, trembling from the inside out.

As he walked around to the driver's door of the truck,

he slammed a fist into the side of the camper, making the pickup rock and denting the metal. No sound came within. But then, he hadn't expected one.

His hand ached, funneling some of his energy into physical pain rather than anger as he climbed into the pickup, slid in the key and started the engine. Prudence forced him to drive calmly, carefully, not to draw attention or suspicion by peeling out in the gravel or driving as fast and erratically as he'd have liked.

He felt as if he might explode if he didn't let off some of the pressure. But still he drove slowly. Out past the last adobe building. Out to the paved two-lane blacktop. He turned onto it and headed toward the Texas border. The road would fork fifteen miles ahead, the fork to the right going to the closest border crossing at Piedras Negras, the left continuing on north to Cuidad Acuna.

In his rearview mirror he watched a beater of an old car approaching fast. He slid down a little, keeping his face shaded by the hat and his itchy foot from flattening the gas pedal. The speedometer wavered at forty-five when the car swept up beside him. He could feel the gazes of whoever was inside, just as he could feel the trigger of the double-barreled shotgun he'd pulled onto his lap.

He pretended to pay no attention to the car beside him. He pretended to sing loudly with the radio, turning up the Texas station, blasting redneck noise.

After a moment, the car sped on past. Four men inside. Ramon and three of his goons. Jake wondered about the other men he'd seen guarding the motel. Where were they? Or had he taken them out in the van crash?

He watched the car disappear into the flat, tan desert horizon and kept the pickup at forty-five, letting it lumber along as he turned down the radio and listened to the soft murmur of voices behind him in the camper.

His Spanish was rusty. Abby had been fluent because of her Spanish grandmother, who'd raised her. She'd often reverted to Spanish when she was angry. He'd learned from her. But it had been a long time. He'd forgotten a lot.

"There's food and water in the cooler for you," he said over his shoulder.

After a moment's silence, the woman said, "Thank you."

The little girl said something in Spanish he didn't catch.

He turned up the radio and tried not to think about them. Or what they might have been discussing. Unfortunately, he couldn't forget the trusting, fearless look on the little girl's face as she'd opened her big green eyes to meet his.

Isabella had hoped Elena would fall back to sleep and let her alone so she could think. Her head ached from exhaustion and fear and confusion.

"I told you he would come to save us," Elena whispered in Spanish next to her.

She didn't have the heart to tell her daughter that Jake Cantrell hadn't necessarily saved them. More than likely they were just prisoners of a different man now. But still prisoners. Possibly worse. If what she'd read from the information in the envelope about the man was true, she and Elena could be in worse trouble than they had been before.

"I told you he was my daddy," Elena said, daring Isabella to disagree.

She didn't have the energy. Nor the conviction. There had been so little she'd understood about her marriage to Julio. Or her past, the one he'd filled in for her after the fire.

But the moment she'd looked into Jake Cantrell's eyes she'd known one clear truth.

Jake Cantrell was Elena's father.

She'd seen her daughter in the deep green of his eyes. But also in the familiar way his brow furrowed in a narrowed frown. In the intense intelligence she'd glimpsed behind all that green. In the small telltale mannerisms that genetics passed from one generation to the next.

Jake Cantrell was Elena's father.

But if she accepted that as truth, didn't she have to accept the rest as well? That she was Abby Diaz. Former FBI agent. Former partner and lover of Jake Cantrell.

That was where her mind balked. She had given birth to Elena, hadn't she? Wouldn't she have known if Elena wasn't her child? Felt something…wrong if the babies had somehow been switched at the hospital?

Her head ached and she knew she was trying to come up with an explanation other than the one staring her in the face.

She closed her eyes. Was it possible? Was she Abby Diaz?

She had to admit, she'd never believed brown-eyed Julio was Elena's father, any more than Elena had. It wasn't just Elena's green eyes, though they certainly did make Isabella suspicious. But Julio had told her that his brother, who'd died at birth, had had the same green eyes, that they ran in the family.

She'd suspected it was a lie and the reason her husband wanted nothing to do with her or their beautiful baby was because Elena was the result of an affair Isabella had had before the fire. It would have explained a lot. Especially Julio's coldness and her baby's green eyes.

But now she could no longer cling to that explanation any more than she could keep telling Elena that she was wrong, that the man in the front of the pickup wasn't her father.

"Go to sleep for a little while, *chica suena,*" she told Elena, and closed her eyes. Beside her, Elena began to sing the songs Isabella had taught her. Songs Isabella believed she remembered from her grandmother. But now she wasn't even sure that was true.

If she was this FBI agent Abby Diaz, then why didn't she feel it? She knew nothing about being an FBI agent. Why hadn't she remembered her training? Was it possible she'd been burned from an explosion during an FBI investigation in Texas instead of a house fire in Mexico?

And if there'd been any chance that she'd survived, why hadn't the FBI come looking for her years ago? Why hadn't they rescued her from Julio? Why hadn't Jake?

Her head ached and her stomach roiled. She didn't want to be Abby Diaz. Not a woman—if it was true—whom someone had tried to kill six years ago. Especially if that someone had been her partner, her lover, Jake Cantrell.

But the real question was, did he still want her dead?

Chapter 5

Isabella jerked awake as she felt the pickup slow. She reached for Elena, thankful and relieved when she found her daughter sleeping deeply beside her, her face peaceful, almost content. In the pickup's cab, the radio played softly. A country-and-western station out of Del Rio. How close were they to the border?

She pushed herself up into a sitting position. She couldn't have been asleep for long. Through the windshield she could see that the sun still hung low on the horizon, the cactus casting dark extended shadows.

With a start, she realized that Jake had turned off the paved highway onto a road that appeared to be little more than a dust trail. What was he planning to do with them? It crossed her mind that he might be looking for a place to kill them. No one would be the wiser out here in what was a very isolated part of the Mexican desert.

But did a man who planned to kill people offer them food and water first? Did he rescue them from drug dealers and killers? Who knew with *this* man? If he'd set Abby Diaz up to die six years ago and if he thought there was even a chance she *was* Abby—

Feeling at a distinct disadvantage in the back of the pickup, she asked in English, "Do you mind if I come up front?"

He turned with a start as if he'd forgotten she was back there. Or wished he could. "Up to you," he said, but she was already slipping through the adjoining window and down onto the bench seat of the cab.

He didn't look over at her as she fastened her seat belt, but she saw his jaw tense and his hands grip the wheel tighter, his gaze fixed straight ahead on the ribbon of dirt road that wove through the cactus and scrub brush.

Covertly, she studied him from the corner of her eye, prodding her memory for some hint of recognition. Some glimmer of remembered emotion. If there was any chance this man had been her lover...

But she felt nothing. Except a tightrope of tension that stretched between them. Hers was from fear. But what about him? He seemed anxious. Why was that? Did he have something to fear from Abby Diaz?

It gave Isabella a chill to think that he might still have some reason to want his former lover dead—if she could believe what she'd read in the envelope. And why wouldn't she believe it? The evidence had been damning. Dates and receipts and phone transcripts. All compiled by the FBI. Proof that Jake Cantrell had tried to kill his partner.

But why? she wondered as she stared at the narrow dusty road and the desert that stretched to the horizon. What had Abby done to him to make him hate her so that he'd want her dead? The mother of his unborn child. Or had he known about the baby?

If only she could remember. Right now, she'd have been happy to remember that she was Isabella Montenegro. Her only one clear memory was her grandmother. Surely the wonderful grandmother she recalled had been real. Or had Julio made her up, the way he might have made up her past as Isabella Montenegro?

"Where are you taking us?" she asked quietly over the music playing on the radio, not wanting to wake Elena.

"The first phone booth I come to across the border," he said without looking at her. "The FBI will take it from there."

The FBI. Fear shot through her. Shouldn't she feel relieved? Why did the mere thought of him turning her and Elena over to the FBI spike her heart rate and make her sick and scared inside?

"What's in this for you?" he asked suddenly, reaching over to turn off the radio.

She could feel his gaze on her, hard, unforgiving. "I don't know what you mean."

His intent stare narrowed into a frown. He looked like Elena when she was upset. "What were you promised for pretending to be Abby Diaz?"

"I'm not pretending to be anyone." *Except maybe Isabella Montenegro,* she thought. She heard herself repeating what Julio had told her about her past, how she was born in a small Mexican town, how her parents died when she was young and her grandmother raised her, how at sixteen she married Julio and finally, how her grandmother and Julio's mother and sister had perished in the fire that scarred her face and one shoulder.

"That's quite the story," he said, glancing over at her, his expression as unbelieving as his tone. "You certainly speak good English for a woman who's spent her whole life in Mexico. Are you also going to tell me that your husband didn't work for Tomaso Calderone? Or that you just happen to resemble an FBI agent named Abby Diaz who Calderone killed six years ago?"

He blamed Calderone for Abby's death? "My husband, Julio, worked for Señor Calderone," she admitted. How did she explain the way she'd lived the last six years? Trying hard to keep herself and Elena invisible when Julio and his men were around. "I cannot tell you why I resemble this woman, the FBI agent. I had nothing to do with my husband's dealings and until yesterday, I didn't even know of Abby Diaz's existence."

He held her gaze for a long moment, then looked back to his driving. "I suppose you also don't know where the money is that your husband stole from Calderone."

"If I knew that, I would have tried to buy my freedom from my husband's employer."

Jake laughed.

"What is it you find so amusing?" she demanded in a flare of anger. She'd learned to control her emotions around Julio, especially her temper. So why was she letting it show with a man who was possibly even more dangerous?

"Buying your freedom would have been like trying

to buy your soul back from the devil." He looked over at her. "Tell me something. This woman you described, this Isabella Montenegro, this woman you say you are, how is it she recognized me today in the alley? How do you know me?"

She didn't want to tell him about the manila envelope she'd found under Julio's body.

"Your picture was in the locket," said a small voice from the back of the truck in perfect English. Julio had forbidden Isabella to speak English under his roof, having long ago explained away why Isabella had awakened in the hospital six years ago, knowing both English and Spanish.

But she'd taught her bright daughter both languages in secret, warning the child never to speak English except to her and only when they were alone. She now regretted teaching her.

They both turned to see Elena sitting just behind them at the open window. Isabella wondered how long her daughter had been awake and how much she'd heard and understood.

"What locket?" he demanded.

Elena produced the heart-shaped piece of worn silver from her pocket and held it out as if it were a rare jewel.

He slammed on the brakes, bringing the pickup to a teeth-rattling stop, and snatched the locket from the child's hand.

His strong features seemed to dissolve in either pain or anger. Isabella couldn't tell which. He bent his head, running his thumb over the engraved letters of the locket, as dust settled around the pickup.

Then slowly, he opened the tiny silver heart.

His eyes closed as his fist closed over the locket. "Where did you get this?" he demanded, his voice breaking, as he swung around to face Elena.

"I gave it to her," Isabella said quickly, realizing she had no other choice now but to tell him about the envelope. If he looked into her bag, which he was bound to do before long, he'd find the envelope anyway.

"I found an envelope with the locket in it after my hus—after Julio was killed." Whether Julio had really been her husband or not, she refused to think of him in those terms. Not anymore.

He shot her a look. "How did your husband get it?"

"I don't know." She could see he didn't believe her. She couldn't really blame him. She knew so little. And yet she had much more than Jake's former lover's locket. She had her face. And her baby. No wonder he was so mistrustful.

"I want to see the envelope," he said.

She nodded and asked Elena to hand it to her.

Still sitting in the middle of the narrow dirt road, he dug through the contents, scanning the material inside, glancing at her periodically and finally letting out a curse when he found the evidence against him. He closed his eyes, the top of the envelope crushed in his large fist.

Then slowly his grip relaxed and he shoved everything but the locket back into the envelope and handed it to her.

"If you were Abby Diaz, it appears you would have something to fear from me," he said quietly, bitterness layered on top of anger.

She realized she'd been holding her breath. She let

it out now and met his gaze. "But neither of us believes I am Abby Diaz."

He stared at her, his gaze probing hers. What was he looking for? His lost love? Or a hint of recognition on her part? She could give him neither.

"Even if you are who you say you are, the evidence in that envelope would make you think you couldn't trust me," he said carefully.

She said nothing. Trusting Jake Cantrell was the last thing she planned to do.

"For all I know, you aren't even Isabella Montenegro," he said after a moment. "Of course you have some identification, some proof of who you are."

She nodded and pulled out the only piece of identification she had with a photo of her on it, taken after the fire. All other photos and identification of her prior to that had been burned in it.

"This is all you have?"

It did sound unbelievable, but not for a woman who never left the house except in the company of one of her husband's associates. "I've never had need for much identification."

"But you have Abby's passport, her driver's license, a copy of her birth certificate," he pointed out.

"I found them in the envelope only yesterday."

He nodded as he pocketed the locket.

Elena started to protest but Isabella stopped her with a warning look. "Play with your doll," she told Elena.

Jake got the truck moving again as Elena did as she was told and moved farther back. A few moments later, Isabella heard her talking softly to the rag doll.

The pickup rolled along for a few miles, the silence inside the cab heavy, laden with uncertainty.

She couldn't help thinking about the FBI. If Julio really had been working for them as the information in the envelope showed, how could the Bureau not have known about her and Elena? Why did she feel that at least someone in the FBI had known she was alive and kept it a secret?

"I don't understand why the FBI would be interested in Elena and me," she said.

He looked at her as if she were joking. "You've been living with one of Tomaso Calderone's top distributors, a man who knew enough of Calderone's business to steal millions from him."

Millions? Julio? She glanced out her side window at the passing desert, the sun already hot and stifling, even this early in the morning. Why did she find it impossible to believe? Because Julio had always been so fearful of Calderone, a man who would kill his own mother for money. No, Julio was not the kind of man who'd risk stealing that much money, knowing the consequences.

But if Calderone believed it, it would explain why his men were after her and Elena.

She jerked her gaze back around to Jake as another realization struck her. And Cantrell's next words made her feel he had read her thoughts.

"That's right, if you were Abby Diaz, the FBI would want to know what you've been doing the last six years, why you were living with Julio Montenegro as his wife, why you were pretending to be someone else and if you'd been helping Calderone. They'll also want to know where Julio hid the money."

She swallowed, her mouth suddenly dry. In other words, they'd think that she'd sold out her country and fellow agents. What were the chances they'd believe she couldn't remember even her name? About as much as Jake would if she told him about her loss of memory.

"But I'm not Abby Diaz," she said.

He gave her a humorless smile. "Lucky you."

She stared out at the dirt road ahead, trying to still her hammering heart. Even as Isabella Montenegro, the FBI wanted her. Planned to use her. To get Calderone? Or the missing drug money? Or both?

She realized Jake was looking at her.

"What are you afraid of?" he asked. "That the FBI can prove you're an imposter? That they'll arrest you for aiding and abetting a criminal?"

"What does *imposter* mean?" Elena asked from the back.

Isabella tried to hush her daughter, but Elena wasn't having any of it. "Imposter is—"

"It means fake, fraud," Jake said, his gaze on Isabella. "That's why the FBI has DNA tests, fingerprint comparisons, ways to expose the truth."

"Are you sure you can handle the truth?" she snapped, unable to hold back her anger. It was one thing to deny that she might be his former lover, but it was another to deny his child. What kind of man was he that he didn't acknowledge his own child? "Don't you already know? Can't you see what is right before your very own eyes?"

Elena crawled up into the front seat, into her lap. "My doll!" she cried as she realized she'd forgotten it in the back. Elena and the doll had been inseparable since Isabella had made it for her. "Get my Sweet Ana, Mommy. Please."

Jake felt as if he'd been kicked by a mule. "What is the doll's name?" he asked, telling himself he hadn't heard correctly.

"Sweet Ana," the woman said.

He could feel her gaze on him, feel the kid watching him too. *Sweet Ana.* "The kid come up with that?"

"Mommy named her. Mommy made her for me for Christmas when I was a baby."

He glanced at Elena, a little bowled over by her English and her confidence. She was smart. He could see that. Smarter than five, that was for sure. "How old are you now?"

"Four and three-quarters."

He smiled at that and her, and went back to his driving. Damn, she was a cute kid. All little girl.

"Why don't you want to be my daddy?"

"What?" He swung around to look at her.

Her eyes were big as CDs and that incredible all-too-familiar green, and she was looking at him with an expression that battered his heart with a club.

He shot Isabella a furious look over the top of the child's head. This was her doing.

"I'm not your father," he said more harshly than he'd intended. He thought the kid would burst into tears. He thought she'd at least leave him alone now.

"She's just a child. Don't hurt her because of how you feel about me," the woman whispered angrily.

How he felt about her? He stared at her, seeing Abby. Passion burning in her gaze. Even if it was only anger, it stirred something in him, confusing him, making him doubt everything, especially what he'd thought had happened six years ago.

"Why do you think you're not my father?" Elena asked, drawing his gaze again. She didn't sound upset, just curious, as if he were only trying to fool himself.

"Look, kid—" He met her gaze, feeling cursed with the same green eyes. She looked up at him, those eyes so filled with trust. With innocence. With longing for the father she wanted to see in him. "Why do you think I am?"

She smiled as if his question was just plain silly.

He pulled his gaze away from her, realizing he'd just driven off the road. Not that it mattered. This wasn't much of a road, anyway. This kid was rattling him more than he wanted to admit.

"Look," he said, "I don't know if I'm your father or not." He shot the woman a hostile glance, angry with her for putting him in this spot, angry with himself.

She just stared back at him as if he were the biggest fool on earth. He couldn't argue with that.

He told himself he didn't see Abby in those dark eyes. Didn't hear her in the woman's voice. Didn't sense her in the tension that arced between them. What had made him think this would be easy? An open-and-shut case. One look and he would know if she was Abby.

Elena smiled up at him and hugged the worn, homemade rag doll in her arms. Her Sweet Ana. "You are my daddy," she said with conviction, those green eyes gazing up at him with open affection. "You'll see."

Damn, he thought as he looked away. This woman already had him doubting himself enough, without seeing those Cantrell green eyes in this little girl. What the hell was wrong with him? He was letting a little kid con him. He was damned glad the gang from Texas Confidential wasn't here. Wouldn't they love this. He sped up the truck, anxious to turn these two over to the Feds.

"We're almost to the border," he said. "You'd better get your things together." He was grateful when they climbed into the back again. He concentrated on his driving, speculating on what might lie ahead at the border, rather than thinking about the woman and little girl in the back of his truck.

He stopped just outside of Cuidad Acuna and disposed of the Umberto's Produce signs, the produce, the mattress, his serape, instructing Isabella and Elena to get into the front again. He hid his weapons in the truck, changed the plates back to Texas ones, then climbed in again, unable to shake a bad feeling that he'd been led into a trap—just as he'd suspected.

The evidence in the envelope had been compiled by the FBI. So that meant that Frank knew about it. Damning evidence that made him question his own innocence. So why was he still walking around? Why wasn't he behind bars?

But the bigger question was, why had Frank chosen him for this job?

It made him nervous. Something wasn't right.

His original plan had involved help from the FBI to get across the border with the woman and kid. But that was no longer necessary. Nor his first choice. The woman could use Abby's identification at the border. Her likeness to the photo was enough to convince any immigration officer. Not that they paid that much attention. An American and her child could easily cross the border. An American and her husband and child could cross even easier.

And right now, he didn't want to tip off the FBI. He had a bad feeling he couldn't trust Frank Jordan.

"Abby was born in Dallas," he said to the woman as they neared the border, taking the truck route through the industrial part of town. "For the moment, you're Abby Diaz." He looked over at her.

She nodded but said nothing, her gaze on the border town.

"Elena," he said, using the child's name for the first time. "If the border guard says anything to you, speak English."

"I understand," Elena said.

"Good," he said. Her smile made him ache. He turned back to his driving, watching his rearview mirror as well as the side streets and the town ahead, telling himself he'd better be ready for trouble. Like he already didn't have enough in the cab of the pickup.

He was counting on Ramon and his men going to the closest border crossing, some fifty miles away. Unless he missed his guess, they'd still be there, waiting, expecting the woman and child to take the fastest route to the States. He told himself Ramon wasn't smart enough nor did he have enough men to cover both border crossings.

Lost in those thoughts, Jake didn't see the man step out into the street in front of the pickup until it was almost too late. He hit his brakes. The truck skidded to a stop and died just inches from the man. As the man turned, Jake saw the pistol in his hand and realized belatedly that Ramon Hernandez was a lot smarter than he'd originally thought.

"Get down," Jake cried to Isabella as he shoved Elena to the floorboards.

But it was too late. Before he could get the truck started, Ramon put a round into the pickup's engine.

One of Ramon's armed thugs jerked open the passenger door and grabbed Isabella by the arm. As she struggled to fight him off, Elena screamed for Jake to help her. Jake slammed down the lock on his door as another man came around to his side of the truck.

"Put your head down," he yelled at Elena as he groped under the pickup seat for the semiautomatic he'd duct-taped there, wrestled it free and fired, dropping the man beside Isabella with two quick shots that reverberated through the cab like dual explosions.

The driver's-side window shattered behind him. Before he could turn, his door was jerked open and he was grabbed from behind in a half nelson, the man's free hand on Jake's pistol as he tried to wrestle it away.

The man was strong and had Jake pinned in the pickup in a position where he could do little to free himself. The arm at his throat was cutting off his air. He felt his fingers weakening on the weapon and heard Elena cry out something in Spanish to her mother. Darkness edged his vision as the pressure from the man's arm cut off his air.

He heard the shot, felt the arm around his neck loosen, the hand on his weapon release. The first shot was followed quickly by a second. The man behind him made a small grunt before he hit the ground with a lifeless thud. The third shot, which came within seconds of the other two, made a hollow sound as it punctured the windshield, driving a clean hole through the glass and instantly turning the glass around it into a thick white web.

Jake heard the sound of someone running, the roar of a large car engine and the screech of rubber as the sound of the engine died away.

Beside him, one of Ramon's men lay in a pool of blood, staring up, a neat little black hole between his eyes.

Jake swung around to look at Isabella as he gasped for breath, his throat on fire where the man had choked him.

She sat perfectly still, except for the trembling of the hand that held the pistol. A pistol she must have taken from the man he'd killed on her side of the truck. He looked quickly at Elena, still huddled on the floor.

"Are you all right, Elena?" he asked, his voice hoarse.

She lifted her face from her knees, her doll clutched to her thin chest, and nodded, eyes wide.

In the distance, he could hear the sound of police sirens. He knew he wasn't going anywhere in this truck and now, more than ever, he needed to get out of Mexico. "Come on," he said to Isabella.

She still hadn't moved. She seemed in shock. No more than he was, he thought.

"We have to get out of here," he said, touching her arm.

She stirred at his touch, her gaze settling on him for a moment, then quickly flicking to Elena. Tears welled in her eyes as she dropped the gun and reached for her daughter.

Jake shoved his pistol into the waist of his jeans,

then took Elena from her mother's arms. "We're going to have to run. Are you up to it?" he asked Isabella.

She nodded and pulled her bag from the back. A second later she was out of the truck and running beside him down a side street.

He ran with Elena, her one small arm wrapped around his neck, the other around her Sweet Ana. As he wound through the narrow streets, he looked for a vehicle to steal, trying to ignore the voice in his head, the one that kept reminding him of the perfectly placed bullet hole and the only other woman he'd known who could shoot like that.

Abby Diaz.

Chapter 6

The red short-box Toyota pickup was almost too easy. It had Texas plates, was parked at the edge of the industrial area and was one vehicle he could hot-wire in less than a minute.

Jake would have much preferred something a little less flashy than bright red. But beggars couldn't be choosers.

However, when he got closer, he realized hot-wiring it wouldn't be necessary. Not only was the truck unlocked, the keys glittered in the ignition. He glanced around nervously. When things went too easily it made him nervous. When they went this smoothly, it scared the hell out of him.

Jake quickly ushered the woman and child into the front bench seat, worried either that the owner hadn't gone far and would return too soon or that he'd just walked into an ambush. He hurried around to the driver's side and slid behind the wheel. The truck started on his first try.

The Mexican town still dozed in the warm, early-morning sun. He drove toward the border, avoiding the part of town where he could still hear police sirens. Three minutes later, he pulled into the short line of commercial trucks and several cars at the border crossing, still looking over his shoulder. For Ramon. For the owner of the pickup. Afraid someone would stop them before they could reach the States.

The line moved as slow as mesquite honey. When their turn came, the border guard ambled over to Jake's side of the pickup and leaned down to peer at the three of them. He asked the standard questions. Were they American citizens, where they were born, what had they been doing in Mexico and had they purchased anything.

Jake wondered if Frank had alerted the border guards to watch out for him and his companions. That would be like Frank. If Frank had his way, he'd have Isabella and Elena in protective custody the moment they stepped on U.S. soil.

But the guard barely glanced at them or their drivers' licenses before he waved them on through.

Still, Jake found himself holding his breath as he drove into Texas. He watched the highway ahead and behind them, expecting—hell, that was just it. He didn't know *what* he expected.

Well, at least he was back in Texas. Home. He'd done what he'd been assigned to do. Find the woman and child, get them to the States. Now all he had to do was call Frank and have the Feds pick them up. Job done.

He glanced down at the speedometer and quickly

lightened his foot on the gas pedal. *Don't be a fool, Cantrell. All you need to do is get picked up for speeding in a stolen vehicle.*

But he couldn't deny the need to put distance between them and Mexico. Or the unaccountable urge he felt to run.

The question was: run from what? He watched the highway. No Ramon. No nondescript car with occupants who looked like agents. He told himself he could relax now. He was back in Texas. Safe.

He looked over at the little girl, her face lit with excitement as she stood on the seat, staring ahead at the town of Del Rio. Then past her to her mother. The woman's eerie resemblance to Abby struck him like a blow—just as it always did. Now, though, after what he'd witnessed in Ciudad Acuna—

"That was some shot," he said.

Yes, it had been. She'd thought of little else since. "I can't believe I did that. It just happened so fast."

Her hands had stopped trembling but she was still shaking inside. She'd killed one man and would have killed the other one if he'd given her the chance.

Even now it didn't seem like her hand that had wrenched the pistol from the dead man's fingers and fired without hesitation. She didn't even know she knew how to shoot let alone could hit anything.

But she'd more than just hit something, hadn't she?

"I just pulled the trigger," she said, trying to convince herself as much as him. "Anyone could have hit such a large target at that close range." Was that true?

She dragged her gaze from the Texas town to look over at him, afraid of what she'd see.

He stared at her openly, suspicion in his gaze as he searched her face. She knew what he was looking for. Abby Diaz. He was beginning to suspect what she'd feared.

"You must have shot a pistol before," he said.

She noticed the careful way he chose his words. "Not that I can remember," she answered truthfully.

He nodded, eyeing her intently before turning back to his driving. "Lucky shot, for your first time."

She said nothing. She'd shot the man between his eyes. No hesitation. The pistol in her hands had felt almost…natural. She looked out her side window and watched the city of Del Rio rush past in a blur, remembering the look on the man's face, the shock when she'd turned the pistol on him and fired.

Dear God. She closed her eyes. Who was she? Certainly not Isabella Montenegro, housewife and mother, prisoner of Julio Montenegro in a loveless marriage.

She opened her eyes. Why couldn't she accept what had to be the truth?

She glanced over at Jake. A thought struck her, taking her breath away. She'd always wondered why she couldn't remember anything before the fire. At first she'd thought her loss of memory was due to the accident. But the doctors had told her it was psychosomatic, caused instead by trauma or repression due to possible shock. In other words, she'd blanked out the past because she couldn't face it.

Couldn't face that someone close to her, someone she'd trusted, maybe even loved, had betrayed her?

The thought sent a chill through her. If that were true, then Abby Diaz knew her killer. Knew him and trusted him. Just as she might have her lover. The father of her child. If Jake really was guilty, then wouldn't he now be afraid she'd identify him to the FBI?

If only she could remember. Dear God, what had happened six years ago?

She realized Jake hadn't stopped at a phone booth yet. Hadn't he said he was taking her to the first phone booth, calling the FBI and turning her and Elena over to the Feds?

But he seemed to be driving straight through Del Rio as if he had no intention of stopping. Her heart took off at a gallop. He'd been so anxious to wash his hands of her and Elena. What had changed?

Had he changed his mind because of what had happened in Ciudad Acuna? Did he suspect that she was Abby Diaz? Is that why he'd changed his plans?

Her pulse throbbed at her temple, the morning sun blinding. She pulled Elena closer, fear making her chest tighten, her mouth dry.

They passed another phone booth. "Are you going to call the FBI or take us to the nearest office?" she asked, trying to keep the anxiety out of her voice.

"I'm not taking you to the FBI just yet," he said without looking at her.

Her heart thudded dully in her chest. She looked out at the small Texas town, fighting panic. Once they left these streets and were out in the open desert again— She leaned down and whispered into her daughter's ear. Elena whispered back.

"Elena has to go to the bathroom," she told Jake.

He glanced over at them, not looking happy about the prospect, then glanced at the gas gauge. "All right. We need gas, anyway. Can she hold it just a little longer? I'd really like to get to the other side of town."

She nodded and reached down to pick up her bag from the floor.

"But you'll have to make it quick," he added. "We have a long way to go." His gaze locked on hers, suspicious.

He didn't trust her. Not that he probably ever had. But now he'd be careful. Cautious. More watchful. And he'd changed his plans.

She could think of only one reason he'd decided not to take them to the FBI yet.

We have a long way to go. She hated to think where he might be planning to take her and Elena.

He stopped at a small, deserted gas station on the far edge of Del Rio. "Just a minute," he said as Isabella started to get out, her bag in one hand, Elena's small hand in the other. He took the bag from her. "You won't need this, right?"

She looked up at him. Compliant was a look she'd perfected with Julio. "I just need a change of clothing for Elena and me. These clothes still reek of smoke."

He nodded, seemingly reassured as she pulled out what she needed, then she let him take the bag and put it behind the pickup seat.

She climbed out and, taking Elena's hand, walked toward the ladies' room. She heard his door open, heard him begin to fill the gas tank. She knew he was watching them. She knew she'd have to be careful. Just as she had been with Julio.

Ten minutes later, Jake saw her and the little girl come out of the ladies' room. The two of them made a striking pair and he couldn't deny the resemblance between mother and daughter. If he even considered that Elena might be his daughter, then—he caught the woman's eye. She quickly looked down at the child as the two advanced.

He didn't know what to think. What to believe. Right now he was just scared and not sure exactly what it was he feared the most.

A dust devil whirled across the pavement to shower the side of the nearly derelict building with Texas dust. He glanced at the road, unable to shake that uneasy feeling. But there was little traffic out this way and they had the gas station to themselves.

When he turned back, the woman and child were almost to him. He finished filling the tank with unleaded and waited until she'd led Elena around to the passenger side of the truck before he went in to pay. In his pocket, he jingled the keys just to assure himself he hadn't left them in the ignition. And he kept an eye on the pair. Not that he thought the woman was fool enough to take off on foot. Not with the child.

While he paid the cashier, a teenage boy watching a rerun on an old black-and-white TV, he had the feeling of being observed. He looked out at the pickup. Elena stood at the driver's-side window, staring at him with an intensity that unnerved him. He suddenly realized he couldn't see the woman.

Hurriedly, he took the change the teenager absently handed him, the TV still squawking in the corner, and left the office, his anxiety growing with each step he took toward the pickup.

She came around the front fender with a squeegee in her hand and began to wash the windshield. He almost laughed in relief and surprise. Someone had certainly trained this woman well. Then he remembered the way she'd fired the gun and wondered just how trained she really was.

"Here, let me do that," he said, going around to the passenger side of the truck to where she scrubbed enthusiastically at the bugs on the dirty windshield.

She'd changed into a Mexican embroidered top and jeans. The top billowed out, hiding her curves as she worked. She turned to look at him, her gaze quickly dropping behind the veil of dark lashes.

He studied her a moment, wondering. One moment she was so passive, so subservient, a woman whose will had been broken. And the next? She was shooting a man between the eyes with a pistol as if it was the most normal thing in the world.

She handed him the squeegee, her fingers brushing against his. He was hit with that sudden unmistakable twinge again. The same one he'd felt the first time he'd seen her, the first time he'd touched her. And he had the most irresistible desire to pull her into his arms and kiss her. If he kissed her, he'd know. He felt certain of it. And wasn't that what was driving him crazy? Not knowing for sure?

Their bodies were so close that her scent filled his senses, reminding him of something rare and exotic. And...familiar.

The feel of the cold hard barrel of the pistol pressed into his ribs caught him completely by surprise. He blinked. Too shocked to comprehend what was happening for a moment. Where had she gotten a gun? He had his on him and—the other gun. What a fool. He'd just assumed when he hadn't seen her with the pistol she'd taken from Ramon's henchman that she'd left it in the produce truck. Dropped it like a hot potato.

He closed his eyes and groaned. What the hell was wrong with him? But he knew the answer to that as he opened them again and looked at the woman.

"The keys to the truck, please," she said.

He stared into her dark eyes and saw an intelligence that he'd somehow missed before. No, that she'd kept hidden, just as she'd hidden the anger and determination that now burned as bright as dazzling sunlight in her gaze.

"This is a mistake," he whispered, and felt the steel dig a little deeper into his flesh.

"The mistake will be yours if you don't give me the truck keys," she said calmly, her eyes locking with his.

The last thing he wanted to do was give her the keys to the pickup. But he realized she could kill him where he stood in an instant and from the look in her eyes, he didn't doubt she would. She probably believed the evidence in the envelope. Believed he was a killer.

Then she couldn't possibly be Abby Diaz. Abby would never have believed that he could hurt her—even if the information *had* come from the FBI.

"Easy," he said as he slowly reached into his pocket for the keys. He handed them to her, wondering, *now what?*

She produced a pair of handcuffs from the waistband of her jeans, cuffs that had been concealed under her billowing blouse. *His* handcuffs. The ones he'd unclipped from his belt and slipped under the seat of the pickup just before they'd reached the border.

She handed him the cuffs. "One on your right wrist, the other to the pump handle."

"You and the kid don't stand a chance on your own."

"I'll take my chances. The cuffs, please."

He glanced toward the gas-station office. The attendant was probably watching the TV he'd been glued to earlier. Not that the boy could see what was happening on this side of the pickup even if he'd bothered to look. No doubt that was the way she'd planned it. If only someone would stop for gas. But then he'd purposely chosen this rundown station because it *wasn't* busy.

He let out a curse as the pistol barrel pressed deeper into his flesh beneath his shirt, drawing his attention quickly back to the woman.

"The cuffs," she reminded him.

Completely gone was the passive female he'd originally thought he was taking to the FBI. This woman had a fireworks show of anger and pent-up aggression in her dark eyes.

And she had the pistol in the perfect spot to kill a man before he could make a move to save himself. Just luck, like the shot she'd fired between the man's eyes? *Right.*

He cursed himself for the fool he'd been as he snapped one cuff to his right wrist, the other to the gas pump. He'd underestimated her. Whoever the hell she was.

He met her gaze. She seemed to hesitate and in that instant, he felt something arc between them, strong and fierce and—this time no mistaking it—passionately familiar.

"Abby?" he whispered.

And then the lights went out.

Chapter 7

Ramon Hernandez was not having a good day. His half-finished breakfast hadn't agreed with his stomach, the van was demolished, and three of his men were dead and another two hurt too badly to be of much use.

He swore to himself as he stepped gingerly into the hot, cramped phone booth, watching his back. Outside, one of his remaining, least-injured men stood guard; little consolation, all things considered.

He quickly dialed the number, nervous, sick to his stomach and frightened. Who was the gringo with Isabella Montenegro? DEA? Or a drug dealer? He didn't like this added complication, whoever the man was, and wished he'd killed him when he'd had the chance.

A gust of wind whirled dirt against the weathered glass, making him jump. He mopped his brow, the slanted early-morning sun bearing down on the booth, making him feel like a target.

"We have a problem," he said when Tomaso Calderone came on the line.

"*You* have a problem," Calderone snapped.

Yeah. Well, Calderone didn't know the half of it. "Isabella Montenegro and her whelp pulled a fast one and got away, but someone is helping her."

"Who?"

"I don't know. A gringo. He grabbed her and the kid."

"Where were *you* when this happened?" Calderone demanded.

"Staking out the front of the motel," he lied quickly. "I had two men behind the motel." He wished. Who would have thought she'd set some sort of fire as a diversion and go out that tiny bathroom window? "The gringo killed three of my men, then shot out the tires on our van when we were in pursuit, destroying it." Lying came easy. It was probably his second best talent, lying on his feet. Killing was his first.

"I had to commandeer a car," he continued quickly, wincing at the sight of the large, older-model American car lounging like a lizard in the street. He wasn't about to tell his boss that he'd had the gringo in his sights and had foolishly killed his pickup instead. It was so hard to get good help these days.

"What did this man look like?" Calderone asked quietly.

Ramon described him.

"Why would *he* be interested in Julio's wife and child?" Calderone muttered almost to himself. "Listen to me, Ramon. This man is very dangerous. I want him. And I want my money. You do understand?"

"Si," he said, feeling sicker. Surely he'd heard wrong. "You don't want him...*alive?"*

"Oh, yes. I want them *all* alive."

Ramon swore silently. This would be very difficult and a waste of his true talents.

"What do you know of this woman and child?" Calderone asked.

Ramon shrugged to himself and looked out into the street. What did he know of Julio's life? Like Calderone, he lived farther south in Mexico. He had only seen the woman briefly and had paid little notice to her or the child with her.

"She looked like...a wife," he answered lamely.

"Mexican?"

"Si."

"I wonder...." Calderone mused.

"Who is this gringo?" Hernandez asked, a little concerned since he'd now be chasing him into the States.

"Jake Cantrell. He used to be an FBI agent."

"But he's not anymore," Ramon said, relieved he wouldn't be dealing with the FBI.

"He'll head for someplace he feels safe," Calderone said, as if still thinking out loud. "Let me make a call. Give me your number. I will get back to you when I know where he has gone."

Ramon hung up, wondering how Calderone knew so much about this gringo. Had recognized him immediately from Ramon's description.

The phone rang a few minutes later. What Calderone told him more than surprised him. Maybe this wouldn't be so difficult after all. As long as he got the credit for bringing in Jake Cantrell, former FBI agent.

"Do not fail me, *amigo*," Calderone said after he'd promised to send him several more men. The line went dead.

As dead as Ramon Hernandez himself would be if he failed. The only good news was that the former FBI agent was traveling with a woman and child. That would hamper any man. And now Ramon would have help.

Isabella's body trembled, her knuckles white on the steering wheel.

"You're scaring me, Mommy," Elena cried.

"I'm sorry, *chica suena,* I don't mean to scare you."

"But you hurt him," she cried, turning to stare out the back window at Jake on the ground beside the gas pump.

"He'll be fine," she assured her daughter. "He'll just have a headache when he wakes up." How did she know that? How did she know to hit him the way she had and not kill him?

She stared for a moment at her hands gripping the wheel as if they belonged to a stranger. She feared that they did.

Elena swung back around, tears glistening on her sweet face.

Isabella reached over to thumb the wetness from her daughter's cheeks. The child's lower lip trembled and big tears welled in her green eyes like pools of spring water. "He *is* my daddy."

"Yes," she agreed. "He is your father."

"Then why did you do that?" Elena demanded.

"Because I'm not sure we can trust him." He hadn't harmed her or Elena. But he'd changed his plans to turn them directly over to the FBI. Because he was afraid she really was Abby? Afraid she remembered that it had been Jake Cantrell who'd tried to kill her six years ago?

She thought of the way Jake had reacted to the locket. He'd appeared almost ready to break down with grief. A strange reaction for a man who'd tried to kill his lover.

She shook her head. She wasn't sure of anything at this point. Especially her reaction to him. That was why she wasn't taking any chances. But she couldn't shake off the memory of what had happened back at the gas pumps. That almost remembered feeling of… what? Passion?

Whatever it had been, it was gone again. And now she couldn't be sure what she'd felt. If anything.

"You are acting so…different," Elena said.

"I know, but I have to be strong right now. And you have to be strong. There are people who want to hurt us."

Elena wiped at a tear. "The people who killed Julio?"

"Yes. And others. I have to keep you safe, no matter what else I have to do. Do you understand?

The child nodded. "You always keep me safe."

Her eyes burned. "I have always tried."

"Where are we going?" Elena asked, looking out at the highway ahead.

Good question. As soon as Jake woke up, he'd either figure out a way to free himself or raise such a ruckus, the station attendant would hear him and call someone. Either way, it wouldn't be long before he'd be after them again. This time, with the help of the FBI, unless she missed her guess.

She'd have to ditch the pickup and get another means of transportation before she could leave Del Rio. How would she do that? Did she know how to hot-wire a car? She thought not. Nor did she expect to be as lucky as Jake had been in Ciudad Acuna.

She pulled up to a stop sign and rolled down her window, letting in the morning air, already hot although it wasn't even eight yet. In the distance, she heard a train's whistle.

Jake woke with a start to find the gas station attendant standing over him, holding a dripping empty bucket and wearing a perplexed expression.

"How come you're handcuffed to my pump?" the boy asked.

For a moment, he couldn't remember. Or maybe he just didn't want to. "My girlfriend and I had a little falling-out."

"Really?" the kid said. "You must have really ticked her off."

"Yeah." He sat up. His head ached, and unfortunately, the memory of what had happened came back in minute detail. He still couldn't believe it. Might not have, except for the bruised skin just below his ribs where she'd jabbed him hard with the gun, and the raised, painful lump on his head where she'd nailed him.

Nor could he forget what he'd seen in her eyes just before she'd hit him. He shook his head and groaned, his head aching from more than the blow as he stumbled to his feet.

Besides the headache and still being handcuffed to a gas pump, he was soaking wet from being doused with a bucket of cold water. But the water *had* done the trick. He glanced at his watch. He hadn't been out long. If he hurried—

"Do you have a cell phone?" The boy nodded. "Get it. And bring me a hacksaw, will ya?"

"Amtrak's Sunset Limited from New Orleans pulls out of Del Rio, Texas headed for points west at 8:30 a.m. Sunday, Monday, Thursday and Saturday," the clerk said. It was Thursday.

She had only enough money to buy two coach seats as far as El Paso and just hoped that would be far enough.

"I'm hungry," Elena told her the minute they got on the train.

"As soon as we leave the station, I'll get you something to eat."

She'd gotten a window seat on the station side and pulled down the shade, leaving it open just enough that she could still see the platform. So far she hadn't spotted any of Calderone's men. Or Jake Cantrell. Not that she thought she would. He and the FBI would be looking for the red Toyota pickup, expecting her to still be driving it. But how long would it take them to find the truck parked in the junkyard down the road from the train station?

The train started to move. She leaned back, finally beginning to relax a little. Through the window, she watched the last of Del Rio sweep past. She looked for Jake's face, or Ramon's and the rest of Calderone's men, in the people they passed along the way. But she didn't see anyone who looked familiar.

"Let's get some breakfast," she told her daughter when Del Rio had disappeared entirely and only desert stretched to the horizon.

In the dining car, she ordered the Tucson Morning for Elena, two pancakes, butter and syrup, and the Sunrise Limited for herself, eggs and grits.

They ate in silence, Elena making short work of her pancakes and then finishing most of her mother's eggs and grits. Elena sulked. She'd finally found her father. Only to lose him again. Thanks to her.

When they'd finished breakfast, they went back to their seats and Elena fell asleep to the rocking of the train, while she stared out the window. Miles and miles of flat desert as far as the eye could see. The train clattered along and she had to admit at last, she wasn't the woman she'd believed she was for the last six years.

Jake still had one person in the FBI he thought he could trust. He called Reese Ramsey, a man he'd trusted with his life more than a few times when they'd worked together as agents. Reese, true to form, didn't ask any questions, just listened until he'd finished.

"Two agents will bring you what you need in the next fifteen minutes," Reese said. "If you need anything else—"

"Yeah, I know, *don't* call."

"No, I'm here for you, Jake. I don't believe the rumors going around this place. Not for a minute."

"Thanks, Reese." That meant a lot, since Ramsey had been on the team the night Abby died. His injuries from the explosion had left him with a metal plate in his left leg and a painful limp.

Two Feds showed up ten minutes after Jake's call. By then, he was in the gas-station office drinking a soda and watching a rerun on the black and white.

"Reese put an APB out on the woman and the pickup," one of the federal agents informed him. "He suggested you might want to check in with Frank."

Yeah, right. Jake only nodded and took the items he'd requested with a hurried "thanks." He handed them a plastic bag with the handcuffs in it. "You'll find two sets of fresh prints on these. Ask Reese to check them against the files and let me know what he comes up with."

He went into the john and changed quickly into the dry new clothing: jeans, socks, boots, shirt and jean jacket. Then he strapped on the shoulder holster, pocketed the money and slipped the cell phone and extra clips for the weapons into his coat pocket.

As he walked out to the nondescript car waiting for him beside the gas pump, he asked himself: what would Isabella Montenegro do? Probably try to hightail it out of town in the pickup. Just like Reese thought she would. In that case, it would just be a matter of waiting for a call from Reese that she'd been pulled over.

But he no longer believed he was dealing with Isabella Montenegro. He was looking for a woman who'd escaped from a rundown motel in broad daylight, who'd put a shot between a man's eyes without hesitation, who'd pulled a gun on him, handcuffed him to a gas pump, knocked him out and stolen his weapon, money and previously "stolen" truck.

He thought he knew now who he was dealing with. But still, he just couldn't be sure. Not yet. The fingerprints on the handcuffs would tell the tale. But he knew he couldn't wait for that. There was one other way to find out exactly who she was.

He walked to the car and laid his arms over the top. The metal was hot to the touch, the sun low and blinding, the air scented with unleaded gasoline and Texas dust.

That woman, the one who'd known exactly where to point the barrel end of the gun, was too smart not to ditch the truck. But was she smart enough to steal another rig? Did she have the know-how? Abby hadn't been good at appropriating automobiles.

Then what? Another bus? A sound from earlier seemed to echo through his aching head. A train whistle off in the distance.

"Hey," he called back to the gas station attendant. "Is there a passenger train that comes through town?"

The boy nodded, his eyes still glued to the tube. "The Sunset Limited," he called back.

"The one I just heard? Where is it headed?"

"Los Angeles, California." He turned to look at Jake then, as if the words held some sort of magic.

"Do you know what time it left?"

"Eight-thirty. Only time it comes through, headed west."

Jake glanced at his watch. "What's its next stop?"

Chapter 8

She dozed, waking abruptly to the swaying of the train, and reached automatically for her daughter, fear seizing her for those few seconds before her hand touched warm skin.

Elena slept, curled toward her in the adjacent seat, the morning light on her precious face.

It was impossible now *not* to see Jake in her daughter. For a long time, she just stared down at that face, trying to make sense of everything. Jake was Elena's father. Any fool could see that. But even if she hadn't seen it with her eyes, her heart now knew it was so. Then why didn't her heart tell her that she and Jake had once been lovers?

Her head ached. She felt as if she were trying to put together a puzzle with most of the pieces missing and no idea of the finished picture. Was there any chance at all that Elena *wasn't* her own child?

She thought back to the difficult birth, trying desperately to remember the exact moment she'd first seen her daughter through the flurry of doctors and nurses and the pain. Such pain. The doctor had given her something to help with the birth. He said there was *"una problema."*

She opened her eyes with a start. She *hadn't* seen Elena until after the birth. Long enough after it that she couldn't be sure Elena was the child she'd given birth to.

She felt sick. And weak. And scared. Was it possible? But who would want to do such a thing to her? Calderone had the power, there was no doubt about that. But why would he? Why go to so much trouble? And for what? It made no sense.

She studied Elena, searching for signs of herself in the child, then sighed. It didn't matter if the babies had been switched. Elena was hers. Would always be hers. Calderone be damned. He might have set the wheels in motion, but she was now at the controls.

The thought almost made her laugh. What did she know about control? For the last six years she'd had no control at all over her life.

Just the thought of Julio—had anything he'd told her been true? It didn't appear so. Not based on what she'd seen of herself lately.

She shivered, thinking she should be shocked by her behavior. But she wasn't. She definitely liked this woman better than the defenseless and frightened Isabella Montenegro. But that was the past, she told herself. She wasn't Isabella Montenegro, the woman who took whatever she had to to survive. Not anymore. She was—

She wasn't Abby Diaz, either. Even if she *had* been

six years ago, she wasn't that Abby anymore. She didn't know who she was. A stranger. A stranger who was in a lot of trouble, but who was resourceful and strong. It was heady stuff. She liked this new feeling. A lot.

Now all she needed was a plan.

When the sunrise limited stopped in Sanderson, Texas, Jake Cantrell was waiting at the station. He'd driven fast and furiously to beat the train and now kept out of sight, watching to make sure that Isabella and Elena didn't get off. If they were even on the train. His instincts told him that they were. And that wasn't all his instincts told him.

He waited until the last moment before he boarded, getting on the end car. He knew Frank Jordan would be expecting a call. The FBI bureau chief would be furious that he hadn't heard from him.

But Jake didn't work for Frank Jordan anymore. He reported to Mitchell Forbes now and Mitchell gave him free rein. Probably because Mitchell knew him and knew that was the way he worked best. The *only* way he worked now.

Frank should know Jake, too. At least well enough not to be waiting by the phone. They'd once been friends, Frank a mentor, a father figure. They'd worked closely together. Right up until the last case. Right up until the night Abby was killed.

Right or wrong, he blamed the FBI, blamed Frank, for what happened that night. It was supposed to have been part of a routine investigation. They'd been undermanned, not realizing what they'd walked into. One long-time agent, Buster McNorton, had been killed, along with rookies Dell Harper and Abby Diaz. Reese Ramsey had been injured.

Only he and Frank had walked away without injury.

There'd been an investigation, but it hadn't turned up anything at the time. Just bad luck that they'd stumbled onto one of Tomaso Calderone's operations.

Jake had quit the Bureau, bitter as hell because he'd lost everything when he'd lost Abby.

Frank had gone on to work his way up the FBI ladder. So had Reese Ramsey.

He hadn't seen Frank in six years. Hadn't talked to him. And he wasn't ready just yet to call him. Especially after seeing the so-called evidence against him collected by the FBI. Why now, after all these years?

He took a seat by the train window, unable to shake the feeling he'd had since he woke up handcuffed to a gas pump: that he had to get to the woman and kid, pronto. The feeling was so strong, it took everything in him to wait until the train got moving. What if his instincts were wrong? What if she and the kid weren't on the train?

Then that would mean he was wrong about a lot of things.

The train finally pulled out of the station. He watched to make sure she hadn't gotten off. And that Ramon Hernandez hadn't gotten on. At least not while Jake had been sitting at the window. For all he knew, Ramon could have boarded the train at Del Rio.

The thought did nothing to dispel his fears.

He got up and started through the cars.

He hadn't gone far when he spotted the back of the woman's head a few seats ahead and to the right. He'd have recognized that hair and the shape of her head anywhere.

Relief coursed through him. At least he'd been right about her taking the train. Abby had always liked trains. They'd made love the first time on one a lot like this one.

He shook that thought out of his head. He didn't think of her anymore as Isabella Montenegro. But he also hadn't accepted she was Abby. Not yet. He wished he could see the little girl. She had to be with her mother, no doubt sitting in the adjacent seat. As badly as he wanted to make sure, he took a seat a few rows back and off to the left, where he could watch them from behind the magazine he'd bought in the station. He wanted to be ready to move quickly if he had to.

The train rolled along the tracks, with a gentle rocking motion and a faint clickity-clack. With the woman in view, Jake began to relax a little. They appeared to be in no current danger. The car was about two-thirds full and there was no sign of Ramon or any of his men.

Jake leaned back in the seat, willing his heart to slow, his anxiety to recede. They were fine. His instincts had been right about the train, but wrong about the danger. So where did that leave his other instinct, the one that told him Abby Diaz was alive?

Abby looked out the train window, seeing nothing. She dug in her memory, sifting through the faint and painful nightmares she'd woken with six years before, searching for Abby Diaz, searching for the woman she'd been, frantic to find the skills the FBI agent must have possessed.

She willed herself to remember, needing that training desperately if she hoped to save herself and Elena. But she found nothing in the ashes of her previous life. Except for a few faint recalled feelings.

She had only one memory from before the fire. She cherished it like an old family quilt, wrapping herself in the comforting warmth. Let that one good memory be real, she prayed, as she recalled the feeling that was her grandmother. It filled her with a strange kind of peace. The same kind of peace she'd seen on Elena's face when she looked at her father.

But even the memory of her kind, compassionate, loving grandmother was hard to hold on to. Had she invented the woman just to help her get through the last six years?

What about the only other feeling she could recall? Passion. Had that been with Jake? Was that why she'd blanked out her life prior to six years ago? Because she couldn't face his betrayal?

She felt suddenly bereft. She had no way of knowing who to trust. There was no one to turn to. It was just her and Elena. Just as it had always been. Just as she had always had only one thought: keeping Elena safe. But how?

For a moment, she thought about turning herself over to the FBI. Didn't that make more sense than taking the chance that Calderone's men would capture her and Elena?

She had the sense that she couldn't trust the FBI and absolutely nothing to back up that fear. But the feeling was all she had to go on until she could find out who'd tried to kill her six years ago. And why.

* * *

Jake saw the woman rise, then the little girl stepped out into the aisle. He felt his heart jump at the sight of the child. She started toward him, her mother right behind her.

He quickly hid behind the magazine, his heart pounding. Any moment they'd walk right by him. Where were they going? Probably just to the bathroom. They were headed in the wrong direction for the dining car. He held his breath as first the child passed by within inches of him, then the woman. She was carrying the bag with the envelope in it.

He wanted to turn and watch them, but waited until he was sure they'd stopped at the bathroom. When he did turn, he saw the waiting line, but no sign of the woman and child. He got to his feet and caught a glimpse of them going into the next car, no doubt hoping to find an empty rest room. He wanted to follow but knew it'd be too risky. Who knew what the woman would do if she spotted him? He couldn't take the chance. Not until the train stopped, anyway.

He sat back down and picked up the magazine again, feeling antsy. Anxious. That feeling he'd had earlier about the woman and child being in imminent danger was back. Only stronger. He glanced around the car. Nothing out of the ordinary. He would bet his horse that Ramon and his men weren't on the train. Then what? What had him so worried?

He turned in his seat to look back. He didn't like letting them out of his sight. But what choice did he have if he hoped to keep his presence a secret? He told himself he could protect them much better at a distance.

When the train stopped in Alpine, he'd get them off. One way or another. At least this time, he knew the woman wouldn't go quietly, as she had in Mexico. He let out a soft laugh. No, he thought, he wasn't dealing with the same woman anymore and they both knew it.

He glanced down at his watch. How long did it take for the two of them to use the bathroom? Even if there had been a line in the next car—

Alarm hurtled through him. It had been too long. They should have been back by now. Something was wrong.

He stood and felt the train begin to slow. They must be nearing the Alpine, Texas station. He moved faster. Out the car and into the next. The car was only about half-full.

He passed the women's bathroom. Vacant. Panic sent a jolt of adrenaline into his system like a strong drug.

There was only one more passenger car. If she wasn't in there— The oppressively hot car was empty. The air-conditioning must have gone out. No wonder it was empty. This bathroom was vacant, as well. He caught a movement outside the railroad car—a flash of bright-colored, billowing fabric and the dark sleeve of a man's suit in the space between the cars. That was when he heard the muffled cry. Then he was running, his weapon drawn.

The train whistle blasted in his ears as he reached the end of the railroad car. In that instant, just before he burst through the door into the enclosed area between the cars, he saw the woman backed against a corner, Elena tucked protectively behind her. A man in a dark suit stood holding a gun on the pair in one gloved hand, his broad back and one shoulder visible through the glass.

Jake hit the door, banging it open, driven by his forward motion and fear. The man in the suit never saw him coming. Never heard him over the blast of the train whistle.

Jake hit the man hard, slamming him into the wall. The gun clattered to the floor. Before the man could reach for it, Abby kicked it away. But the man hadn't been going for the gun, Jake realized belatedly. Instead, he dove for the emergency exit.

Jake grabbed for him, but missed and he was gone, leaping from the slow-moving train into nothing but hot, dry Texas air.

Through the opening, Jake saw him hit the ground and roll, then get to his feet and, limping, disappear behind a parked freight train. Jake gripped the edge of the opening, staring after him, a bad feeling pressing on his chest.

He turned. The woman he no longer thought of as Isabella Montenegro had dropped to her knees and now cradled her daughter in her arms, her eyes tightly closed as she rocked back and forth, murmuring softly. A tear squeezed from beneath her dark lashes to glisten on her cheek.

Just watching her try so hard not to cry—he didn't want to feel this much. He stood for a long moment, letting his heart slow, his fear subside, then he holstered his weapon and reached down with his shirtsleeve over his fingers to pick up the man's gun from the floor. It was a service revolver like the ones used by FBI agents.

The train rolled to a stop, signaling their arrival in

Alpine, Texas. The Hub of Big Bend, the sign over the station read, Home of the Last Frontier.

Jake slipped the man's gun into his jacket and picked up the bag she'd dropped, knowing there was little chance of fingerprints since the man had been wearing gloves.

He watched her rise to her feet again, her hands on her daughter's small shoulders as the two turned their gazes to him. Elena smiled at him through her tear-stained face, the look of admiration in her eyes almost his undoing.

"I knew you'd come," she said confidently. "How is your head?"

"OK. Are you all right?"

She nodded and hugged her doll to her, still beaming up at him, her smile contagious. "But Sweet Ana and I still have to go to the bathroom."

He chuckled and shifted his gaze to her mother.

"Thanks," she said.

He wanted to tell her not to thank him. He'd only saved her temporarily and he wasn't sure how long he could keep doing that, because he was no longer sure just who was after her.

But he only nodded and opened the door to the train car, stepping back to let her and Elena enter ahead of him.

Through the window, he could see that the car was still empty. He wondered where Ramon and his men were. But mostly he wondered about the man in the dark suit.

He moved to the door marked ladies' rest room, pulled it open to make sure it really was as vacant as the sign said, then motioned that it was all right for Elena to go on in. "If you don't need your mother's help, she and I will wait here for you."

Her mother's gaze jerked up to his, but she said nothing as Elena closed the door behind her, leaving the two of them alone in the small space between the seats.

"What did that man want with you?" he asked quietly.

She shook her head. "He planned to take us off the train when it stopped. That's all I know."

"You didn't recognize him? He wasn't one of Ramon's men?"

Again she shook her head. "I'd never seen him before." She seemed to hesitate. "But he knew *me*. He was startled when he saw me. It was obvious the way he stared at my face. He called me Abby."

Jake nodded, his heart pounding, as he put down the woman's bag on the floor beside him.

"I'm sorry about earlier." She lowered her gaze. "Back at the gas station."

"Sure you are."

She looked up as if surprised by his reply.

He smiled in answer, searching her face. "We both know that if you had it to do over again, you would."

She said nothing but this time she held his gaze, no longer pretending to be someone she wasn't.

He needed to ask her more about the man who'd been holding them at gunpoint. He needed to ask her a lot of things. But there was one question that couldn't wait. He needed it answered. And he needed it answered now.

Before she knew what was happening, he caught her shoulders and pulled her into him, dropping his lips to hers.

* * *

It happened too fast. One moment he was simply looking at her. The next he was kissing her. She'd been too stunned. Too shaken from her close call. Too relieved at the sight of him coming to her rescue. Again.

She just hadn't been prepared. But the moment his lips touched hers, she realized nothing could have prepared her for his kiss.

His mouth closed over hers, stealing her breath away. His kiss was at first tentative. Then ravenous. He kissed her deeply, completely, his lips unlocking a memory so pure, so strong, that she felt dizzy and weak under the freedom of it.

His arms enveloped her, pulling her against him, crushing her breasts to his hard muscular chest, kissing her, tasting her, igniting a fuse of desire that quickly spread through her until she thought she'd explode.

It was over far too quickly. He pulled away abruptly, staggering back in the narrow space, his gaze locked on her, his eyes wide.

She leaned against the wall, not trusting her legs as she fought for breath. *This. This* was the feeling she'd told herself she couldn't possibly have remembered.

"Abby," he said.

It was no longer a question. Nor a curse. It was simply a statement of fact.

She was Abby Diaz. And now they both knew it.

Chapter 9

"Why?" Jake asked in a hoarse whisper. "Why didn't you come back to me?"

She looked into his handsome face, the taste of him still on her lips, the memory of his strong arms around her still making her tremble. His eyes reflected the same hurt and confusion as she felt.

"Abby?" He touched her arm and she shuddered. "Abby, you know me. You know I would never hurt you. Why are you afraid of me?"

"Because I *don't* know you," she cried.

He stared at her, uncomprehending. "You believe that stuff in the envelope about me? Even after that kiss?"

She believed she was Abby Diaz. That she'd been crazy in love with this man. That they shared an incredible passion. But did she really believe he'd tried to kill her six years ago? No. But that was her body talking, and she knew she couldn't trust it right now.

"Are you telling me that kiss meant nothing to you?" he asked, his voice rough with pain.

She shook her head, tears welling in her eyes. "No. Jake, I don't remember anything before waking up in a hospital six years ago."

His jaw dropped. He stared at her openmouthed.

"I woke up to find Julio Montenegro beside my bed. He said he was my husband. All I had of my past was what he told me and some faint memories that made no sense."

Jake shook his head, disbelieving. "You don't still think you're Isabella Montenegro?"

"How can I after everything that's happened? After—" The kiss. She unconsciously ran her tongue over her upper lip, the memory still fresh, the feeling still intoxicating.

"But you're afraid of me because of what you found in the envelope."

She was afraid of him because of the power she knew he had over her, because of the obvious passion they shared. And because she couldn't remember what had happened between them six years ago. But something had. She felt it.

"I don't know who or what to believe at this point," she said, looking away.

From outside, the conductor called, "All aboard!"

"If you could remember what you and I had, you'd know the truth," he said softly. "I loved Abby Diaz. I would never have hurt her. We were going to get married. We were going to have a child."

"We *did* have a child," she said.

"Yes." The bathroom door opened and Elena stepped out between them, her doll locked in the crook of her arm.

He seemed to hesitate only a moment before lifting their daughter up into his arms, his face twisted in pain, and hugged her tightly to him. His eyes closed as he buried his face in her hair and breathed in deeply, as if inhaling her essence.

"Daddy," Elena sighed and hugged him around the neck.

Tears burned her eyes, her throat choked closed with emotion, as she watched Jake with his daughter. All those years lost. She felt a surge of anger. Why? Elena had desperately needed a father. Where had Jake been?

"All aboard!" the conductor called again. She could hear the sounds of the train getting ready to move again. Passengers were settling into their seats, voices and laughter drifting down to them.

"We have to get off the train," Jake said and looked up at her as if he expected an argument.

How could she argue? Staying on the train would be foolhardy since someone, whoever he'd been, knew where she was. But was going with Jake any less foolhardy?

She met his gaze, wondering where he planned to take them. What he planned to do with them. Turn them over to the FBI? She looked at her daughter's face. Elena's green eyes glowed as if filled with inner sunshine. After everything that had happened in her young life, all was now right in her world. She'd found her father.

Abby nodded to Jake as her gaze flicked back to him. He wasn't the only one who wanted answers. And while she wasn't ready to trust him with her heart or even her life, she knew she could trust him with Elena's. For now, that was enough. She picked up her bag and started toward the exit.

With Elena still in his arms, he followed Abby through the car, the full weight of responsibility making him tense. Anxious. He didn't know who was after Abby and Elena. Nor what they wanted with the pair. All he knew was that he had to find a safe place to hide them until he could figure it out.

The glaring noonday sun spilled in the windows, blinding and hot. Any moment the train would start moving and they wouldn't be able to get off.

He was right behind her as she scrambled to the platform just seconds before the train started out of the station.

As soon as his feet touched the ground, he was scanning the platform and the cool darkness behind the sun-glazed windows of the station, wary, worried. By now the man who'd jumped from the train could be waiting for them. Or Ramon and his men. Or the Feds. He felt scared. Abby and this child in his arms were everything he'd ever wanted. And now someone was trying to take them away from him—again.

"Here, give me, Elena," Abby said quickly.

The last thing he wanted to do was let go of his daughter. But he was smart enough to know he wouldn't be able to get to his weapon fast enough with the child in his arms. Still, it was all he could do to relinquish her.

The sun hovered overhead. No breeze moved along the tracks. Only the sound of the train leaving the station filled the late morning air.

"On your right," Abby whispered as she took Elena and, smiling, started walking in the other direction.

He glanced out of the corner of his eye and saw the security guards. They were looking at him and talking quickly. One had his hand on the butt end of his gun.

Jake quickly caught up to Abby, slipping his arm around her and leaning closer, as if to share a private thought with her. "Keep moving. They aren't sure yet."

Just before they rounded the corner of the station, Jake called out, "Mom! We almost missed our stop! I hope you haven't been waiting long." Then they were around the blind corner where the guards couldn't see them, couldn't see that no one was waiting to pick them up. "Run!"

Abby didn't relax until Alpine, Texas, disappeared behind them, distant as the rugged volcanic-born mountains that cradled it. The day was hot and dry. They were headed south on Farm Road 118 in the four-wheel drive Explorer Jake had rented, leaving behind grassland and commercial orchards for the rough, seemingly endless mountain country ahead, the road behind them almost empty.

"Stealing a car is too risky and it won't buy us any more time than renting one," he'd said a few blocks from the train station after they were sure the security guards hadn't followed. "Not with Calderone *and* the FBI after us now. They'll be on top of anything we do."

She thought of the guards at the train station and wondered who had alerted them. They'd seemed more interested in Jake than her and Elena. Unlike the man on the train. He seemed to know exactly who he was after. The question was why? What had he wanted?

By now she wasn't sure who was actually after them. Everyone, it seemed.

She glanced back at Elena, strapped into her seat, her gaze focused on the country outside the window. The child seemed to have gotten over her earlier fear of the sudden change in her mother. Now she watched the rugged terrain flash by, her eyes large, her expression excited. Elena had never been outside the small town in Mexico where she'd been born. Nor had she ever seen mountains before. Elena always made the best of any situation. But this situation continued to get worse.

Abby felt sick to her stomach with fear for her daughter. The people after them were trained killers. They wanted the money Julio had stolen. But did they also want Abby Diaz for some reason? And her child?

Jake turned on the radio and adjusted it so most of the sound came out of the back speakers. "There isn't anywhere we can leave Elena that would be safe," he said quietly as if reading her mind.

She nodded, the lump in her throat making it impossible to speak for a moment. "I'm just worried."

"So am I." He gave her a reassuring smile. "But she should be safe with two former FBI agents taking care of her, don't you think?" His smiled faded in an instant and his eyes darkened to deep jade. "You really don't remember *anything?*" he asked quietly.

She shook her head.

He stared at her for a moment, then the road ahead. "I've heard of cases where there's partial or total memory loss due to a brain injury."

"Mine's not due to an injury."

His gaze ricocheted back to her face. "Then—"

"The doctors said there was nothing physically wrong with me. They think my memory loss was due to shock or repression," she said, watching his face. "Now that I know who I am, I think it was from discovering someone close to me had tried to kill me." She met his gaze and held it.

Jake stared at her for a moment, then looked back to the road ahead. "I didn't try to kill you, Abby. And I'll prove it to you. I'll find out who did."

"*We'll* find out."

He drove in silence for a moment. "You can't remember what happened six years ago?"

"No," she said, hoping she wasn't making a mistake telling him this.

"Or remember…us?"

That was the hardest to admit. "I woke up in a Mexican hospital, burned and in terrible pain, with no memory at all. It's as if my life began six years ago. Julio told me things, but none of the pieces ever fit. I sensed—" A lost passion? "That there was more. Something I'd lost. Something…important."

His gaze softened, and his glance at her was almost a caress. He let out a sigh. "Abby, I can't tell you how much I've missed you. After what happened, I—" He waved a hand through the air. "I didn't want to go on. Not without you."

"But you did." She hadn't meant it to sound like an accusation.

"Yeah, I guess I did." He glanced over at her. "And I guess you still aren't sure about me, are you?"

She wasn't sure about anything. Except that she was Abby Diaz. That Elena was Jake's father. That she and

Jake had shared a passion that made her body come alive. Her past played at her memory, bits and pieces that left her worried and afraid of what she'd find when her memory returned. *If* it returned.

"Didn't you ever wonder if I might be alive? Question the idea I was dead?" she asked, hearing the hurt in her words.

"Good Lord, no," he said, reaching over to cup her cheek in his large hand. The hand of a man who worked at hard labor. There was something comforting about that. Strong and solid.

"I saw the end of the building where you'd been just moments before go up in a ball of flame," he said quietly as he turned back to his driving. "I knew you couldn't have survived that."

"But when my body wasn't found—"

"But it was. A body of a woman was found the next day. We just assumed it was yours."

She nodded and hugging herself against the sudden chill, looked away. "I wonder who she was."

"We'll know soon enough," he told her. "Frank is having the body exhumed. But Julio said it was some woman who worked with him."

"How do you explain the evidence I found in the envelope?" she asked, wondering why Julio had planned to burn it. Could he have been trying to protect her? Or someone else?

"I can't," he said simply. "All I can tell you is none of it is true."

They drove along for a few miles to only the sound of Elena singing softly along with the radio.

"Tell me about Abby, the one you knew," she implored. "Tell me what I was like. Who I was. But first, Jake, tell me—was I raised by my grandmother?" She held her breath, terrified of the answer. If that memory hadn't been real, then—

"Ana," he said.

She looked startled.

He nodded. "Yes, the same name you gave Elena's doll."

She frowned. "Julio told me my grandmother was named Carmela. The name sounded wrong. When Elena wanted help naming her doll, I suggested Ana. I liked the name." She looked over at Jake. "The grandmother I remember was a very kind, generous, loving woman."

"She was," he agreed. "You adored her."

Tears filled her eyes. "Is she still alive?"

He shook his head. "Ana Fuentes passed away a year before you were—lost," he finished.

She sighed, relieved to hear that her grandmother hadn't died while she'd been held captive in Mexico. That would have been too painful to bear. "And my parents?"

He shook his head again. "Your father died before you were born. Your mother when you were just a baby."

How odd to lose both parents at such a young age. "From accidents?"

Jake nodded, but kept his eyes on the road. Was there more to it?

She stared out at the rugged scenery. "Then I had no one."

"Just me," Jake said.

She realized they were nearing some sort of town. She could see a handful of adobe and rock dwellings, but they seemed deserted.

"Study Butte?" Elena said, leaning over the front seat, to read the sign.

"Stew-dy Butte," he corrected.

As they drew closer, Abby saw that the town was abandoned, the buildings mostly in ruin. "A ghost town," she whispered and looked over at Jake, wondering why he'd brought them here, of all places.

He didn't say anything as he drove through the deserted town, then took a narrow dirt road that led up into the hills.

He glanced over at her. "Remember any of this?"

She shook her head. Nothing in the harsh landscape looked familiar. Just isolated and hostile.

"This is where I was raised," he said after they'd driven up the windy road for a few minutes. "Study Butte was a mining town. My grandfather got in on the last of the quicksilver just before it died out." He glanced over at her. "Like you, I was raised by a grandparent."

She heard something in his voice she recognized. Regret. Pain. Loss. "What happened to your parents?"

"They weren't into parenting," he said tightly. He brought the car to a stop in front of a small adobe building. "My grandfather came to the house one night and brought me here."

She swallowed, her eyes burning, and reached across to squeeze his hand on the seat between them.

"It wasn't that bad," he said, and withdrew his hand, pushing away her sympathy. "I learned to love it here. My grandfather was a lot like your grandmother. He saved me."

"So we were both orphans," she said.

"Yeah." He glanced over the seat at Elena, the lines

in his face softening. "Come on," he said to the child as he shut off the engine. "There's something I want to show you."

Elena scrambled from the car to be hoisted up into his strong arms. He looked over at Abby as she got out of the car and tilted his head toward the steep hillside behind the house. The trail up the mountain was faint from lack of use. She glanced back the way they'd come, at the ghost town, now miniature in the distance. Then she followed Jake and Elena up the path through the rocks and cactus.

She could hear Jake pointing out mountains and flowers to Elena.

"What is that smell?" Elena asked, wrinkling up her nose.

He laughed. "Creosote bush," he said, pointing to the short evergreen with tiny yellow flowers on it. "That is the smell of the desert."

They topped the ridge, stopping in the hollow of a rock outcropping. Jake moved to the edge where the rocks opened. She joined him and caught her breath at the sight before her. The landscape was honeycombed with canyons and caves against a backdrop of jagged mountains, some reddish with the cinnabar that had contained the mercury, the substance that had given the town life—and killed it. Beyond Study Butte, she could see the river that marked the boundary between Texas and Mexico.

"The Rio Grande," he said proudly as if it was his.

In some way, she realized it was. This was Jake's home. That place he could always come to that resonated with another time. Did she have such a place?

"The Rio Grande is one of the longest rivers in North America," he was telling Elena.

She felt his gaze on her.

"You should see the sunsets up here," he said quietly.

She met his eyes and felt a heat hotter than even the fiery sun hanging in the endless blue overhead. And she knew they'd seen a few sunsets up here, that they'd made love in the hollow of these rocks.

He seemed lost in her eyes as if he could see things she couldn't, feel things she could only imagine.

"I'm hungry," Elena said. "Is this where we're going to eat the food we bought?"

He dragged his gaze away and laughed. "This is the place."

He started back down the mountainside, but Abby stayed behind for a few moments, trying to see Jake Cantrell as a boy here, wanting to feel the strong roots that had helped form the man.

Something caught her eye. She leaned closer and saw the small hollow in the rocks where the sun glistened off one side. Initials had been laboriously dug into the stone. J.C.

Jake took the trail down to the house, surveying the dirt road and the familiar hills around it. Elena was at his side. He knew he hadn't been followed from Alpine. Traffic had been light, and once he'd turned at Study Butte, he'd had the road to himself.

Nor did anyone know about this place. Not even Mitchell. Or the FBI. The only person he'd ever shared it with was Abby. And now his daughter.

As he pointed out the different mountains in the distance to Elena, he felt himself beginning to relax. He hadn't been back here in years. But he *had* kept the place after his grandfather died. A couple from town took care of the upkeep and he kept his name off the title, burying it under a variety of company names and addresses.

He hadn't done it out of paranoia, but the simple desire for privacy. Study Butte was too much of himself. He hadn't wanted to share that part of him with anyone. Except Abby.

He turned to look back at her. Her dark hair shone in the sunlight. It swung around her shoulders as she moved toward him, her hips swaying, thighs strong and muscular against the denim of her jeans, the soft hint of her breasts beneath the embroidered top.

"Did you see the mountains?" Elena asked excitedly. "Daddy says they named a canyon in Big Bend just for me. Santa Elena Canyon. He says the walls of the canyon are so high and narrow that the river roars through it. The Apaches used to believe that anyone who went into the canyon would never be seen again."

Abby laughed, the sound heartrending.

Jake wished there was a place that the three of them could go and never be seen again.

"Can we go there someday? Can we see it?" Elena pleaded.

Abby ran a hand over her daughter's dark hair and smiled. "Yes," she said after a moment. "I suppose we could someday." She looked up at him for confirmation.

"Definitely. The three of us."

Elena squealed in delight and ran to the car to help with the groceries.

He could see the doubt on Abby's face. "No one knows about this place but you and me. It's going to be all right."

She nodded.

"Or is it me who has you worried?"

She seemed to study him for a moment, then shook her head.

He stepped closer to her, his fingers caressing her smooth cheek as he brushed back her dark hair. Her body came to him as if drawn by magnetism. Or something much more powerful.

He turned her, spooning her body to his as he wrapped her in his arms so they were both facing east. "That's Big Bend," he whispered. "And someday we'll take our daughter there to see her canyon."

Abby leaned back against him. Her scent mingled with the desert's. He closed his eyes, breathing it in, letting himself believe for that moment that she was finally starting to trust him and that they were safe.

The adobe dwelling was small but cozy—and almost familiar, Abby thought, with its tiled floors and wood and wicker furniture.

Jake motioned to the huge claw-foot tub in the bathroom. "If you ladies would like to get a hot bath, I'll get dinner started."

A bath. At that moment, Abby couldn't imagine anything she wanted more.

"Can we have bubbles?" Elena asked excitedly.

Jake produced a bottle of purple bubble bath from the bag of groceries. "Just for you," he said handing it to Elena. "I *thought* a girl like you would appreciate a bubble bath."

Elena giggled as she took the plastic bottle and ran into the bathroom. Jake handed Abby the other supplies he'd bought while she was purchasing clothing for her and Elena. Their fingers brushed and she felt a rush both chemical and electrical. Her breath caught in her throat as a memory flashed bright as Texas sunlight.

"What is it?" Jake asked, suddenly wary.

She stared at him. "I… I think it's a memory. You and me on a…train? Just the two of us."

He smiled, relief softening his strong, masculine face. "What do you remember?" he asked gently, seductively.

She felt her face flush with heat, the images so provocative, so sensual, so…sexy. She swallowed. "Just that we were on a train together before today."

He nodded, studying her as if he didn't quite believe that was all she'd seen.

"Mommy! Come on!" Elena called from the bathroom.

Face burning, she hurried in to join her daughter, closing the bathroom door behind her. In the mirror over the sink, she saw her high color and knew he'd seen it as well. The images of their lovemaking had burned into her brain like a brand. Her skin tingled with the memory, her breasts heavy and aching, need making her weak. How odd to remember such intimacies with a man who was still a stranger to her! Worse yet, to want him so desperately.

She filled the tub, bathing Elena first, then shooing her daughter out to help Jake with dinner so she could be alone. She poured in the purple bubble bath. It smelled of lilac. She stepped into the warm water and cool lilac bubbles and slid down with a satisfied *"Ahhhhhh."*

Closing her eyes, she reclined in the tub, bubbles up to her chin, and tried not to think about the man in the next room. Impossible! She opened her eyes, remembering the two of them on that other train, remembering enough to make her ache with unbearable longing.

Over dinner, Jake talked about his childhood while they ate fried catfish, hush puppies and coleslaw. Then he told Elena about her great-grandmother Ana. Abby listened, her eyes tearing. She wished Ana could have lived to see Elena, but more than anything, she wished Elena could have known her great-grandmother.

Elena listened, eyes wide, to Jake's stories, giggling one minute, bashful the next when he turned the full power of his smile on her. Abby's heart ached watching the two of them.

After dinner, Jake carried a tuckered-out Elena up to one of the two bedrooms. Abby stood in the doorway, listening to the two of them talking quietly, their voices blending in a sweet lullaby.

She watched him lean down to kiss the child on the cheek. Elena grasped him around the neck with both of her small arms and pulled him close.

"Good night, Daddy." She kissed his cheek.

Jake straightened. Abby could see the effect the words had on him. The effect his daughter had on him. He cleared his throat. "Good night, *chica suena.*"

Elena giggled. "That's what Mommy calls me."

"I know. It's what her grandmother called her."

"Good night, Mommy," she called out as she circled

an arm around Sweet Ana, snuggled down under the comforter he pulled over her, and smiled up at him.

Abby had to turn away. She walked out onto the portico and stared up at the magnificent sky. Earlier, the purple tint of twilight had softened the rough edges of the mountains. Now they were etched black against the vast Texas horizon. Stars shimmered in the deep dark blue overhead, dusting the quiet evening in silver starlight. The breeze was warm and dry, perfumed with a mixture of desert scents that pulled at her memory.

She hugged herself and looked up at the heavens, asking the one question that had haunted her since she'd learned of Jake Cantrell's existence.

"Wishing on a star?" he asked from behind her.

Startled, she swung around. His broad shoulders filled the doorway, blocking out the faint glow of the light he'd left on inside. Slowly he stepped into the starlight.

"Abby." His fingertips found her face, warm and gentle.

She lost herself in his look, in his touch, stepping into his powerful embrace as if opening a familiar door.

His kiss was both soft and seductive, passionate and potent. He traced her lips with the tip of his tongue. She opened to him, breathless, heart pounding, body aching.

"Jake," she whispered against his lips. A plea.

He pulled back just enough to look down into her face. Then he swept her up in his arms and, opening the screen door with the toe of his boot, carried her into the bedroom and laid her carefully on the bed.

"It's been a long time," she whispered as he joined

her. Starlight filtered in through the curtains along with the sweet warm scent of the night breeze.

His gaze touched her face gently. "How long?"

"Six years."

He frowned. "You don't mean—"

"Julio was never a husband to me."

He drew her to him. "I wish I could say I was sorry," he said huskily. Then his lips dropped to hers and he took her mouth with a hunger that could only match her own.

Frantically they made love, stripping away clothing to get to bare skin, kissing and caressing, wrapped up, locked together, unwilling to relinquish even a naked inch of the other's body until the moment when they lay spent, hearts pounding in unison.

Abby sighed and looked up into his handsome face. "Jake." Her one question had been answered. She remembered him...them. Their shared passion. This had been the one feeling she'd recalled, the feeling she hadn't trusted. She'd been afraid to trust it, for fear it had never existed.

They made love again, this time, slowly, seductively. She explored his body, he explored hers. The night waned outside the window, they reveled in rediscovering what they'd thought they'd lost forever.

How could she question any longer who she was? Or that Jake had been the man she'd shared such passion with? How could she still wonder if he'd been the one who'd tried to kill her?

She lay curled in his arms, sated and satisfied, feeling blessed. Feeling lucky. Both feelings scared her. She'd learned with Julio never to feel safe. Never to let her guard down. With Jake, could she and Elena learn to feel safe again?

She left the warmth of his arms to check on Elena. The child slept, Sweet Ana beside her. Abby covered her with the thin blanket and padded back across the hall to Jake.

He must have seen the worried look on her face.

"You and I are the only ones who ever knew about this place," he said. "If we aren't safe here, Abby, we aren't safe anywhere."

She nodded, fearing the latter was true as she got back into the bed, back into his arms. But she couldn't shake the worried feeling that this wouldn't last. Couldn't last.

"Tell me about the last six years," he whispered against her hair. "Please."

She stared up at the fan turning hypnotically above them, the air cool on her naked skin. "Elena and I were virtually prisoners. I tried to leave once." She hesitated. "Julio caught me and Elena. I knew then that he'd kill us both if I tried again. I also knew he was involved with Calderone. I hoped pretending would keep Elena safe."

He didn't say anything for a long time, just held her. "I'm sorry. Why do you think he pretended to be your husband for all those years?"

She shook her head. "I guess he planned to use me and Elena to get him out of Mexico with Calderone's money." Why did she feel it was much more than that? "I suppose once he realized I had amnesia and was pregnant, it was an easy way to keep an eye on me. Plus he had his own built-in housekeeper and cook."

She saw Jake's jaw clenched with anger and changed the subject.

"Tell me about my life. The key has to be in my past and you're the only one who can help me."

He told her about a strong, capable, sexy, interesting, unique woman named Abby Diaz and she had to laugh, knowing that no such woman had ever existed, except in Jake's mind. Or maybe his heart.

She tried to imagine even a scaled-down version of that woman, that life, but still couldn't.

"Has any of your memory come back?" he asked.

"Just feelings more than actual memories. Images." She frowned. "I keep seeing an older, blond woman, a striking woman."

"Crystal Jordan. Frank's wife. We spent quite a lot of time at their place. The four of us and some of the other agents."

She frowned, trying to pull up something that seemed just on the edge of her memory. But gave up after a moment and closed her eyes, her head aching.

"Give it time, Abby."

"I might not have time," she whispered. "Jake, there is someone in my past who I can't trust, who might still want me dead—and I won't even recognize him when he comes for me."

"What about the man on the train? You still can't place him?"

She shook her head. "I just know that he was shocked to see me. He definitely recognized me, and it surprised him."

He told her about the six-agent team that had gone into the building the night she disappeared, then described the agents.

"Buster McNorton was older, a veteran, experienced and levelheaded," he said summing it up.

"He's one of those who died?"

Jake nodded. "The other agent who died was Dell Harper."

She felt a small stir of memory. "Dell?"

Jake seemed to be watching her closely. "Dell Harper was the quiet type. Average Joe. You were closer to him than anyone else on the team."

That surprised her. "Really?"

He looked away. "You were on his baseball team. You always said he was like the little brother you never had."

She studied Jake, sensing something she couldn't put her finger on as she tried to picture Average Joe Dell Harper. "Was Dell married?"

He shook his head. "I think I heard something about a fiancée once. But I guess she was killed in an accident." He seemed to hesitate. "You were always real protective of him. He might have told you about it."

She said nothing, wondering if she'd heard something in Jake's voice. Jealousy?

"Frank and Reese Ramsey stayed with the Bureau," Jake continued. "Both have moved up. You remember Reese?"

She shook her head. She didn't remember any of this. It seemed as foreign as the stories Julio had told her. She wondered if she and Jake would have still been with the Bureau if that night hadn't gone so badly.

"Reese is a nice guy. Smart, easygoing, dedicated, but not like Frank."

"You don't like Frank?" she asked, surprised considering that he'd just told her they'd spent a lot of time with Frank and his wife, Crystal.

"I used to, but everything changed when you—"

"Were lost," she suggested, using his words.

"Yeah."

"Frank was with us that night?" she asked.

He let out a sigh. "Frank had gone around to the side of the building with Reese. You and I were taking the front." He looked up, his gaze meeting hers for an instant. "I'm not sure what happened. One minute you were behind me. The next you'd gone around to the back after Buster and Dell."

A chill raced over her skin like a long-legged spider. She shivered. Why had she gone with Buster and Dell instead of staying with Jake? She wouldn't have disobeyed orders, would she? She snuggled into him, suddenly terrified.

"You think Frank ordered me to go with Buster and Dell?"

He said nothing, just pulled her close and kissed the top of her head.

"If that's true, then what are we going to do? That would mean that Frank—"

His cell phone rang, startling them both. He looked at her for a long moment, then he reached for the phone where he'd left it beside the bed. He acted as if he knew who was calling. A man they both suspected they now had to fear.

Chapter 10

But it wasn't Frank Jordan's voice on the other end of the line. "Jake?"

"Reese." He sat up, glancing over at the clock beside the bed. Two-fifteen in the morning. What was Reese doing calling at this hour?

"Do you have Isabella Montenegro and her daughter with you?" Reese said without preamble, his tone hurried.

"Yes, what—"

"Jake, you're in danger."

He almost laughed. He'd been in danger since the moment he took this assignment.

"You need to get the woman and child to us as soon as possible," Reese was saying. "Tell me where you are and I'll send—"

"Reese, what's going on?"

"Jake, you've been set up. The woman isn't Abby Diaz. Your life is in danger as long as—"

"What the hell are you talking about?" he demanded.

"The fingerprints you sent us from the handcuffs," Reese said. "They *aren't* Abby Diaz's."

He felt the blood rush from his head, the earth drop beneath him as if he were suddenly marooned in outer space. He glanced over at her, lying beside him on the bed. She looked up at him, fear in her eyes.

"What is it?" she whispered.

"That's not possible," he said into the phone.

"Abby's dead, Jake. We exhumed the body. It's her. There's no doubt. You've got to bring the woman in. And the kid. And you have to hurry."

He fought for breath, his mind screaming, *no!*

"Jake, it's a trap. Don't be a damned fool. Wherever you are, get the hell out of there. Now. Before it's too late. I'll send men to meet you. Just tell me where—"

He closed his eyes. "I'll take care of it myself," he said and clicked off the phone, dropping it to the floor.

"Jake," she whispered beside him. "What is it?"

He didn't look at her. He couldn't. He got up and pulled on his jeans. "It was Reese Ramsey. I sent him the handcuffs you used to cuff me at the station. He checked the prints." He turned then to face her. "He says they aren't Abby Diaz's prints."

She stared up at him, looking stunned, confused, then dropped her gaze to the crumpled bedsheets.

"The body they exhumed from the grave," he continued. "It's been positively identified by the FBI as Abby Diaz's."

She shook her head, her eyes filling with tears as her

gaze rose again to his. "The person who called, he's the one you said you trusted?"

Jake nodded, sick at heart. And scared. He tugged on his shirt, his flesh still alive with the feel of her, his body already aching for her.

"Of course, it's a lie," he said quietly. "Someone falsified the report. There's no other explanation."

She nodded, her eyes on him. "Frank?"

"He'd have the authority." He stood, fighting the need to flee, fighting the question that haunted him. If he didn't believe what Reese had told him about Abby, then why did he believe the part about the trap, about being in immediate danger?

"I think we'd better get out of here," he said, feeling the weight of his words, the implications weighing on him.

"I'll get Elena." She rose and dressed quickly, no longer looking at him.

He watched her leave the room, his heart hurting, the pounding too loud. Reese had to be wrong. About everything. He hadn't even realized how hard he'd been listening until he heard the sound outside. A sound as distinct as a heartbeat and as ominous as a gunshot. Someone tried the back door.

If we aren't safe here, we're not safe anywhere. His words had come back to haunt him.

Moonlight made a silver path on the tile floor as she padded quickly across the hall to Elena's room. She felt numb. All except her heart, which seemed to struggle with each labored beat. *Not Abby Diaz.*

Jake's words had stunned her. Not Abby Diaz? Just

when she'd finally found herself? Just when she'd found Jake and the passion she'd remembered from before?

It was one thing to want to take away her new-found strength, to take away her identity, to take Jake and the love she'd once shared, but to take her child, to make her believe the babies *had* been switched and that Elena wasn't hers—because Elena was so obviously Jake Cantrell's daughter.

She looked down at her daughter. Elena lay curled in the narrow bed, burrowed deep in the blankets, only the top of her dark head showing. Anger made her weak. Who was playing with her life like a puppeteer, pulling her heartstrings? If only she could remember the past. The answer had to be there. The person behind this. The person responsible for trying to destroy her.

But what made her heart ache was what she'd witnessed in Jake's eyes. She'd seen that moment of doubt. That moment of distrust.

As she reached down to pick up her daughter, a shadow moved across the window on the other side of the curtain. She froze as the outline of one man, then another, crept along the side of the house. Hurriedly she scooped Elena up, covers and all.

Elena's eyes widened as she came awake.

"Shhh," she whispered to the child. "Not a sound."

She started out of the room, desperate to get back to the bedroom and Jake. But as she reached the hall, Elena in her arms, Elena cried out. "Sweet Ana! I dropped Sweet Ana!"

Then the air exploded with the crash of shattering glass and splintering wood as the house was breached.

She looked up to see Jake framed in the bedroom

doorway across the hall, a gun in his hand. She heard him call a warning. Out of the corner of her eye, she caught movement. Shielding Elena, she ran toward him.

Jake got off one shot before he took the bullet. She felt it whiz past her, saw it strike him, his head jerking back, and watched in horror as he went down.

She lurched toward him but was grabbed from behind before she could reach his side or the weapon he'd dropped to the floor next to him. Elena was pulled from her arms and she was dragged backward. The last thing she saw was one of Ramon's men kneel beside Jake and shake his head.

She started to scream. But a hand closed over her mouth and nose, the cloth wet and cold, the smell strong and blinding. Her knees gave way beneath her. And she fell, dropping into blackness as if falling down a deep, dark bottomless well.

Abby woke to the dark and the silence and the pain. So much like six years ago when she'd awakened in the Mexican hospital. Only this time, she knew what she'd lost. This time, she remembered too much.

"Elena?" she whispered as she sat up and felt around on the cold floor for her daughter. "Elena?"

She felt nothing but the rough adobe of her prison. Panic seized her as she stumbled to her feet, windmilling her arms in the blinding blackness. "Elena!"

Her knuckles scraped the wall. Pain shot up her arm, but her real pain centered in her pounding heart. She took slow, deep breaths, but they came out as sobs. Where was Elena? Her baby? What had they done with her?

Elena was gone. Jake was dead. Shot dead. Jake. Oh,

God. Jake. Had he died believing her an imposter? Part of a plot to get him killed?

She closed her eyes against the thought. Someone with the FBI had falsified the fingerprint and autopsy reports. It had to have come from the top. Frank. But why?

She fought the urge to scream. But screaming wouldn't bring Jake back. Hysteria wouldn't help Elena. She had to think of her daughter now. She dropped to her hands and knees, her legs too weak to hold her, her head hurting too much to think of anything but her child.

She felt her way around the room. It was small, no more than a cell, and completely empty. The walls were adobe like the floor, rough and cold to the touch. On one wall, she found a door, thick and made of wood. She put her shoulder to it. It didn't budge.

She sat back down on the floor, dizzy from the darkness and the chloroform or whatever they'd used to knock her out. She felt cold and nauseous, sick soul-deep. Jake was dead. Elena lost. Defeated, she wrapped her arms around her knees, laid her head down and cried.

The sound of the bolt scraping in the lock on the other side of the door made her lift her head. Hurriedly, she dried her eyes, wishing she had something to use as a weapon. The door slowly swung open, bringing with it the night breeze. And light. She blinked. A man stood silhouetted in the doorway, holding an old-fashioned lantern. He shone the light into the room, blinding her. She heard his sharp intake of air.

"Get her out of there," he ordered in Spanish.

His voice was at once familiar—and frightening, because she couldn't place it. She got to her feet, pulling herself up the rough wall, shielding her eyes from the light. Two men came into the room and, taking her arms, dragged her out into a hallway of sorts. Some of the walls had eroded away, leaving dark holes open to the night.

She only half feigned the weakness that made it hard for her to stand. They held her up in the light of the lantern. Slowly, she lifted her head.

He stood only inches away, studying her. When she dared look up into his face, she was afraid she'd know him and afraid she wouldn't.

He was tall, with brown hair and a kind face. But his angry expression and the intense look in his dark eyes made her recoil inwardly. She told herself she'd never seen him before. But the look in those eyes assured her it was not mutual.

"My God," he said in English. "Abby?"

"Where is my daughter?"

He seemed taken back by her tone. "Don't worry about her. She's fine. Being well cared-for." He shook his head, his gaze studying her face with astonishment. "Jake must have been shocked when he saw you."

Something in his words... A memory dropped into place. A flash of knowledge she didn't question. As sure as the shots she'd fired from the pistol. "Isn't that the way you planned it, Frank?"

Jake woke to an unbearable sense of loss that blunted his physical pain.

Death, he realized, came in many forms. He felt the crease where the bullet had grazed his head. He was weak from loss of blood. It took all of his strength to crawl into a sitting position. He leaned back against the wall. Blood ran down into his left eye. Images moved across his memory, dark and debilitating. Abby. He swallowed and tasted blood. A trap.

His, it seemed, was a death of despair.

Slowly, he shrugged out of his shirt and, balling it up, pressed it to the shallow ditch-like wound that started at his forehead, ending just over his left ear.

The breeze flapped at the curtains of the broken window. The front door stood open at an odd angle. It had been a trap, all right. And he'd walked right into it.

He felt too weak to move, too heartsick to know what to do if he did. He knew now that he'd been fighting an uphill battle against a power much stronger and more far-reaching than himself. Even if he knew who'd taken Abby and Elena, even if he could find them, he wasn't sure he could save them. He wasn't even sure he could save himself at this point.

Then in the shaft of moonlight that spilled across the tile floor, he saw something. His heart constricted. He rolled over onto his right elbow and scooted along the floor, still holding the shirt to his head, still unable to stand, barely able to see.

When he was close enough, he sat back against the wall again, sucked in hard breaths, and slowly pulled the object he'd spotted to him. Sweet Ana. He pressed the worn rag doll to his face. It smelled of lilac bubble bath. It smelled of Elena.

Emotion choked off his throat. He closed his eyes and tipped his head back, wanting to howl like the coyotes in the night. He'd lost so much. He couldn't lose any more. He crushed the doll in his hands, the way he wanted to crush the people who'd done this.

With all sensation centered on the pain in his head and heart, at first he didn't feel the tiny, cold, stabbing pain in the palm of his right hand. Slowly he opened his eyes and focused on the doll and his large sun-browned hands gripping it.

He opened his fists. The soft fabric was forgiving. He brushed his fingers over the handmade dress. It matched the one Elena had worn just yesterday. He stared down into Sweet Ana's face, for the first time noticing her stitched eyes. Cantrell green. And with a cold chill, he realized how Julio had planned to get out of Mexico with the money—and his life.

He tossed aside his bloody shirt and struggled to his feet, moving as quickly as he could before blood blurred his vision again. Stumbling into the kitchen, he set the doll down on the counter and dug in the drawer for a sharp knife. Lifting the hem of the doll's dress to expose the stitching along the right side of the stuffed body, he carefully cut through the threads until he saw the sharp edge of the key hidden inside.

Chapter 11

"You know who I am?" Frank Jordan sounded surprised.

"Just like you know who *I* am."

He raised a brow, the light from the lantern flickering in the warm night breeze. He looked older than she remembered him. His hair grayer. His eyes more anxious.

"Not Abby Diaz. She's dead." His words sent a chill through her.

"I guess you'd probably know that better than anyone."

He frowned and motioned for the men to release her and leave.

She straightened, willing herself to stand taller in front of him, to show no fear. An impossible task, knowing now the influence a man in his position could wield.

She recognized the guards as two of Calderone's men

as they left, disappearing down the long, dark hallway toward a faint light, leaving her alone with Frank.

She looked at him and swallowed, her throat dry, her eyes burning with tears at the memory of Jake lying on the floor and with anger at seeing Frank Jordan here with Calderone's men. If she'd had a weapon she'd have used it on Jordan without a second thought. If she could have taken him with her bare hands, she'd have tried.

"I want to see my daughter," she repeated.

"She has Jake's eyes," he mused. "And your beauty." His gaze seemed to focus on her and soften. "And you have Abby's face and her temper."

"That's odd, since the FBI is trying to convince me I'm an imposter."

Frank's gaze narrowed. "Too bad you didn't listen."

Another memory came out of nowhere just like the last one had. *Frank calling her into his office the morning of the explosion. Acting upset with her and threatening to suspend her from duty.* The realization made her heart pound. But why? She couldn't remember why.

"Let's go out here where we can talk in private," he said and motioned to an opening in the wall that led to an old courtyard. In the lantern's glow, she could see the courtyard had fallen into ruin, just as it appeared the rest of the building had over the years.

He indicated a rock bench near a crumbling fountain and she gladly sat down, still weak from the drug they'd used on her and a little disoriented. She realized the building reminded her of the ones they'd driven by in Study Butte. She sniffed the breeze and smelled creosote. Was it possible they were still in the ghost town?

He put the lantern down on the edge of the fountain

and sat down next to it. No one would have ever guessed he was FBI, dressed as he was now in a T-shirt, light-weight jacket, jeans and hiking boots. Except for the bulge of his service revolver under his jacket.

"Your men killed Jake," she said, her voice no more than a whisper. She remembered enough about Frank to know he wouldn't have done it himself. And surprisingly found it a flaw in his character. But she knew from the way Calderone's men were taking orders from him that he was responsible.

"If Jake had done as he was supposed to…" His voice broke. "He was never good at following orders."

"Who do you take your orders from, Frank?" she asked. "Tomaso Calderone?"

He raised his gaze to meet hers, his jaw tightening, but said nothing as he studied her, as if he really wasn't sure who she was. Or maybe, he was just worried about how much she'd remembered.

"Why did you try to suspend me that day? Because you knew the team was walking into a trap?"

He seemed surprised that she'd remembered their last meeting. His face flushed. "I thought you had amnesia. Julio said—"

"I thought you said Abby Diaz was dead." The anger bubbled up, hot as liquid lava. "You *knew* I was alive in Mexico. Maybe you were even the one who ordered me captured and held prisoner all those years."

He flinched at the words. "Do you really think I'd have left you there if I'd known?"

"You're doing your best to make people think I'm dead," she snapped. "I wouldn't put anything past you."

He met her gaze in the lantern light, his eyes hard.

"You were always so smart, one hell of an FBI agent. Too bad you've forgotten your training."

She stared at him. "Don't worry, it's coming back. I know Julio was working for you." Was Frank the man Elena said Julio used to call in the States? "Are you going to stand there and tell me you didn't know I was his prisoner for the last six years?"

"I only found out you might be alive a few days ago when Julio Montenegro told me," he said evenly. "I didn't believe him."

"Then why did you send Jake? Why not come yourself?"

He got to his feet and moved away, never completely turning his back on her. The man was no fool. She listened for Elena and sounds beyond the thick adobe walls, but heard nothing that would indicate where Elena was being held or if her daughter was even here. She watched Frank and waited for an opportunity.

"Why did I send Jake?" He turned to meet her gaze. "Because I couldn't face doing it myself."

She saw something in his eyes. A weakness that ran bone-deep. And guilt. "You were in charge of that routine investigation that night. How did it turn out to be one of Calderone's warehouses? You had to have set us up. But why? Why would you get involved with Calderone? Didn't you have enough power, enough money, enough influence over enough lives? Or is there just no limit for you?"

His eyes darkened in the lantern light as if her words cut him to the quick. "You're wrong, Abby."

It was the first time he'd called her by name and something in his tone stilled her. She watched him glance up at the sky that had just begun to lighten over the tile roof top.

"We don't have much time," he said quietly. "You need to tell me where Julio hid the money. It's the only hope you and your daughter have of staying alive."

"You need a doctor," the elderly Mexican woman said as she pressed the wet cloth to Jake's head and turned a worried eye on what the attackers had done to his house.

He held on to the chair waiting for the dizziness and darkness to subside. "No doctor." He'd called the Mexican couple who took care of his house because he knew if anyone could patch him up and get him on his feet it would be Guadalupe.

She shook her head, her lips pursed in disapproval. "You are lucky you are not dead."

"I thought I *was.*" He closed his eyes as she applied the alcohol, gritting his teeth.

"There is much blood, but the bullet only grazed your hard head," she said. "You have the lives of a cat."

He'd gotten himself to the bathroom mirror and had almost passed out at the sight of the blood and the wound. That's when he'd called her. She was right. He was damned lucky to be alive. But it meant nothing without Abby and Elena.

While Guadalupe bandaged his head and gave him three extra-strength pain relievers, her husband boarded up the windows and door of the house. When she'd finished, he thanked her.

"If you bleed to death, you don't thank me," she said.

He smiled at her. "You and Alejandro are good friends." He walked her to the door. Alejandro had finished his temporary repairs to the house and now stood looking back down the road toward Study Butte.

"What is it?" Jake asked, joining the elderly man.

"Lights," he said. "In the old mining building."

Jake looked to where he pointed. "You're sure no one is living there? Squatters?"

Alejandro shook his head. "It is uninhabitable."

"Take the back way home to Teringua," he told his friend. "Be careful."

"Vaya con Dios," Guadalupe said as they left. Go with God.

Jake went back inside and picked up the key he'd found in the doll from the table. Stamped on the metal were the words El Paso Central, locker No. 19. He pocketed it and tucked Sweet Ana into Abby's bag along with the rest of their clothing, the cell phone and the manila envelope about Abby, then zipped the bag shut.

How had someone known about Study Butte? Known he would come here? No one could have.

"I'm not telling you anything until I see my daughter," Abby said, assuring herself Frank Jordan didn't have the stomach for torture.

He rubbed his hand over his face, then studied her as if she were a problem he didn't have an answer for. "Fine. But you're wasting valuable time."

"Does Elena know—"

"About Jake?" He shook his head.

She nodded, thankful for that, and rose to her feet to be led through the abandoned adobe building. It didn't appear to be a house; it was too large for that and arranged all wrong.

At one point she caught sight of a mountainside through a hole in the wall. They *were* still in Study Butte! She felt her heart soar with hope. If she could reach Elena and get away, she could find a place for them to hide. But those were some pretty big ifs.

Elena was sitting on a wooden stool at an old desk, picking at a peanut-butter-and-jelly sandwich when Abby came into the room. She recognized the large Mexican man who stood over the child and the two others sitting in the glass-less windowsill appearing to watch the road below. All three were armed. All three were Calderone's men.

Elena's face lit up when she saw her. She jumped down from the wooden stool to run into her mother's arms.

"Mommy," she cried and hugged her tightly. "Sweet Ana is lost and I'm scared and you know I don't like peanut butter."

She smiled down at her daughter. "Don't worry about Ana. We'll find her." She eyed the large man still standing guard near the table and could feel Frank's presence behind her. She ignored the others. "She doesn't like peanut butter. Do you have anything else she could eat?"

The large man looked put upon. "What kind of kid doesn't like peanut butter?"

"A kid raised on tortillas and goat cheese," Ramon said, and laughed as he got up and walked toward Abby.

She recognized his voice. He greeted her in Spanish as if they were old friends. In fact, now that she could put his voice with his face, she realized she had seen him at the villa with Julio on more than one occasion.

"Did she tell you where the money is?" Ramon asked Frank.

"Not in front of the child," Frank said under his breath. "Carlos, get the girl something decent to eat from the store. Bring us all something."

The large man seemed to hesitate, his gaze going to Ramon for approval. "The store won't even be open this time of the morning."

"Then break in," Frank snapped.

Ramon moved, just inches from Frank's face. His voice dropped, a warning in his look, in his words. "I don't like being here. We should have taken the woman and kid and gotten away from here. But I agreed to do it your way. Now I want to know what the holdup is. Let's get what we need from the woman and get out of here. If you can't persuade her to talk, *I* can."

"We do this my way," Frank said, his voice low, threatening.

The men tensed visibly. Abby stepped back, pulling Elena with her. Ramon touched the butt of the gun sticking out of the waistband of his pants, his eyes never leaving Frank's face.

"Your way will get us all killed," Frank said quietly.

Ramon stared at him for a long moment, his face motionless, then suddenly he smiled and shook his head. "Then I will go to the store myself. I'll bring food, and some beer and tequila. I need a drink." He ordered his men to stay and not let Frank and the woman and child out of their sights.

As Ramon left, Frank offered Abby the stool and turned to the men. "You're scaring the little girl," he said in Spanish. "Go outside. You can guard just as well from there."

With obvious reluctance, they moved out into a smaller courtyard than the one Frank had taken her to earlier. It looked as if someone had been camping in it. There was a fire pit in the center and some boxes that might have been pulled up for seats. Through the crumbling wall, Abby saw them sit down on the boxes, and watch sullenly from the darkness at the edge of the lantern light as the sky over Big Bend began to lighten.

Abby sat down on the stool, pulling Elena up into her arms, hugging her, wondering how Frank had gotten involved with these men and just who was in charge. Elena sucked on her thumb, something she still did when she was tired. Or scared. Or without Sweet Ana.

She thought she heard a noise in the distance. A faint buzzing sound. It seemed to be coming from behind the house. She looked at Frank and realized he was listening, too. She could almost feel him tense. Hadn't he said they didn't have much time?

"Do you know where the money is?" he whispered, still watching the men.

"No," she admitted quietly, suddenly on guard.

"I was afraid of that," he said, sounding genuinely sorry. There was no doubt; he'd been waiting for something. He now looked spring-loaded, like a diamond-back rattler getting ready to strike.

Fear sent a shudder through her. "Frank, what—"

The sound of a helicopter suddenly filled the air. It rose up from the backside of the mountain and dropped down on them. *Whoop. Whoop. Whoop.* Then, suddenly, there was a blast of artillery fire.

Abby dove with Elena to the floor. She saw Frank draw his weapon. She scrambled to her feet and, shielding Elena, ran hunched-over down the hall, looking for a way out as bullets exploded behind her.

She heard Frank call out, his voice lost in the crack of gunfire and the steady whoop of helicopter blades hovering overhead.

Jake heard the helicopter just as he reached the left side of the old mining building. The adobe structure sat against the mountainside overlooking Study Butte, the walls deteriorating, part of the roof gone, a dim light glowing from its center.

He thought he could make out two vehicles parked in some scrub brush off to the right and wondered how many men he'd find inside. He knew he wouldn't be able to handle many in his condition. His only hope was getting in the first shots, and that was mighty optimistic.

Then he heard the chopper. It rose up out of the darkness over the rough edge of the mountains silhouetted against the dawn sky. The large military helicopter crested the mountain and swooped down on the mining building like a giant wasp.

He ducked behind a wall as the big bird hovered over the center of what was left of the structure and started firing. Weapon drawn, he worked his way toward the rat-a-tat-tat of firearms, praying Abby and Elena weren't in there.

Abby could hear footfalls on the broken tile floor behind her, but she didn't turn. She ran harder, seeing an opening ahead, the faint light of day bleeding through a pale gray. She hit the opening and burst through with Elena in her arms. Daybreak washed the rough mountains of Big Bend in quicksilver, but night's shadows still pooled, dark and cool, at the edges of the buildings hidden from daylight.

She didn't see the helicopter until it was almost on her. It came in a deafening roar of whirling dust and noise. Suddenly it was in front of her, hovering just above the ground. A dark figure leapt out. Before she could turn and run, strong arms grabbed Elena from her and swung the child up into the dark cavity of the chopper. Abby screamed, the sound lost in the whoop of the blades as she rushed the chopper. The dark figure jumped back inside, the helicopter started to rise.

Abby grabbed hold of the man's leg, struggling to see her child in the whirling dust, frantic to learn who had taken her, as she tried to pull herself up into the chopper.

A face came into focus just above her. It was the same man who'd pulled a gun on her on the train.

Jake had seen Abby burst out of the building running, with Elena in her arms. He'd dashed toward her, knowing he wouldn't get to her in time. He'd called out, trying to warn her as he watched the helicopter swoop down on her and Elena. But he knew she hadn't heard him. The noise of the chopper drowned out everything but the erratic gunfire still coming from the mining building.

He ran, his heart thudding as his feet pounded the earth. Helplessly, he watched as someone jumped from the helicopter and grabbed Elena. All his attempts to assure himself that the chopper was the cavalry come to save Abby and Elena failed when a second man swung out the side and opened fire on him.

He got off one shot, then stopped, afraid he might hit Elena inside the aircraft. It was a lucky shot. The man tumbled off, hitting the ground in a puff of dust.

He ran all out, closer now, but not close enough. His head pounded harder than his boot soles. His vision blurred. A numbness seemed to wash through his limbs and just lifting his feet took all his energy.

As he reached the chopper, he saw that Abby had a death grip on the man's leg and was desperately trying to pull herself up into the chopper.

The aircraft started to lift off. He jumped up and grabbed onto the chopper's skids, his body swinging, making the craft wobble in the air. He looked up, unable to see the men inside, only the man's hand trying to loosen Abby's grasp on his leg.

For a moment, it looked as if the man would drag Abby up into the helicopter. Instead, he broke her hold on him. She dropped to the ground and into the dust storm a half dozen feet beneath the chopper.

With the last of his strength, Jake grabbed the undercarriage and tried to climb up into the helicopter. But a boot heel swung down on his hand, breaking his tenuous hold.

He fell, dropping hard into the dust, the fall knocking the air from his lungs. He lay in the dirt, gasping for breath, watching as the helicopter hovered for a moment overhead. Then the big bird was gone. With Elena inside it.

Chapter 12

"Elena!" Abby cried. "Elena! Oh, God, no."

He pulled her to him, burying her face into his shoulder, searching for words of comfort, but he could find none. The bastards had taken his daughter.

"Oh, Jake," Abby cried. "I thought you were—"

"Yeah," he said grimacing. "Damned near."

He breathed in the scent of her, relishing the feel of her, holding on to her for dear life.

"I thought I'd never see you again," she whispered.

This was the second time he'd thought he'd never see *her* again. "I know what you mean." He gazed into her dark eyes as the sky over Big Bend lightened with the approaching sunrise.

"They took Elena," she said, her voice thick with tears.

He nodded and struggled to sit up. But who were

they, anyway? And what the hell did they want? All this for the stolen drug money? He found that hard to believe.

"Are you sure you're all right?"

"Yeah," he lied, his heart breaking with worry over Elena. He could barely see and realized his gunshot wound had started bleeding again. He pressed his shirt-sleeve to the bandage, and it came away wet and dark. Several shots echoed from the old mining office.

"This might be a good time to hit the road," he said, trying to keep his voice light. Trying hard to keep her from knowing just how worried he was about Elena. Or about their own chances of getting out of this.

She helped him up, supporting him, as she urged him toward one of the abandoned buildings just ahead of them.

He stumbled through the thin morning light spilling over the ghost town. The air around him felt too heavy, the dawn too bright, the buzzing in his ears too loud. He didn't know how much farther he could go.

She must have sensed his fatigue as she hustled him to the dark side of one of the ruins. "Let's stop for a minute." She let go of him and he dropped into the shadows, weak and dizzy and bone-chilling cold.

Abby knelt beside him, fear tightening her throat and making her heart ache. His bandage was soaked in fresh blood. She didn't know how badly he was hurt, but she knew he wasn't going far. Not on his feet, anyway.

She slipped to the edge of the building and glanced back up the hillside, memory playing again the horrible moments when Elena was pulled into the helicopter.

Elena. Oh, God. Elena. Her tears tasted bitter and her

aching heart labored in her chest. She had to get Jake out of here. Get him to a doctor. Then she could figure out what to do. If only she could remember her training. She'd never needed it more than she did right now.

She focused again on the large building set back against the mountainside. She didn't think anyone had followed them. But she couldn't be sure someone hadn't seen them, knew where they were and would be coming soon.

Several more shots drifted down from the hillside. Who was still up there, still exchanging volleys? She didn't even know who was fighting whom.

"We can't stay here," Jake whispered behind her.

"I know. Just for a few minutes." She went to him. "Until you catch your breath."

He smiled up at her, his fingers lifting to touch her cheek, tears welling in his eyes and in her own. She quickly touched her fingers to his lips and shook her head. If he even mentioned Elena, she would fall apart.

He kissed her fingers, his gaze understanding. "I found this hidden in Sweet Ana," he whispered as he dug something out of his pocket. He handed her a small key. "I want you to have it, just in case something happens to me."

"Nothing is going to happen to you." Oh, God, how badly was he wounded? Did he know something she didn't? She stared at the key for a moment. It could be the key to getting Elena back. "You found it *inside* the doll?"

"The stitching was a different color and crudely sewn on that side of the cloth body," he said.

She closed the key in her fist, the sharp metal digging into her palm. Elena's lost doll. It had been lying beside Julio's dead body. "Julio was going to take Elena with him. He was planning to use her." And the doll. A man and his daughter looked less suspicious than a man traveling alone.

He started to get up. "I hid the Explorer behind the old church. If we could—"

"Are the keys in it?"

He nodded.

"Stay here, I'll be right back."

She left before he could argue, running along the shadowed sides of the buildings, keeping out of sight, until she reached the Explorer. She started it quickly and drove back to where she'd left Jake.

He'd gotten to his feet and stood propped against the adobe wall. She leaned over to shove open the passenger-side door. He slid in and slammed the door just as the glint of a chrome bumper appeared from behind a stand of brushy trees up on the mountainside. The vehicle came out of a cloud of dust, moving fast, headed her way.

She hit the gas, tires spinning in the dirt as she flipped a cookie. Dust rooster-tailed behind the Explorer, as she headed south toward the Rio Grande.

"I think you should know, Abby Diaz was one helluva driver, especially in this kind of situation," Jake said.

She glanced over at him, not at all sure that was true. He'd buckled his seat belt and was now leaning back into the seat, his eyes closed, his face ashen in the glow of the dash lights. "You'd better hope so."

She skidded onto Farm Route 170 headed west, the pavement disappearing under the hood in a blur, and looked back to see not one, but two vehicles in hot pursuit.

"Are you all right?" she asked, knowing if he'd been all right he'd have been driving.

He opened his eyes and gave her a wan smile. "Good enough."

The truth was, he felt light-headed, his pulse throbbing to the buzzing in his head, and he couldn't seem to keep his eyes open.

"Do you have any idea who that might be behind us?" she asked.

"Not a clue. At this point, I just figure *everyone* wants us dead. How about you?"

She shook her head. "Could be Frank. He's the one who took Elena and me from the house after you were shot."

"Jordan?"

"He was with some of Calderone's men, including possibly the man who killed Julio, a man named Ramon."

Ramon Hernandez and Frank Jordan in Study Butte, working together. "I was afraid Frank was involved when we got the report on you," he said quietly, cursing silently to himself. Frank.

"He swears he didn't have anything to do with what happened six years ago or my abduction by Julio. Nor does he admit he knew I was being held in Mexico," she said, sounding as disbelieving as he was.

His anger made him weaker, more worried for Elena, more worried for Abby. Frank had to be behind Elena's kidnapping, but he'd never seemed like the kind of agent who could be corrupted by mere money. The FBI had always been too important to him, his rise to the top and the power that came with that. What had changed?

He swore as he looked out at the road ahead. Just when he'd thought things couldn't get any worse, they were on the wrong road out of town!

He looked over at the speedometer, then back at the two cars on their butt. He closed his eyes again, no longer worried about his gunshot wound or his health. He'd never survive this car ride.

They flew through the town of Lajitas, an old army post built to protect this part of Texas from Pancho Villa. The irony didn't escape him, even in his weakened state. They raced through the frontier-style town with its plank sidewalks and hitching rails, the streets empty at this hour, the two pursuing vehicles staying right with them.

Jake wondered where the cops were. Probably in bed. He wished that was where he was. With Abby. With Elena just across the hall, sleeping peacefully. He squeezed his eyes tight, fighting the pain, fighting images of Elena, the feel of her small hand securely in his, the scent of lilac on her skin as he leaned down to kiss her good-night—

He opened his eyes at the sound of Abby's shocked curse. She'd reached El Camino del Rio, a fifty-mile stretch of pavement that wound like a dark and dangerous snake beside the Rio Grande from Lajitas to Presidio. The narrow blacktop twisted and turned up and down and around the volcanic and limestone rock formations of the Bofecillos Mountains, finally dumping out into the fertile river valley at Presidio.

If they were that lucky.

But there was no turning back. Not with whoever was right behind them.

"You've driven this road before," he told Abby, trying to sound confident and unconcerned. Driving the road going the speed limit in broad daylight was precarious. At close to a hundred miles an hour at first light, it was beyond dangerous. Add two carloads of probable killers and you had a very bad situation.

She shot him a look.

"Don't worry," he assured her. "You can handle this with your eyes closed."

"Right." She let out a small, scared laugh, but at least it was a laugh and he knew the old Abby Diaz was at the wheel. He felt a little better, a little more optimistic about their chances. At least Isabella Montenegro wasn't driving.

The route was the same one Pancho Villa used for his mule trains during the Mexican Revolution. He doubted it had changed much. Someone had just thrown a little blacktop on it and called it a scenic route.

Abby took the first hairpin curve with a determined look and a white-knuckled grip on the wheel. The Rio Grande stayed with them, quicksilver in the early light. So did the vehicles behind them.

He noticed that the first one, a green Dodge pickup, was gaining. Moving in for the kill? The way they were driving, they knew the road well. He'd figured their pursuers had been waiting for this hazardous stretch of highway to make their move.

The pickup came up fast behind them.

"Jake!" Abby cried.

He braced himself. The truck slammed into their

back bumper. Metal crunched as they were thrown forward. But Abby kept the rig on the road.

"Never fear, darlin'," he said as he hurriedly rolled down his window. The early-morning air was already hot and scented with dust. He felt drunk, only running on a couple of cylinders, not all pistons firing. But he thought he could still shoot.

Unbuckling his seat belt, he leaned out the car window and fired back at the truck. The bullet made a clean entry into the windshield, leaving a web of white the size of his head in the glass but on the passenger side instead of the driver's. *Settle down.* The pickup backed off, but not fast enough. He fired again.

The left front tire exploded in a puff of gray smoke. The pickup began to rock, the front veering from side to side. Rock and roll. The truck took the ditch flying, smacked into the side of the mountain and disappeared in a rolling cloud of dust.

One down, he thought grimly. He flopped back into his seat, almost too weak to roll up the window.

Abby let out a breath. "Nice shooting."

"Thanks." He saw the second vehicle, a Chevy Suburban, come up fast in the side mirror. The gleam of a shotgun barrel came out the passenger-side window.

"Get down!" he yelled.

The blast shattered the rear window sending glass showering over the backseat. He swung around and fired through the gaping hole, putting one in the grill and doing only cosmetic damage to the hood with the second.

The Suburban roared up beside the Explorer. Another shotgun blast took out the back side window.

Jake swore as Abby took a curve on two wheels and for a moment he thought this would be it. *Adios.* He pulled up and fired as the Suburban dropped back only a little for the curve, then started to make another run at them.

The gun felt too heavy, his finger too weak on the trigger, his vision blurred, the whole scene surreal. But he got off another shot, then another. The Suburban was too close to take out a tire. It moved up the left side of them again. The barrel of the shotgun glinted dully in the dawn as it leveled at Abby.

He threw himself over the back of the seat and emptied the clip through the missing side window. The man with the shotgun saw it coming and ducked, but the driver didn't. He slumped over the wheel as one shot hit home.

The man with the shotgun came up again, unaware that his driver had been hit. Abby went into a tight right-hand curve. The Suburban left the road going over eighty. But not before the man with the shotgun got off one last blast.

The shot was off-center. It peppered Abby's door with buckshot and got just enough of Abby's side window to shatter it. Glass showered over both of them.

"Are you all right?" Jake cried.

She didn't answer, the Explorer rocking as she fought the wheel.

"Abby?"

"Yeah," she said finally, after she got it back under control. Behind them, the Suburban had dropped off the side of the mountain and was now cartwheeling toward the river.

Abby topped a hill and they dropped down into the farming community of Redford with its collection of adobe and wood-frame houses. A church, the Redford Co-op Goat Cheese Factory and the Cordera Store blurred past, seeming too normal.

Abby slowed the Explorer. He crawled back into the front seat, buckled up again and took a deep breath, no longer feeling much of anything. Abby didn't say a word. He watched the side mirror, but no other vehicles appeared. It wasn't over and he knew Abby was more than aware of that. It wouldn't be over until they got their little girl back. And they *would* get her back. He wouldn't let himself think anything else. Couldn't.

He felt sick, more tired than he'd ever remembered being, and cold, as if his body had caught fire and was burning from the inside out.

They rolled into Presidio as the sun rose over the tops of the rugged mountains. The "Hottest Town in Texas" was just waking as they drove in. Across the border, Ojinaga, its Mexican sister city, dozed in the sunshine.

"Neuvo Real Presidio de Nuestra Senora de Betlena y Santiago de Las Amarillas de La Junta de Los Rios Norte y Conchos," he said, then singsang the words like a mantra, feeling oddly light as if he were floating. Or drunk.

Abby looked over at him and frowned. "New Royal Garrison of Our Lady of Bethlehem and St. James on the Banks of the Junction of the Rio Grand and Conchos Rivers?"

He nodded. "Wonder why they shortened it to Presidio? Just doesn't have the same ring, does it?" His gaze fell on her and he smiled. It felt crooked even to his lips. "You are one hell of a woman behind a wheel. I take back everything I ever said about your driving." He laughed. It sounded to his ears as if he were down in a well. "You are one hell of a woman."

"Are you sure you're all right?" he heard her ask from a distance. She reached across the seat to touch his forehead. "Jake, you're freezing."

He laughed. At least he thought he did. It had a carnival-midway feel to it inside his head. Then he remembered something. "Abby, there's something I should have told—" He lost the thought as he lost consciousness.

His tanned, square-jawed, handsome face was pale against the white hospital sheets. He opened his eyes. They'd never looked more green. Never looked more like Elena's, she thought, with a stab of pain.

She smiled down at him. "How ya doin'?"

He returned her smile. "You tell me."

"Just fine," she said softly as she brushed a dark lock of hair back from his forehead. He felt warm. But he'd lost a lot of blood. "Looks like you might make it."

"Good." He started to get up. "Let's get out of here, then."

She pushed him back onto the bed easily and pulled up a chair beside him, holding his hand in hers. "You're not going anywhere. Doctor's orders." He started to argue. "I'm serious, Jake. You've got to get your strength back. They just want to keep you overnight and get some fluids in you."

"Elena—"

"There isn't anything we can do until we get you well."

She lowered her voice, although only the two of them were in the room. "Or until we hear from the kidnappers."

"Yeah." He frowned as he glanced toward the window. It was afternoon. He'd slept all morning. "You haven't heard anything yet?"

She shook her head. Like him, she'd thought they'd have called by now. She'd taken Jake to the safest hospital she could find, a small private one outside of town. Then she'd waited, praying he'd be all right, praying the kidnappers would call.

She'd just assumed they had Jake's cell-phone number because of Frank. She couldn't bear to think the kidnappers had no way of contacting them.

"I still can't understand how they found us," Jake said.

She recalled his words: *If we aren't safe here, then we're not safe anywhere.* "If you can't trust the Feds, then who can you trust?" she said.

Why hadn't they called? It scared her. Who had her daughter? And what did they want?

The obvious answer was the stolen drug money. So why did she think there had to be more to it?

"This morning reminded me of when the two of us used to work together," Jake said.

She nodded, wishing she could remember. "My memory is starting to come back," she told him, disturbed by the bits and pieces she kept seeing in her mind's eye. Some memories made no sense but left her anxious and worried, as if they were important things she desperately needed to remember. Jake was hurt and someone had their little girl. That was all she knew for sure.

"The harder I try to remember that night, the less clear anything is," she told him.

"There's no reason for you to remember that night," Jake said quickly, squeezing her hand. "Forget the past, Abby. All that matters now is the future."

She wished that were true. But she couldn't throw off the feeling that the answer to everything that was happening now was hidden in her past.

"It's funny, I keep thinking I remember you and me arguing about something the afternoon before," she said, confused by a glimpse of memory. "I just feel like something happened, something I need to remember."

He shook his head slowly and reached up to cup her cheek in his large palm, his thumb moving in slow circles, caressing her skin. "It was a stupid fight. But believe me, it didn't have anything to do with what's happening now."

She studied him, concerned he was holding something back. But why? "What about?"

He glanced away for a moment. "Dell Harper."

"Dell?"

He took a breath and let it out slowly. "Like I said, it was a stupid fight. I just felt that you were being too protective of him and that it was affecting your work." He met her gaze. "I was a little…jealous, too."

She wondered about her relationship with Dell. Did Jake have anything to be jealous of? She tried to pull up an image of Dell. A feeling. Nothing came.

"Is that what you were going to tell me earlier?" she asked. "About our fight?"

He nodded. "Not that it has anything to do with what happened later."

The nurse came in and told Abby she'd have to leave, the patient needed his rest. Before Jake could protest, the nurse gave him a shot.

"You'll be here when I wake up?" he asked, already sounding groggy.

She nodded. "You get better," she said and slipped a gun under his pillow when the nurse wasn't watching.

He smiled up at her, acknowledging the weapon and his possible need for it. "Abby, I— Just watch your back."

"Rest. I'll be fine." As she let go of his hand, she felt a sense of loss. For a moment, she almost changed her plans. The doctor had told her Jake would sleep through the night and she should get some rest. Rest was the last thing on her mind.

She'd seen to it that the doctor's report of the gunshot wound would never reach its destination. Not that she could see any reason why the men who had Elena would be searching for her and Jake. But even if they were, and even if they suspected how badly Jake was hurt and checked local hospitals, they wouldn't find a patient listed by the name of Jake Cantrell.

The moment the hospital-room door closed behind Abby, Jake thought about their argument six years ago. Looking back, it had been foolish. He'd been foolish. Arguing over Dell Harper.

He wished he'd never said anything to her. But the fact was, he'd been jealous of Dell and her friendship with him. Abby had been overly protective of the young FBI agent and Dell—well, Dell had always seemed too...interested in Abby.

But Jake still wished he'd kept it to himself. He'd

regretted their argument for six years. In the end, a man's biggest regrets in life would involve a woman, he thought. He already had his share when it came to Abby.

Dell Harper was dead. Gone. He needed to concentrate on getting Elena back. On getting Abby to trust him again.

But at the back of his mind something warned him that he'd just made a terrible mistake. One he would live to more than regret.

Chapter 13

On the drive to El Paso in the rental car, Abby pooled together everything she could remember and waded through it. Only a few fragmented memories remained from the day of the explosion, just enough to make her feel troubled and tense. She could sense something important buried deep in her memory. Her subconscious teased her with it, holding it just out of reach.

Was it as the doctors at the hospital had told her six years ago, something she'd repressed because she couldn't face it? Whatever it was, the harder she tried to remember, the more it evaded her.

Beside her on the seat was Sweet Ana, the cell phone the FBI had given Jake and the envelope she'd found under Julio's body. Just the sight of the doll made her cry, but she wiped at her tears, stubbornly determined to find her daughter and put the cherished doll back into the child's arms, just as she would take her daughter in hers.

Under her jacket, she wore Jake's shoulder holster with the gun she'd taken from one of Calderone's men at the border. When had that been? It seemed like a lifetime ago.

She wished the phone would ring. That the kidnappers would call and name their price. But she didn't sit around and wait. She couldn't.

She drove into El Paso in the early afternoon. El Paso was a big sprawling city with a combination of cultures that made her very aware that Mexico was just across the border. It reminded her of her own Spanish heritage. At a convenience store, she asked for directions to the El Paso Central bus station.

She found it easily but drove around the block several times before she parked. She didn't think she'd been followed—at least not that she'd seen, and she'd been watching closely.

Her instincts told her that no one would be waiting here for her, either. If they knew where the money was stashed, they wouldn't have kidnapped her daughter. But still, she felt the hair rise on the back of her neck, her skin prickle with apprehension, as she walked into the large bus terminal.

According to the schedule, the bus to San Antonio had just left and buses going to Albuquerque and Phoenix wouldn't be leaving for a few hours.

Passengers loitered in the lobby, some standing around looking restless, others mesmerized by the large TV mounted on the wall. A few, probably waiting for even later buses, dozed on the uncomfortable chairs or curled up on the floor.

She walked through the throng toward the back of the building, following the sign that read Rest Rooms to the row of old beat-up green metal lockers. As she walked, she searched the faces of the people she passed.

She didn't see anyone she knew. Or at least anyone she recognized. That was one of the real drawbacks of amnesia, she thought.

She felt edgy, even with the reassuring feel of the gun against her ribs, as she wandered through the rows of lockers. A few passengers or possibly homeless people slept at the ends of the rows, as unrecognizable as bundles of clothing. Any of them could be staking out locker No. 17, waiting on her to show with the key.

But one good look at the lockers themselves and she knew no one would sleep in a huddle on a bus-station floor to wait for her to open a door that the most amateur crook could crack with a hairpin in a matter of seconds.

The thought did settle her down some as she walked to locker No. 17. She stood looking at it for signs that the lock had been tampered with. Even after a half dozen coats of dark green paint, the metal locker front was dented and scratched, banged-up and defaced, but the lock looked fine.

She dug into her jeans, glancing around. No one seemed the least bit interested and yet she felt as if she was being watched. She waited a few moments, then pulled out the key and tried it in the lock. She turned it, heard a click and felt the door give. One thought struck her: what man in his right mind would put several million dollars in a bus locker? Would that much money even fit in a locker this size?

But then she still couldn't imagine Julio stealing that much from Calderone.

She swung the door open and stared into the shadowy darkness of the locker, instantly surprised by how empty it was. Cautiously, as if she thought there was a diamondback rattler coiled inside, she reached in.

The money was stacked in the back, each bundle of bills fastened with a rubber band. Without pulling it out, she thumbed through one. All used hundreds in U.S. dollars. The bundle was a good three inches thick or more, so she knew it had to be more than ten thousand dollars.

Hurriedly she thumbed through several more, then quickly estimated the number of bundles. Just over three hundred thousand dollars. Definitely nowhere near millions.

So where was the rest of the money? Maybe he'd hidden it in a variety of places, just in case he had any trouble getting to one of his stashes. Or maybe this was all there was.

From inside her jacket, she took out two brown shopping bags and began to slide the money into the largest of the two, watching out of the corner of her eye for movement.

But as she filled the bag, no one approached. No one even seemed to pay her any mind. She slid the last wad of money into the bag, then covered the bundles of bills with the second bag, and felt around in the locker to make sure she'd gotten it all.

Her fingers brushed over a scrap of paper. A note

reminding Julio where he'd left the rest of the money? Not likely. She withdrew a folded piece of newsprint, yellowed and ragged. Unfolding it, she saw that it was nothing more than a clipping torn from the Houston Chronicle, and she almost put it back without even looking at, thinking it had been left by a previous renter. But three letters in the headline caught her eye. *FBI.*

Bystander Dies in FBI Raid. She glanced at the publication date. Almost twenty years ago. Surely this couldn't have anything to do with—a name leapt out of the copy. Frank Jordan. Then a name Jake had mentioned to her. Hal "Buster" McNorton. The man who'd died six years ago in the same routine investigation Abby herself had almost died in.

She stared at the photo. So faded and worn, it was impossible to make out the faces, but it appeared to be of a man beside a body on the ground in front of a restaurant. She could almost make out the neon sign reflected in the plate-glass window out front.

She heard someone approaching and quickly stuffed the newspaper article into her bag, raked a hand over the rusted bottom of the inside of the locker to make sure she'd gotten everything, then locked it again.

It was hard to walk slowly out of the bus terminal. Harder still not to look over her shoulder. But somehow, she did it.

When she reached her car, she tossed the bag onto the floor on the passenger side, got in and locked the doors. She desperately wanted to look more closely at the newspaper clipping, but she started the car and slipped into the traffic, watching behind her.

After driving for twenty minutes in an ever-widening

circle, she pulled into a fast-food drive-through and ordered a large coffee. She realized she hadn't eaten all day, and amended her order to include a cheeseburger and fries.

With her coffee and food, she parked in the lot where she could watch the street and dug out the newspaper clipping again and turned on the dome light. She read it as she ate.

The article was pretty straightforward. The FBI had raided a business believed to be manufacturing cocaine. During the chase that ensued, a young woman bystander was killed. Her name was being withheld until notification of relatives. FBI agent Frank Jordan refused to comment on the raid or the death of the bystander.

She reached into the bag and finished off the last of the fries, not even aware that she'd eaten all of her burger. Downing the last of the coffee, she studied the photo again, wondering what this article could possibly have to do with Julio and the money she'd found.

It probably didn't. But she also didn't believe that it just happened to be in the bottom of the locker, not the way it had been carefully ripped from the paper and folded. Or the fact that the newspaper clipping was almost twenty years old. Or that the article just happened to mention Frank Jordan. And Buster McNorton.

Too many coincidences.

Then she saw something that made her heart pound. The byline. The article had been written by Crystal Winfrey. Had Crystal Jordan been a newspaper woman before she became a TV anchorwoman? Before she married Frank Jordan? It seemed likely.

Was she still an anchorwoman for a San Antonio

television news station? Or had she gone on to something else in the last six years?

She made a few calls on the cell phone and found Crystal working for a small, obscure public TV station in Houston. The former anchorwoman now worked behind the camera on the night shift. For a few minutes she sat in the parking lot trying to talk herself out of it. When she called Jake, the nurse told her he was sleeping, his condition improved.

She'd thought about calling Crystal. But she wasn't sure Crystal would talk to her. She wasn't even sure what she hoped to accomplish by contacting Crystal in the first place.

But the newspaper clipping nagged at her. It had to have some significance, and Crystal Winfrey Jordan was her only lead. And Abby wanted to surprise her.

All the way to the airport she told herself this was nothing more than a wild-goose chase. Worse, she wouldn't be able to get a call from the kidnappers during the short flight. But thirty minutes later she was on a jet winging its way across Texas, trying desperately not to think about Elena and the man who had her or about Jake. Trying to think like an FBI agent. Not a mother. Not a lover.

As Abby got out of her car, locked it and headed toward the TV station, she felt again as if someone was watching her. But she hadn't seen anyone on the flight who looked familiar and the station parking lot was half-empty, with no one hanging around.

The television station was quiet in the office area,

away from the action of live broadcasting. Her footsteps echoed down the long, windowless hallway.

"Excuse me," she said, sticking her head into the open doorway of the broom-closet-sized office marked Jordan.

The woman behind the desk looked up and Abby remembered her.

Crystal Jordan had once been a beautiful woman. Tall, lean and blond, with a dynamite face that flirted with the camera and a smile that radiated honesty on the screen.

But that was not the woman now sitting behind the cluttered desk at the end of the hallway.

"Yes?" she asked. Her hair was still blond, bleached thin. It hung straight to her shoulders, a style too young for the face it framed. It was a wrinkled, sallow face, the face and voice of a woman who'd spent too much time on a barstool, trying to kill herself with booze and cigarettes. "Can I help you?"

But there was something familiar about that voice, a familiarity that struck a chord with her. She'd once considered Crystal a friend. "Crystal," she said softly. "It's me, Abby. Abby Diaz."

Crystal picked up a pair of glasses from the desk. As she hurriedly settled them on her nose, she jerked back, eyes wide, an expression that held both surprise and fear on her face. And in that instant, Abby wondered how long Crystal Winfrey Jordan had known she was alive.

Crystal got awkwardly to her feet. "My God, it *is* you."

Abby closed the door behind her and leaned against it. "When did Frank tell you I was alive?"

The older woman stepped back. "Frank and I are divorced. He doesn't tell me—"

"Don't lie to me, Crystal. I've been a prisoner in Mexico for six long years, my daughter's been kidnapped and someone is trying to kill me. I'm not in the mood for any more lies. You knew I was alive. You knew I'd be coming here. Why is that?"

Crystal reached for her intercom, but Abby jerked it out of her hand, ripping it from the wall and tossing it into the corner. She did the same with the phone, knocking the piles of papers on the desk to the floor.

The former anchorwoman wobbled for a moment on her high heels, then dropped into the chair behind the desk again. "What do you want from me?"

"The truth," Abby snapped.

Crystal looked as if she might cry, but she no longer appeared fearful, just resigned. "Frank told me a couple of days ago. He was in shock. He couldn't believe it."

Abby just bet he *was* in shock.

She pulled the folded newspaper clipping from her jacket pocket. Unfolding the yellowed paper, she laid it on the desk. "Do you remember this?"

Crystal drew the clipping closer. "Where did you get it?"

"I found it in a bus-station locker with three hundred thousand dollars of stolen drug money."

The older woman paled under the fluorescent lighting and her fingers trembled as she shrank back from the newspaper clipping.

"Frank was the one who shot the bystander, wasn't he?" Abby said, voicing what she'd suspected from the moment she'd read it.

Crystal nodded. "It was an accident. She was just a kid. Maybe sixteen. Pretty little thing. Frank never got over it."

"Who is that in the photo, leaning over her?" Something about the blurry figure looked almost familiar to Abby although his face was hidden.

"Her boyfriend. He was hysterical. I felt so sorry for him."

"Do you remember his name?"

Crystal shook her head. "It's been years."

"What about the girl's name?"

Again the newswoman couldn't recall.

Abby folded the newspaper clipping. Frank had shot the bystander. But what did that have to do with anything? What did the clipping have to do with Julio? With the stolen drug money? With getting her daughter back?

She watched Crystal pull out a drawer in her desk, knowing instinctively the woman wasn't reaching for a weapon. Crystal dug out a pint of vodka and poured two fingers into her dirty coffee cup.

"You know, I always envied you," the older woman said. "You had everything I wanted."

Abby watched her in surprise, wondering how a woman like Crystal Winfrey Jordan could have wanted for anything back in her heyday.

"You had Frank's respect," Crystal said, lifting the cup in a mocking toast. She downed the clear liquid without a blink and licked her lips. "I used to think he was half in love with you."

The words hit Abby like ice water. She shivered in the confined, hot room. She'd seen Frank as a mentor.

Surely Crystal couldn't mean that he'd had a romantic interest in her.

Crystal poured herself another drink and downed it. "I do remember the name of the barbecue place, now that I think of it. The girl worked there, was a good friend of the family. It was called H's Second Avenue Barbecue." Crystal seemed to focus on Abby. "But what does this have to do with getting your daughter back?"

"I'm not sure it does," she admitted, hating to think she'd wasted her time coming here.

Crystal looked up at her, tears welling in her eyes.

Abby felt the old kinship, a remembered closeness with this woman. "Frank's involved with a drug lord name Tomaso Calderone and he or Calderone's men have my daughter."

Crystal shook her head. "Not Frank."

"Maybe you don't know him as well as you think." But she could see that Crystal didn't believe it. The woman was still in love with her ex-husband. Love was blind and deaf, it appeared.

"I'm sorry about what happened to you, but Frank would never have hurt you," Crystal said. "Nor your little girl."

"I'm sure he didn't know I was alive in Mexico these past six years either." Abby wrote down the cell phone number on a scrap of paper and laid it on the desk. "If you hear *anything* about my daughter, will you call me?"

Crystal's faded blue eyes welled again with tears. "Frank doesn't have your daughter, Abby. He's in intensive care in a hospital in San Antonio. He's not expected to live. He was shot trying to save you and your daughter."

Chapter 14

With her flight not leaving for several hours and still stunned by what Crystal had told her, Abby drove around Houston, feeling lost. She kept thinking back to last night, replaying Frank's words in the dilapidated building in Study Butte. Searching for the key to finding Elena. He'd wanted to know where the money was. Said it was the only way she could save her life and Elena's. She'd gotten the impression he'd been expecting someone. He'd said she was wasting valuable time. But had he been expecting the men in the helicopter? The men who had taken Elena?

What bothered her most was that Frank might have been trying to save her and Elena. Was that possible? She'd heard shots behind her and Elena as she fled, but she couldn't be sure Frank had been shooting at her. Nor could she explain what he'd been doing with Calderone's men.

She called the Presidio hospital on the cell phone from her car, hoping to talk to Jake but the nurse said he was still out, sleeping peacefully and still improving.

Relieved he was better, she hung up and sat for a moment looking out into the darkness. It had been easier, thinking Frank was behind the kidnapping. But if he wasn't, then who had her daughter? And why hadn't they called?

She tried calling the hospital in San Antonio but couldn't even find out if Frank Jordan was a patient.

Bereft and more frightened than she wanted to admit, she dialed directory assistance, desperately needing something to occupy her mind—and the time—before her flight.

Surprisingly, H's Second Avenue Barbecue was still in business after all these years. Like many Texas barbecue joints, it was small, nondescript and out-of-the-way. She smelled the meat cooking over the hickory as she got out of her car. There were only a few tables and half a dozen stools at a counter, most empty this time of the night.

She sat down at the counter and opened the menu, looking the place over before she settled on a barbecued pork sandwich and a cola.

As a young waitress wearing the name tag Jennifer took her order, she noticed the framed photographs on the walls, some of them quite old. She studied one—a picture of two people holding large platters of food.

She got up for a closer look. "Who are these people?" she asked as Jennifer rushed by.

"The original owners." The girl carried two huge plates of barbecued pork ribs that smelled wonderful as they passed. "The Harpers," she added over her shoulder.

Harper? She told herself there had to be thousands of Harpers in the country as she sat down again. When Jennifer brought her sandwich and cola, she asked, "Did they have a son named Dell Harper by any chance?"

She could tell immediately the girl was too young to know, but an older waitress had overheard and came over. "You knew Dell?" Her name tag said she was Suzie.

"Maybe. Was he with the FBI?"

"Unfortunately." Suzie pulled down one of the photos from the wall and walked over to where Abby was sitting. She used the hem of her uniform top to clean the glass.

"Dell was a friend of mine," Abby said, recalling what Jake had told her, wishing she could remember Dell. "I used to be an FBI agent in the same division."

"The FBI did nothing but hurt Dell," the woman said bitterly. "First his girlfriend was killed. Then Dell, dying like he did." She wagged her gray head. "Pretty near destroyed that family. Bud and Lenore sold the place and left. Couldn't blame them."

"It was *Dell's* girlfriend who was shot by an FBI agent out front?" Abby repeated, her heart thudding.

The woman nodded. In the back, the cook called out "Order up," and the waitress handed her the framed photograph as she hurried to the kitchen.

She looked down into the faces. A smiling couple in their forties, a tall, lean young boy of about eleven standing with them. All three held platters of barbecued ribs in front of them.

She stared at the boy's face and felt a small nudge of memory. A prickling feeling of warmth and fondness, almost a memory. And something else. Something darker, colder, more frightening.

If she and Dell had really been close, then he must have told her about losing his girlfriend. She felt a ripple of apprehension crawl up her spine. What a coincidence that Dell ended up working for the man who'd killed his girlfriend. If you believed in coincidence.

Suzie came back and put the photograph on the wall again without a word.

Abby took a bite of her barbecued pork sandwich out of politeness. She no longer felt the least bit hungry, even though the barbecue was delicious. Why on earth had Dell gone into the FBI after what had happened to his girlfriend? How had he ended up working under Frank Jordan? And what was the clipping doing in the bus-station locker?

She feared none of it had anything to do with Elena's kidnapping. Dell Harper was dead. He'd died in the explosion that had almost killed her and *had* killed Buster McNorton. With a start, she realized that Buster McNorton was the other agent who'd been on the scene when Dell Harper's girlfriend was killed. Now Buster was dead, as well.

She put down the half-eaten sandwich, paid her bill, leaving a good tip, and started out of the restaurant, her heart pounding. She couldn't wait to get back to Jake.

But near the door, she spotted another photograph. Her footsteps slowed. She stared at the smiling faces.

Bud and Lenore Harper with their son Dell and another young man. The two boys wore baseball uniforms.

She grabbed Suzie's arm as the older woman was going past. "Is that another Harper son?" she asked, her heart a deafening drum in her ears.

"No, Dell was their only child."

"Then who—" She pointed at the second young man in the photograph.

"That was Dell's best friend, Tommy Barnett. The two grew up here in the neighborhood."

Abby swallowed. "Does he still live around here? Or have family?"

Suzie shook her head. "The Harpers *were* his family. The boy lived with an old-maid aunt who died years back, but he spent all of his time here with Dell." She studied the photograph for a moment and smiled. "Tommy idolized Dell. Did whatever Dell did. If Dell jumped off the roof, then Tommy did. Lenore called him Dell's shadow, always following Dell around like a puppydog."

She dragged her eyes from the photo, her gaze hardening as it settled on Abby. "Tommy always did what Dell did. He would have joined the FBI too, but couldn't get in. Probably doesn't know how lucky he is."

Abby stared at the photo of Dell Harper and his best friend, Tommy Barnett, the man who'd held her at gunpoint on the train, the man who'd kidnapped her daughter.

Jake woke with a start and looked around the room, confused for a few moments, before he remembered where he was. The hospital room was empty. No Abby.

His heart pounded furiously in his chest and he felt weak with fear. Hurriedly he buzzed the nurse.

"Yes?" she said, a dark silhouette in the doorway. He realized it was dark outside. How many hours had he been asleep? How long had it been since he'd seen Abby? His fear heightened. "Would you get Abby, my—"

"Your wife isn't here, Mr. Cooper." His wife? Mr. Cooper? He blinked. Of course Abby would have been too smart to admit him under his own name. And only a wife could come and go freely.

"Did my wife say where she was going?" he asked, his throat dry, his heart thudding in his chest.

"She left earlier. She called a few minutes ago to check on you and we told her you were sleeping peacefully. I'm sure she'll be here soon."

But he knew better. He knew Abby. And now that he felt stronger, his head clearer, he had a feeling he knew where she'd gone. After the money, so she'd be ready when the kidnappers called. But they wouldn't be calling. "She didn't say where she was?"

"No, but earlier she did ask where she could rent a car, and she left her cell-phone number, in case we needed to contact her. Try to get some more rest. I'm sure she'll be here soon." She closed the door.

Jake reached for the phone beside the bed and hurriedly dialed the cell-phone number, scared sick for Abby. He knew now how Frank had tracked him to Study Butte. The same way, he feared, Abby was being tracked right at this very moment.

At the door of the restaurant, Abby hesitated. She looked out into the growing darkness and knew Tommy

Barnett was out there somewhere. She'd felt his presence before El Paso. Except now, she knew who he was. She knew who had her daughter, who'd led her here. She just didn't know why.

The door opened and a couple came in, bringing with them the warm evening air. She looked past them to the pockets of darkness pooling in the parking lot and stepped back. Not yet.

Turning, she made her way to the ladies' rest room. It was vacant. Inside, she locked the door and reached into her purse for the cell phone.

She dialed the FBI number, not even realizing that she'd remembered it until her fingers had tapped out the once-so-familiar digits. She asked for Reese Ramsey, said it was urgent and waited as her call was transferred.

Reese came on the line, a little groggy, but he woke up quickly when she told him who she was.

"Abby Diaz is dead," he said, sounding suspicious.

"Guess again."

"Yeah? Well I have two reports that say otherwise."

Just the sound of his voice brought back a memory, crystal clear. "How about that party at Frank's when you got drunk and confessed to me your deepest darkest secrets on the back steps?"

Silence. "ABBY?"

"Tommy Barnett. I need to know everything you have on him." She waited for him to boot up his laptop.

If only she could remember what'd happened six years ago. If she was right and Dell was the one who'd tipped off Calderone to try to get Frank, then why was Frank still alive and Dell dead? And why did his best friend now have her daughter? If Crystal had told the truth and Frank Jordan was on his deathbed, what more did Tommy want? The money?

"Sorry," Reese said after a few minutes. "No Tommy Barnett."

"Are you sure? Keep in mind that according to the FBI, I'm dead."

"Look, Frank gave me the results of those tests himself. Take it up with him," Reese said. "Hold on, I've got your boy. Yep. He tried to get into the FBI, but failed psychological testing."

She gripped the phone tighter. Nutcase. A nutcase had her daughter.

"Oh boy. I just ran his name through the crime computer. He did three of fifteen in a Texas prison."

She caught her breath. "What was he in for?"

"Selling illegal substances. And Tommy was no small-time operator either."

Drugs? Conceivably Tommy could have found out about her and Elena from Julio. They *were* in the same business. Maybe even associates.

"Is Jake there with you?"

"He can't come to the phone right now," she lied, not sure why. But she knew she wasn't telling anyone where Jake was. Not even someone Jake trusted. "Thanks for the information." She hung up, her fingers shaking. What kind of man had Elena? She didn't want to think.

Someone knocked at the bathroom door. She knew she couldn't stay here. She thought about calling the police, but couldn't risk it. Tommy Barnett had Elena. And she thought she knew what he wanted. Eventually she'd have to deal with him if she hoped to get her daughter back.

She opened the bathroom door, half expecting to see him waiting for her. A small gray-haired elderly woman gave her a smile as she hurried into the rest room and closed the door behind her, leaving Abby standing outside in the hallway.

She walked through the restaurant toward the front door, studying the patrons out of the corner of her eye. No Tommy Barnett. No, he'd be waiting for her outside.

But as she walked to her car she saw no one, and yet she swore she could feel him out there, watching her, waiting. Waiting for what?

She opened her car door, her fingers trembling, and climbed in, locking the door behind her. The cell phone rang, startling her. Tommy? Or Reese trying to reach Jake?

"Abby." The sound of Jake's voice brought tears to her eyes. "Where are you?"

"Houston. Jake, are you all right? I—"

"Abby, listen. I know how they found us in Study Butte. It's the cell phone. There must be a tracking device in it."

She stared at the phone in her hands, realization making her heart pound harder.

"You have to get rid of it, and quick. Frank—"

"It's not Frank, Jake. A man named Tommy Barnett has Elena. He was a friend of Dell Har—"

Her words were lost in an explosion of glass as her side window imploded. The cell phone was jerked from her hand. She turned and saw the familiar face just before she felt the blow.

Chapter 15

"Abby!" Jake heard the glass break, heard her cry out, then a loud thunk came over the receiver as if the phone had been dropped to the pavement. He listened to the deadly silence, his heart slamming against his chest as he heard another sound. Abby being dragged from the car. A car door opened, then slammed closed. An engine revved, then faded away. He thought he'd die. He closed his eyes, squeezing the phone in his hand. Not again. God, please, don't let me lose her, not again.

Houston. She'd said she was in Houston. What the hell was she doing there? He couldn't imagine. Something to do with Dell Harper and another man he'd never heard of. Tommy Barnett. He realized he was still listening. At first all he heard was silence. Then he picked up another sound. It took him a moment to realize it was the loudspeaker coming from a ballpark. A base-ball game! He could hear the crowd now.

He listened, concentrating hard. *Give me a name.* *Give me just one team name.* Then he heard it. The Texas Red Devils were up by three.

He hung up and called Reese.

"I thought you were Abby calling back," Reese said. *"Abby called you?"*

"Yeah, she's alive."

He only hoped.

"She needed me to run a name through the computer," Reese was saying. "Tommy Barnett."

"Who is he?"

"A pretty big-time drug dealer here in Houston."

Great. "Any connection to Dell Harper?"

"Not that I know of," Reese said, sounding surprised.

Dell was dead and had been for six years. What could it matter now anyway? "Listen, I need a jet. I need to get to Houston and quick. You can fill me in when you meet me at the airport. We've got to find Abby before it's too late." If it wasn't already.

Abby had said it wasn't Frank. Then why would he falsify the reports to make her look dead? Why would he be working with Ramon Hernandez? "Just hurry." He hung up and slipped out of bed to dress. He felt stronger. Or maybe he just told himself he did. Either way he was going after Abby.

The world came back slightly out of focus. In the fuzzy grayness, Abby remembered. It all came back fast and furious. Scenes racing through her mind, conversations, the past flooding her memory.

She was outside the warehouse in the darkness, waiting with Jake, her weapon drawn. When she looked down the side of the building, she saw Dell and her heart leapt into her throat. Had she really seen him signal someone out in the darkness?

Buster and Dell disappeared inside the warehouse. She followed, a terrible feeling taking possession of her. Dell hadn't been himself lately but he wouldn't talk about what was bothering him.

She slipped through the side door behind the two agents and stopped to let her eyes adjust to the semi-darkness. The warehouse was large and full of wooden crates. The air smelled musty and dank. Only a dim light burned near the center. She crouched behind a stack of crates for a moment, then moved toward the light and the sound of whispered voices.

As she neared, she realized Dell was talking with someone. Whoever it was, it wasn't Buster.

"You aren't changing your mind now," a male voice snapped. "We've worked too hard. Think of Amy."

"Amy's dead, Tee." Dell sounded weary.

She edged closer.

"If you don't have the stomach for this, I can do it for you."

"No, I can handle it," Dell said. "Let's just get it finished. Your part ready? Then you'd better get out of here. They'll be coming in any minute."

Oh, God. What kind of trouble was Dell in? Finish what? She slipped to the edge of the crate and peered around the corner. Her heart caught in her throat.

Buster lay sprawled on the warehouse floor. Dell stood over him with another man, both with their backs to her. Dell had his weapon drawn and didn't seem to even notice Buster's body beside him. No, Dell wouldn't— No!

"Make it look good," Tee said, handing Dell a large clear plastic bag filled with white powder. Then Tee turned and disappeared between two crates.

She felt the hair on her neck rise. She rose to her feet and stepped out, gripping her weapon as she pointed it at her friend. "Dell, tell me Buster isn't dead. Tell me you didn't kill him."

Dell turned slowly.

The memory jerked to a halt, then began again in slow motion.

She could feel tears burn her eyes. Her legs felt weak, the gun in her hand too heavy and awkward. "Dell?" Her voice came out a whispered plea. She could hear the others coming. They'd be here any minute.

"I'm sorry, Abby. You and Frank are next." He raised his weapon, aiming it right at her.

No!

She saw herself dive to the floor and roll and come up firing. A trained reaction. Instinctive. She felt Dell's shot whiz past her head, too shocked to even realize how close he'd come to killing her. She saw him take the hits as her finger squeezed off the shots. One in the neck just above his bulletproof vest. The other snapping his head back as he went down.

She watched as if underwater, everything surreal, everything happening in microseconds, nothing making any sense. Someone grabbed her, pulled her back, struggling to get the weapon out of her hand. She fought him off and ran toward the sound of Jake's voice calling to her.

The building exploded around her. Flames and fire. Someone dragging her out, wrapping her in a rough, smelly fabric. Someone she didn't know. Pain. Terrible, terrible pain. Then darkness.

She blinked and swallowed. She'd killed Dell. Oh, God. She squeezed her eyes shut. No wonder she hadn't been able to remember. No wonder. Her heart ached as she recalled how close she and Dell had been. Like the little brother she'd never had. She'd loved Dell.

She opened her eyes and saw Tommy Barnett. Tee. He sat across from her in a small room with a low ceiling and dirt floor, watching her. Had he felt the same way about Dell once? What had made him push Dell into doing what he did? Or was he just being protective toward Dell, the same way she'd been?

The difference was, Tommy would kill for Dell. And there was a good chance he knew that she'd been the one who'd fired the shots that had taken his best friend's life. *Her* best friend's. Was that why he'd kidnapped her daughter? Abducted *her?* Had he seen her shoot Dell that night?

She sat up, using the rough wall behind her for support, her eyes on Tommy Barnett.

"The game's almost over," he said. He leaned casually against the opposite wall, facing her. He didn't appear to be armed. He wore a baseball cap. Both of his hands were in the pockets of his jacket. "I was afraid you were going to miss the last inning."

Game? She heard the cheering then. The echo of the loudspeaker. Someone had just made a home run. She glanced around in confusion. They appeared to be in an old dugout.

She swallowed, her tongue feeling thick, dry as Texas dust. "Where is my daughter?" Her voice broke as all her fears welled up like tears inside her.

"She's at the ball game," he said matter-of-factly. "Where else would she be on a spring night like this?"

She frowned.

"Don't worry, you'll see her soon."

He seemed so...normal, she thought. Not like a kidnapper at all. Not even like a drug dealer. He looked like the boy next door.

"What is it you want?" she asked, sitting up a little straighter. Her head ached from where he'd hit her. "The money?"

"I make my own money," he said, waving off even the idea. "I'm just finishing what Dell started."

He made it sound as if he was talking about a project, like rebuilding an old car or refinishing a boat. Not about kidnapping a child. Not about murdering people.

"This is about his girlfriend, the one who was killed."

He nodded. "Amy. Dell loved her more than anything. They were going to get married right after graduation, couldn't wait. Then we were going to take over the barbecue joint so Bud and Lenore could have some fun. Dell'd always wanted that. His parents had worked so hard for so many years." He smiled. "Dell was going to make me a partner. We were going to franchise and open up H's Barbecue restaurants all over Texas. It would have worked, too." His smile faded.

"I don't understand."

"Frank Jordan killed Amy," Tommy said as if it all

made perfect sense to him. She was sure it did. Because Frank had killed more than Dell's girlfriend. He'd killed the boys' dream, their planned futures.

She stared at Tommy, wondering desperately why she and Elena were a part of this. Frank was dying in a hospital in San Antonio. Maybe was already dead. Dell and Tommy had gotten their revenge. What more did Tommy want? Unless he'd seen her kill Dell. Was that what this was all about?

"What does my daughter have to do with this?" she asked, afraid of the answer.

He stared at her. "You really don't know?"

She felt her heart lurch.

"Dell always said how smart you were. He admired you a lot. He really liked you," Tommy assured her. "He said you were the best agent he'd ever met, because you were smart but you also cared. It tore him up knowing he had to kill you."

She thought of that moment of hesitation before Dell fired at her. It had cost him his life. But he *had* fired. He *would* have killed her. If she'd let him.

"Why?" she asked, tears welling in her eyes. "What was the point? All those years, working so hard to get into the FBI, getting put into Frank's division, why didn't Dell just kill him years ago?"

Tommy shook his head. "Dell always said that anything worth doing, was worth doing right. He wanted to get close to him, get to know him. He wanted Frank to know him as well. At first Dell was just going to gain his trust and then tell him who he was and execute him for murdering Amy, but then we realized how much help Dell could be to me in his position so we thought, why hurry?"

So Dell had been helping his drug-dealing friend. "Frank didn't mean to kill Amy. It was an accident in the line of duty," she said, but Tommy didn't seem to hear her.

"Then, Dell realized that killing Frank was almost like putting him out of his misery."

She stared at Tommy. It was true. The Frank Jordan she knew was not a happy man. She'd always thought it was Crystal's drinking that had made him that way. Now she wondered if Frank's unhappiness was what had caused Crystal's drinking. "His ex-wife told me that Frank never got over Amy's death.

Tommy shook his head. "It wasn't Amy who was eating him up inside. It was you."

"Me?"

"You still don't get it, do you? You figured out so much. Just like Dell said, you're smart. But you can't see what's been right in front of you the whole time. Just like Frank didn't see Dell."

She frowned as she looked up at Tommy, seized by a terrible premonition. Frank had covered up how Dell and Buster had died that night in the warehouse. It had never come out that they'd been shot by one of the other agents. Why had Frank done that?

Tommy nodded as if he could see her coming to the realization. "You were Frank's favorite. You wouldn't believe the strings he pulled to get you on his team. He was so proud of you. Dell said only a fool couldn't have seen it. Dell was no fool."

She swallowed, fear making her numb. Outside the dugout the crowd was screaming. Where was Elena?

Somewhere out there watching the game? Eating popcorn, drinking a soda, waiting for her mommy and daddy to show up with Sweet Ana? Abby prayed so.

"What are you trying to tell me?" Her words came out in a hoarse whisper.

"Frank Jordan is your father."

Chapter 16

Her father? Abby stared at Tommy. "My father died before I was born."

He shook his head. "Dell found out that Frank Jordan sent checks monthly to a woman named Ana Fuentes in Galveston, Texas."

The ground beneath her no longer felt solid. "No. That can't be. He'd have told me."

Tommy lifted a brow. "He ran out on your mother when she was pregnant with you. Why would he tell you that? Especially after your mother killed herself."

Her head spun. No. She wanted to argue. Dell had gotten it wrong. But she couldn't find the words. She remembered the way Jake had hesitated when she'd asked about her mother. She closed her eyes, unable to will it away. Frank. Her father. On some level, she knew it was true. The way her grandmother had never told her how her father and mother had died. Why they'd died so young.

And later, the way she'd gotten into the FBI and quickly become part of Frank Jordan's team. The special treatment Frank had always given her. The odd argument they'd had the day of the explosion. The conversation they'd had in Study Butte. She *had* been his favorite and she'd known it. She just hadn't known why. Until now.

She let her gaze fall on Tommy's face. Oh, God. Now she understood. She understood it all. An eye for an eye. Take from Frank the one thing he valued most. Or in this case, the two things. His daughter and granddaughter.

She felt such a sudden sense of loss, not just for a father she hadn't known, but for the wasted years. Like Elena, she'd yearned for a father. There had been a time when she'd have given anything for one. Why had Frank walked out on her mother? Why had he never told her who he really was?

"I had hoped Frank would be here to see this," Tommy said. "But it will just have to be enough that he knew I'd taken his granddaughter before he died."

So much lost and for what? "Is Frank—"

"Dead?" Tommy shrugged. "One way or the other." He pulled a pistol from his jacket pocket and glanced out of the dugout. "The game is over. We'd better go get Elena." He motioned with the gun for her to lead the way.

She struggled to her feet, fighting back the grief, the loss, the fear. She had to think of Elena now. Elena had found *her* father and she'd be damned if she'd let anyone take that away from her. Jake would be on his way.

She'd told him she was in Houston. And she knew Jake. He'd find her. Somehow. Even as she thought it, she knew it was inconceivable that he'd find her and Elena in a city this size. Even if he *could* get here in time.

But she wanted to see him, to look into his handsome face, to touch him again. After all these years they'd been apart, she couldn't bear the thought that she might not see him one more time.

"Don't plan on Jake," Tommy said as if he'd read her mind.

She looked back at him in surprise.

He smiled. "I figured you were thinking he'd be coming to your rescue soon." He shook his head. "Not this time."

Jake flew into Houston in the dark, desperately trying to put all the pieces together quickly. Reese met him at the airport.

"You were right," Reese said as they hurried to the car. "The Texas Red Devils are playing at Bayview Field. It's about twenty minutes from here. You wanna drive?"

"No, you drive," Jake said getting into the passenger side. "You know Houston much better than I do."

Jake watched the city pass in a blur through his window. On the flight, he'd had a long time to think. Too long. Someone at the FBI had falsified the fingerprint and autopsy reports. Frank. But if he didn't have Elena, then why had he tried to make everyone think Abby was dead?

"Why would Frank lie about Abby's real identity?" he asked Reese.

Reese shrugged. "Maybe he got the wrong information. Or had some reason to not want anyone to know the truth."

Jake shook his head, remembering that moment of doubt when he'd heard the news. "You personally had the reports done, right?"

"Yeah, but Frank got wind of them," Reese said. "I didn't see the results until they'd gone through him."

Jake nodded. "What else did you find out about this Tommy Barnett?"

"Other than the fact that he's a drug dealer? Not much."

"Abby said he was a friend of Dell Harper's."

"Tommy Barnett *is* from Houston, Dell's old neighborhood."

"The same neighborhood we're headed for, right?"

Reese nodded. "You think he took Abby and Elena to the ball game?"

"Just a feeling," he said, praying his instincts were right. Dell had loved to play baseball. Jake recalled a photograph of Abby and Dell after a game, Dell's arm around Abby's shoulder, their heads close together, both smiling broadly. The memory clutched at his stomach.

Jake could kick himself now for not digging into Dell's background, for not being more suspicious of the man. But he'd thought it was just jealousy that had made him suspect Dell, and hadn't listened to his instincts.

Reese turned into the baseball field parking lot and could see the ballpark ahead. It was deserted. His heart lunged in his chest. His instincts had been wrong. Or he hadn't gotten here in time.

"The game got out early," he said.

"No." Reése pointed to an adjacent ballpark where the lights still glowed on the field but only a couple of cars remained in the lot. "Looks like you're right on target."

As Abby walked across the field, she saw that they were in an older field. The lights of another park shone down on the deep green of the diamond in the distance. Earlier she'd heard cars leaving, the sounds diminishing. Now the lights blinked off, pitching the park into darkness except for a shaft of light spilling out from beneath the concession area below the stands.

Under a moon cloaked in clouds, she walked ahead of Tommy across the dew-damp field, her eyes on the light, her heart pounding. Elena. *Oh, God, let her be all right.* At that moment, she had just one wish. To hold her daughter in her arms. Even for one last time.

The stands stood empty and dark. Quiet settled over the ballpark and the humid spring night, as they crossed the deserted diamond.

Suddenly she spotted Elena in the dark bleachers. A man sat next to her. Elena waved excitedly when she saw her. The man rose and took Elena's hand. They started down the steps toward the field.

Her heart leapt into her throat at the sight of her daughter. All her FBI training hadn't prepared her for this. She knew better than to try to talk Tommy out of the finale he'd planned. His loyalty to Dell was unconditional. And she'd heard enough that night at the warehouse to know that it had been Tommy who had forced Dell to go through with his plot against Frank Jordan and Buster McNorton.

Nothing she could say would change Tommy's mind. She understood his commitment. While misplaced, it reminded her of the commitment she felt for her daughter. The same one she'd made years ago to Jake Cantrell. She would kill for Elena and Jake.

But she also knew that the odds of getting herself and Elena out of this weren't good. While she might be able to get the better of Tommy, she didn't stand much of a chance against two men.

And all the training in the world couldn't make her forget that this was her little girl running toward her. Her daughter who trusted and loved her without question.

She felt paralyzed at the thought of risking Elena's life. Because anything she did would be risky at best.

She glanced back at Tommy. He'd put the gun into his pocket again along with his hand. His look warned her to be very careful of what she did or said.

"Mommy!" Elena cried as she ran to her. "I flew in a helicopter all over and I got sick and threw up and I slept funny and I cried and I saw a baseball game and I ate hot dogs and popcorn and cotton candy and I so wanted my Sweet Ana and you, Mommy, and Daddy. They said you'd come. Where's Daddy? Why didn't he come with you?"

Abby fell to her knees and wrapped her arms around her baby, hugging her desperately. "Oh, Elena." What a resilient child, always finding that silver lining.

"I missed you, Mommy," Elena whispered.

"I missed you, too, *chica suena*." She felt Tommy behind her.

"Let's go down to the concession stand," he said. She

heard him take a deep breath. "Dell did love the game of baseball. He would have loved a night like this."

She heard the break in Tommy's voice, the anguish. As she pulled Elena up into her arms, she thought of Dell, the little brother she'd always wanted. "I loved Dell, too," she whispered and looked over at Tommy.

For an instant, their eyes met in the dim light. She saw his terrible pain, his remorse, his regret, his need for revenge at any price. It was a debt that had to be paid.

"Karl," he said to the man who'd been sitting with Elena. "Let's go check out the cotton candy." She felt his hand on her arm. He pushed her toward the concession stand.

Jake jumped out of the car and ran toward the ballpark, his heart thundering in his chest. He could hear Reese behind him, his limp slowing him down.

He drew his weapon as he neared the stands. From inside, he heard the tinkle of laughter. Elena's sweet laughter. And the sound of voices.

As he neared, he spotted something white lying on the ground. He bent down to pick up the baseball and stuffed it into his pocket without thinking. Slowly, he made his way toward the voices.

The air smelled of popcorn and fresh-mown grass. He slipped onto the field, moving along the edge of the stands. The voices grew more distinct as he neared the concession area. He stopped, glancing around for Reese, but he didn't see him. The ball field lay empty. Nothing moved on the breeze. No sounds other than the ones coming from beneath the stands.

He moved closer, weapon drawn.

* * *

"Karl, make sure we're not interrupted," Tommy said to the other man after he'd checked to make sure they were alone in the cool concrete concession area.

Karl nodded and moved to the bottom of the stairs leading up to the stands, his tread heavy and slow. The two men stood a few feet away, both facing her and Elena.

Abby hugged her daughter and looked around, hoping to see something she could use for a weapon, some way she could protect Elena. The room was large. Its cold concrete walls were painted with bright colors. A long line of metal counters ran the length of the room on the right. Nearer stood a cotton-candy machine. But not close enough that she could reach it.

Tommy stood for a moment, just looking around as if the room held a plethora of memories. Or he was waiting for something. But she knew he was watching her closely.

She lowered Elena to the floor, her hands on the child's small shoulders, half listening to her daughter recount the baseball game and the food she'd eaten. Half listening to Tommy's breathing.

His gaze finally settled on her and Elena.

Abby swallowed, praying for a miracle. It was the only thing that could save her and Elena now.

Tommy drew the pistol from his jacket. Elena's body stiffened beneath Abby's fingers.

Behind him and Karl, in the shadows, Abby thought she caught movement. She froze. Jake. He moved toward her, carefully sneaking up behind Tommy and Karl. If either of them turned, they would see him.

She met Jake's gaze, that old feeling arcing between them, strong as their passion for each other, strong as their need to save their daughter. Together. Just like old times.

"Stall," he mouthed.

"You realize that Dell was like a little brother to me," she said as she looked down the dark barrel of the pistol in Tommy's hand. "Dell—" The catch in her throat was real. "He was my best friend. I had no idea how much pain he was in. I just wish he'd told me. Maybe I could have helped."

Tommy shook his head. "There wasn't anything anyone could have done. Not from the moment Frank Jordan fired the shot that killed Amy."

Out of the corner of her eye, she saw Jake pull a baseball from his pocket. He motioned to her.

"Anything you want me to tell Dell when I see him?" she asked quickly.

Tommy seemed taken back by her question.

The instant Jake threw the ball, she cried, "Under the counter!" in Spanish to Elena and hurled the child toward the metal concessions. Abby dove after her.

The ball hit Tommy in the back. He let out a loud "Ufft!" and got off a wild shot as he stumbled and fell to his knees from the blow.

Abby rolled as gunfire ricocheted through the concession area. She came up behind the cotton-candy machine. Karl had turned and fired at Jake. She drove the cotton-candy machine into the thug's side as she scrambled to her feet, driving Karl back. Jake fired. Karl dropped like a rock, his pistol rattling to the floor.

She grabbed his gun and swung around.

Tommy was gone.

Behind her, she caught a glimpse of Elena scrambling toward a large cooler. Tommy came around the end of the counter and grabbed Elena before Abby could get off a shot.

"Jake!" she cried as Tommy came up too quickly with Elena in his arms, the barrel of his pistol to the back of the child's head.

"Drop the gun," he ordered. "Now!"

She let the pistol fall to the floor.

"You too, Jake," Tommy said as he moved from behind the counter, using Elena as a shield. The child's eyes were wide but lit up when she spied her father.

"Daddy!" she cried.

"Hi, baby," he said. "Everything's going to be fine." He lowered his gun to the floor and stepped away from it as Tommy instructed. The room grew impossibly quiet.

"Dell wouldn't have wanted this," she said, knowing she was wasting her breath.

With a shudder of relief she saw Reese appear behind Tommy. He limped toward them, his weapon drawn.

"Reese?" Tommy said at the limping sound behind him. "What kept you? I could have used some help."

"Looks like you're doing just fine," Reese said.

She heard Jake swear under his breath behind her as Elena squirmed in Tommy's hold.

She stared at Reese. Hadn't he been the one who'd given Jake the cell phone with the tracking device in it? The one who'd told Jake she wasn't Abby Diaz? He'd made them believe Frank was behind it. Frank, her father. Could what Crystal have told her be true?

"I should have known," Jake said. "If I hadn't figured out that Abby was here, you would have helped me out, huh, Reese? You've been so helpful. Like the cell phone with the tracking device. Nice touch."

Reese shrugged and gave a slight bow. "I do try to please."

"And telling me that Abby really wasn't Abby," Jake said as he moved up behind her and put a hand on her back. "That was good!" She realized it wasn't just his hand. He pressed the cold steel of a knife flat to her back. She reached back, as if to cover his hand with her own, and took the knife and slipped it down into the waistband of her jeans. "You have a flare for the dramatic!"

"Please, you're making me blush," Reese said. "Now, kindly step away from Abby." He motioned with his gun.

Jake stepped a few feet away from her in Tommy's direction. A clear signal. She'd recognized the knife as well. It was the one she'd pulled from Julio's body, the one she'd had in her bag. She knew, the same way she knew Reese didn't know Jake had had the knife.

"But you did figure it out," the agent said. "You just thought Frank was behind it. Him putting the tracking device in the cell phone made it so easy for me."

"Don't tell me you're doing this for Dell Harper, too," Jake said conversationally.

Reese shook his head. "Naw, I'm just in it for the money. Crass, huh?" He shrugged. "The thing about being on a drug task force, you see so much money and after a while you realize if you put one drug dealer away, another one just comes along to take his place. What's the point?"

"That's bull, Reese, and you know it," Jake said congenially enough. "It's greed, plain and simple."

Reese's look darkened. "The FBI owes me something for this bum leg."

"The FBI didn't blow up that warehouse," Abby interjected.

"Enough already," Tommy snapped. "Let's get this over with."

She had to get Elena away from Tommy. "Please, just let me hold my baby one last time. Then you can—do what it is you have to do."

"Don't do it," Reese warned. "You don't know her like I do. She might try something."

Tommy shot Reese a disgusted look. "Like what? She isn't armed and she can't do much with a child in her arms."

He slowly let Elena down, turning the pistol on Jake. "And I'll be forced to kill her lover and the father of her baby if she does." Elena ran to her.

She scooped her daughter into her arms and hugged her tightly, aware of the knife wedged against her spine.

"Keep your hands where I can see them," Reese warned Jake.

She waited for a sign from Jake.

"You're getting awfully paranoid, Ramsey," he said.

Now! With one swift desperate move, she held Elena with one arm and reached back with her free hand, pulled the knife and threw it in a once expert, long-practiced movement. It appeared knife throwing was right up there with bike riding. You never quite forgot how.

The blade glittered in the concession lights for an instant, then hit home, burying itself to the hilt in Reese's chest.

Reese gasped in surprise and stumbled back, getting off a wild shot that ricocheted through the room.

Abby whirled around, trying to shield Elena, as she dove for the stairs.

At that same instant, Jake went for Tommy's weapon.

A shot echoed through the building. Then another. She waited for the pain as she clutched her daughter to her breast and launched herself and Elena under the stairs.

For a moment, she thought she might have been hit. She stared down at Elena, seeing the wide eyes, but feeling the child's sweet breath against her cheek as she pulled her back under the open stairwell.

Silence filled the concession area. She waited with her heart lodged in her throat. She had no weapon. And she and Elena were trapped.

"It's all right, Abby."

She felt tears rush her eyes at the sound of Jake's voice. It was over.

Slowly she climbed out with Elena. Tommy lay on the floor at an odd angle. Blood leaked out like motor oil onto the concrete. Reese was sprawled not far away, his weapon still in his hand, his eyes open and sightless, the same knife that had killed Julio stuck in his chest. There was something symbolic about that, she thought.

She turned away, shielding Elena, and felt Jake's arm come around her shoulders.

"Daddy!" Elena cried as she encircled his neck with her arms. "I knew you'd come. I wasn't even scared."

Jake hugged them both to him, then led them up the stairs and out into the night.

"The thing is," Jake said as they walked across the ballfield. "I have this place north of here on the Smoking Barrel Ranch where I work. Right now the cabin isn't much but I was thinking, we could always add on to it."

Abby looked up. The first star of the night glittered brightly in a sky warm and rich with the promise of summer. She stumbled to a stop, realization rushing over her in a drowning wave of relief. Tears blurred the night and great sobs rose in her chest. They were alive. They were together. At last.

Jake pulled her and Elena into his arms. The three of them stood in the middle of the baseball diamond, cloaked in the darkness as the rest of the stars came out, one after another.

Chapter 17

Frank Jordan had come out of his coma. He was asking for his daughter.

"This is something I need to do alone," Abby told Jake. She reached up to cup his jaw in her hand. His face was warm, his dark eyes full of promise.

She stood on tiptoe to meet his kiss. It fired that now-familiar passion. Just a look. A touch. A whisper. She wondered if she would always yearn for him and suspected she would until the day she died.

"I'll take Elena to the park across street," he offered. "Take your time. You can meet us there."

She smiled and squeezed his hand, then knelt down to hug her daughter. She still feared letting Elena and Jake out of her sight, but she knew she had to learn to trust again. To believe that they'd lived through this for a reason. And that now, nothing could keep them apart.

As she stepped gingerly into Frank's room, she was filled with so many emotions. And even more regrets.

He looked older against the white of the pillow, his face drawn and pale. But his eyes lit up when he saw her and tears welled and spilled down his cheeks.

She moved to his bedside.

"I'm so sorry," he whispered. "If I had married your mother—" His voice broke.

She sat down in the chair next to his bed. He reached for her hand. It felt cold, as cold as her heart toward him. "Tell me about you and my mother."

Slowly, he proceeded to tell her a story of a young, ambitious man and a beautiful Mexican girl named Rosa Louisa. Her mother. He faltered when he reached the part where Rosa Louisa told him she was pregnant with his child.

"I made the biggest mistake of my life," he said, his voice no more than a whisper. "I abandoned her. I thought a wife and a child would keep me from reaching my dreams." Anguish contorted his face. "I have regretted leaving your mother every day of my life."

"You could have gone back," she said, wishing that were true.

He shook his head. "She wasn't strong. She took her life right after you were born. I never got to tell her how I felt. How sorry I was."

"Why didn't you come for me?" Abby asked, her heart breaking.

He shook his head. "You were better off with your grandmother."

"But still, you could have—"

"I couldn't face you with the truth. Not then, not

later." He told her how he'd watched her from a distance, watched her grow up. How he'd planted the seed about the FBI when he'd sent her career information after graduation. How delighted he'd been when she'd unknowingly followed in her father's footsteps, becoming an FBI agent. No wonder her grandmother had been so upset about that choice.

"I couldn't believe it when I had the chance to get you on my team," he said. "I was so proud of you. To be near you—"

"That day I disappeared, you called me in your office."

He nodded. "I was worried about you. I'd seen how protective you were with Dell."

"Did you know about Dell?"

He shook his head. "I knew you were pregnant with my grandchild." He waved away her question of how he'd known. "I just didn't want anything to happen to the two of you."

"You covered up what happened." It sounded like an accusation even to her ears.

"I did what I thought was best. It wasn't until later that I put it all together and realized it was my fault. That Dell had ultimately killed you and the baby because of me. But I thought it was over."

All he'd had after that was his work, he said. He'd thrown himself into it. Crystal began to drink more, feeling disconnected from him, and they'd finally divorced. His fault. She'd realized all his emotions were tied up in the past and the family he'd lost.

"Then you really didn't know Julio Montenegro abducted me?" Abby asked.

"No, I was knocked out in the blast. I believed the body we found in the ashes was yours. I never dreamed you might be alive. Until Julio contacted me. He'd been there that night. He'd taken you and the knowledge of what had happened to use when he had enough money to make a move against Calderone."

"I only found three hundred thousand dollars," she said.

"Who knows how much he stole?" Frank said. "I have a feeling Ramon knew a lot more about Calderone's missing money than Julio. I would imagine Ramon used Julio as his scapegoat."

"Ramon?"

"Dead. Killed in the shootout in Study Butte."

"You saved my life and Elena's," she said, knowing that now to be true.

"I'm the one who jeopardized it in the first place," he said bitterly. "I did everything I could to protect you, including hiring Jake to go after you. He was the one man I believed I could trust although I'd been given evidence to the contrary. I knew Jake. I knew how much he loved you. If he couldn't get you and Elena out of Mexico alive, no one could."

"You also falsified the fingerprint and autopsy reports," she said.

He nodded. "I thought if no one knew you were Abby Diaz—"

"But Tommy knew."

He nodded. "Because of Reese."

He'd even made a deal with the devil, Calderone, providing the information where Ramon could find Jake in Study Butte. In exchange, he got to call the shots.

But things had gone badly at Study Butte because he hadn't known about Tommy Barnett. Nor about Reese.

"How did you know about Study Butte?" she asked, remembering that Jake thought no one had.

Frank looked chagrined. "When you started seeing him, I found out *everything* about him. I'm also the one who put the tracking device in the cell phone Reese gave Jake. I thought I could protect you."

He'd acted like a caring father, she thought. She squeezed his hand, touched by his attempts to protect her and Elena. He'd risked his life. He'd even risked his job, his reputation with the Bureau, something that had meant so much to him.

"We're fine," she said. "Elena is—" She shook her head and smiled, not sure how to describe her daughter. "She bounces back easily. It's as if she came into the world expecting nothing, so she's always amazed by what life has to offer her." Tears filled her eyes. "She has the father she's always wanted. She'll mend."

Frank squeezed her hand. "I would like to be part of your lives, but I know I have no right to ask."

Abby looked into his face, her feelings all too close to the surface. "We're going to need some time. Jake is taking us up to the Smoking Barrel Ranch where he works. He has a place up there on Ash Pond. Elena loves it. He's promised to teach her to ride. And the people on the ranch, well, they're quite the bunch. They've become Jake's family."

He nodded. "I understand."

She got to her feet. "The thing is," she said, feeling tears rush her eyes. "Elena would love having a grandfather."

"What about you, Abby? Is it too late for us to be father and daughter?"

Was it ever too late to find the father you'd always yearned for? "I was thinking," she said, hearing her voice break, "you might like the Smoking Barrel Ranch and I know you'd find the people who live there very interesting. Maybe when you're feeling better, you could come up."

He burst into a smile, his eyes swimming in tears. "I'll do that."

Epilogue

From the porch of the Smoking Barrel Ranch, Jake watched the helicopter touch down on the front lawn. Behind him in the house, he could hear Rosa and Elena in a discussion about what to make for dessert. Jake only half listened to their running conversation. They were both speaking in lightning-speed Spanish, as Elena trailed along behind the good-natured cook.

He watched as a man jumped down from the chopper and, keeping low, ran toward the house.

Behind him, the rugged Texas plains ran to the vast horizon. The waning sun turned the distant Davis Mountains to pale purple.

The federal agent stopped at the bottom of the porch steps. "The new director asked that I see you get this personally." He held out a large manila envelope marked Confidential.

Jake took it and, with a slight nod, the man retreated to the helicopter. Once he was back inside, it lifted off again. Jake watched until the chopper was no more than a dark speck against the pale sky.

He turned at the sound of footsteps behind him as Abby came through the screen door to join him. She was dressed in jeans, boots and a western shirt that hugged her lush curves. He pulled her to him, thinking about the baby growing inside her. Their child. A sister for Elena. Or a brother. Not that it mattered. They'd have more children. Maybe they'd fill this old ranch house.

They'd already outgrown his cabin on the acreage he'd bought from Mitchell. The place sat overlooking Ash Pond and now rang with the sounds of laughter and little girl giggles. He'd been working all summer on an addition, excited about the nursery he'd built and Abby had decorated.

"What is it?" she asked when she noticed the envelope in his hand.

"The original reports on the fingerprints from the handcuffs, the autopsy on the body in Abby Diaz's grave and DNA on Elena," he said.

"You haven't opened it?"

He leaned down and kissed her. "I already know everything I need to know. How about you?"

She looked up at him and shook her head as she wrapped her arms around his neck.

"I love you, Abby," he whispered against her hair. "After dinner I intend to show you just how much."

She laughed and curled into the crook of his arm as they headed back into the house. Her memory had returned. And along with it, her love for him. It blazed in her eyes, in her touch. He couldn't quit looking at her. He especially couldn't quit touching her. It had taken a while, but he was finally beginning to believe that Abby and Elena were safe.

As he opened the screen door and drew her inside the house, he tossed the envelope on the table. Elena came running, wrapping herself around their legs.

"We're going to have flan for dessert. Rosa said I could help. I get to break the eggs and stir and I helped with the enchiladas. Rosa says I'm a great cook."

Jake laughed as he ran a hand over the child's sleek black hair. She'd blossomed since they'd arrived at the ranch. He'd never seen a child like her. She amazed him every day and thrilled him. He had never known such love. Except for the love he felt for her mother.

He glanced up to see that most everyone had gathered in the kitchen. He could smell enchiladas cooking in the oven, Elena's favorite, and hear their neighbor Maddie Wells arguing with Mitchell about his health.

"He doesn't take care of himself," Maddie called after Mitchell as he came out into the foyer. He winked at Jake and Abby as he passed.

"The woman loves me," Mitchell said, shaking his head.

His impossible executive assistant Penny Archer trailed right behind him, complaining that someone had been in her computer files. "We need better security around here, Mitchell."

Jake led the way into the big, bright country kitchen, his arm still around Abby, Elena riding along on the tops of his boots. Catharine, Brady Morgan's new bride, was making a salad, or at least trying to. Brady couldn't seem to leave her alone. Rosa was laughing at something Slim, their Romeo of a ranch hand, had said, her face flushed.

Jake pulled out a chair for Abby, then drew one up for himself as he pulled Elena onto his lap. His heart swelled at the sight of his family.

The other room, Penny picked up the manila envelope marked Confidential from the front table. "Isn't this the proof the FBI promised on Abby and Elena?"

Mitchell nodded.

"Jake didn't even open it," she said.

Mitchell smiled as he looked back into the kitchen. "Jake knows everything he needs to know." He took the envelope from her and tossed it into the fireplace. The flames quickly devoured the pages.

Penny gasped as she watched them burn.

"Mitchell, you might want to hear this," Maddie called from the kitchen. "Jake has an announcement."

Mitchell offered his arm to his assistant.

Penny took it but mugged a face at him as she did. "What now?" she grumbled.

"Oh, I have a pretty good idea," he said. "I'd suggest you get busy and learn how to knit baby booties."

"Not likely," she groaned. "I have enough to do around here."

"Abby and I are getting married," Jake announced when they were all in the large ranch kitchen. He turned to Abby and, reaching into his pocket, pulled out a heart-shaped locket on a silver chain. The silver gleamed as he put the locket around her neck. "She's said she'll have me."

Everyone applauded but he held up a hand to silence them. "That's not all," he said with a laugh. "Elena is going to have a brother or sister come next spring." He smiled at Abby and Elena. Mitchell had never seen him so happy.

Elena cheered and clapped. "Mommy says I can be a flower girl and dance with Daddy at the wedding and wear a really pretty dress." She danced around the room, then stopped as a thought hit her. "I want a brother *and* a sister *and* a horse."

Everyone laughed.

"Anyone seen Rafe?" Cody, the youngest agent, asked from the doorway. Rafael "Rafe" Alvarez was the charmer of all the agents, Cody often the sullen, moody one.

"He's out riding patrol, why?" Slim asked.

Cody shook his head. "What's going on here?"

"Just the usual," Mitchell said as he let his gaze fall on his ever-growing family. "This calls for a toast."

He broke out the champagne and filled glasses, promising Maddie he'd only have a little.

He lifted his glass. It surprised him, the lump he felt in his throat as he looked around the room. He wished Rafe was here for this. And Daniel Austin, the agent they'd lost last year.

He touched his glass to Maddie's. "To everlasting love."

* * * * *

STONE COLD
UNDERCOVER AGENT

Nicole Helm

The first romance novel I ever read
was a romantic suspense, and I never thought
I'd be able to write one. Thank you, Helen and
Denise, for helping me prove past me wrong.

Chapter 1

Gabby Torres had stopped counting the days of her captivity once it entered its sixth year. She didn't know why that was the year that did it. The first six had been painful and isolating and horrifying. She had lost everything. Her family. Her future. Her *freedom*.

The only thing she currently had was…life itself, which, in her case, wasn't much of a life when it came right down to it.

For the first four years of her abduction, she'd fought like a maniac. Anyone and anything that came near her—she'd attacked. Every time her captor got up close and told her some horrible thing, she'd fought in a way she had never known she could.

Maybe if the man hadn't so gleefully told her that her father was dead two years into her captivity, she might have eventually gotten tired of fighting. She might have accepted her fate as being some madman's kidnapping victim. But every time he appeared, she remembered how happily he had told her that her father had suffered a heart attack and died. It renewed her fight every single time.

But the oddest part of the eight years of captivity was that, though she'd been beaten on occasion in the midst of fighting back, mostly The Stallion and his men hadn't ever forced themselves on her or the other girls.

For years she'd wondered why and tried to figure out their reasoning...what their *point* was. Why she was there. Aside from the random jobs The Stallion forced her and the other girls to do, like sewing bags of drugs into car cushions or what have you.

But she was in year eight and tired of trying to figure out why she was there or what the point of it was. She was even tired of thinking about escape.

She'd been the first girl brought to the compound and, over the years, The Stallion had collected three more women. All currently existing in this boarded-up house in who knew where. Gabby had become something like the den mother as the new girls tried to figure out why they were there, or what they had done wrong, or what The Stallion wanted from them, but Gabby herself was done with wondering.

She had moved on. After she'd stopped counting every single day at year six, the past two years had been all about making this a reality. She kept track of Sundays for the girls and noted when a month or two had passed, but she had accepted this tiny, hidden-away compound as her life. The women were as much of a family as she was ever going to have, and the work The Stallion had them doing to hide drugs or falsify papers was her career.

Accepting at this point was all she could do. If sometimes her brain betrayed her as she tried to fall asleep, or one of the girls muttered something about escape, she pushed it down and out as far as it would go.

Hope was a cancer here. All she had was acceptance.

So when just another uncounted day rolled around and The Stallion, for the first time in all of those days, brought a man with him into her room, Gabby felt an icy pierce of dread hit her right in the chest.

Though she'd accepted her fate, she hadn't accepted *him.* Perhaps because no matter how eight years had passed, or how he might disappear for months at a time, or the fact he never touched her, he seemed intent on making her *break.*

Quite honestly, some days that's what kept her going. Making sure he never knew he'd broken her of hope.

So, though she had accepted her lot—or so she told herself—she still dreamed of living longer than him and airing all his dirty laundry. Outliving him and making sure he knew he had never, *ever* broken her. She very nearly smiled at the thought of him dead and gone. "So, who are you?"

The man who stood next to The Stallion was tall, broad and covered in ominous black. Black hair—both shaggy on his head and bearded on his face—black sunglasses, black shirt and jeans. Even the weapons, mostly guns, he had strapped all over him were black. Only his skin tone wasn't black, though it was a dark olive hue.

"I told you she was a feisty one. Quite the fiery little

spitball. She'll be perfect for you," The Stallion said, his smile wide and pleased with himself.

The icy-cold dread in Gabby's chest delved deeper, especially as this new man stared at her from somewhere behind his sunglasses. Why was he wearing sunglasses in this dark room? It wasn't like she had any outside light peering through the boarded window.

He murmured something in Spanish. But Gabby had never been fluent in her grandparents' native language and she could barely pick out any of the words since he'd spoken them so quickly and quietly.

The Stallion's cold grin widened even further. "Yes. Have lots of fun with her. She's all yours. Just remember the next time I ask you for a favor that I gave you exactly what you specified. Enjoy."

The Stallion slid out of the room, and the ominous click of the door's lock nearly made Gabby jump when no sounds and nothing in her life had made her jump for nearly two years.

While The Stallion's grin was very nearly…psychotic, as though he'd had some break with reality, the man still in her room was far scarier. He didn't smile in a way that made her think he was off in some other dimension. His smile was… Lethal. Ruthless. *Alive.*

It frightened her and she had given up fear a very long time ago.

"You don't speak Spanish?" he asked with what sounded almost like an exaggerated accent. It didn't sound like any of the elderly people in her family who'd grown up in Mexico, but then, maybe his background wasn't Mexican.

"No, not really. But apparently you speak English, so we don't have a problem."

"I guess that depends on your definition of problem," he said, his voice low and laced with threat.

What Gabby wanted to do was to scoot back on the bed as far into the corner as she possibly could, but she had learned not to show her initial reactions. She had watched The Stallion get far too much joy out of her flight responses in the beginning, and she'd learned to school them away. So even though she thought about it, even though she pictured it in her head complete with covering her face with her hands and cowering, she didn't do it. She stayed exactly where she was and stared the man down.

He perused the bedroom that had been her life for so long. Oh, she could go anywhere in the small, boarded-up house, but she'd learned to appreciate her solitude even in captivity.

The man opened the dresser drawers and pawed through them. He inspected the baseboards and slid his large, scarred hands up and down the walls. He even pulled at the boards over the windows.

"Measuring for drapes?" she asked as sarcastically as she could manage.

The man looked at her, still wearing his sunglasses, which she didn't understand at all. His lips curved into an amused smile. It made Gabby even more jumpy because, usually, the guards The Stallion had watching them weren't the brightest. Or maybe they'd had such rough lives they didn't care for humor of any kind. Either way, very few people, including the women she lived with, found her humor funny.

He was back to his perusal and there was a confident grace about him that made no sense to her. He wasn't like any of the other men she'd come into contact with during her captivity. He was handsome, for starters. She couldn't think of one guard who could probably transfer from a life of crime into a life of being a model, but this man definitely could.

It made all of her nerves hum. It gave her that little tingle that mysteries always did—the idea that if she paid enough attention, filed enough details away, she could solve it. Figure out why he was different before he did her any harm.

She'd begun to wonder if she hadn't gone a little crazy when she noticed these things no one else seemed to. She was pretty sure Tabitha thought she was out of her mind for having theories about The Stallion's drug and human trafficking operations. For coming up with a theory that he spent three months there and split the other seasons at three other houses that would ostensibly be just like this one.

She'd been here for eight years and she knew his patterns. She was sure of it. Things puzzled together in her head until it all made sense. But the girls all looked at her like she was crazy for coming up with such ideas, so she'd started keeping them to herself. She'd started trying to stop her brain from acting.

But it always did and maybe she had gone completely and utterly insane. Eight years ago her life had been ripped away from her, but she didn't even get to be dead. She had to be here living in this weird purgatory.

Wouldn't that drive anyone to the brink of insanity? Maybe her patterns and theories were gibberish.

Finally the man had looked through everything in the room except her bed where she was currently sitting. He advanced on her with easy, relaxed strides that did nothing to calm the tenseness in her muscles or the heavy beating of her heart. She couldn't remember the last time in her captivity she'd felt so afraid.

He didn't say anything and she couldn't see his eyes underneath the sunglasses, so whatever he was thinking or feeling was a blank-expressioned mystery.

Finally, after a few humming seconds, he lifted a long finger up to the ceiling. She frowned at him and he made the gesture again until she realized he wanted her to get off the bed.

Since most of the guards' preferred way of getting her to do something was to grab her and throw her around, she supposed she should feel more calm with this man who hadn't yet touched her.

But she wasn't calm. She didn't trust him at all.

She did get up off the bed and, instead of scurrying away, tried to measure her steps and very carefully move to the farthest corner from him.

The man lifted every single blanket on her bed and then, in an easy display of muscles, the heavy mattress and box spring, as well. He got down on all fours and looked under the bed and, finally, she realized he was searching for something in particular.

She just had no idea what on earth he could be looking for.

"No bugs?"

She stared at him. What, did he have some weird fear of ladybugs or ants or something? Then she realized the intensity with which he was staring at her and recalled how carefully he had looked through every inch of this little room. Yeah, he wasn't looking for insects.

"I've been here for eight years. As far as I know, he's never bugged or videotaped individual rooms."

The man raised his eyebrows. "But he films other rooms?"

Gabby trusted this man almost less than she trusted The Stallion, which was not at all. She offered a careless shrug. The last thing she was going to do was to share all of her ideas and information with this stranger.

"Tell me about your time here."

There was a gentleness to his tone that didn't fool her at all. "Tell me who you are."

He smiled again, an oddly attractive smile that was so out of place in this dire situation. "The Stallion told me you'd be exactly what I was looking for. I don't think he knew just how perfect you'd be."

"Perfect for what?" she demanded, trying to keep the high-pitched fear out of her voice.

"Well, he thinks you'd be the perfect payment. A high-spirited fighter—the kind of woman who would appeal to my baser instincts."

This time Gabby couldn't stop herself from pushing back into the corner or cowering. For the first year she'd been held captive, she'd been sure she'd be sexually assaulted. She'd never heard about an abduction that hadn't included that, not that she'd had any deep knowledge of abductions before.

But no one had ever touched her that way and she'd finally gotten to a point where she didn't think it would happen. That was her own stupid fault for thinking this could be her normal.

The man finally took off his sunglasses. His eyes were almost as dark as his hair, a brown that was very nearly black. Everything about his demeanor changed; the swagger, the suave charm, gone.

"I'm not going to hurt you," he said in a low voice.

Maybe if she hadn't been a captive for eight years, she might have believed him. But she didn't, not for a second.

"You're just going to need to play along," he continued in that maddeningly gentle voice.

"Play along with what?" she asked, pushing as far into the corner as she could.

"You'll see."

Gabby wanted to cry, which had been an impulse she'd beaten out of herself years ago, but it was bubbling up inside her along with the new fear. It wasn't fair. She was so tired of her life not being fair.

When the man reached out for her, she went with those instincts from the very first time she'd been brought there.

She fought him with everything she had.

Jaime Alessandro hadn't worked his way up "The Stallion's" operation by being a particularly *nice* guy. Undercover work, especially this long and this deep, had required him to bend a lot of the moral codes he'd started police work with.

But thus far, he'd never had to beat up or restrain a woman. This woman was surprisingly agile and strong, and she was coming at him with everything she had.

He was very concerned he was going to have to hurt her just to get her to stop. He could stand a few scratches, but he doubted The Stallion was going to trust him with the next big job if he let this woman give him a black eye—no matter how strong and "feisty" she was.

God, how he hated that word.

"Ma'am." He tried for his forceful FBI agent voice as he managed to hold one of her arms still. He didn't want to hurt the poor woman who'd been here eight years—a fact he only knew because she'd just told him.

He shouldn't have been surprised at this point. He'd learned very quickly in his undercover work that what the FBI had on Victor Callihan, a.k.a. The Stallion, was only the tip of the iceberg.

If he thought about it too much, the things The Stallion had done, the things Jaime had done to get here... Well, he didn't, because he'd had to learn how to turn that voice of right and wrong off and focus only on the task at hand.

Bringing down The Stallion.

That meant if she didn't stop flailing at him and landing some decent blows, he was going to have to restrain her any way he could, even if it caused her some pain.

Though he had her arm clamped in a tight grip, she still thrashed and kicked at him, very nearly landing a blow that would have brought him to his knees. He swore and, though he very much didn't want to, gave her a little jerk that gave him the leverage he needed to grab her from behind with both arms.

She still bucked and kicked, but with his height advantage and a full grip on her upper body, he could maneuver her this way and that to keep her from landing any nasty hits.

"I'm not going to hurt you. I'm going to help you, I promise."

She spat, probably aiming for him but missing completely since he had her from behind. It was only then he realized he'd spoken in Spanish instead of English.

He'd grown up speaking both, but his work for The Stallion and the identity he'd assumed required mostly speaking Spanish and pretending he struggled with English.

It was slipups like that—not realizing what language he was speaking, not quite remembering who he was—that always sent a cold bolt of fear through him.

He needed this to be over. He needed to get out. Before he lost himself completely. He could only hope that Gabriella Torres would be the last piece of the puzzle in getting to the heart of The Stallion's operation.

"I'm not going to hurt you," Jaime said in a low, authoritative tone. Certain, self-assured, even though he didn't feel much of either at this particular moment.

"Then let go of me," she returned, still bucking, throwing her head back and narrowly missing headbutting him pretty effectively.

He tried not to think about what might have happened to her in the course of being hidden way too long from the world. It was a constant fight between the human side of him and the role he had to play. He wouldn't lose his humanity, though. He refused. He might have to bend his moral code from time to time, but he wouldn't lose the part of him that would feel sympathy. If he lost that, he'd never be able to go back.

Jaime noted that though Gabriella still fought his tight hold, she was tiring.

"Be still and I'll let you go," he said quietly, hoping that maybe his outer calm would rub off on her.

She tried to land a heel to his shin but when that failed she slumped in his arms. "Fine."

Carefully and slowly, paying attention to the way she held herself and the pliancy of her body, Jaime released her from his grip. Since she didn't renew her fight, he took a few steps away so she could see he had no intention of hurting her.

When she turned and looked at him warily, he held his hands up. Her breathing was labored and there were droplets of sweat gathered at her temples. She had a pretty face despite the pallor beneath her tan complexion. She had a mass of dark curls pulled back and away from her face, and he had to wonder how old she was.

She looked both too young and too world-weary all at the same time, but he couldn't let that twist his insides. He'd seen way worse at this point, hadn't he? "I'm not going to harm you, Gabriella. In fact, I want to help you."

She laughed, something bitter and scathing that scraped against what little conscience he had left.

"Sure you do, buddy. And this is the Taj Mahal."

Yeah, she'd be perfect for what he needed. Now he just had to figure out how to use her without blowing everything he'd worked for.

Chapter 2

Gabby was wrung out. Physically. Emotionally. It had been a long time since she'd had something to react so violently against. Her breathing was uneven and her insides felt scraped raw.

She wanted to cry and it had been so long since she'd allowed herself that emotional release.

She couldn't allow it now. Not with the way this man studied her, intently and far too interested. She had become certain of her power in this odd world she'd been thrust into against her will, but she didn't believe in that power in the face of this man.

She closed her eyes against the wave of despair and the *need* to give up on this whole *surviving* thing.

"Gabriella. I know you have no reason to trust me, but I'm going to say it even if you don't believe it. I will not hurt you."

The worst part was that she was so exhausted she *wanted* to believe him. No one had promised her safety in the past eight years, but just because no one had didn't mean she could believe this one.

"I guess it's my lucky day," she returned, trying to roll her eyes, but exhaustion limited the movement.

"I know. I know. I do. Don't trust me. Don't believe. I just need you to go along with some things."

"What kind of things? And, more important, *why*?" She shook her head. Questions were pointless. The man was going to lie to her anyway. "Never mind. It doesn't matter. Do whatever you're going to do."

"You fought me."

"So?"

He stepped forward and she stumbled away. He shook his head, holding his hands up again, as if surrendering. "I'm sorry. I won't. I'm not going to touch you." He kept his hands raised as he spoke. Low, with a note to his voice she couldn't recognize.

Panic? No, he wasn't panicked in the least. But there was something in that tone that made her feel like time was running out. For what, she had no idea. But there was a *drive* to this man, a determination.

He had a goal of some kind and it wasn't like The Stallion's goals. The Stallion had a kind of meticulous nature, and he never seemed rushed or driven. Just a cold, careful, step-by-step map in his head to whatever endgame he had. Or maybe no endgame at all. Just... living his weird life.

But *this* man in her room had a vitality to him, an energy. He was trying to *do* something and Gabby hated the way she responded to that. Oh, she missed having a goal, having some *fight* in her. The weary acceptance of the past two years had given her less and less to live for. Helping the other girls was the only thing that kept her getting up every morning.

"What do you want from me?"

"Just some cooperation. Some information. To go along with whatever I say, especially if The Stallion is around."

"Are you trying to usurp him or something?"

He released a breath that was almost a laugh. "N—" He seemed to think better of saying no. "Who knows? Right now, I need information."

"Why should I give you anything?"

He seemed to think about the question but in the end ignored it and asked one of his own. "Is it true…?" He trailed off, giving her a brief once-over. "They haven't touched you while you've been here?"

She stared hard at the man. "One time a guard tried to touch my chest and I knocked his tooth out."

The man's full mouth curved a little at that, something so close to humor in his expression it hurt. Humor. She missed…laughing. For no reason. Smiling, just because it was a nice day with a blue sky.

But she couldn't think about all the things she missed or her heart would stop beating.

"What happened to the guard?"

Gabby shrugged, hugging herself against all this *feeling*. Thoughts about laughter, about the sky, about using her mind to put the pieces of the puzzle together again.

You gave that up. You've accepted your fate.

But had she, really, when the fight came so easily and quickly?

"I don't know. I never saw him again."

"Was it only the one time?"

Gabby considered how much information she wanted to give a stranger who might be just as evil as the man who held her captive. She could help him boot The Stallion out...and then get nothing for her trouble. She wasn't sure if she preferred to take the risk. The devil you knew and all that.

But there was something about this man... He didn't fit. Nothing about his demeanor or mannerisms or his questions fit the past eight years of her experience. What exactly would be the harm in telling him what she knew? What would The Stallion do? He'd been the one to leave her with this man.

"As far as I know, they can knock us around as long as they don't break anything or touch our faces. If they go overboard, or get sexual, they disappear."

The man raised an eyebrow. "How many have disappeared?"

Gabby shrugged, still holding herself. "It was more in the beginning. Five the first year. Three the second. Only one in the third. Then five again the fourth. Two the fifth, then none since."

Both his eyebrows raised at this point, his eyes widening in surprise. "You remember it that specifically?"

Part of her wanted to brag about all the things she remembered. All the specifics she had locked away in her brain. All the patterns she'd put together. None of the girls had ever appreciated them. She had a feeling this man would.

But it would be showing her hand a little too easily for comfort. "Not a lot to think about in this place. I remember some things."

"Tell me," he said, taking another one of those steps toward her that made her want to cower or run away to whatever corner she could find. But she stood her ground and she shook her head.

If she told him, it would be in her own time, when she thought telling might work in her favor in some way.

He stood there, opposite her, studying her face as though he could figure out how to get her to talk if he simply looked hard enough.

So she looked right back, trying to determine something about *him*.

He had a sharp nose and angular cheekbones, a strong jaw covered liberally with short, black whiskers. His eyes looked much less black close up, a variety of browns melding to the black pupil at the center.

He had broad shoulders and narrow hips and even the array of weapons strapped to him didn't detract from the sexy way he was built. Sexy. Such an odd thing. She hadn't thought about sex or attractiveness or much of anything in that vein for eight long years.

She didn't know if she was glad she could still see it and recognize it or if it just made everything more complicated. Far more lonely.

The eerie click of a lock interrupted the moment and he looked back at the door, then at her. His expression was grave.

"I'm not going to hurt you," he whispered. "But this may scare you a little bit. That's okay. Fight back."

"Fight ba—"

He reached out and grabbed her by the shirt with both large hands. She screeched, but he had her shirt ripped in two before she landed the first punch.

Jaime pretended to laugh as Gabby pounded at him. He glanced at The Stallion, doing his best to stand between the man and his view of Gabby. He'd tried not to look himself, but he needed the illusion of a fight. A sexual one.

He couldn't let his disgust at that show. *"Senor?"* The Stallion always got some bizarre thrill when Jaime called him that, so he'd done it with increasing regularity. Being the egomaniac that he was, The Stallion never got tired of it. "An hour, no?"

"I'm sorry to interrupt, but I need you immediately. Your hour will have to wait."

Jaime scowled. He didn't have to fake it, either. He wanted more information from Gabriella. If the woman had remembered how many guards were dismissed every year...who knew what other kind of information she might have.

Jaime inclined his head as if he agreed, though he didn't at all. He wanted to get information out of Gabriella as soon as possible. The more he got and the sooner he got it, the less he'd have to do for The Stallion.

He gave her a fleeting glance. Those big, dark eyes were edged with fury, and she crossed her arms over her chest. The bra she wore was ill-fitting and he couldn't help but notice the way her breasts spilled over the fabric even under her crossed arms.

He quickly looked back at The Stallion. He handed

Gabriella the remains of her shirt. *"Perdón,"* he offered, making sure he didn't sound sorry in the least.

The Stallion chuckled as Jaime walked to meet him at the door. "You could be so much better at your job if you weren't so easily distracted," the man said, clapping him on the shoulder in an almost fatherly manner as he pulled the door closed, leaving Gabby alone in the room.

He didn't lock the door this time and Jaime was surprised at how much freedom he allowed the women he kept there. Of course, the front and back doors were chained and locked even when The Stallion was inside, and all the windows were boarded up in a permanent, meticulous manner.

There were no phones in the house, no computers. Absolutely no technology of any kind aside from kitchen appliances. But even that was relegated to a microwave and a refrigerator. No stove and no knives beyond dull butter ones.

He wondered if the women inside knew that only a couple of yards away, in a decent-size shed, The Stallion kept all the things he denied the women. Computers and phones and an array of weapons, which was where The Stallion was leading Jaime now.

"We have a situation I want you briefed on. Then you may go back to our Gabriella and finish your…" He trailed off and shook his head as he locked and chained the back door they'd exited into an overgrown backyard. "Sex is such a *base* instinct, Rodriguez. Women are a worthless expense of energy. I'm fifty-three, for over half my life I have searched for the perfect woman and failed time and time again. Though, I will admit the women I've kept are of exceptional quality. Just not quite there…"

The man got a far-off look on his face as they walked through the long grass toward his shed. It was the kind of far-off look that kept Jaime up at night. Void of reason or sense, completely and utterly…incomprehensible.

The Stallion patted his shoulder again, tsking. "I know this is all going over your head. You really ought to work on your English."

Jaime shrugged. It suited his purpose to be seen as not understanding everything that went on because of a language barrier, and at times it had been hard to remember he was supposed to barely understand.

But when The Stallion started going on and on about women, Jaime never had any problems keeping his mouth shut and his expression confused. It was broken and warped and utter nonsense.

The Stallion unlocked the shed and stepped inside. Two men were sitting on chairs around The Stallion's desk, which was covered in notes and technology. The man strode right to it and sat on his little throne.

"Herman's gone missing," he said without preamble, mentioning The Stallion's most used runner in Austin. "He didn't deliver his message today, and so far no one has figured out where he disappeared to. Wallace, I'm giving you the rest of today to find him. He can't have gone too far."

The fair-haired man in the corner nodded soundlessly.

"If he *somehow* gives us the slip that long…" The Stallion continued. "Layne, you'll take him out."

Layne cracked his knuckles one by one, like he'd

seen too many mobster movies. "Be my pleasure. What happens to him if Wallace finds him, though? I wouldn't mind getting some information out of him."

The Stallion's mouth curved into a cold, menacing line that, even after two years, made Jaime's blood run cold. "Rodriguez will be in charge if we find him. I'd like to see what he can do with a...shall we say, recalcitrant employee. *¿Comprende?*"

"Sí, senor."

"Wallace, you're dismissed. Report every hour," The Stallion said with the flick of his wrist. "Layne, have the interrogation room readied for us, please."

Both men agreed and left the shed. Jaime stood as far from The Stallion as he could without drawing attention to the purposeful space between them. The man steepled his hands together, looking off at some unknown entity Jaime was pretty sure only he could see.

Jaime stood perfectly still, trying to appear detached and uninterested. "Did you need me, *senor*?"

The Stallion stroked his forehead with the back of his thumb, still looking somewhere else. "Once we figure out what's going on with Herman, I'll be moving on to a different location." His cold, blue gaze finally settled on Jaime. "You'll stay here and hold down the fort, and Ms. Gabriella will be yours to do whatever you please with her."

Jaime smiled. "Excellent." He didn't have to fake his excitement about that, because Jaime was almost certain Gabriella had exactly the information he'd need to pull the sting to end this whole nightmare of a job.

And then Jaime could go back to being himself and figuring out...who that was again.

Chapter 3

Gabby considered taking a nap in lieu of lunch. Her little *visit*, which she couldn't begin to understand, however, had eradicated any appetite she'd had.

That man had acted like two different people. Even the way he talked when The Stallion was present and when he wasn't was different. His voice, when he'd spoken with her, had only the faintest touches of Mexico, reminding her of her parents' accents—a sharp, hard pang of memory.

But when he spoke to The Stallion, it was all rolled R's and melodic vowels. Even his demeanor had changed. That goal or determination or whatever she thought she'd seen in him just…disappeared in the shadow of The Stallion. He was someone else. Something more feral and menacing.

But, despite the very disconcerting shirt-ripping, and the way his gaze had most definitely lingered on her chest, he had been honest with her thus far.

He hadn't hurt her, but he'd let her hurt him. Blow after blow. Considering she'd gotten into the habit of exercising to keep her overactive mind from driving her crazy, she wasn't weak. She had punched him with everything she had, and though he hadn't made too much of an outward reaction, it had to have hurt.

She shook away the thoughts, already tired of the merry-go-round in her head. If she couldn't nap or eat, she'd do the next best thing. Exercise until she was too exhausted to think or to move or to do anything but sleep.

She rolled to the ground, then pushed up, holding the plank position as she counted slowly. It had become a game, to see how long she could hold herself up like this. The counting kept her brain from circling and the physical exertion helped her sleep better.

A knock sounded at the door, which was odd. No one here knocked. Except the girls, but that was rare and only in case of emergency.

Before she could stand or say anything, the door squeaked open and in stepped the man from earlier.

She scowled at him. "I only have so many clothes, so if you're going to keep ripping them, at least get me some duct tape or something."

He pulled the door closed as he stepped inside. "I won't rip your clothes again...unless I have to." He studied her arms, eyebrows pulling together. "You're awfully strong."

"Remember that."

"It could definitely work in our favor," he muttered. "Now, where were we?"

She pushed into a standing position. "You don't want to go back to where we were. I'll hit you where it *really* hurts this time." Why he smiled at that was completely beyond her.

"You might literally be perfect."

"And you might literally be as whacked as Mr. Stallion out there."

He shook his head in some kind of odd rebuttal. "Now—"

"You act like two very different people."

He froze, every part of his body tensing as his eyes widened. "What?"

"You act like two completely different people. In here alone. With him. Two separate identities."

He was so still she wasn't even sure he breathed.

"Two separate identities, huh?"

"Your accent is different when he's not here. The way you hold yourself? It's more…relaxed when he's with you. Rigid with me. No…almost…" She cocked her head, trying to place it. "Military."

She knew she was getting somewhere at the way he still didn't move, though he'd carefully changed his wide-eyed gaze into something blank.

Yeah, she was right. "You were military."

"No."

"Police then?"

"You're an odd woman, Gabriella." He said her name with the exaggerated accent, and it reminded her of her long-dead grandfather. He hadn't been a particularly nice man or a particularly mean man. He'd been hard.

Very formal. And while everyone else in her family had called her Gabby, he'd been the lone holdout.

He'd never appreciated the "Americanization" of his family, even though he'd immigrated as a young man.

"I'm right. You're…" Her eyes widened as she put it all together. Him not hurting her. Him gathering information. Being someone else with The Stallion.

He gave a sharp head shake so she didn't say anything, but she did step closer. "But you are, aren't you?"

"No," he returned easily, nodding his head as he said it.

Her heart raced, her breathing came too shallow. He was an undercover police officer. She had to blink back tears. "Tell me what it means, that you're here. Please."

He let out a long breath and stepped toward her. This time she didn't scurry away. She needed to know more than she was afraid of him. He'd checked the room for bugs before, and she knew they were safe to talk in there, but she also understood how a man like him would have to be inordinately careful. *Undercover.* What did it mean? For her? For the girls?

He inclined his mouth toward her ear, so close she could feel his breath against her neck. "I can't promise you anything. I can only tell you that I am trying to end this, so whatever information you can give me, whatever you can tell me, it'll bring me closer to finishing out my job here."

He pulled back, looking at her, his gaze serious and that determination back in his dark eyes.

She tried to repeat those first five words. *I can't promise you anything.* It was important to remember, to not get her hopes up. Just because he was an undercover police officer…just because he wanted to take The Stallion down…it didn't mean he *would*. Or that he'd get her out in the process.

"How did you put it all together?" he asked. "I'm not…"

"You're very good. Very convincing. I'm probably the only person you let your guard down for, right?"

He nodded, still clearly perplexed and downright worried she'd figured it out.

"I don't know, ever since I got here… I remember things, and I can see…patterns that no one else seems to see. I thought I was going crazy. But… I don't know. I was always good at that. Observing, remembering, figuring out puzzles and mysteries. It just works in my head."

"Clearly," he muttered. "Hopefully you're the only one around here with that particular talent or I'm screwed."

"How long?" she asked. Was he just starting out? He was so close to The Stallion, surely…

"Two years."

She let out a breath. "That's a long time."

"Yes," he said, a bleak note in his voice that softened her another degree toward him. He'd voluntarily held his own identity hostage, separated himself from his life. He'd probably had no idea the things he'd end up missing or wanting.

God help her, she hadn't had a clue in that first day, week, month, even year. She'd had no idea the things that would grow to hurt her.

She felt a wave of sympathy for the man and, even if it was stupid or ill-advised, she had to follow it. She had to follow this first possibility in *ages* that there might be an end to this. "How can I help?"

"So, you trust me?"

"I don't trust anyone anymore," she returned, feeling a little bleak herself. "But I'll try to help you. Because I believe you are what I think you are."

"That'll work. That'll work. But there's something you have to understand. Being a different person means being a *different* person. The ripping-your-shirt thing..."

"It was for him to think that you were...having your way with me." She shuddered a little at the thought, at how close they might have to come to...proving that.

"Yes. There may be times I have to push that a little bit. Because he is..." He cleared his throat. "What do you understand about your position here? Is there a reason you were kidnapped? Is there a reason he's kept you girls...untouched?"

"I'm not really sure. I have no idea why I was taken. I was waiting at my dad's work for him to get off his shift and all of a sudden there were all these people and men talking and I was grabbed and thrown into a van with some other people. They took us somewhere that I don't know anything about. It was all dark and sometimes we were blindfolded or there were hoods put on our heads."

Gabby felt ill. She didn't relive the kidnapping anymore. She'd mostly gotten beyond *that* horror and lived in the horror of her continual imprisonment. Going back and thinking about coming here brought up all sorts of horrible memories.

How awful she'd been to her mother that night when she'd had to cancel her date to pick up Dad. All that fear she hadn't known what to do with or how to survive with when she'd been taken, moved, inspected. But she had. She had survived and lived, and she needed to remind herself of that.

"Eventually, after I don't know how long... Actually that's not true." She didn't have to lie to this man about her memory or pretend she didn't know exactly what she knew like she did with so many people. "It was two days. It was two days from the time they took me and put me in the van to the time they took me to this other place, kind of like a warehouse. They took me—and all the people from that first moment—there and then we were sorted. Men and women went to different areas. And then The Stallion came."

"Keep going," he urged, and it was only then she realized she'd stopped because she could see it. Relive every terrifying detail of not knowing what would happen to her, or why.

"I didn't know that's who he was at the time, but he walked through and he asked everyone if we knew who he was. One woman in my group said yes and she was immediately taken away."

"Did he say his name or offer any hints about who he was beyond The Stallion?"

"No. I've gone over it a million times in my head. He must've...he must be someone, you know? He had to be someone with some kind of profile?"

"Yes, he is."

"He is?" She stepped toward the man who could mean freedom, a scary thought in and of itself. "Who? What's his name? Why is he doing this?" she demanded, losing her cool and her calm in an instant.

"I can't answer those questions."

She grabbed his shirtfront, desperate for an answer, a reason, desperate for those things she'd finally given up on ever getting. "Tell me right this second, you miserable—"

"I'm sorry," he said so gently, so *emotionally*, she could only swallow a sob.

"He kidnapped me. He brought me here. He separated me from my family for eight years, and you can't tell me who he is?" she demanded, her voice low and scratchy but measured. She was keeping it together. She would keep it together.

"Not now. There are a lot of things I can't tell you, because everything you know jeopardizes what I'm doing here. You deserve the answers, you do, but I can't give you what you deserve right now. But if you help me, you'll have the answers, and you'll have your *life* back."

Odd *that* prompted a cold shudder to go through her body. "You can't promise me that."

"No, I can't, but I promise to put my life on the line to make it so."

She didn't know what to do with that or him, or any of this, so she turned away from him, hugging herself, trying to calm her breathing.

There were no promises. There were no guarantees. But she had a *chance*. She had to believe in it. She had to *fight* for it. With everything she had. If not for herself, for the three girls she shared this hell with. For their family's, and hers, even if they probably thought she was dead.

She owed it to a lot of people to do what this man said he would do: put her life on the line to make it so.

*　*　*

Gabriella was clearly brilliant. The way she described remembering things and figuring out patterns no one else did, to the point she thought she was crazy... It sounded like a lot of the analysts he knew. Because when you saw things no one else saw, it was very easy to convince yourself you were wrong.

But she wasn't wrong, and she had *so* much information in that pretty head of hers... Jaime was nearly excited even though she now had the power to end his life completely.

He didn't care because he was so close now. So damn close to the end of this.

She might be brilliant, but he was a trained FBI agent, after all. He wasn't going to let her figuring him out be the end. No way in hell.

"Tell me about what happened after the woman who knew who he was disappeared."

Gabriella nodded. "She was taken away from the room. She had no chance to say anything at all. After that, the rest of us women were separated into groups, and I tried to find a rhyme or reason for these groups, but I really couldn't. Except that all of the women in my group were young and reasonably fit. Dark hair, though none of the same shade—it ranged from black to light brown."

Jaime thought back to The Stallion's odd statement about searching half his life for the perfect woman. He couldn't make sense of it, but that had to be connected to this.

"At that point, it was just six of us. The Stallion lined us up and, one by one, he inspected us."

"Inspected you how?"

Gabriella visibly shuddered, and Jaime hated that she had to relive this, but she did. If they were going to put The Stallion away, she'd probably have to relive it quite frequently.

"He touched our hair and…smelled it." She audibly swallowed, hugging herself so tightly he wished he could offer some comfort, some support.

But he was nothing to her.

"He had one of his cronies measure us."

"Measure you?"

"You know, like if you've ever been measured for clothes?" She turned to face him again, though her dark eyes were averted. But she gestured to her body as she spoke. "Shoulders, arms, chest, hips, legs, inseam, and the guy yelled out each number and The Stallion wrote it all down on this little notepad."

She was quiet for a few seconds and instead of pushing this time, he let her gain her composure, let her take the time she needed.

Time wasn't on his side, but he couldn't…lose the humanity. That was his talisman. *Don't lose your humanity.*

"He dismissed everyone except me."

Jaime didn't know how to absorb that. He could picture it too easily after everything he'd done with and for The Stallion. The fear she must have felt having been taken for no reason, having been chosen for no reason that she understood.

It was dangerous to fill her in on the things he knew. But he had already entered dangerous territory when he had allowed himself to behave differently enough with her for her to figure out who he was. *What* he was.

"He's a sick man," Jaime offered.

"A sick man who is very, very smart or very, very lucky since he hasn't gotten caught in eight years. Probably more than that."

"Yes. Listen, there are a lot of things The Stallion does. But this thing you're involved in… He told me something just now about how he spent over half his life looking for the perfect woman. That women are basically stupid and you shouldn't dirty yourself with them unless you find this perfect specimen."

"Oh, how lovely. I'd love to show him how *stupid* I can be. With my fists."

He smiled at the irritation in her tone because it was *life*. A spark. It wasn't that shaky fear that had taken over as she had relived her kidnapping experience.

"Let him have his delusions. They might get us out of this mess." He wanted to reach out and take her shoulders or…something. Something to cement this partnership, but he was still a strange man in her room who'd ripped her shirt. He had to be careful. Human. "Between what you said and he said, I think that's what he's been doing with this arm of things. Searching for the perfect woman."

"So that's what the measuring was, then. He has a perfect size, I just bet." Gabriella rolled her eyes. "Disgusting pig. And then when we got here he, like, tested me. He would ask these questions, and I never answered. I only fought. For weeks, every time he opened his mouth, I'd just attack. I thought maybe that's why…"

She took in a shaky breath, still hugging herself.

Jaime hadn't been lying when he'd said she might be perfect. She was smart, she was strong—not just physically. Strong at her core.

"I thought for sure I would be raped, but I never have been, and I've never understood why."

"He thinks women are dirty. At least, in this context of looking for the perfect woman. I can't rationalize a madman, but the point is that you were brought here because he thought you *could* be the perfect woman. The fighting, I guess, proved to him that you weren't."

"I thought that for the longest time, but that isn't it. Jasmine—she was brought here my second year—she didn't fight him at all. She told him she'd do whatever he wanted as long as he would let her go. I was the only one who fought, but he hasn't touched any of us. No matter what our reactions were, he found us lacking in some way, I guess."

Gabriella shook her head. "So, he brought us here because we were a possibility, then he tests us and decides we're not perfect, but then why does he keep us?" She looked up at him for answers.

Jaime hated that he couldn't give them to her—and that hate kept him going. Because at least he still had a conscience. He'd started to worry. "That's where I come in. I've been working my way up to get close to figuring out who he was. When I did that, it was decided I'd stay and get enough information on him that we can arrest and prosecute."

"And you don't have that yet?"

"Not to the extent my superiors would like. Which is why we came up with a plan."

"Let me guess. You can't tell me about the plan."

"Actually, this one I can. A little. You're a gift to me."

She physically recoiled and he could hardly blame her.

"Excuse me?"

"I've slowly become his right-hand man and as I learned about the girls he keeps locked up… I wanted to get close to one of you to figure out how I could get you out. How we could all work together to get you out. So I convinced him that a woman would be better payment than drugs or money. I mean, I get paid, too, bu—"

"Of course you do. I'm sure you get money and a horse and forty acres of land. The payment of a woman is simply pocket change, right?"

"Gabriella."

She began to pace the tiny room, her irritation and anxiety so *recognizable* to him he started to feel the same build in his chest.

"This is insane," she muttered. "This is so impossible. These things don't happen! They don't happen to people in my family. They don't happen to people! This is movie craziness."

"No. It's your life," Jaime returned firmly. He needed her to focus, to get past the panic. "There's one of his compounds that has the most evidence on his whole operation, and it's the only one that I don't know where it's located. So, as I work with him right now, that's what I'm trying to figure out. If you've been watching, paying attention, listening…you might have the answer. But we have to pretend like…"

"Like I'm the gift to you. And you can do whatever you want with me," she said flatly.

"Yes. But the key here is that it's pretend. I'm not

going to hurt you. I've done a lot of things that will stick with me for a very long time." He stopped talking for a few seconds so he could regain his composure. He didn't like to think back at some of the chances he'd had to take or some of the people he'd had to hurt. Though he hadn't actively killed anyone, he had no doubt some of the things he'd been involved in had led to the death of someone else.

There were a lot of terrible things you could do to a person without killing them.

He had to get hold of himself, so he did. He forced himself to look at Gabriella. She was studying him carefully, as though she could see the turmoil on his face.

To survive, he had to believe this was a very special woman who could see things no one else could. Because if she could see these things and other people could, as well, they would probably both end up dead.

"I know it sounds crazy," she said carefully, "but I know what it's like. I've helped hide drugs that I'm sure have killed people. I've had to dig holes that I think were…so he could bury people. I've had to do terrible things, and sometimes I'm not even sure that I had to. Just that I did."

"No." He took a step toward her and though he knew he had to be careful so he didn't startle her, he very slowly and gently reached out and took her hand in his. He gave it a slight squeeze.

"We've done what we had to do to survive. In my case, to bring this man to justice. We have to believe that. Above everything else."

She looked down at their joined hands. He had no idea what she saw or what she felt. It had been so long since he'd been able to touch someone in a kind way, in a gentle way, it affected him a bit harder than he'd expected.

Her hand was warm and it felt capable. She squeezed his back as though she could give him some comfort. This woman who'd been abducted from her family for eight years.

When she raised her gaze to his, he felt an odd little jitter deep in his stomach. Something like fear but not exactly. Almost like recognizing something or someone, but that didn't make sense, so he shook it away.

Chapter 4

Gabby looked at her hand, encompassed by a much larger one. She wondered if the small scars across his knuckles were from his undercover work or if he'd got them before.

What would he have been like before his assumed identity?

And what on earth did *that* matter?

She forced her gaze back to him, his dark brown eyes somehow sure and comforting, when nothing in eight years had been *comforting*. It shouldn't be potent. It was probably part of his training—looking in charge and compassionate.

She'd never been too fond of cops, though that may have been Ricky's influence. Her first serious boy-friend. A poster child for trouble. Gabby had been convinced she could change him, that everyone saw him all wrong. Her parents had been adamant that she could *not* change what was wrong with that boy.

They'd barred him from their house. Insisted Gabby live at home through her coursework at the community college, and had been making noise about her not transferring to get her bachelors.

It had all seemed like the most unjust, unfair fate. They didn't have enough money, they didn't have any trust. The world had seemed cruel, and Ricky had been nice...to her.

She was twenty-eight now and that was the only relationship she'd ever had. A boy, really, and she'd only been a girl.

This man holding her hand was no *boy*, but she wasn't sure what she was. Except a little off her rocker for having this line of thought.

She cleared her throat and pulled her hand away. "So. What is it you need from me?"

He was quiet for a moment, studying his hand, which he hadn't dropped—it still hovered there in the air between them.

"My main goal is to find the last compound," he finally said, bringing his hand down to his side. "It's the one he's the most secretive about. So much so, I'm not sure he takes any of his employees there."

"I don't know if I can help with that. I did have this theory..." She trailed off. "I wish I had something to write on," she muttered. She searched her room for something...something to illustrate the picture in her head.

She opened one of her drawers and retrieved her brush, pins and ponytail holders, some of the few "extras" The Stallion afforded her. A giddy excitement jumbled through her and maybe she should calm it down.

But this was something. God, *something* to do. Something real. Something that wasn't just pointless fighting but actually working toward a *goal*.

Freedom.

She settled herself at that word. It had come to mean something different in eight years. Or maybe it had come to mean nothing at all.

She shook those oddly uncomfortable thoughts away and looked around for a place to create her makeshift map. "I can't explain it without props," she said, setting a brush on the center of the floor.

"Let's do it on the bed instead of the floor, so if anyone comes in we can…" He rubbed a hand over his unkempt if short beard. "Well, cover it up."

Right. Because to The Stallion she was a *gift*. No, that was too generous. She was a thing to be traded for services. She shuddered at the thought but…the man kneeled at the bed. The man who hadn't used her as payment but was using her as an informant.

The man whose name she didn't know.

"What should I call you?" she asked suddenly. Because she was working with this man to free—no, not to free anything, but to bring down The Stallion—and she hadn't a clue as to what to call him.

He glanced at her and she must be dreaming the panic she saw in his expression because it disappeared in only a second.

"They call me Rodriguez," he said carefully. "But my name is Jaime A— I…" He shook his head as he focused, as he seemed to push away whatever was plaguing him. "Call me Rodriguez. It's safest."

She knelt next to him, biting back the urge to repeat *Jaime.* Just to feel what his name would sound like in her mouth.

Silly. "All right, Rodriguez." She placed the brush at the center of the bed. "This is Austin. The bed is Texas. I don't have a clue…" She trailed off, realizing this man would know where they were. He hadn't been blindfolded or hooded. He actually *knew* if they were still in Texas, if they were close to home.

She breathed through the emotion swamping her. "Where are we?" she whispered.

"An hour east of El Paso. Middle of nowhere, basically. Only a few small towns around."

She blinked. El Paso. She'd had theories about where they could be, and El Paso had factored into them, but theories and truths were…

"Take your time," Jaime said gently.

"But we don't have much time, do we?" she returned, staring into compassionate eyes for the first time in eight years. Because as much as all the girls felt sorry for each other, they felt sorry for themselves first and foremost.

Jaime nodded toward the bed. "Technically, I don't know how much time we have. I only know the quicker we figure it out, the less chance he has of hurting people. More people."

She took a deep breath and returned her focus to the bed. "The brush is Austin. I get the feeling that's something like…the center. I don't know if it's a headquarters or…"

"Technically, he lives in Austin. His public persona, anyway."

His public persona. Though it fit everything she knew or had theorized, it was hard to believe The Stallion went about a normal life in Austin and people didn't see something was wrong with the man. Warped and broken beyond comprehension.

"So, we've got his personal center at Austin," Jaime continued for her, taking one of the rubber bands she'd piled next to her. He reached past her, his long, muscular arm brushing against her shoulder. "And this is the compound close to El Paso."

"Right. Right." She picked up another rubber band. "He seems to work by seasons, sort of. I started wondering if he had a place in each direction. If this is west, he has a compound in the north, the south and the east. Unless Austin is his east." She placed rubber bands in general spots that represented each direction, creating a diamond with Austin at the somewhat center.

"He has a compound in the Panhandle. Though I haven't been there, he's talked of it. I've been to the one on the Louisiana border. I didn't think he had women there, but… Now that I've seen this setup, maybe he did and I just didn't know about it."

The idea that there'd been women to help and he hadn't helped them clearly bothered him, but he kept talking. "But south… He's never mentioned any kind of holdings in the south of Texas." He tapped the lower portion of her bed. "It has to be south."

"It would make sense. The access to drugs, people."

"It would make all the sense in the world, and you,

Gabriella, are something of a miracle." He grinned over at her.

"It's… Gabby. Everyone, except *him*, calls me Gabby."

His grin didn't fade so much as morph into something else, something considering or…

The door swung open and the next thing Gabby knew, she was being thrust onto the bed and under a very large man.

Jaime hadn't had a woman underneath him in over two years, and that should not at all be the thought in his head right now. But she was soft underneath him, no matter how strong she was…soft breasts, soft hair.

And a kidnapping victim, jackass.

"Rodriguez. Boss wants you." Layne's cruel mouth was twisted into a smirk, clearly having no compunction about interrupting…well, what this looked like, not so much what it was.

Damn these men and their interruptions. He was getting somewhere, and he didn't mean on top of Gabriella.

Gabby.

He couldn't call her that. Couldn't think of her like that. She was a tool, and a victim. Any slipups and they could both end up dead. He glanced down at her, completely still underneath him, and it was enough of a distraction that he was having trouble deciding how to play things in front of Layne.

She blinked up at him, eyes wide, and though she wasn't fighting him, he'd scared her. No matter that she understood him, his role here, he didn't think she'd be trusting him any time soon. How could he blame her for that?

Wordlessly he got off Gabby and the bed and straightened his clothes in an effort to make Layne think he was more rumpled than he really was.

"We'll finish this later," he said offhandedly to Gabby, hoping it sounded to Layne like a hideous threat.

Jaime sauntered over to the door, not looking back at Gabby to see what she was doing, though that's desperately what he wanted to do. He grabbed his sunglasses from his pocket and slipped them on his face as he stepped out into the hallway with Layne.

"Awfully clothed, aren't you?" Layne asked.

Jaime closed the door behind him before he answered. "Still trying to knock the fight out of her. Wouldn't want to intimidate her with what's coming." Jaime smirked as if pleased with himself instead of disgusted.

"It's a hell of a lot better when there's still a little fight in them," Layne said, glancing back at Gabby's door as they walked down the hall.

Jaime's body went cold, but he reined in his temper, curling his fingers into fists, his only—and most necessary—reaction.

"Do you think *senor* would be pleased with that world view?" he asked as blandly as he could manage.

Layne's gaze snapped to Jaime and his threat. The man sneered. "Not every idiot believes your Pepe Le Pew act, buddy."

Jaime flashed his most intimidating grin, one devoid of any of the *humanity* he was desperate to believe he still had. "Pepe Le Pew is French, *culo.*"

"Whatever," the man said with a disinterested wave. "You know what I mean."

"I know a lot of things about you, *amigo,*" Jaime

said, enjoying the way the man rolled his eyes at every Spanish word he threw into the conversation.

Layne didn't take the hint. "Maybe you want to pass her around a bit. Boss man's been pretty strict about us getting anything out of these girls but you——"

Jaime stopped and shoved Layne into the wall. What he really wanted to do was punch the man, but he knew that would put his credibility in jeopardy, no matter how much dirt he had on Layne. He wrestled with the impulse, with the beating violence inside him.

No matter what this man might deserve, he was not Jaime's end goal. The end goal was to make this all moot.

So, he held Layne there, against the wall, one fist bunched in the man's T-shirt to keep him exactly where he wanted him. He stared down at the man with all the menace he felt. "You will not touch what is mine," Jaime threatened, making his intent clear.

"You've already stepped all over what's mine," Layne returned, but Jaime noted he didn't fight back against Jaime's hold—intelligence or strategy, Jaime wasn't sure.

"I ran this show before he brought you in," Layne growled.

"Well, now you answer to me. So, I'd watch your step, *amigo*. I know things about you I don't think The Stallion would particularly care to hear about. A hooker in El Paso, for starters."

Layne blustered, but underneath it the man had paled. This was why Jaime preferred everyone think of him as muscle who could barely understand English. They underestimated him. But Jaime hadn't walked in here blindly. He knew The Stallion's previous head honchos wouldn't take the power share easily. So he'd collected leverage.

Thank God.

"Now, are you ready to keep your disgusting tongue and hands to yourself?" Jaime asked with an almost pleasant smile. "Or do I have to make your life difficult?"

Layne ground his teeth together, a sneer marring his features, but he gave a sharp nod.

"Muy bueno," Jaime said, pretending it was great news as he released the piece of garbage. "Let's proceed, then." He gestured grandly down the hall to the back door.

Layne grumbled something, but Jaime was relieved to see concern and fear on the man's face. He could only hope it would keep the man in line.

They exited the house and Jaime waited while Layne chained everything up. The late summer sun shimmered in the green of the trees, and if Jaime didn't know what lurked in the shed across the grass, he might have relaxed.

As it was, relaxing wasn't happening any time soon.

Jaime let Layne lead the way to the shed. He preferred to touch as little as possible in that little house of horrors.

Both men stepped in to find The Stallion pacing, hands clutched behind his back, and Wallace looking wary in the far corner.

The Stallion looked up distractedly. "Good. Good. We've gotten news of Herman before Wallace even got anywhere." The man's hands shook as he brought them in front of him in fists, fury stamped across his face.

The usual calm calculation in his eyes something darker and more frenzied. "With the Texas Rangers and a hypnotist." The Stallion slammed a fist to the desk that made the creepy-ass dolls on the shelf above shake, their dead lifeless eyes fluttering at the vibration.

Jaime forced himself to look away and stare flatly at his boss. *Fake boss*, he amended.

"Luckily, Mr. Herman doesn't know enough to give them much of a lead, but he certainly represents a loose end." The Stallion took a deep breath, plucking one of the brunette dolls from the shelf. He cradled it like a child.

It took every ounce of Jaime's control and training to keep the horror off his face. Grown men capable of murder cradling a doll was not…comforting in the least.

"I've sent a team to get rid of Herman. Scare the hypnotist. I don't think I want to extinguish her yet. She might be valuable. But I want her *scared*." He squeezed the doll so tight it was a wonder one of its plastic limbs didn't break off.

"There we are, pretty girl," The Stallion cooed, re-settling the doll on the shelf and brushing a hand over its fake hair.

Jaime shuddered and looked away.

"Until this mess is taken care of, you are all on lock-down. No one is leaving the premises until Herman is taken care of."

"Then, boss?" Layne asked a little too hopefully.

The Stallion smiled pleasantly. "And then we'll decide what to do about the hypnotist."

Lockdown and death threats. Jaime tried to breathe

through the urgency, the failure, the impossibility of saving this man's life.

He'd try. Somehow, he'd try. But he had the sinking suspicion Herman was already gone.

Chapter 5

Gabby couldn't sleep. It wasn't an uncommon affliction. Even in the past two years, exercising herself to exhaustion, giving up on things ever being different, avoiding figuring out the pieces of The Stallion puzzle, insomnia still plagued her.

Because no matter how she tried to accept her lot in life, she'd always known this wasn't *home*.

But what *would* be home? Her father was dead. Her sister would be an adult woman with a life of her own. Would Mom and Grandma still live in the little house on East Avenue or would they have moved?

Did they assume she was dead? Would they have kept all her things or gotten rid of them? The blue teddy bear Daddy had given her on her sixth birthday. The bulletin board of pictures of friends and Ricky and her and Nattie.

Her heart absolutely ached at the thought of her sister. Two years apart, they hadn't always gotten along, but they had been friends. Sisters. They'd shared things, laughed together, cried together, fought together.

Tears pricked Gabby's eyes. She hadn't had this kind of sad nostalgia swamp her in years, because it led nowhere good. She couldn't change her circumstances. She was stuck in this prison and there was no way out.

Except maybe Jaime.

That was not an acceptable thought. She could work with him to take down The Stallion, and she would, but actually thinking she could get out of there was... It was another thing altogether.

She froze completely at the telltale if faint sound of her door opening. And then closing. She closed her hands into fists, ready to fight. She couldn't drown that reaction out of herself, no matter how often she wondered if giving in was simply easier.

"Gabby."

A hushed whisper, but even if she didn't remember people's voices so easily, she would have known it was Jaime—*Rodriguez*—from a man calling her Gabby.

Gabby. She swallowed against all of the fuzzy feelings inside her. Home and Gabby and what did either even mean anymore. She didn't have a home. The Gabby she'd been was dead.

It didn't matter. Taking The Stallion down was the only thing that mattered. She sat up in the dark, watched Jaime's shadow get closer.

The initial fear hadn't totally subsided. She wasn't *afraid* of him per se or, maybe more accurately, she wasn't afraid he would harm her. But that didn't mean there weren't other things to be afraid of.

She had sat up on the bed, but he still loomed over her from his standing position. She banked the edgy nerves fluttering inside her chest.

He kneeled, much like he had earlier today when they'd been putting together her map. Except she was on the bed instead of her makeshift markers.

"Do you have any more ideas about the locations? Aside from directions?" he asked, everything about him sounding grave and...tired.

"I have a few theories. Do we...do we need to go over all that tonight?"

"I'm sorry. You were sleeping."

"Well, no." She had the oddest urge to offer her hand to him. He'd taken her hand earlier today and there had been something... "Is something wrong?"

He laughed, caustic and bitter, and she didn't know this man. He could be lying to her. He could be anyone. Then there was her, cut off from normal human contact for *eight* years. The only place she had to practice any kind of compassion or reading of people was with the other girls, and she'd been keeping her distance lately.

So she was probably way off base to think something was wrong, to feel like he was off somehow.

But he stood, pacing away from the bed, a dark, agitated shadow. "It doesn't get any easier to know someone's going to die. I tried..." He shook his head grimly. "We should focus on what we can do."

"You tried what?" Gabby asked, undeterred.

"I tried to get a message to the Rangers, but..." He

kneeled again and she couldn't see him in the dark, found it odd she wanted to.

"But?"

"I think it was too late."

Gabby inhaled sharply. Whether she knew him or not, whether she'd lost all ability to gauge people's emotions, she could all but *feel* his guilt and regret as though it were her own.

She didn't know what the answer to that was…what he might have endured in pretending to be the kind of man who worked for The Stallion. Gabby couldn't begin to imagine… Though she'd ostensibly worked for the man, she'd never had to pretend she liked it.

"If we're an hour west of El Paso, I would imagine each spot would be likely the same distance from the city in its sector," she said, because the only answer she knew was bringing The Stallion down.

It couldn't bring dead people back, including herself, but it could stop the spread. They had to stop the spread.

She kept going when he said nothing. "He's very methodical. Things are the same. He stays here the same weeks every year. He eats the same things, does the same things. I would imagine whatever other places he has are like this one. Possibly identical."

In the dark she couldn't see what Jaime's face might be reflecting and he was completely and utterly still.

"Jaime…"

"Rodriguez. We have to…we can't be too complacent. There's too much at stake. I am Rodriguez."

"Okay," she returned, and she supposed he was right, no matter how much she preferred to call him something—anything—other than what The Stallion called him.

"But you're right. The eastern compound was around an hour west of Houston. I wonder... He is methodical, you're right about that. I wonder if the mileage would be exactly the same."

"It wouldn't shock me."

"Have you seen the dolls?"

Gabby could only blink in Jaime's shadow's direction. "Dolls?"

"He has a shelf of dolls in his office. They sit in a row. I'd always thought they were creepy, but today..." Jaime laughed again, this one wasn't quite as bitter as the one before, but it certainly wasn't true humor. "You should get some rest. I didn't mean to interrupt you. We can talk in the morning." He got to his feet.

She didn't analyze why she bolted off the bed to follow him. Even if she gave herself the brain time to do it, she wouldn't have come up with an answer.

He was a lifeline. To what, she didn't know. She didn't have a life—not one here, not one to go back to.

"I wasn't sleeping." She scurried between him and the room's only exit. "What about the dolls?"

He was standing awfully close in his attempt to leave, but he neither reached around her for the door nor pushed her out of the way. He simply stood there, an oppressive, looming shadow.

Gabby didn't know what possessed her, why she thought in a million years it was appropriate to reach out and touch a man she'd only met today. But what did it *matter*? She'd been here eight years and worrying about normal or appropriate had left the building a long time ago.

So she placed her palm on his chest, hard and hot even through the cotton of his T-shirt. Such a strange sensation to touch someone in neither fight nor comfort. Just gentle and…a connection.

"Tell me about the dolls," she said in the same tone she used with the girls when she wanted them to listen and stop whining. "Get it off your chest."

His chest. Where Gabby's hand was currently touching him between the vee of straps that kept his weapons at hand. Gently, very nearly *comfortingly*, her hand rested in the center of all that violent potential.

Jaime was not in a world where that had happened for years. His mother had hugged him hard and long that last meal before he'd gone undercover, and that had been it. Two years, three months and twenty-one days ago.

He had known what he was getting himself into and yet he hadn't. There had been no way to anticipate the toll it would take, the length of time and how far he'd gotten.

That meant bringing The Stallion to justice was really the only thing that could matter, not a woman's hand on his chest.

And yet he allowed himself the briefest moment of putting his hand over hers. He allowed himself a second of absorbing the warmth, the proof of beating life and humanity, before he peeled her hand off his chest.

"He cradled the doll like a baby. Talked to it. Damn creepiest thing I've ever seen—and I've seen some things." He said it all flippantly, trying to imbue some humor into the statement, but it felt good to get it out.

The image haunted him. A grown man. A doll. The threat on a man who would most certainly be dead even if Jaime's secret message to his FBI superiors made it through.

Dead. Herman, a man he'd never met and knew next to nothing about, was dead. Because he hadn't been able to stop it.

"Dolls." Gabby seemed to ponder this, and though her hand was no longer on his chest, she still stood between him and the door, far too close for anyone's good.

"If there are identical dolls in every compound, I'll never be able to sleep again after this is all over."

Even in the dark he could see her head cock, could *feel* her gaze on him. "Do you think of after?"

"Sometimes," he offered truthfully, though the truth was the last thing they should be discussing. "Sometimes I have to or I'm afraid I'll forget it isn't real."

"I stopped believing 'after' could be real," she whispered, heavy and weighted in the dark room of a deranged man's hideout.

He wanted to touch her again. Cradle her small but competent hand in his larger one against his chest. He wanted to make her a million promises he couldn't keep about *after*.

"I...I can't think about after, but I can think about ending him. If we're an hour west of El Paso, give or take, and the western compound is an hour west of Houston, then what would the southern compound be? San Antonio?"

"If we're going from the supposition it's the closest

guarded one because it's closest to the border, I think it'd be farther south."

"Yes." She made some movement, though he couldn't make it out in the dark. Likely they could turn on the lights and no one would think anything of it, she had been a gift to him, after all, but he found as long as she didn't turn on the lights, he didn't want to, either.

There was something comforting about the dark. About this woman he didn't know. About the ability to say that a man's life wasn't saved probably because of him. Because who else could he express that remorse to? No one here. No one in his undercover life.

He finally realized she had moved around him. She wasn't exactly pacing, but neither was she still in the pitch-black room.

He couldn't begin to imagine how she'd done it. This darkness. This uncertainty. For eight years she had been at someone else's mercy. As much as he sometimes felt like he was at someone else's mercy, it was voluntary. It was for a higher purpose. If he really wanted to, if he didn't care about bringing The Stallion down, he could walk away from all this.

But she was here and said she couldn't even think about after. Instead she lived and fought and puzzled things together in her head. Remembered things no one would expect her to.

She was the key to this investigation. Because she'd been that strong.

"Laredo, maybe?" she offered.

"It's possible," Jaime returned, reminding himself to focus on the task at hand rather than this woman.

"Doesn't quite match the pattern of being close to bigger cities like Houston and El Paso."

"True, and he does like his patterns." She was quiet for a minute. "But what about the northern compound? There isn't anything up there that matches Houston or El Paso, either. Maybe whatever town in the south it's near matches whatever town is north."

"I haven't been to the northern one, so I don't know for sure, but one would assume Amarillo. Based on what I know."

"Laredo and Amarillo would be similar. Was the place west of Houston similar to this?"

It was something Jaime hadn't given much thought to, but now that she mentioned it... "I never went in the house, but there was one. It didn't look the same from the outside, but it's very possible that the layout inside was exactly the same."

"If you didn't go in the house, where did you go there?"

It confirmed Jaime's suspicion that the girls didn't know anything about the outside world around them. "He has a shed for an office outside."

"It must be in the back. He had us dig holes in the front."

It shouldn't shock him The Stallion used the women he kidnapped for manual labor, and yet the thought of Gabby digging shallow graves for that man settled all wrong in his gut. "Did you ever see...?"

"We just dug the holes and were ushered back inside," she replied, her tone flat. Though she had brought it up yesterday when they'd first met, so clearly it bugged her. "It's the only time I've been out..." She shook her head. "The office shed. Is the one here the same as the one in the west?"

He wanted to tell her she'd make a good cop—focusing on the facts and details over emotions—but that spoke of an after she couldn't bring herself to consider. So he answered her question instead.

"The one he has here is a little bit more involved than the one he had there. And no dolls."

"The doll thing really bothers you, huh?"

"Hey, you watch a grown man cradle and coo at a doll the way a normal person would an infant and tell me you wouldn't be haunted for life."

Though it was dark and Jaime had no idea if his instincts were accurate without seeing her expression, he thought maybe she was teasing him. An attempt at lightening things a little. He appreciated that, even if it was a figment of his imagination.

"As long as I'm on lockdown, I can't share any of this information with my superiors. It would be too dangerous and too risky, and I've already risked enough by trying to warn them about…" He trailed off, that inevitable, heavy guilt choking out the words.

"If the man ends up dead, it has nothing to do with you," Gabby said firmly.

"It's hardly nothing. I knew. And I didn't stop it."

"Because you're here to bring down The Stallion. Doing that is going to save more men than saving one man. Maybe I wouldn't have thought about it that way years ago, but… You begin to learn that you can't save everyone, and that some things happen whether it's *fair* or not. I hate the word *fair*. Nothing is fair."

That was not something he could even begin to argue with a woman who'd been kidnapped eight years ago.

"Do you know who this man was?" she demanded in the inky dark.

"He delivered messages for The Stallion."

"Then I don't feel sorry for him at all."

"You don't?" he asked, surprised at her vehemence for a man she didn't know.

"No. He worked for that man, and I don't care who you are or how convincing he is in his real life, if you work for that man, you deserve whatever you get."

She said it flatly, with certainty, and there was a part of him that wanted to argue with her. Because he knew things like this could make you hard. Rightfully so, even. She deserved her anger and hatred and her uncompromising views.

But he could not adopt them as his own. He was afraid if he did that he would never find his way out of this. That he would become Rodriguez for life and forget who Jaime Alessandro was. It was his biggest fear.

He felt sorry for Gabby, but it made him all the more determined to make sure she got out. He would make sure she had a chance to find her compassion again.

"Until I can get more intel to my superiors, the next step is to keep gathering as much information as we can. The more I can give them when the time comes, the better chance we have of ending this once and for all."

"End." She laughed, an odd sound, neither bitter nor humorous. Just kind of a noise. "I'm not sure I know what that word means anymore."

"I'll teach you." That was a foolish thing to say, and

yet he would. He would find a way to show her what endings meant. And what new beginnings could be about.

Because if he could show her, then he could believe he could show himself.

Chapter 6

Gabby was tired and bleary-eyed the next day. Jaime had stayed in her room for most of the night and they had talked about The Stallion, sure, but as the night had worn on, they'd started to veer toward things they remembered about their former lives.

She'd kept telling herself to stop, not to tell yet another story about Natalie or not to listen to another about the birthday dinners his mother used to make him. And yet remembering her family and the woman she'd been years ago—which had never been tempting to her in all these years—had been more than just tempting in a dark room with Jaime.

She should think of him as nothing but Rodriguez. She shouldn't be forming some odd friendship with a man whose only job was to bring down The Stallion.

Knowing those things seemed to disappear when she was actually in a room with him.

He was fascinating and kind. She missed kindness. In a way she hadn't been able to articulate in the past eight years. The other kidnapped girls were mostly nice. Alyssa was a little hard, but Gabby had spent many a night holding Jasmine or Tabitha as they cried. She had reassured them they wouldn't be hurt and hoped she wasn't lying. She had given them all kindness and compassion, but there was something about being the first—the older member, so to speak—that meant none of the girls offered the same to her.

Gabby was the mother figure. The martyr to them. Everyone thought she was strong and fine and somehow surviving this. But she wasn't. She was broken.

Jaime saw the victim in her, though. It should be awful, demoralizing, and yet it was the most comforted she'd felt in eight years.

But it would weaken her. It *was* weakening her. There was this war in her brain and her heart whether that weakening mattered.

Maybe she should be weak. Maybe she should lean completely on this strange angel of a man and let him take care of everything. If it all worked out in the end and The Stallion was brought down, and she was free—

She wasn't going to go that far. She'd save thinking about freedom for after.

So she sat at the kitchen table with Jasmine, Tabitha and Alyssa eating breakfast and wondering what Jaime would be up to this morning. Would he be as exhausted as she was? Would he be thinking of her?

Foolish girl. But it nearly made her smile—to feel

foolish and stupid. It was somehow a comfort to know she could be something normal. Stupid felt deliciously normal.

At Jasmine's sharply inhaled gasp, Gabby glanced up from her microwaved oatmeal. All the girls were looking wide-eyed at the entrance to the hallway.

Jaime stood there in his dedicated black, weapons strapped against his chest. Those sunglasses on his face. Gabby wondered if there was a purpose to always wearing them. So no one could see the kindness in his eyes. Because even in the dark she had to think that kindness would radiate off a man like him.

Since the girls seemed scared into silence, she nodded toward him. "Rodriguez."

"You know him?" Jasmine squeaked under her breath.

"He's The Stallion's new right-hand man." She looked back at Jaime and tried to work on the sarcastic sneer she sent most of the guards. "Right?"

Jaime's lips quirked and she could almost believe it was in pride, but she saw the disgust lingering underneath it.

Was she the only one who saw that? Based on the way Jasmine scooted closer to her, as though Gabby could protect her from the man, Gabby wondered.

"Senorita."

It took everything in her not to roll her eyes at him and smile at that exaggerated accent.

"You're wanted privately, Gabriella," he said with enough menace she should have been scared. She didn't think the little fissure of nerves that went through her was *fear*.

"But, please, finish your *desayuno*. I am nothing if not gracious with my time."

Gabby began to push her chair back, the crappy packet oatmeal completely forgotten. But Jasmine's fingers curled around her arm and held on tight.

"Don't go, Gabby. Fight."

Gabby looked down at Jasmine, surprised that none of the women seemed to see the lack of threat underneath Jaime's act. But then, they didn't know what she knew. Maybe that made all the difference.

"It's all right. When have I ever not been able to handle myself?" She smiled reassuringly at... Sometimes she thought of the girls as her friends. Sometimes as her charges. And sometimes simply people she didn't really know. She didn't know what she felt today. But she patted Jasmine's arm before peeling the woman's fingers off her wrist. "I'll be back for lunch."

"Don't make promises you can't keep, *senorita*."

She shot Jaime a glare she didn't have to fake. He didn't have to make these women more scared. They already did that themselves.

She walked over to where Jaime stood in the entrance to the hallway. He made a grand gesture with his arm. "After you, Gabriella."

Again she had to fight to mask her face from amusement. He should go into acting once this was all over. The stage where his over-the-top antics might be appreciated.

As she began to walk down the corridor to her room, Jaime's hand clamped on her shoulder. Hot and hard and tight. She didn't have to feign the shiver or the wild worry that shot through her.

It wasn't comfortable that he could turn himself on and off so easily. It wasn't comfortable that, though she was intrigued by the man and convinced of his kindness, she didn't know him at all. Anything he'd told her so far could be lies.

When he acted like this other man, she could remember she shouldn't trust him. She couldn't believe everything he said. He could be as big a liar as The Stallion, and just as dangerous.

But they walked to her room with his hand clamped on her shoulder and somehow in the short walk it became something of a comfort. A calming presence of strength. She missed someone else having strength. True courage. Not the strength The Stallion or his guards exerted. Not that physical, brute force.

No, Jaime was full of certainty. Confidence. He was full of righteous goodness and she wanted to follow that anywhere it would lead.

She wanted to believe in righteous goodness again. That it was possible. That it could save her.

And what will happen after you're saved?

Jaime closed the door behind them, taking off his sunglasses and sliding them into his pocket. Immediately his entire demeanor changed. How did he do it? She opened her mouth to ask him but he seemed suddenly rushed.

"We don't have much time. There's a meeting in ten minutes and Layne will be sent to fetch me. I need… when he comes…"

She cocked her head because he didn't finish his sentence. He studied her and then he swallowed, almost nervously. "I'll have to, uh, do what I did the other day."

"The other day?"

"I'll try not to rip your shirt, but I'm going to need to…er, well, grab you."

"Oh." She let out a shaky breath, the white-hot fear of that moment revisiting her briefly. "Right. Well, okay. But, uh, you know, not ripping my clothes would be preferred, if only because I don't have many."

His lips almost curved, but mostly something heavily weighted his mouth and him. She supposed he could play the part of Rodriguez easily enough in front of whoever walked through, but demonstrating the physical force expected of him? No. She couldn't imagine Jaime ever getting comfortable with that.

Maybe she was wrong. Maybe she was making everything up. Maybe he enjoyed scaring women and she was stupidly coping by turning him into a hero.

If a hero hadn't saved her in the past eight years, why would she think one would now?

"What do you know about his schedule? You said something about him staying certain times in certain places. Is he usually here, at this location, at this time?"

Gabby filtered through her memories. The ways she used to count days. Her many theories about The Stallion's yearly travel.

"Yes. He'd usually be here, but getting ready to leave." She tried to work out the days that would be left, but she'd stopped paying such close attention to the days and—

The thought hit her abruptly—a sharp blow to the chest as she met his intense brown gaze. "You know what day it is." She'd meant that to be a question, not the shaky accusation it had turned into.

He blinked down at her. Something in his face softened and then shuttered blank. "August 23, 2017."

She did the math in her head, trying to get through

the shaky feeling of knowing what day it was. What actual day. For so long she'd known, but in the past two years she'd let it slide to seasons at most.

It was 2017. She'd been here for the entirety of the 2010s.

"Gabby." He touched her shoulder again, not the hard clamp of a guiding hand but a gentle laying of his palm to the slope of her arm. It was weird not to flinch. Weird not to want to. She wanted to lean into the strong presence. To the way he seemed to have everything under control…even when he didn't.

"August twenty-third. I would say usually he leaves for the southern compound on the twenty-sixth. I think. Around there. Never quite at the end of the month, but close."

Jaime smiled down at her, clearly pleased with the information.

When was the last time she'd seen a smile that wasn't sarcastic? When had anyone tried to smile at her reassuringly in eight long years? It hadn't happened.

She quashed the emotional upheaval inside her. Or, at least, she tried. It must've showed on her face, though, because he moved his hand up to her cheek, a rough, calloused warmth against her skin.

She knew he wanted to fix this for her. To promise her safety. But she didn't want to hear it. Promises… No, she wanted nothing to do with those.

Jaime was losing track of time and it wouldn't do. But she looked so sad. So completely overwhelmed by the weight of her existence here. He wanted to do something, anything, to comfort her. To take the tears in her eyes away, to take the despair on her face and stamp it out. He wanted to promise her safety and hope and a new life.

But he could promise none of those things. This was dangerous business, and they could easily end up dead. Both of them.

No matter that he would do everything in his power to not let that happen, it didn't mean it wasn't possible. It would be worse to promise something he couldn't deliver than to fail his mission.

"That means we'll have to wait about three more days. If he has me stay here while he goes to the southern compound, it gives me the opportunity to get this new information to my superiors. If he wants me to go with him, then I'll know where it is. Either way, we win."

"We may win the battle but not the war," she stated simply, resolutely. He wondered if she was just a little too afraid of getting hopes up herself.

He brushed his thumb down her cheek, even though it was the last thing he should've done. But though she was probably more gaunt than she would have been had she been living her actual life, though she was pale when the rich olive of her complexion should be sun-kissed, she was soft. And something special.

Her eyebrows drew together, but she wasn't looking at him. She was looking at the door and she mouthed something to him, but he couldn't catch what it was. She didn't hesitate. She grabbed him by the shoulders and pulled him close, her big brown eyes wide but determined. She mouthed the words again and this time he thought he caught them.

The door. Someone was at the door. Behind the door. That meant there was only one thing he could do. He choked back his complicated emotions and dropped his mouth to her ear.

"I'm going to kiss you. It won't be nice. The minute the door opens, shove me away with everything you've got. Understand?"

Her eyes were still wide, her hands on his shoulders. As if she trusted him.

She gave a nod and all he could do was say a little prayer that this would not be…complicated. But if someone was listening at the door, he had to prove he was Rodriguez and nothing more. That meant not being nice. That meant taking what he wanted whether it was what she wanted. And then, somehow, not getting lost in that. Humanity. His calling card. To keep his humanity.

But first… First he had to be Rodriguez. That meant he could not gently lower his mouth to hers. He had to take. He had to plunder.

And he had to stop talking to himself about it and do it.

He slid his arm around her waist and pulled her to him roughly. It was both regret and something far darker he didn't want to analyze that twined through him. He crushed his mouth to hers if only to stop his brain from moving in this hideous circle.

He focused on the fact that it wasn't supposed to be nice or easy. It was supposed to scare and intimidate. If she trembled, he was only doing his job. He was proving to everyone that he was Rodriguez—awful and mean, a broken excuse for a human being.

He thrust his tongue into her mouth and tried not

to commit her taste to memory. But when was the last time he'd tasted a woman? Sweet and hot. Uncertain, and yet, brave with it. She let his tongue explore her mouth and she did not fight him.

He scraped his teeth along her plump bottom lip and fought to remember who he really was. Not this man, but a man with a badge. A protector. A believer in law and order.

Gabby's fingers tensed on his shoulders and then relaxed. She did something that felt like a sigh against his mouth, and then he was being pushed violently back and away from sweet perfection.

He allowed himself two steps from the shove before stopping. He did everything to ignore the way his body trembled. Ignored the desperate erection pressing against his jeans. Ignored the inappropriate desire running through his blood. It was wrong and it was cruel but surely his body's natural reaction to that sort of thing after such a long absence.

Or so he told himself.

He didn't look at Gabby because it would surely unman him completely. Instead he turned to face the interruption with a sneer on his mouth.

Layne didn't need to know the hatred in his expression was for himself, not the interruption.

"You have the worst timing, *amigo*," he said, trying to eradicate the affectedness from his voice. "I grow weary of it."

Layne snorted. "You knew I was coming to fetch you at one. And here you are, yet again, clothed and being pushed around by a woman. Starting to question your strength, Rodriguez."

"Question all you want. Then test me. I'd love you to."

Layne merely crossed his hands over his chest. "Boss wants us now."

"Sí." Jaime strode to the door, making sure never to look back at Gabby. The only reason Jaime paused in the hallway instead of going straight to The Stallion was to ensure Layne left Gabby's room without saying a damn thing. Because if that man said something to her...

Jaime balled his hands into fists. He had to get his temper under control. He wasn't pissed off at Layne. The man had done exactly what he was supposed to.

Jaime was pissed at himself.

Much like the afternoon before, Jaime let Layne lead him down the hall and outside. When they entered the shed this time, The Stallion's demeanor was calm rather than the unhinged anger of yesterday. He was sitting at his desk all but smiling.

"You're late. I suggest you get that kind of impulse under control. I demand timeliness in all things, gentlemen."

"Sí, senor."

"Now that that's been taken care of, we have our next target."

"The hypnotist?" Wallace asked from the corner.

"Yes, but not just her. A Texas Ranger has taken it upon himself to protect this young woman. I sent two men to follow them and to bring her to me." The Stallion reclined in his chair, his smile widening.

"What about the Ranger?" Jaime asked.

"He's of no use to us. I want her," The Stallion said with a sneer. "I hate when law enforcement try to get in my way. Bunch of useless pigs. We'll get rid of him and take the girl. The girl is *very* important." The Stallion's empty blue eyes zeroed in on Jaime. "There is a message I want you to deliver to our Gabriella, Rodriguez."

Jaime tried to maintain a blank expression, but it was hard with the addition of Gabby into the conversation. That should be a warning in it of itself that he was letting himself get too wrapped up in this whole thing.

"The hypnotist has quite the interesting connection to our oldest guest."

"Connection?" Jaime repeated, hoping he covered the demand with enough confusion in his tone to make The Stallion think it was a language barrier issue.

"Natalie Torres is our hypnotist. Whatever Herman told her and this Ranger, I want to know it. But more, I want the girl." The Stallion turned his computer screen to face Layne and Jaime. "The resemblance. Do you see it?"

Jaime schooled himself into complete indifference. *"Sí."* The woman in the picture was more slight of build than Gabby and she had a softer chin and a sharper nose. But she had the same mass of curly black hair. The same big brown eyes.

"Tell our Gabriella her sister will be joining us soon. Make sure you mention how close she was to being the perfect woman. Perhaps her sister will fit the role she could not." The Stallion leaned back in his chair, smiling a self-satisfied smirk.

Jaime tried to match it, afraid it only looked like a scowl. But if he failed, The Stallion was too happy with himself to notice.

Chapter 7

Gabby knew it was beyond foolish to wait in the dark and hope Jaime would come to her again. She'd answered the questions he'd needed answered and he probably had henchman things to do.

Besides, she didn't really want to see him. Not after that kiss, which was hardly fair to call a kiss since it wasn't real. Like her life. It was a shallow approximation of something else. No matter how his mouth on hers had rioted through her like some sort of miracle.

She was clearly delirious or crazy. Maybe it was some sort of rescue-fantasy type thing that all kidnap victims succumbed to. She didn't know, and it wouldn't matter. Because it had all been fake. It had been a show.

Layne was... Gabby didn't know if "suspicious" was the right word, but he clearly didn't like Jaime and that was going to be dangerous. Because he would be watching him and making sure that whatever moves he made matched up with the man he was supposed to be. Making enemies as an undercover agent had to be incredibly dangerous and Layne was clearly Jaime's enemy.

Maybe she should think up something that could help Jaime in that regard. Surely there had to be something she'd witnessed or put together that would make all of this moot. Something he could tell his superiors that would make sure they felt like they had enough to prosecute.

Maybe if she told him the exact location of the holes she'd had to dig two summers ago, Jaime could find out what was buried there. Maybe that would be enough. Surely a dead body or two would be something.

If they could get through the next two days, and The Stallion left, surely Jaime could do a little figurative and literal digging.

She could make a map, like the one they'd made when trying to figure out the locations of the other compounds. But it would be difficult without paper. It would be difficult without being outside and working through landmarks. Maybe Jaime could sneak her out once The Stallion was gone.

She very nearly laughed at herself. Yes, after eight years she was going to sneak outside and bring The Stallion down with an undercover FBI agent. That was about as plausible as getting kidnapped, she supposed. But then what? She'd go back to her life? Eight years missing and she'd just waltz back into her old life? Twenty-eight with eight years of absolutely no education or work experience. Eight years without a *life*.

Maybe she could add digging shallow graves to her

résumé. *Excellent seamstress. Knows just where to hide the drugs.*

This was such stupidity. Why was she even going down this road? The future had never held any appeal, and it still didn't. Jaime was here to do a job, and she'd do whatever he needed, but she certainly wasn't going to allow fantasies about escaping. About helping him or saving him from his gruesome undercover work.

The door opened and Gabby's heart jumped to her throat. Not as it had the night before. That night, she'd been scared. This night she was anything but.

She scrambled into a sitting position. But instead of staying in the dark, or saying her name, Jaime turned on the light. She blinked against the sudden brightness.

"I apologize," he said, his tone strangely bland, maybe a little tense. "I should've warned you."

"It's all right," she replied carefully, trying to read the blank expression on his face. He was tense and not like she'd ever seen him before. Because this wasn't his Rodriguez acting, and it wasn't exactly the honest and competent Jaime, either.

"Is everything all right?" she asked after he stood there in silence for ticking seconds.

"I want you to know that it will be. But there is some uncomfortable information I have to share with you."

Her heart sank, hard and sharp. She realized who this Jaime was. FBI Agent Jaime. A little aloof, delivering bad news. Probably how he delivered the news to a family that someone was dead.

"Uncomfortable?" she repeated, because surely if another one of her family members was dead it would be more than *uncomfortable*.

"If I could spare you this, I would," he said, taking a step toward her, some of his natural-born compassion leaking through. "But I have to do what The Stallion asks right now."

A shiver of fear took hold of her, with deep awful claws, and she pressed herself into the corner of where her bed met the wall.

But this was Jaime, and he wasn't going to hurt her just because The Stallion told him to. She wanted to believe that. But for a moment she wondered if something in her would have to be sacrificed to take The Stallion down.

"It's just a message, Gabby," he said softly. "I won't hurt you. I promise. No matter what."

Part of her wanted to cry. Over the fact he could see through her so easily. The fact she could feel guilty over making him think that she thought he was going to hurt her. She wanted to cry at the unfairness of it all, and that was just…so seven years ago.

She straightened with a deep breath and fixed him with her most competent I-can-handle-anything expression. "Just tell me. Say it outright."

"The Stallion is after your sister."

Gabby thought she couldn't be surprised at what horrors The Stallion could do. After all, he'd gleefully informed her of her father's heart attack. Made it very clear she had been the cause. She knew The Stallion killed, and extorted, and hurt people.

He was after her sister. Her Nattie. There was no way to be calm in the face of it. She jumped off the bed and reached for Jaime.

"He doesn't have her," he said calmly. So damn calm.

"And she's with a Texas Ranger who will do everything in his power to protect her—that, I know for sure."

"But he's after her. He's after *her*. Purposefully. Why? Why?"

Jaime took her by the shoulders, looking her directly in the eye. She could see all of that compassion and all of the right he wanted to do. No matter how she told herself not to believe in it. No matter how she told herself it was a figment of her imagination and that he couldn't really be good, she felt it. She *believed* it and knew it. No amount of reason seemed to change the fact that she trusted him.

"She has something to do with the dead messenger. I don't know the whole story yet, but I think she knows something. She's a hypnotist working with the Rangers, and if she's with the police... This could be... It could be a positive development. I know it doesn't feel like that, but this could be a positive."

"Is she...is she looking for me?" Gabby asked, ashamed that her voice wavered. But Nattie, a hypnotist, working with the Rangers? It didn't make sense. And Gabby was afraid of whatever the answer would be. If Natalie was looking for her, Nat had wasted eight years of her life. If she wasn't and this was some cosmic coincidence...

Jaime's strong hands squeezed her shoulders. Comforting. Strong. "I don't know. I don't know why your sister was in that interrogation room with The Stallion's messenger. I don't know why..." He shook his head, regret and frustration in the movement. "I wish I knew more, but I don't. But The Stallion wants you to know he's after your sister because he wants to break you."

Maybe if it had been her and The Stallion alone delivering his message, it would have succeeded in breaking her. But something about having Jaime there, something about feeling his strength and his certainty that this could work out…

"He won't break me," Gabby said firmly.

Jaime's mouth curved, one of those kind smiles that tried to comfort her. It made her feel as though…as though there was hope. That was dangerous. Hope was such a dangerous thing here.

"You're an incredibly brave woman," Jaime said, giving her shoulders yet another squeeze.

The compliment warmed her far too much. Much more so than when the girls gave it to her. Then it felt like a weight, a responsibility, but when Jaime said it, it sounded like an *asset*.

"It's not exactly brave to survive a kidnapping. You don't get much of a choice." No, choice was not something she had any of.

"There is always a choice. And the ones you've made have made this possible, Gabby. The things you remember, the theories you've come up with… You're making this all the more possible. I know you don't believe in endings, or maybe you can't see the possibility of them, but I am going to end this. One way or another, we will end him."

We. It was that final straw, a thing she couldn't fight. To be a "we" after so long of feeling like an I. Like the only one who could do something or be something or fight something.

"I believe you," she whispered. *Too much.* She shouldn't feel it, and she shouldn't say it. She should feel none of the things washing through her at the way his face changed over her saying she believed him.

She shouldn't want to kiss this man she'd known for two days. She shouldn't want to feel what it would be like for him to kiss her for real. Without weapons and fake identities between them.

But there was something kind of beautiful about being a kidnap victim in this case. That she had no life to ruin, no self to endanger. Nothing to lose, really. There was only her.

What choices did she have? Jaime thought she had a choice, but he was wrong. She was nothing here. A ghost at best. What she did or didn't do didn't truly matter.

Even now, with The Stallion after Natalie, there was nothing she could do except hope and pray the Texas Ranger with her was a smart man, and a good man, and would protect Natalie the way Jaime was protecting Gabby right now.

Because no matter that he shouldn't, she knew that was the decision he'd made. He would protect her above himself.

Tentatively she touched her fingertips to the vee of his chest between the straps of guns. She could feel underneath her fingertips the heavy beating of his heart. A little fast, as though he had the same kinds of swirling emotions inside him that she had inside her. She glanced up at him through her lashes, trying to read the expression on his face. A face she'd memorized. A face she thought she would always remember now.

There was enough of a height difference that she would have to pull him down to meet her mouth.

It was such an absurd thought, the idea of wrapping her arms around his neck and pulling his lush mouth to hers. She smiled a little at the insanity of her brain. And he smiled back.

"Thank you for that," he said.

She had lost the thread of the conversation and had no idea what he was thanking her for. All she could think about was the fact he was stepping away from her. Letting her shoulders go and making enough distance that her fingers fell from his chest.

"I should let you sleep," he said, backing slowly away and toward the door.

Gabby should leave it at that. She should let him go and she should sleep. But instead she shook her head.

"Please don't go. Stay."

It was wrong. It would be wrong to stay. It would be wrong to let her touch him. It would be wrong to let her belief in him change anything. It didn't matter. All that mattered was doing his duty. His duty included protecting her, not…

"There are things I could tell you," Gabby offered, for the first time in all their minutes together seeming nervous without fear behind it. "More things to help with making sure we can end this."

It didn't escape him the way she halted over the word "end." Like she still didn't quite believe a life outside these walls could exist, but she was trying to believe in one. For him? For herself? He had no idea.

He only knew that everything he should do was tangled up in things he shouldn't. Right and wrong didn't always make sense anymore, and it would take nothing at all for him to lose sight of the fact that anything more than a business partnership with her was a gross dereliction of duty. It was taking advantage of a woman who had already been taken so much advantage of.

But she wanted him to stay. She wanted him to stay. Not the other way around.

"I was just thinking before you got here that if I could tell you where the holes were that we dug two years ago, you might be able to connect it all together. If The Stallion does go in a few days, you'd be able to dig it up or something, and… Maybe that would be… Surely finding a body would be enough. Your superiors would want to press charges at that point, wouldn't they?"

The way she cavalierly talked about digging holes for bodies scraped him raw. It had always been hard to accept that there were people in the world who could hurt other people in such cruel and unusual ways. He'd always had a hard time reconciling the world as he wanted it—with law and order and good people—to the world that was with people who broke those laws and that order and had no good intentions whatsoever.

He didn't know what to do with the kinds of feelings that twisted inside him when he knew that nothing should have ever happened to her. She had been a normal girl, picking her father up from work, and she'd been kidnapped, measured and emotionally tortured into this bizarre world of being hidden away. Not touched, but put to work digging graves and hiding drugs.

"Don't you think?" she repeated, stepping closer to him.

She reached out to touch him and he sidestepped.

He was too afraid if she touched him again, all of the certainty inside him would simply disappear and he would do something he would come to deeply regret. Something that would go against everything he'd been taught and everything he believed.

He was there to protect her, and that meant any deeper connection—physical or otherwise—was not ethical. It was screwing with a victim, and he wouldn't allow himself to fall that low. He had to keep a dispassionate consideration for her own good, not develop a passionate one.

"It's possible that evidence would be sufficient," he finally managed to say, his voice sounding raw. "But even if The Stallion goes to another compound, Layne and Wallace will still be here. Me doing any kind of digging is going to be hard to explain."

"Not if you told them that The Stallion ordered you to do it. He stays away for three months. So you'd have time before they'd tell him, wouldn't you?"

"I don't know how they communicate with him when The Stallion isn't here. I'm sure there'd be a way for them to keep tabs on me, and we both know that's exactly what Layne will be doing whether he's supposed to be or not."

"What about Wallace?" Gabby demanded.

Jaime scratched a hand through his hair. "I don't think Wallace is the brightest, but he's the most loyal. Layne is out to get me. Wallace will do whatever it takes to protect The Stallion. Either way, I don't think I have much hope of getting anything past them. At least, not anything tangible like digging."

Noticing her shoulders slump, he hurried on.

"But that doesn't mean it's not useful information. Maybe we can't use it right this second to shut this whole thing down, but every last shred of evidence we have when we finally get to that point is another nail in The Stallion's coffin. Men like him—powerful, wealthy men with connections... They're not easy to take down. We need it all. So it's still important."

"Right. Well. What else could I tell you that would help?" she asked hopefully.

A million things, probably, but he thought distance might do them both a bit of good. Too close, too alone, too much...bed taking up a portion of the room. "Don't you want to sleep?" Because he wanted to convince himself sleep was why he was thinking about beds.

She looked at him curiously. "I haven't had much to do in eight years except sleep. Day in and day out."

"Right, but..." He struggled to find a rebuttal and failed.

The curious look on her face didn't disappear and he couldn't exactly analyze why he suddenly felt bizarrely nervous. He'd been prepared for a lot of things as an undercover FBI agent, but not what to do with nerves over a woman.

A woman he'd known for all of two days. Who knew his secret now, and was thus her own dangerous weapon, but even in his most suspicious mode, he couldn't believe she'd turn him in. They were each other's best hope.

"Is it hard to switch back and forth?" she asked earnestly.

"Switch back and forth?" He'd been so lost in his own thoughts he was having a hard time following hers.

"Between the real you and this character you have to play?"

"Are you sure they're so different?" He'd tried to say it somewhat sarcastically, or maybe even challengingly, but the minute it came out of his mouth, he knew what he really wanted to hear was that she could tell the difference. That she absolutely knew he was two separate people. Because if she could see it, if this stranger could see it, then maybe it was true. Maybe he really hadn't turned into someone else altogether.

"I've been nothing but Rodriguez for two years. You're the only one who knows any different. I don't know if it's easy. I only know that… This is the first time I've had to do it."

She stepped toward him again and he should side-step again. He knew he should. Everything about Gabby called to him on a deep cellular level, though, and he didn't know how to keep fighting that call. There was only so much fighting a man could do.

She brushed her fingertips across his chest again. "Do you always wear these?"

Jaime looked down at the weapons strapped to his chest. "I try to. Not a lot of trustworthy men around."

Her fingertips traced the leather strap, which was strangely intimate considering the fact he never let anyone touch his weapons. It was a part of the persona he'd created. Slightly paranoid, always armed and always dangerous. No one touched his weapons.

Yet, he was letting her do just that. Touching them in ways she couldn't begin to understand he was touched.

"You could take them off in here." She looked up at him through the long spikes of her eyelashes.

It was tempting enough to lose his breath for a moment. "Wouldn't be smart," he rasped, surprised how visceral the reaction was to the thought of not being strapped to the hilt with guns and ammo. What would that feel like? He'd forgotten.

"Right. Of course not." She offered him a smile, something he supposed was an attempt at comfort, and that, too, was out of the ordinary. Something he didn't remember.

"I have to go."

"Why?"

He should lie. Tell her he had important henchman duties to see to, but the truth came out instead. "I can't stay in my own skin too long. It's too hard to go back otherwise."

Then she did the most incomprehensible thing of all. She rolled up on her tiptoes and brushed her lips across his cheek. His cheek. Soft and sweet. A soothing gesture. She came back down to be flat-footed and gave him a perilous smile.

"Then you should go. Good night, Jaime."

That, he knew, to be a challenge. He should correct her. Tell her that she absolutely had to call him Rodriguez. Lecture her until she wished he'd never come into her room.

Instead he returned her smile and said, "Good night, Gabby," before he left.

Chapter 8

Gabby didn't know the last time she'd felt quite so light. Probably never here. It was probably warped.

Maybe if Jaime had showed up in her first year, it wouldn't be quite so easy to fall into comfort or friendship or even pseudo-flirting. Maybe there would have been enough of the real world and non-ghost Gabby to keep her distance or to keep her head straight.

But she had been here eight years, and all of those things before ceased to exist. All she had was these past eight years, and they had been dark and dreary and horrible. It was nice to have something to feel *light* about.

It didn't mean she wasn't worried about Natalie. It didn't mean she was happy to be kidnapped. It didn't mean a lot of things, but it did give her the opportunity to feel somewhat relaxed. To breathe. To smile as she thought of Jaime's bristled cheek under her mouth.

She made breakfast for the girls, which she did every Sunday. Even after she'd stopped counting the days, she made sure to know what days were Sundays so she could do this for them. Give them something, if not to look forward to, something that felt like this was home and not just prison.

She didn't know if any of them still believed in home. She didn't. This was a prison no matter what, but sometimes it was nice to feel like it wasn't.

"We've been talking," Alyssa announced with no preamble, which was her usual way of broaching a subject. She had only been here for two years and one of the illuminating things about being imprisoned with other people was the realization that victims could be good and bad people themselves.

Alyssa was a bit of a jerk. Had been from the first moment, continued to be these two years later. She was too blunt and always abrasive, never kind to the softer girls. In real life, Gabby thought she might have ended up punching the woman in the nose.

But this wasn't real life.

"What about?" Gabby asked pleasantly, as if she cared.

"Rodriguez and his interest in you."

That certainly caught her off guard, but she feigned interest in her breakfast. "Interest?"

"He's traipsing in and out of your room at all hours."

Gabby slowly turned to face the trio of women in the exact same situation as her. They should be friends and yet all she felt like was an irritable babysitter. "Are you watching me, Alyssa?" Gabby asked, not bothering to soften the threat in her voice.

She wouldn't let anyone figure out what was going

on, mostly because she didn't think the girls could hack it, but also because she didn't trust any of them. Perhaps same circumstances should have made them something like sisters, but when you were struck by senseless tragedy it was damn hard to remember to be empathetic toward anyone else.

"I've been watching *him*," Alyssa said with a sniff. "Are you sleeping with him?"

Gabby blinked. She couldn't tell if it was jealousy or fear or *what* that sparked Alyssa's interest. She only knew she was tired. Tired of navigating a world that didn't make any sense, and yet she barely remembered one that did.

She sighed. "The Stallion has *gifted* me to Rodriguez. I'm supposed to do whatever he wants." She almost smiled thinking about how surprised The Stallion would be to discover what Jaime really wanted.

Alyssa's eyes narrowed at the information but Jasmine gasped in horror and Tabitha looked frightened.

"Why you?" Alyssa demanded.

"I'm sorry, did you want to be offered up as payment for a job well done to any bad guy who walks through?" Gabby snapped.

Alyssa fidgeted, her expression losing a degree of its hostility. "Will it get you out?"

Gabby didn't know what to say. What little pieces of her heart that were left cracked hard for Alyssa thinking there was any possible way of getting out. And then there was the very fact that if anyone was ever going to get them out, it would be Jaime.

But not like Alyssa meant. "No," Gabby replied flatly. "Nothing we do for them gets us anything. We're things to them, at best. Certainly not people."

"What do we do then?" Jasmine asked, her voice wobbly and close to tears.

"We wait for him to die," Tabitha said morosely, lowering herself to a seat.

Jasmine sniffled and sat next to Tabitha, but Alyssa still stood, staring at the girls and then at Gabby. "Maybe we hurry that along."

Gabby's eyebrows winged up. It wasn't that she'd never wondered what it might take to kill The Stallion and escape on her own. It was just… She never thought the other women would have the same thoughts.

But Alyssa's face was grim and impassive, and the other girls were contemplatively silent.

"There's four of them, though," Tabitha offered in a whisper, as though they were plotting and not merely… thinking aloud.

"And four of us," Gabby murmured. A few days ago she would have shut this conversation down. She would have reminded them all that there was no hope and they might as well make the best of their fates.

She would have been wrong. Wrong to squash their hope, and their fight, like she'd been wrong to squash her own.

Jaime had brought it back, had reminded her that life did in fact exist outside these walls. Natalie, on the run. Blue skies. Freedom.

A dangerous kind of hope built in her chest. An aching, desperate need for that freedom she'd tried to forget existed. Even as Jaime had talked of ends and bringing him down, she had tried to fight this feeling away.

But it was all his fault she'd lost the reserves, because he'd appeared out of nowhere and trusted her in his mission. He'd somehow crashed into her world and opened her up *to* life again, not just existence.

"How would we do it?" Tabitha asked, her eyes darting around the kitchen nervously.

Alyssa eyed Gabby still. "Rodriguez wears a lot of guns, and if you are a gift, it means he gets awfully close to you."

"I couldn't steal his gun without him noticing."

Alyssa shrugged easily. "That doesn't mean you couldn't get it and shoot before he had a chance to notice."

The three women looked at her expectantly and she wondered if they hadn't all gone a little crazy. "Or, he stops me and shoots me first."

Alyssa raised a delicate shoulder. "Maybe it'd be worth the risk."

"Then you risk it," Jasmine said, surprising Gabby by doing a little standing up for her. "It was your idea, after all."

This time Alyssa smirked. "But Gabby is the one with access to his *guns.*"

Gabby couldn't think of what to say to that. She had access to a lot of things, but she couldn't and didn't trust Alyssa with the information, and she wasn't sure she could trust Jasmine or Tabitha, either. All it would take was one woman to slip up or break and Jaime could end up dead.

It wasn't safe to let them into this, and it wasn't fair to refuse these women some hope, some power.

Leave it to Alyssa to make an already complicated, somewhat dangerous, situation even more twisted.

Gabby took a deep breath and tried to smile in some appropriate way. Scheming or interested or whatever, not irritated and nervous. Not...guilty. "I'll see what I can do, okay?"

"Don't put yourself in harm's way, Gabby," Jasmine said softly. "What would we do without you?"

Alyssa snorted derisively, but Gabby pretended she didn't notice and smiled reassuringly at Jasmine. "I'll be careful," she promised.

A whole lot of careful.

Jaime stood in the corner of The Stallion's well-lit shed while the man paced and raged at the news Wallace had just delivered.

"How did they get away? How did my men get arrested? I demand answers." He pounded on his desk, the dolls shaking perilously, like little train wrecks Jaime couldn't stop staring at.

"I don't know," Wallace said, shrinking back. "I guess the Ranger tangled 'em up with the local cops."

The Stallion whirled on Wallace. "Who is this Ranger?"

"Er, his name's V-Vaughn Cooper. With the unsolved c-crimes unit. Uh—"

Jaime lost track of whatever The Stallion's sharp demand was at the name. Vaughn Cooper. He *knew* Vaughn Cooper. Ranger Cooper had taught a class Jaime had taken in the police academy.

Christ.

"Rodriguez." It took Jaime a few full seconds to engage, to remember who and where he was. Not a kid in the police academy. Not an FBI agent. Rodriguez.

"*¿Senor?*" he offered, damning himself for his voice coming out rusty.

"No. Not you. Not yet," The Stallion muttered, wild eyes bouncing from Jaime to the other men. "Wallace. Layne. You find them. You track them down. The girl, you bring to me. The Ranger, I don't give a damn about. Do what you will."

Layne grinned a little maniacally at that and Jaime knew he had to do something. He couldn't let Cooper get caught in some sort of ambush. He couldn't let a man who'd reminded them all to, above all else, maintain their humanity, get killed. Especially with Gabby's sister.

"*Senor*, perhaps you could allow me to take care of this problem." He smiled blandly at Layne. "I might be better suited to such a task."

The Stallion gave him a considering once-over. "Perhaps." He paced, looking up at his collection of dolls then running a long finger down the line of one's foot.

Jaime barely fought the grimace.

"No, I want you here, Rodriguez. We have things to discuss."

That wasn't exactly a comfort, though he did remind himself that as long as he was here, Gabby was safe. He wasn't so sure Layne would leave her be if Jaime wasn't around, even with The Stallion's distaste over hurting women.

Jaime assured himself Ranger Cooper knew what he was doing, prayed he knew what he was up against. If the man had outwitted the first two of The Stallion's men, surely he could outwit Wallace and Layne.

"You have three days to bring her to me. The consequences if you fail will be dire. I would get started immediately."

The other two men rushed to do their boss's bidding,

hurrying out of the shed, heads bent together as they strategized.

Jaime remained still, trying to hide any nerves, any concern, with cool disinterest.

The Stallion turned to him, studying him in the eerie silence for far too long.

"I hope you're being careful with our Gabriella," The Stallion said at last.

"Careful?" Jaime forced himself to smile slyly. He spread his arms wide, palms up to the ceiling. "Care was not part of our bargain, *senor*."

The Stallion waved that away. "No, I'm not talking about being gentle. I'm talking about being *careful*. Condoms and whatnot."

Jaime stared blankly at the man. Was he...giving him sort of a sex-ed talk?

"Women carry diseases, you know." The Stallion continued as though this was a normal topic of conversation. "And she's not a virgin, according to her."

"I..." Jaime couldn't get the rest of the words out of his strangled throat. The "according to her" should be some kind of comfort, but why had the man been quizzing her on the state of her virginity? Why did he think Jaime—er, Rodriguez, would care?

"Perfect in every way, save for that," The Stallion said, shaking his head sadly. "Oh, well, then there were her toes."

"Her...toes?"

"The middle one is longer than the big toe. Unnatural." The Stallion shuddered before running his fingers over his dolls' feet again.

Jaime knew he didn't hide his bewilderment very

well, but it was nearly impossible to school away. What on earth went through this man's head? He ran corporations. Jaime doubted very much anyone in Austin knew Victor Callihan was really a madman. Perhaps eccentric, somewhat scarce when it came to social situations, but he was still *known*. Somehow he could hide all this…whatever it was, warped in his head.

"Regardless, if you are to be my right-hand man, and insist upon indulging in these baser instincts inferior men have, I expect you to keep yourself clean."

"I… *Sí*." What the hell else was there to say?

"Good. Now, I held you back because I have some concerns I didn't want to broach in front of Layne and Wallace. I think we've been infiltrated."

There was a cold burst of fear deep within Jaime's gut, but on the outside he merely lifted an eyebrow. "Where?"

"Here," The Stallion said grimly, tapping his desk. "I don't believe that Ranger was smart enough to outwit my men unless he was tipped off. This is why I sent Layne and kept you with me."

"I do not follow."

The Stallion sighed exhaustedly. "You're lucky you're such a good shot, but I suppose I wouldn't want anyone too smart under me. How could I trust them to follow my lead?" He shook his head. "Anyway, if Layne and Wallace fail, I will be assured it's one of them, and they'll be taken care of. If they succeed, then I know my suspicions are wrong and we can carry on."

Jaime inclined his head and breathed a very quiet sigh of relief.

"If they fail, you will be in charge of punishing them

suitably." The Stallion frowned down at his desk. "I don't like to alter my schedule…"

"If there's somewhere you need to be, I can be in charge here. I can mete out whatever punishments necessary, gladly."

The Stallion made a noise in the back of his throat. "This situation is priority number one. I need to do some investigating into this Ranger, and I want to be here for the arrival of Gabriella's sister to do my initial testing. For now, you're free to fill your time with our Gabriella. Get it out of your system before her sister gets here, if you would, please."

Jaime bowed faintly as if in agreement.

"You did give her my message, didn't you?" The Stallion asked, his gaze sharp and assessing.

"Sí."

"And how did she react? Were there tears?"

The Stallion sounded downright ecstatic, so Jaime lied. *"Sí."*

He sighed happily. "I should have done it myself, though I do like you telling her and then doing whatever it is you must do with her. Yes, that's a nice punishment for the little slut."

Jaime bit down on his tongue, hard, a sharp reminder that defending anyone wasn't necessary, no matter how much it felt it was.

"May I go, *senor*?" he asked through clenched teeth.

The Stallion inclined his head. "Do what you can to make her cry again. Yes, I like the idea of proud Gabriella crying every night. And when her sister comes… well, I'll bear witness to that."

All Jaime could think as he left the shed was *like hell he would.*

Chapter 9

Gabby didn't see Jaime all day. She'd expected him—to pop into her room, to come into the kitchen at dinner, something. But she'd eaten with the girls nearly an hour ago and she'd been in her room ever since…waiting.

She shouldn't be edgy, yet she couldn't help herself. The more time she had alone—or worse, with the other girls—the more her mind turned over the possibility of actually killing a man.

Actually escaping.

But she had Jaime for that, didn't she? Alyssa's cold certainty haunted Gabby, though. Should she have thought of this before? Not just as angry outbursts, but as a true, honest-to-God possibility?

Of course, this was the first time in eight years Gabby'd had access to anything that might act as a viable weapon. If she could count Jaime and his guns as accessible.

Where was he? And what was he doing? Had The Stallion sent him on some errand? Was he gone for good?

Her heart stuttered at that thought. Somehow it had never occurred to her that something might happen to him or that he might get sent elsewhere, but Layne and Wallace, and the other three men who sometimes guarded them were forever leaving for intervals of time. Some never to return.

Oh, God, what if he never came back and she'd missed all her chances? What if she was stuck here forever? What if all that hope had been a worthless waste of—

Her door inched open and Jaime stepped inside, sunglasses covering his eyes, weapons strapped to his chest. Strong and capable and *there*.

She very nearly ran to him, to touch him and assure herself he was real and not a figment of her imagination.

The only thing that stopped her was the fact that in three short days she'd come to rely on this man, expect this man, and in just a few minutes she'd reminded herself why she couldn't let that happen.

He could be shipped out. He could be executed. Anything—*anything* could happen to him and if she didn't make a move to protect herself and Jasmine, Alyssa and Tabitha…they'd all be out in the cold.

She tamped down the fear that made her nauseous. Jaime seemed to remind her of the best and worst things. Hope. Freedom. An end to this hell. Then how it could all be taken away.

"I have a bit of good news for you," he said, slipping his glasses off and into his pocket.

Some of the fear coiled inside her released of its own accord. It was so hard to fear when she could see his dark brown eyes search her face as if she held some answer for him. Some comfort.

"Okay," she said carefully, because she wasn't sure she had any for him.

"Your sister and the Texas Ranger she's with escaped The Stallion's first round of men."

"First...round."

"And I know the Texas Ranger she's with. He's a good man. A good police officer."

"But he's sending another round of men," Gabby said dully, because though she'd not spent a lot of time with The Stallion, she knew his habits. She knew what he did and what he saw. When he saw a challenge, he didn't back down.

"Layne and Wallace," Jaime confirmed, crossing to where she sat on her bed. He crouched in front of her and, after a moment, took her hands in his. "I tried to get him to send me, but he thinks Layne is leaking things to the cops."

Gabby jerked her gaze up from where it had been on their joined hands. "He thinks there's a leak," she gasped. That meant Jaime was in danger. That meant once The Stallion figured out it wasn't Layne, he'd figure out it was Jaime and then—

Jaime squeezed her hands. "I don't actually think he thinks that because of anything I've done. He thinks it too convenient that Ranger Cooper and your sister outwitted those men, but he's underestimating the Ranger."

"Maybe he's underestimating my sister."

Jaime smiled, and not even one of those comforting ones. No, this seemed closer to genuine. A real feeling, not one born of this place. It smoothed through her like a warm drink on a cold day, which she barely remembered as a thing, but his smile made her remember.

"Maybe that is it. He certainly underestimates you."

"But you don't." She touched his cheek, brushed her fingertips across his bristled jaw. Five seconds in his company and she'd forgotten all the admonitions she'd just made to herself. But in his presence—calm and strong and comforting—she forgot everything.

Her gaze dropped to the weapons strapped to his chest and she sighed. Well, not everything. Alyssa's words were still there, scrambling around in her brain.

She dropped her fingers from his face to his holster of weapons. She traced her hand over a gun. She didn't know anything about guns. He'd have to somehow teach her to fire one, and it wasn't as if she'd be able to practice anywhere.

But maybe one of the other girls knew how to shoot. If she got one to them…?

She sighed, overwhelmed. This was why she'd given up making a plan. Too many variables. She could analyze a problem, remember a million facts and figures, puzzle together disparate pieces, but when it came to all the unknown fallout of her possible actions…

It made her want to curl up in her bed and cry.

"What's wrong?"

She had to put it all away. Emotion had never gotten her anything in this place. Unless it was anger. Unless it was fight.

"Would they notice?" she forced herself to say strongly and evenly. "If you gave one of these to me, would anyone notice it missing?"

His expression changed into something she didn't recognize. Into something almost like suspicion. "You want one of my guns?" he asked, moving out of his crouch and into a standing position. He folded his arms across his chest and looked down at her, and it was a wonder anyone who really paid attention didn't see the way his demeanor screamed *law enforcement.*

"What do you want to do with it?" he asked carefully, the same way she thought he might interrogate a criminal.

She wasn't sure what she'd expected, but she didn't like *that*. Trust was a two-way street, wasn't it? Didn't he have to trust her for her to trust him?

"What's going on, Gabby?"

She looked away from his dark brown gaze, from the arms-crossed, FBI-agent posture. She looked away from the man she didn't know. Hard and very nearly uncompromising.

She shouldn't tell him about the girls' plan. It felt like a violation of privacy, and yet, if she kept it from him he could just as easily be hurt, or accidentally hurt one of the girls.

It was a no-win situation, which should feel familiar. She'd been living "no win" for eight years.

Then his finger traced her cheek, so feather-light, before he paused under her chin, tilting her head up so she would look at him.

She was tired of hard things and no-win situations and *this*. But Jaime… It was as though he looked at her as neither just another kidnapping victim nor as the strong leader, not as anything but herself.

"What do you know about me, Jaime?" she asked, not even sure where the question came from but knowing she needed an answer. She needed something.

He cocked his head, but he didn't ask her to explain herself. Instead he pulled her up into a standing position, gripping her shoulders and staring down into her eyes. Everything about him intense and strong and just...*him*.

"I know you're brilliant. That you're beyond strong. I know you love your family, and it eats at you that you can't protect Natalie from this. I know you've been hurt, and you're tired. But I also know you'll endure, because there is something inside of you that cannot be killed. No matter what that man does. You're a fighter."

It was a torrent of words. Positive attributes she'd thought about herself, questioned about herself. All said in that brook-no-argument, no-nonsense tone, his gaze never leaving hers. She knew he had to be a good liar to have survived undercover for two years, and yet she couldn't believe this was anything but the truth.

Jaime saw who she was—not what she'd done or how long she'd been here. He saw her. In all the different ways she was.

"The girls want to—" Gabby swallowed. She had to trust him. She did, because he was her only hope, and because he saw her like no one else had in eight years. "They want me to try to get a gun from you, and then go after The Stallion."

Jaime's forehead scrunched. "They can't do that."

"Why not?" she demanded, something like panic

pumping through her. She wanted to be out of there. She wanted a *life*. Even if it wasn't her old life, she wanted…

Him. She wanted him in the real world, and she wanted her.

"I'm here to take him down, Gabby. I'm here to make sure he goes to jail, not just for justice, but so we can put an end to all the evil this man is doing. We can't shoot him in a blaze of glory. That just leaves a power vacuum someone else can take."

"I don't care," she whispered, feeling too close to tears for even her own comfort. But she didn't care in the least. The Stallion was going after her sister and she just wanted him *dead*.

"I understand that. I do. But—"

"My freedom isn't your fight." She sat back down on the bed, slipping through his strong grasp. He could see her. Maybe he even felt some of the things she felt, but her fight was not his fight.

He crouched again, not letting her pull into herself. He took her hands and he waited, silent and patient, until she raised her wary gaze to his.

"It's part of my fight," he said, not just earnestly but vehemently, fervently. "It's a part I don't intend to fail on. I will get you out of here. I will. But I need to do my job, too. It is why I'm here."

A tear slipped out, and then another, and she felt so stupid for crying in front of him, but everything ached in a way she hadn't let it for a very long time.

He brushed one tear off with his thumb then he leaned forward, his mouth so close she inhaled sharply, drowning a little in his dark eyes, wanting to get lost in the warm strength of his body.

"Don't cry," he said on a whisper before he brushed his mouth against another tear, wiping it from her jaw with his mouth.

He pulled his face away from hers, shaking his head. "I shouldn't—"

But she didn't want his shouldn'ts and she didn't want him to pull away, so she tugged him closer and covered his mouth with hers.

He'd dreamed of this. Gabby's mouth under his again. Not because he was trying to be someone else. Not because he was trying to convince *anyone* he was taking what he wanted.

No, he'd dreamed of her mouth touching his because they'd both wanted it, not from anything born of this place. On the outside. Free. Themselves. He'd imagined it, unable to help himself.

Even having dreamed of it, even in the midst of allowing it to happen in the here and now, he knew it was wrong. Not just against everything he'd ever been taught in his law-enforcement training, but against things he believed.

She was a victim. No matter how strong she was. No matter how much he felt for her. She was still a victim of this place. Kissing her, drowning in it, was like taking advantage of her. It was wrong. It flew in the face of who he was as an FBI agent, as a law-enforcement agent.

But he didn't stop. Couldn't. Because while it went against all those things he was, it didn't go against who he was. Deep down, this was all he wanted.

Her tongue traced his mouth and she sighed against

him. Melting, leaning. Crawling under all the defenses he wound around himself. False identities. Badges and pledges. Weapons and uniforms and lies.

He should pull away. He should stop this madness.

He curled his fingers into her soft hair. He angled her head so that he could taste her better. He ignored every last voice in his head telling him to stop. Because she was touching him. Tracing the line of his shoulders. Pressing her hand to his heart. She scooted closer, brushing her chest against his.

She whispered his name against his mouth. His real name. And he wanted to be able to be that. He wanted to be able to be the man who could give her everything she wanted and everything she deserved.

But he wasn't that man. Not here. Not now. He couldn't even let her have fantasies of ending The Stallion's life.

He mustered all of his strength and all of his righteous rightness. Somehow...*somehow* he did the thing he least wanted to do and pulled away from her.

Her breath was coming in heavy pants, as was his. Her dark eyes were unfathomably warm, her lips wet from his mouth. He wanted to sink himself there again and again until they thought of nothing but each other.

"Jaime," she said on a whisper.

"We can't do this. I can't..." He tried to pull away but her arms were strong around him.

"Do you know how long it's been since someone's kissed me? Since I *wanted* someone to kiss me?"

"Gabby," he returned, pained. Desperate—for her and a way this could be right.

"I know it isn't the time or the place. I know it isn't prudent or whatever, but I have lived here for eight years

without anything I wanted. I survived here without anyone touching me kindly, comfortingly or wanting to.
Without anyone seeing me as anything other than a
thing. If I'm going to believe in an *end*, I have to believe
I can go back to being something real, not just this...
ghost of a person."

"Getting involved with the victim is not an acceptable—"

She pulled away from him quickly and with absolutely no hesitation. She turned her head away, shaking
it. He'd stepped in it, badly.

"I know you don't want to see yourself as a victim,"
he began, trying to resist the impulse to reach for her.
"But in my line of work—"

"I understand."

But she didn't understand. She was angry and she
didn't understand at all. "I do know how you feel," he
offered softly.

She rolled her eyes.

"It hasn't been eight years, but two years is a long
time to go without anyone seeing you for who you are.
There aren't a lot of hugs and nice words for the bad
guy, Gabby. Even the *other* bad guys don't like me because I've been slowly taking them down so that I could
be the one next to The Stallion. It isn't all fun and games
over here."

"Are you asking me to feel sorry for you?" she asked
incredulously.

"Of course not." He raked a hand through his hair,
trying to figure out what he *was* trying to ask of her.
"I'm saying that I understand. I'm saying that I would
love to give you what you want. I would..."

"I'm just a victim. And you can't get involved with the victim. I get it."

"You don't, because if you thought it was that simple… I have never in my entire career even considered kissing someone who was involved with a case I was part of. I have never once been unable to stop thinking about a woman who had anything to do with *work*. I have never been remotely—*remotely*—tempted to go against everything I believe. Until you."

That seemed to dilute at least some of her anger. She still didn't look at him, which was maybe for the best. He wasn't sure if she looked at him that he'd be able to stay noble.

Because her soft lips tempted him. And the defiant look in her eyes… Everything about her was very near impossible to resist.

He hadn't been lying that he'd never wanted someone the way he wanted her. Even if he took the police part out of it. No woman, no matter how short or long a period of time they had been in his life, had made him feel the way Gabby made him feel.

He wondered if that wasn't why she was upset. Not that he'd stopped the kiss, but that she thought he didn't see her the way he did.

She'd asked what he knew about her, and he'd been completely honest and open about all the things he *knew* she was. Maybe he shouldn't have been, but she was everything he'd said, and he knew being attracted to her, caring about her, wasn't as simple as whatever label a therapist would likely put on it.

It was Gabby, not the situation, that called to him.

But the situation was what made everything far too complicated.

"I can't give you a weapon," he offered into her stubborn silence.

"All right," she said, and she didn't sound angry. She sounded tired. Very close to giving up. But then she straightened her shoulders and inhaled and exhaled slowly. Then she met his gaze, fierce and strong.

"I have to have a story for the girls... I have to... They want out, Jaime." Something in her face changed, a kind of empathetic pain. "I used to be able to tell them it wasn't any use to think about getting out, but we can't keep doing this. Alyssa is right. Staying here isn't worth being alive for."

"So what kept you alive for so long?" he asked because he couldn't imagine. He couldn't *fathom*.

"My family, I guess. Daddy died because of his guilt over me. The least I could do was still be alive. The least I could do was get back somehow." She looked down at her hands, clenched in her lap. "I thought I'd given up that hope, but I don't know. Maybe I just convinced myself I had."

He covered her clenched fists with his own. "I'm going to get you back to your family." God, he'd do it. Come hell or high water. If he had to *die* first, he would do it.

"Not so long ago you said you couldn't promise me that."

"Not so long ago I was doing everything by the book." He believed in the book, but he also...he also believed in this woman. "You're right. Things can't stand. It's been too long. We can't keep waiting around. We have to make something happen."

She finally looked at him, eyebrows raised. "Really?"

"As soon as we get word that your sister has escaped Layne and Wallace, we'll…" It was against everything he'd been taught, everything he was supposed to do, but he couldn't keep telling Gabby to wait when he could be getting her out.

"Once we know your sister is safe, we'll figure out an escape plan. You can't tell the others who I am but… Maybe you can tell them I'm sympathetic, if you trust them to keep that to themselves. Tell them that if you work on me for a few days, you might actually be able to get a weapon from me. If anything slips up to The Stallion or anyone else, I'll tell him it's part of my plan. If you get the girls to stand down a few days. I don't want to risk getting out and something happening to your sister."

"Why?" she asked, still studying him, her forehead creased.

"Because you love her."

Something in her face changed and he couldn't read it. But she moved. Closer to him. No matter that he should absolutely avoid it, he let her kiss him again.

Slow and leisurely, as if they had all the time in the world. As if it was just the two of them. Gabby and Jaime. As if that were possible.

And because the thought was so tempting, so comforting in this world of dark, horrible things, he let it linger far too long.

Chapter 10

Gabby had kissed four men in her life. Ricky, of course. Corey Gentry on a dare in eighth grade. A guy at a frat party—she didn't know his name—and now Jaime.

In the past eight years she would've considered this part of her dead. The part that could care about kissing and touching. The part of her brain that could go from that to sex.

It was a miracle and a joy to still have the same kind of desire she'd had before. It was a miracle and a joy to be kissing Jaime, his lips so soft, his touch nearly reverent. As though she were something of a miracle to him.

Ricky had never kissed her like this and she'd been convinced she loved him. But he'd been a boy and she'd been a girl. They'd been selfish and Jaime... Jaime was anything but selfish. A good man. A strong and honorable man.

That somehow made the kiss more exciting, knowing he thought it was wrong but couldn't quite help himself. Knowing he felt the same simmering feelings and that he didn't think it was because of their situation. It was because of who they were.

Gabby. Jaime.

She thought she hadn't known who she was anymore, but she was learning. Jaime was showing her pieces of herself she'd forgotten. He was bending his strict moral code for her and that, above all else, spoke to a feeling most people wouldn't believe could happen in three days. She herself wasn't sure she'd believed something like this could grow in three days.

But here she was feeling things for a man that she'd never felt before. She wanted to be able to make sacrifices for him, and she wanted him safe, and she wanted him *hers*.

He pulled away slightly and it was another wondrous thing that every time he pulled away she could *feel* how hard it was for him to do so.

"I have a meeting with The Stallion," he said, his voice very nearly hoarse. "I can't be late again or things could get ugly." He tried to smile, probably to make it sound less intimidating, but it didn't work.

She clutched him harder. "Come back," she blurted. She said it spontaneously, but she still meant it. She wanted him to come back. She wanted more than a kiss.

"So we can..." He cleared his throat. "Plan, right?"

She smiled at him because it was cute he would even think that. "We can plan, too." She watched him swallow as though he were nervous. She didn't mind that the least little bit.

"Gabby."

"Come back tonight. Spend the night with me."

It was a wonderful thing to know he wanted to. That though he was resisting, something deep inside him wanted to or he wouldn't question it at all. It was so against his inner sense of right and wrong, but he wouldn't fight with that if he didn't truly want her.

"It wouldn't be right. To... It would be taking advantage," he said, as though trying to convince himself.

"You're worried about me taking advantage of you?" she asked as innocently as she could manage.

He laughed, low and rumbly. It struck her that this was the first time she'd heard it, possibly one of the very few times she'd heard nice laughter in *years*.

"Gabby, you've been through hell for eight years."

As if she needed the reminder. "I guess that's all the more reason to know exactly what I want," she said resolutely. She knew what she wanted and if she could have it... If she could have him... She'd do it now. She wouldn't waste time. "I want you, Jaime."

He inhaled sharply, but he didn't say anything. "I have to go," he said, getting to his feet.

She gave him a nod, but she thought he'd be back. She really thought he'd return to her. Because he felt it, too. He had to feel it, too. No matter how warped she sometimes felt, this was the most real she'd felt in eight years. The most honest and the most true. The most certain she could survive getting out of this hell. That she wanted to.

That settled inside her like some weird evangelical itch. She wanted to be able to give that same feeling to the other girls. They deserved something, too. Something to believe in. They hadn't spent as much time as her, no, but they had spent enough. They had all spent enough.

Jaime was willing to break the rules and get them there, as soon as Natalie was safe. Not because that helped him any, but because she loved her sister and he knew that meant something to her.

Gabby left her room. She didn't know where exactly Jaime had gone, but she wasn't after him quite now. First, she wanted to find Alyssa. She wanted everyone to know that she was on board, maybe not in the way they thought, but regardless. They were going to find a way out of this.

She walked into the common room, which was basically their workroom opposite the kitchen and dining area.

Tabitha and Jasmine were sitting on the dilapidated couch working on a project The Stallion had assigned them a few days ago. Gabby realized she'd forgotten all about the project and what her role in it was supposed to have been. But ever since Jaime had arrived, it hadn't even occurred to her. Then again, she supposed to The Stallion her job now was to be payment to Jaime. Though she was surprised the girls hadn't asked her for help.

Jasmine looked at her first, eyes wide. She looked from Alyssa, who was riffling through drawers frantically in the kitchen, back to Gabby.

"Did you...?" she whispered then trailed off.

Gabby nodded. "I didn't get a gun or anything, but I think I can. If you give me some time." There was hope. She needed to give them hope.

Alyssa slammed a cabinet door closed and stormed over to them. "What does that mean?" she demanded.

"It means I couldn't quite sneak a weapon off of him, but he seemed a little…sympathetic almost. Like if I keep feeding him our sob story he might…"

"What you really need to do is willingly sleep with him, not fight him off," Alyssa said flatly, giving her a once-over. "When he thinks you're not fighting him, it'll give you time to grab his gun and shoot him."

Gabby couldn't hide a shudder. Maybe if they'd been talking about any of the other men, she wouldn't have felt an icy horror over Alyssa's words. But this was Jaime. Still, she couldn't let even the other girls think he'd gotten to her.

She forced herself to look at Alyssa evenly. "And then what?"

"What do you mean and then what?" Alyssa demanded.

"There are at least three other men here almost at all times. What do you suggest I do after I shoot him? I'm pretty sure gunshots can be heard somewhere else in this little compound, then one of them is going to come running to shoot me. They've got a little more experience with guns and killing people than I do."

Alyssa pressed her lips together, neither mollified nor understanding.

"You just have to give me some time," Gabby said, trying for calm and in charge. "If not to convince him to give me a weapon, then at least time to find a way to sneak one off him without him noticing right away. We do this without a plan, without thinking everything through, then we're all dead. You can't just…"

Alyssa's face was even more mutinous, turning red almost. Gabby tried for conciliatory, though it grated at her a bit. "I know we all want out." She looked at Tabitha and Jasmine, who were watching everything play out from where they sewed on the couch. "And I know once you start thinking about all of the things you could do once you got out of here that it builds inside you and everything feels... Too much. You start to panic. But if we are going to survive getting out of here, we have to be smart. Okay?"

"Does it matter if we survive?" Alyssa asked, all but snarling at Gabby.

Jasmine gasped and Tabitha straightened.

"Of course it matters," Tabitha shouted from the couch. She took in a deep, tremulous breath, calming herself as Jasmine patted her arm. "I'd rather be alive and here for the next *ten* years than die and never get a chance to see my family again." Her voice wavered but she kept going. "We have to have patience, and we have to do this smart. This is the first time any of us has access to a weapon, and we can't waste the chance. It won't happen again. At least, not for a very long time."

Alyssa scoffed, but she didn't pose any more arguments. "I'm going crazy in this place," she muttered, hugging herself.

"Why don't you help us work?" Jasmine offered. "I know it isn't any fun, but it'll at least keep your mind busy."

"You two can be his slave. I have no interest."

Tabitha and Jasmine exchanged an eye-roll and Alyssa stomped back to the kitchen. She riffled through the drawers again, inspecting butter knives and forks.

Gabby hoped Natalie and her Ranger escaped The Stallion's men once and for all, and quickly. Not just for her own sake, and for Jaime's, but because she wasn't certain Alyssa would last much longer.

If she didn't last, if she kept being something of a loose cannon, then they were all in danger. Including Jaime.

Jaime didn't go to Gabby that night. He knew it was cowardly to avoid her. He also knew it was for the best. For both of them. He wouldn't be able to resist what she offered, and it wasn't fair to take it. So he kept himself away, falling into a fitful sleep that was never quite restful.

The next day he busied himself outside. He fed The Stallion a story about wanting to come up with some new security tactics, but what he was really trying to do was to see if he could find any evidence of a shallow grave.

The Stallion was so obsessed with Layne and Wallace's progress in finding Ranger Cooper and Gabby's sister, Jaime felt pretty confident he could get away with a lot of things today.

Including going to see Gabby for only personal reasons.

He shook the thought away as he toed some dirt in the front yard. Unfortunately the entire area, especially in the front, was nothing but hardscrabble existence. Scrub brush and tall, thick weeds. It was impossible to tell if things had been dug, if things had grown over, if empty patches of land were a sign of a grave or just bad soil.

Being irritated with himself over his inability to find a lead didn't stop him from continuing to do it.

Until he heard the scream. A howling, broken sound. Keening almost. Coming from inside. From a woman.

"Gabby," he said aloud.

He forgot what he'd been doing and ran full-speed to the front door. He struggled with the chains on the doors and cursed them. It took him precious minutes to realize the door wasn't just locked and chained, it had been sealed shut with something. There was no possible way of getting to her through this door. He swore even louder and rushed around to the back.

Was The Stallion inside or in his shed? Was he hurting them? Jaime grabbed one of the guns from his chest. If he was hurting Gabby—if he was hurting any of them—this was over. Jaime wasn't going to let that happen. Not for anything. Not for any damn evidence to be used in a useless trial.

He'd just kill him and be done with it.

Nearly sweating, Jaime finally got all the locks and chains undone. He hadn't heard another scream and didn't know if that was a good or bad sign. He ran down the hall, looking in every open door. Gabby wasn't in her room and it prompted him to run faster.

He reached the main room and skidded to a halt at the sight before him. Gabby was standing there in the center of the room looking furious, blood dripping down her nose.

"What the hell happened?" he demanded, searching the room and only seeing the other women.

Gabby's gaze snapped to his and she widened her eyes briefly, as if to remind him he had an identity to maintain. It wasn't Demanding FBI Agent. *Or concerned... whatever you are.*

Either way, he'd forgotten. He'd let fear make him reckless. He'd let worry slip his mask. He very well could have ruined everything if not for that little flick of a gaze from Gabby.

He took a breath, calming the erratic beating of his heart. He moved his gaze from Gabby's bloody face, fighting every urge to grab her and pat her down himself to make sure she wasn't hurt anywhere else.

"Well, *senoritas*?" he demanded, rolling his R's in as exaggerated a manner as he could manage in his current state. He glared at the other three women. The two blondes were holding the brunette down on the couch.

The brunette was breathing heavily, her nostrils flaring as she glared at Gabby. Slowly, she took her gaze off Gabby and let it rest on him.

She sneered and then spat. Right on one of the girls holding her. The slighter blonde shrieked and jumped back, which gave the brunette time to throw off the other woman and jump to her feet.

It wasn't wasted on him that Gabby immediately went into a fighter stance.

"First shot was free, but you hit me again, I will beat you," she said, angry and menacing as the brunette stepped toward her.

Jaime stepped between them. "I will say this only once more. What is going on?" He realized he was still holding his gun and gestured it at the angry brunette threateningly.

The girl who'd been spit on squeaked and cowered

while the girl who'd been flung off the brunette turned an even paler shade of white.

"Let's have story time, Alyssa. Tell our captor here what you're after," Gabby goaded.

"I'm going to get out of here," Alyssa yelled, whirling from Jaime to the blondes. "I don't care if I kill all of you." She pointed around him at Gabby. "I am going to get the hell out of here."

Jaime didn't want to feel sorry for the girl considering she was clearly at fault for Gabby's bloody nose, but he looked at Gabby and watched her shoulders slump and the fury in her eyes dim.

Damn it. He couldn't blame the woman for losing her mind here. Not in the least. But it was the last thing they needed if they were actually going to put something in motion that might get them out.

"You would be dead before you killed anyone, *senorita*. Calm yourself."

She bared her teeth at him. "I can't do this anymore. I can't do this anymore. Shoot me." She lunged toward him. "God, put me out of my misery."

"Hush," he ordered flatly, tamping down every possible empathetic feeling rising up inside him. "I'm not going to kill you. And you are not going to kill anyone. You're going to calm yourself."

"Or what? What happens if I don't?" She got close enough to shove him, even reached out to do it, but Gabby was stepping between them.

Jaime was certain the woman would throw another punch at Gabby and he would have to intervene, but Gabby did the most incomprehensible thing. She pulled the woman into a hug.

And the woman began to sob.

The others started, too. All four of them crying, Gabby with her nose still bleeding.

Jaime had to clench his free hand into a fist and pray for some kind of composure. It was too much, these poor women, taken from their lives and expected to somehow endure it.

"What is all this?" The Stallion demanded and Jaime was such a fool he actually jumped. Where had all his instincts gone? All his self-preservation? He'd lost it, all because Gabby had gotten under his skin.

Jaime steeled himself and turned to face The Stallion.

"Your charges were getting out of hand. I had to do some knocking around," Jaime offered, nodding at Gabby's nose. If any of the girls wanted to refute his story, it would possibly end his life.

But none of them did.

"She is mine, no?" Jaime continued, hoping the fact Gabby was a gift meant he'd forgive him for the supposed violence that had shed blood.

The Stallion was staring oddly at Gabby, and it took everything in Jaime's power not to step between them. In an obvious way. Instead he simply angled his body and hoped like hell it wasn't obvious how much he wanted to protect her.

"Crying," The Stallion said in a kind of wondering tone. "Well, I am impressed, Rodriguez. No one has ever gotten her to cry."

Gabby flipped him the finger and Jaime nearly broke. Nearly ended it all right there.

"I trust our friend has told you that your sister will

be joining us soon," The Stallion said, watching her far too carefully no matter how Jaime tried to angle himself into the picture.

"And yet she isn't here yet. Why is that?" Gabby returned in an equally conversational tone.

Jaime might have fallen in love with her right there.

The Stallion, however, snarled. "You're lucky I don't want to touch your disease-ridden body. But I have found someone who will. Take her away from me, Rodriguez. I don't want to see that face until her sister is here. Make sure to lock her room once you're done with her. She's done with outside privileges."

"And these?" Jaime managed to ask.

The Stallion snapped his fingers. "To your rooms. Don't make me turn you into gifts, as well."

The girls, even the instigator, scattered quickly.

The Stallion squinted at Gabby and maybe it was her unwillingness to cower or to jump that made her a target.

If Gabby cared about that, she didn't show it. So Jaime took Gabby by the arms, as gently as he could while still appearing to be rough to The Stallion. "I will take good care of her, *senor*," he said, donning his best evil smile.

"I'm glad you're willing to soil yourself with this," The Stallion said. "I should have had someone do this long ago. I don't care what you have to do to make her cry. Just do it."

Jaime gave a nod since he didn't trust his voice. He nudged Gabby toward the hallway and she fought him on it, still staring at The Stallion.

"You're a disgusting excuse for a human being. You aren't a human being. You're a monster." And then, apparently taking a page out of Alyssa's book, she spit at him.

The Stallion scrambled away and then furiously scowled at Jaime.

"Are you going to let her get away with that?" he demanded, fury all but pumping out of him.

Oh, damn, Gabby and her mouth. How the hell was he going to get out of this one?

Chapter 11

Gabby had gone too far. She realized it a few seconds too late. She'd wanted to make sure The Stallion didn't think she was happy to go with Jaime. She wanted The Stallion to think she hated Jaime as much as she hated him, and she didn't know how to show it considering she didn't hate Jaime even a little bit.

But she'd put Jaime in an impossible position. The Stallion expected Jaime to hurt her now. In front of him.

And how could he not?

Jaime's jaw tightened and Gabby knew it wasn't because he was getting ready to hurt her. It was because he didn't want to and he was having a hard time figuring out how to avoid it. But he didn't need to protect her.

She lifted her chin, hoping he would understand. "Hit me with your best shot, buddy," she offered.

Much like when he'd come into the room, guns blazing, not using his accent at all, she gave him a little open-eyed glance that she hoped would clue him in.

He had to hit her. There was no choice. She understood that. She wouldn't hold that against him. Besides, he'd pull the punch. It'd be fine.

He raised his hand and she had to close her eyes. She didn't want the image in her head even if she knew he had to do it. She braced herself for the blow, but it never came.

Instead his fingers curled in her hair, a tight fist. Not comfortable, but still not painful, either.

"It appears you need to be taught some respect, *senorita*. Let's go to your room where I can give you a thorough lesson. I teach best one-on-one."

Gabby opened her eyes, ignoring the shaking in her body. She didn't dare look at The Stallion—she didn't want to know if he'd bought that ridiculous tactic or not. She couldn't look at Jaime, because she didn't want anything to give him or her away.

So she sucked in a breath as though Jaime's fingers in her hair hurt and stared at the floor as if he was forcing her. She stumbled a little as he nudged her forward, trying to make it appear as if he'd pushed her. She put everything into the performance of making it look like he was being rough with her when he was being anything but.

"I will come to give you a full report when I'm done, *senor*."

"Excellent." The Stallion sounded pleased with himself. Satisfied.

Jaime continued to nudge her all the way to her room, and she let out a little squeak of faked pain. When Jaime finally gave her a light push into her room, she could only sag with relief.

Jaime closed the door and flicked the lock. Before she had a moment to breathe, to say a thing, she was being bundled into his arms and gently cradled against his hard chest and the weapons there.

She relaxed into him, letting him hold her up. She was shaking more now, oddly, but it was such an amazing thing to be cradled and comforted after everything that had just happened, she couldn't even wonder over it.

"We need to get you cleaned up," Jaime said, his voice low and sounding pained.

She waved him away, wanting to stay right there, cradled against him. "Leave it. Maybe it'll convince him you were suitably rough with me if we let it bleed more."

"He's not going to see you again," Jaime said fiercely, his arms tightening around her briefly. "You're under lock and key now, and if he tries to come in here, I will kill him myself."

She looked up at him curiously. He was… He'd avoided her for days, and Gabby couldn't blame him because she knew he was trying to do something noble. Still, she didn't quite understand his anger.

Frustration or fear, maybe even annoyance, she might have understood, but the beating fury in his eyes, completely opposite to the gentle way he held her, was something she couldn't unwind.

"What was the other woman's problem?" he asked, studying her nose.

"She hit the two-year mark," Gabby stated with a tired sigh.

"What does that mean?"

Gabby sighed. "Oh, I don't know. It just seems that around two years in here you start to realize how stuck you are. How no one's going to come and save you. I think we all have a little bit of a meltdown at two years."

"Did your two-year meltdown include punching another woman in the face?"

"No. I was alone. I did try to use a butter knife to stab a guard," she offered almost cheerfully.

His mouth almost…almost quirked at that.

"I was desperate," she continued. "With that desperation comes a kind of insanity. Alyssa's hitting that same wall. Losing it. Wondering what it's worth being stuck in this horrible place. Of course, she has the worst possible timing, but what can we do? We just have to try and end it as soon as we can."

"You hugged her." Jaime's voice was soft, awe-filled.

Gabby turned away from him and his comforting, strong arms, uncomfortable with the way he said it as though she'd done something special. But she hadn't. Not really.

"You forget sometimes, when you're in here, that a simple hug can be reassuring. She needed someone to be kind. You…you reminded me of that. Humanity. Compassion. So, I did what you've done to me."

"You did it after she punched you in the nose," he pointed out.

"I let her punch me. I thought it would help her get some of the rage out of her system. I'm hoping getting some of it out will stop her from just…losing it completely."

"You are a marvel," he said, like she was some kind

of genius superhero. It shouldn't have warmed her. She should tell him she wasn't.

But she wanted to believe there was something marvelous about her.

"I'm washing you up," he said, taking her arm and pulling her into the little nook that acted as a bathroom. There was a toilet and a sink, but no door, no privacy. Still, Jaime grabbed a washcloth from the little pile she kept neatly stacked in the corner.

He flicked on the tap and soaked the cloth in warm water. He squeezed it out before holding it up to her face gently. Ever so gently, he wiped away the blood that had started dribbling out of her nose after Alyssa had hit her.

"You're lucky she didn't break it," he muttered.

Gabby rolled her eyes. "I *let* her hit me, and I pulled back a bit. I'm a lot stronger than all that bluster."

He cupped her face with his hands, long fingers brushing at her hairline. "That you are," he said with a kind of fervency that had a lump burning in her throat.

"You've been avoiding me," she rasped.

"Yeah," he said. "I'm trying to do the right thing."

"What about instead of doing the right thing, you do what I want? How about you give me something I want?"

He sighed and shook his head. "I don't know how I ever thought I'd resist you." Then his mouth was on hers.

Potent and hot. Not quite so gentle. Gabby reveled in the fact that he could be both. That he could give her everything and anything she wanted.

"Tell me if I hurt your nose," he murmured against her mouth, never breaking contact. His hands trailing through her hair, his body pressed hard and tight against hers.

She could barely feel the ache in her nose. Not with Jaime's tongue sliding against hers. Not with the smell of him and leather and what might be outside if she even remembered what outside smelled like.

She realized whatever this was, it was frantic and needy. It was also something that could be temporary all too easily. The chances she'd have to touch him, to be with him…

She needed to grasp and enjoy and lose herself in this moment, in the having of it. She molded her hands against his strong shoulders, slid them down his biceps and his forearms. Everything about him was honed muscle, so strong. He could've been brutal with someone else's heart, but Jaime was anything but that.

His hands smoothed down her neck and, for the first time, he dared to touch more than just her face or her shoulders. The fingers of one hand traced across her collarbone over her T-shirt. His other hand slid down her back, strong as he held her against him.

She could feel him, hot and hard against her stomach. It had been a long time since she'd done this, and it was possibly the most inappropriate moment, but there wasn't time to think.

She didn't want to think. She wanted to sink into good feelings and let *those* take over for once.

She arched against him and the fingertips tracing her collarbone stilled. Then lowered. He palmed one of her breasts and she moaned against his mouth.

"We can stop whenever," he said, so serious and noble and *wrong*.

"I don't ever want to stop." She wanted to live in a moment where she had some power. Where she had some hope. "Take off your guns, Jaime."

He stilled briefly and then reached up to the shoulder of the harness and unbuckled it. He pulled the strand of weapons off his body, his eyes never leaving hers. He hesitated only a moment before he laid the weapons down next to her bed.

He took a gun from his waistband she hadn't known was there and placed it on the little table next to her bed. Something almost resembling a smile graced his mouth as he reached to his boots and pulled a knife out of each.

There was something not just weighty about watching him disarm, but something intimate. She watched him strip himself of all the things he used to protect himself. All the things he used to portray another man. To do his job, his duty.

"I think that's all of them," he said in a husky voice.

She didn't have any weapons to surrender, so she grabbed the hem of her shirt and pulled it off. She moved her hands to unbutton her pants, but Jaime made a sound.

"Stop," he ordered.

She raised a questioning eyebrow at him.

He crossed back to her, a hand splaying against her stomach, the other sliding down her arm. "Let me."

She swallowed the nerves fluttering to the surface. No, nerves wasn't the right word. It was something more fundamental than that. Would he like what he saw? Would he still be as enamored with her when they were naked? When it was over?

She wanted to laugh at her momentary worry about such things. But, like so many other thoughts, it was a comforting reaction—a real-life response. That she could still be a woman. That she could still care about such things.

His hands were rough against her skin. Tanned against how pale she was with no access to sunlight. She watched as he traced the strangest parts of her, as if fascinated by her belly button or the curve of her waist. But he was still fully clothed, though he'd surrendered all his weapons.

She gave the hem of his shirt a little tug. "Take this off," she ordered, because it was nice to order. More than nice to have someone obey. Power. Equality, really. He could order her and she could order him, and they could each get what they wanted.

He pulled his shirt off from the back, lifting it over his head and letting it hit the floor. He really was perfection. Tall and lithe and beautiful. He had scars and smooth patches of skin. Dark hair that drew a line from his chest to the waistband of his jeans.

She moved forward and traced the longest scar on his side. A white line against his golden skin.

"How did you get this?" she asked.

"Knife fight."

She raised her gaze to his eyes, but his expression was serious, not silly. "You were in a *knife* fight?"

He shrugged. "When I first started out as Rodriguez, I was doing some drug running for one of his lower-level operations. Unfortunately a lot of those guys try to double-cross each other. I was caught in the cross… well, cross-stabbing as it were."

He said it so cavalierly, as if that was just part of his job. Getting stabbed. Horribly enough to leave a long, white scar.

"Did you go to the hospital?"

Again he smiled, almost indulgently now. "There was a man who did the stitching back at our home base."

"A man? Not a doctor?" she demanded.

"Doctors were saved from more…life-threatening injuries. Even then, only if you were important. At that point, I wasn't very important."

Gabby tried to make sense of it as Jaime shook his head.

"It's a nonsensical world. None of it makes sense if you have a conscience, if you've known love or joy. Because it's not about anything but greed and power and desperation."

She traced the jagged line and then bent to press a kiss to it. He sucked in a breath.

"I bet there was no one to kiss it better," she said, trying to sound lighthearted even though tears were threatening.

"Ah, no."

"Then let me." She raised to her tiptoes to kiss him. To press her chest to his. She still wore a bra, but the rest of her upper body was exposed and she tried to press every bare spot of her to every bare spot of him.

She tasted his mouth, his tongue, and she wanted the kiss to go deep enough and mean enough to ease some of those old hurts, some of that old loneliness.

For both of them.

There were things Jaime should do. Things he should stop from happening. But Gabby's kiss, Gabby's heart, was a balm to all the cruelties he'd suffered and administered in the past two years. She was sweetness and she was light. She was warmth and she was hope.

At this point he could no longer keep it from himself, let alone her. She wanted this. Perhaps she needed it as much as he did. Regardless, there was no going back. There was only going forward.

Her skin was velvet, her mouth honey. Her heart beating against his heart, the cadence of a million wonderful things he'd forgotten existed.

Her fingertips were curious and gentle as they explored him, bold as though it never occurred to her she shouldn't.

All of it was solace wrapped in pleasure and passion. That someone would want to touch him with reverence or care. That he wasn't the hideous monster he'd pretended to be for two years. He was still a man made of flesh and bone, justice and right.

And despite her time here as a victim, she was still a woman. Made of flesh and bone. Made of heart and soul.

He smoothed his hands up and down her back, absorbing the strength of her. Carefully leashed, carefully honed.

He reached behind her and unsnapped her bra, slowly pulling it off her and down her arms. It meant he had to put space between them. It meant he had to wrestle his mouth from hers. But if anything was worth that separation, it was the sight before him. Gabby's curly hair tumbled around her face. Her lips swollen, her cheeks flushed.

The soft swell of her breasts, dark nipples sharp points because she was as excited as he was. As needy as he was. He palmed both breasts with his too-rough hands and was rewarded by her soft moan.

Of course this amazingly strong and brave woman before him was not content to simply let him look or touch. She reached out and touched him, as well, her hands trailing down his chest all the way to his waist-band. She flipped the button and unzipped the piece of clothing with no preamble at all.

He continued to explore her breasts with his hands. Memorizing the weight and the shape and the warmth, the amazing softness her body offered to him. And it was more than just that. So much more than just the body. A heart. A soul. Neither of them would be at this point if it wasn't so much more than *physical*. It was an underlying tie, a cord of inexplicable connection.

She tugged his jeans down, his boxers with them. And then those slim, strong hands were grasping him. Stroking his erection and nearly bringing him to his knees.

He needed to find some sort of center. Not necessarily of control but of reason. Sense and responsibility. This was neither sensible nor responsible, but that didn't mean he couldn't take care of her. That didn't mean he wouldn't.

Gently he pulled her hand off him. "I need to go get something. I'll be right back."

She blinked up at him, eyebrows furrowed. Beautiful and naked from the waist up.

He pressed his mouth to hers as he pulled his jeans up, drowning in it a minute, forgetting what he'd been about to do. It was only when she touched him again that he remembered.

"Stay put. I will be right back." When she opened her mouth, he shook his head. "I promise," he repeated, his gaze steady on hers. He needed her to understand, and he needed her to believe him.

She pouted a little bit, beautiful and sulky, but she nodded.

"Right back," he repeated and then he was rushing to his room, caring far too little about the things he should care about. If The Stallion was around… If the other girls were okay… But it hardly mattered with Gabby's soul entwined with his.

He went to his closet of a room and grabbed the box that had been given to him. The box was still wrapped and he had no doubt about the safety of its contents.

And he would keep Gabby safe. No matter what.

With a very quick glance toward the back door, Jaime very nearly *scurried* back to Gabby. That back door was clearly shut and locked. Surely The Stallion had disappeared into his lair to obsess over Layne and Wallace's progress.

Jaime entered Gabby's room once again, closing and locking the door behind him quickly. She wasn't standing anymore. She was sitting on the edge of her bed and she was still shirtless.

He walked over and placed the box of condoms on the nightstand next to his smaller gun. He watched her face carefully, something flickering there he didn't recognize as she glanced at the box.

"We still don't have to," he offered, wondering if it was reticence or something close to it.

Her glance flicked from the box to him. "Why do you have these?"

"If you haven't noticed The Stallion is a little convinced women have—"

"Cooties?" Gabby supplied for him.

Jaime laughed. "I was going to say diseases. But, yes, essentially, cooties."

"So he gave those to you?"

"When I convinced him that only female payment would do, he insisted I take the necessary precautions."

She frowned, puzzling over the box. He didn't know what to say to make her okay. But eventually she grabbed the box and ran her nail around the edge. Pulling the wrapping off, she ripped open the box and took out a packet.

She studied him from beneath her lashes and then smirked. "I think this is where you drop your pants."

He laughed again. Laughing. It was amazing considering he couldn't think of the last time he'd laughed. With Gabby he felt like he wasn't just a machine. He wasn't simply a tool to bring The Stallion down or a tool to help The Stallion out. He'd been nothing but a weapon for so long it was hard to remember that he was also real. Capable of laughing. Capable of humor. Capable of feeling.

Capable of caring. Perhaps even loving.

He'd never been a romantic man who believed in flights of fancy and yet this woman had changed his life. She'd changed his heart and he didn't have to know how she'd done it to know that it had happened.

He pushed his jeans the remainder of the way down, watching her the entire time. Her gaze remained bold and appraising on his erection.

She scooted forward on the bed, tearing the condom packet open before rolling it on him. Finally she looked up at him. Her gaze never left his as she lay back on the bed and undid the fastenings of her pants. She shimmied out of her remaining clothes and then lay there, naked and beautiful before him.

He took a minute to drink her in. Because who knew how much time they would have after the next couple of days. He would save her—he would do anything to save her—and he did not know what lay ahead. He did know he had to absorb all of this, commit it to memory, connect it to his heart.

He stepped out of his jeans and then crawled onto the bed and over her. She slid her arms around his neck and pulled his mouth to hers. The kiss was soft and sweet. An invitation, an enchanting spell.

He traced the curve of her cheek with one hand, positioning himself with the other. Slowly, torturing himself and possibly her, as well, he found her entrance. Nudged against it. Taking his sweet time to slowly enter her.

Joined. Together. As if they were a perfect match. A pair that belonged exactly here. How could he belong anywhere else when this was perfect? When she was perfect?

She arched against him as if hurrying him along, her fingers tightening in his too long hair.

"We have time, Gabby. We have time." He kissed her, soft and sweet, indulging himself in a moment where he was simply seeped inside of her.

A moment when he was all hers and she was all his. And she relaxed, melting. His. All his.

Chapter 12

Gabby had known sex with Jaime would be different for a lot of reasons. First and foremost, she wasn't a young girl sneaking around, finding awkward stolen moments in the back of a car. Second, he wasn't a little boy playing at being a hard-ass bad man.

He was a strong, good, *amazing* man, doing things her ex-boyfriend would have wilted in front of.

But mostly, sex with Jaime was different because it was them. Because it was here. Because it mattered in a way her teenage heart would never have been able to understand. Perhaps she never would have been able to understand if she hadn't been in this position. The position that asked her to be more than she'd ever thought she'd be able to be. Because the truth of the matter was, eight years ago she had been a young woman like any other. Selfish and foolish and not strong in the least.

She would never be grateful for this eight years of hell. She would never be happy for the lessons she'd learned here, but that didn't mean she couldn't appreciate them. Because whether she was happy about it or not, it had happened. It was reality. There was only so much bitterness a person could stand.

With Jaime moving inside her, touching her, caring about her, bitterness had no place. Only pleasure. Only hope. Only a deep, abiding care she had never felt before.

He kissed her, soft and gentle, wild and passionate, a million different kinds of kisses and cares. His body moved against hers; rough, strong, such a contrast. Such a perfect fit.

Passion built inside her, deep and abiding. Bigger than anything she'd imagined she'd be able to feel ever again. But Jaime's hands stroked her body. He moved inside her like he could unlock every piece of her. She *wanted* him to.

The blinding spiral of pleasure took her off guard. She hadn't expected it so quickly or so hard. She gasped his name, surprised at the sound in the quiet room. Surprised at all he could draw it out of her.

He still moved with her. Growing a little frantic, a little wild. She reveled in it, her hands sliding down his back. Her heart beating against his.

She wanted *his* release. Wanted to feel him lose himself inside her.

Instead of galloping after it, though, he paused, as if wanting to make this moment last forever. Satisfied and sated, how could she argue with that? She would stay here, locked with him, body to body forever.

He kissed her neck, her jaw. His teeth scraped against

her lips and she moved her hips to meet with his. But he was unerringly slow and methodical. As though they'd been making love for years and he knew exactly how to drive her crazy. How to make her fall over that edge again and again. Because she was perilously close.

Aside from the tension in his arms, she would have no idea he was exerting any energy whatsoever. That spurred something in her. Something she hadn't thought she'd ever feel again. A challenge. And need.

She tightened her hold on his shoulders, slicked though they were. She sank her teeth into his bottom lip, pushing hard against him with her hips. He groaned into her mouth. She slid her hands down his back, gripping his hips, urging him on. One hand tightened on her hip, a heavy, hot brand.

She looked into his eyes and smiled at him. "More," she insisted.

He swore, sounding a little broken. That control he'd been holding on to, that calm assault to bring her to the brink, snapped. He moved against her with a wildness she craved, that she reveled in.

She'd brought him to this point, wild and a little broken. *She* could be the woman that did this to him, and that was something no one could ever take away. *She* was the woman who had made him hers. Maybe she wouldn't always have Jaime, but she'd always have this.

He groaned his release, pushing hard against her, and it was the knowledge she'd brought him there that sent her over the edge again herself. Pulsing and crashing. Her heart beating heavy, having grown a million sizes. Having accepted his as her own.

He lay against her, and she stroked her hand up and

down his back, listening to his heart beat slowly, slowly, come back to its regular rhythm. He made a move to get off her, but she held him there, wanting his weight on her for as long as it could be.

"Aren't I crushing you?" he asked in her ear, his voice a low rumble.

"I like it," she murmured in return.

He nuzzled into her neck, relaxing into her. As though because she'd said she liked it he would give her this closeness for as long as he could. She believed that about him. That he would always give her whatever he could. Once they knew Natalie was safe, he'd agreed to get her out under any means possible, and she believed.

For the first time in eight years she believed in someone aside from herself. For the first time in eight years she had hope and care and pleasure.

She might've told him she loved him in any other situation, but this was no regular life. Love was… Who knew what love really was? If they got away, back into the real world, maybe…maybe she could learn.

Jaime slept in Gabby's bed. It was a calculated risk to spend the night with her. He didn't know how close an eye The Stallion was keeping on him with everything going on. In the end, perhaps a little addled by her and sex, he'd figured, if pressed, he'd explain all his time as making sure Gabby paid for her supposed lack of respect.

It bothered him to have to think of things like that. Bothered him in a way nothing in the past two years had. That he had to make The Stallion think he was hurting Gabby. It grated against every inch of him every time he thought about it.

So he tried not to think about it. He spent the night in her bed and the next day mostly holed up with her in her room. They made love. They talked. They *laughed*.

It felt as though they were anywhere but in this prison. A vacation of sorts. Just one where you didn't leave the room you were locked into. He wouldn't regret this time. It was something to have her here, to have her close.

They didn't talk about the future or about what they might do when they got out. Jaime would have some compulsory therapy to go through. A whole detox situation with the FBI, along with preparations for the future trial. Any further investigating that needed to be done would at least fall somewhat within his responsibility.

But he was done with undercover work. He'd known that before he'd met Gabby. These past two years had taken too much of a toll and he couldn't be a good law-enforcement officer in this position anymore. He didn't plan to leave the FBI, but undercover work was over.

Once he got Gabby out, he would make sure that "something different" included her. She would need therapy, as well, and time to heal. It would take time to find ways back to their old selves.

He could wait. He could do anything if it meant having a chance with her.

But their time here in this other world was running out. The Stallion would be expecting a full report from Rodriguez, and Jaime had put it off long enough.

He would do all the things he had to do to protect her. To free her.

"You have to go meet with him," she said, her tone void of any emotion.

He turned to face her on the bed. It was too narrow and they barely fit together, and yet he was grateful for the lack of space, for the excuse to always be this close. "How'd you figure that out?"

"You got all tense," she replied, rubbing at his shoulders as though this was something they could be. A couple. Who talked to each other, offered comfort to each other.

He couldn't think of anything he'd ever wanted more, including his position with the FBI.

"He's expecting a report from me."

Gabby frowned and didn't look at him when she asked her question. "Are you going to tell him I cried?"

He'd been planning on it. He knew it poked her pride, but it would be best if The Stallion thought her broken. It would be best if Jaime made himself look like a master torturer.

"Do you not want me to?"

"You would tell him you failed?"

He shrugged, trying to act as though it wasn't a big deal, though it was. "If you want me to. I don't think it would put me in any danger to make it look like I'd failed one thing considering everything else that's currently going down."

"You don't *think*?"

"He's not exactly the most predictable man in the world, no matter how scheduled and regimented he is."

"That's very true," she mused, looking somewhere beyond him.

"Gabby."

Her dark gaze met his, that warrior battle light in them. "Tell him I cried. Tell him I sobbed and begged. What does it matter? I didn't actually."

"If it matters something to you—"

"All that matters to me is you." She blinked as if surprised by the force of her words. "And getting out of here," she added somewhat after the fact.

He pressed a kiss to her mouth. Whatever tension he'd had was gone. Or perhaps not *gone*, but different somehow.

Screw The Stallion. Screw responsibility. She was all that mattered. He wanted to believe that as he fell into the kiss, wanted to hold on to that possibility, that new tenet of his life. Gabby and only Gabby.

But life was never quite that easy. Because Gabby, being the most important thing, the central thing for him, meant he had to keep her safe. It meant that responsibility *did* have a place here. It was his responsibility to get her out. His responsibility to get her *free*.

He started to pull away but she spoke before he could.

"Go have a meeting. Find out if there's any news about Nattie, and make sure you remember every last detail. And then, when you can..." She smoothed her hand over his chest and offered him a smile that was weak at best, but she was trying. For him, he knew.

"When you're done, when you can, come back to me," she said softly.

He brought her hand to his mouth and pressed a kiss to her palm. "Always," he said, holding her gaze. Hoping she understood and believed how much he meant that.

He slid out of bed, because the sooner he got this

meeting with The Stallion over with, the sooner he could find a way to make sure that this was over. For Gabby and for him.

Jaime collected his weapons. He could feel Gabby's eyes on him though he couldn't read her expression. She had perfected the art of giving nothing away and as much as it sometimes frustrated him as a man, he was certainly glad she had built such effective protective layers for herself.

He put the knives back in his boots and then strapped on his cross-chest holster with all of his guns. He buckled it, still watching her expressionless face.

She slid off the bed and crossed to him. She flashed a smile Jaime didn't think had much happiness behind it, but she brushed her lips against his.

"Good luck," she said as though she were scared. For him.

"I have to lock the door," he said, regretting the words as they came out of his mouth. Regretting the way her expression shuttered.

"Yeah, I know." She gave a careless shrug.

Her knowing didn't make him feel any better about doing it, but he had to. There were certain things he still had to do. Things that would keep her safe in the end, and that was all that could matter.

He kissed her once more, knowing he was only delaying the inevitable. He steeled all that certainty and finally managed to back himself out of the room. Away from her smile, away from her sweet mouth.

Away from his heart and soul.

He closed the door and locked it from the outside. He regretted having to add the chain, but any regrets were a small price to pay to get her out. He would keep telling himself that over and over again until he believed it. This was all a small price to pay for getting her out.

He walked briskly down the hall, noting the house was eerily quiet. It wasn't unusual, but often in the afternoon there was a little bit of chatter from the common rooms as the girls worked on their projects or fixed dinner.

Jaime cursed and retraced his steps to check on them. The two calm ones from yesterday were sitting on the couch working on something The Stallion had undoubtedly given them to do. Alyssa was pacing the kitchen.

None of them looked at him, so he could only assume he'd been quiet enough. Satisfied that things seemed to be mostly normal, he backed out of the room. Alyssa's frenzied pacing bothered him a bit. Gabby was right, the girl was a loose cannon, and it was the last thing they needed. But what could he do about it?

There wasn't anything. Not now.

He walked back along the hallway, going through the hassle of unlocking and unchaining the door, stepping out, then redoing all the work. His thoughts were jumbled and he had to sort them out before he actually saw The Stallion.

He paused in the backyard, taking a deep breath, trying to focus his thoughts. He forced himself to hone in on all the strategies he'd been taught in his years as a police officer and FBI agent.

He had to put on the cloak of Rodriguez, get the information he was after, lie to The Stallion about Gabby, then go back to her. Once this was over, he could go back to her.

With a nod to himself, he stepped forward, but it was then he heard the noise. Something strange and faint. Almost a moan. He paused and studied the yard around him.

The next sound wasn't so much a moaning but almost like someone rasping "Rodriguez" and failing.

Jaime started moving toward the noise, listening hard as he walked around the backyard. He held his small handgun in one hand, leaving his other hand free should he need to fight off any attacker.

He rounded the front of the house, still listening to the sound and following the source. When he did, he nearly gasped.

Wallace and Layne were sprawled out in the yard. Layne was a little closer to the house than Wallace, but they were both caked with blood and dirt.

"Rodriguez. Rodriguez." Layne moved his arm wildly and stumbled to his feet. "I've been dragging this piece of shit for who knows how long. Go get The Stallion. And water. By God, I need water."

"Where is your vehicle?" Jaime asked, his tone dispassionate and unhurried.

"Only go so far…" Layne gasped for air, stumbling to the ground again. "Asshole shot our tires. Got as far as I could."

Jaime looked at both men in various states of bloodied harm. "You don't have her."

Layne's dirty, bloody face curled into a scowl, but he gave brief shake of the head.

"I don't know if you want me to get The Stallion if you don't have her."

"He shot us," Layne said disgustedly. "That prick

shot us. Wallace might die. We need The Stallion. We need *help*."

"You may wish you had died," Jaime said, affecting as much detached disinterest as he could.

On the inside he was reeling. Gabby's sister had escaped these men with Ranger Cooper, which meant that it was time. It was time to move forward. It was time to get the hell out. Her sister was safe and now it was her turn.

"Go get The Stallion," Layne yelled, lunging at him. He had a bloody wound on his shoulder and he was pale. Still, he seemed to be in slightly better shape than Wallace who was lying on the ground moaning, a bullet wound apparently in his thigh.

After a long study that had Layne growling at him as he tried to walk farther, Jaime inclined his head and then began striding purposefully back to The Stallion's shed. He knocked and only entered once The Stallion unlocked the door and bid him entrance.

"What took you so long?" The Stallion demanded and Jaime was more than a little happy that he had a decent enough excuse to explain his long absence in a way that didn't have anything to do with Gabby.

"*Senor*, Wallace and Layne are in the yard. Injured."

The Stallion had just sat in his desk chair, but immediately leaped to his feet. "They don't have her?" he bellowed.

"No."

"Imbeciles. Useless, worthless trash. Kill them. Kill them both immediately," he ordered with the flick of a wrist.

Jaime had to curb his initial reaction, which was

to refuse. He might find Wallace and Layne disgusting excuses for human beings, he might even believe they deserved to die, but he was not comfortable with it being at his hand.

"*Senor*, if this is your wish, I will absolutely mete out your justice. But perhaps…"

"Perhaps what?" he snapped.

"You will want to go after the girl yourself, *si*?"

The Stallion frowned as he walked over and stood by his dolls, grabbing one hand as though he was holding the hand of a little girl.

Jaime had to ignore that and press his advantage. "Clearly the Ranger is smarter than your men. But certainly not smarter than you. If you go after him, you can do whatever you want with both of them. Surely you, of all people, could outsmart them."

The Stallion had begun to nod the more Jaime complimented him. "You're right. You're right."

He dropped the doll's hand and Jaime nearly sagged with relief.

"You'll have to go with me, Rodriguez."

Jaime stilled. That was not part of his plan. "Tell Layne and Wallace they're in charge of the girls. We'll leave immediately."

"Their injuries are severe. Shot. Both of them. Surely incapable of watching after anything. You must have other men you can take with you, and I'll stay—"

"No." The Stallion shook his head. "No, you're coming with me. Wallace and Layne, no matter how injured, can keep a door locked. I'll send for another man, and he can kill them and take over here. Yes, yes, that's the plan. I need you. I need you, Rodriguez." The Stallion took one of the dolls off the shelf. He petted the doll's dark hair as though it were a puppy. "If you prove your worth to me on this, there is nothing that I wouldn't give you, Rodriguez." He held out the doll between them.

Jaime was afraid he looked as horrified as he felt, but he kept his hands grasped lightly behind his back. He forced himself to smile languidly at the unseeing doll. "Then I am at your service, *senor*."

"Go tell them the plan," The Stallion said, gesturing with the doll, thank God not making him take it. "Not the killing part, of course, just the watching-after-the-girls part. Pack all your weapons and all your ammunition. Pack up all the water in my supplies and put it in the Jeep. We'll leave as soon as you've gotten everything together. Do you understand?"

Jaime nodded, trying to steady the panic rising inside him. *"Sí, senor."*

It wasn't such a terrible thing. He'd be there to stop The Stallion from getting any kind of hold on Gabby's sister and Ranger Cooper. But it left Gabby here. Exposed.

And he only had limited time to figure out how to fix that.

Chapter 13

Gabby tried to ignore how locked in she felt. She'd been a victim for eight years. A prisoner of this place. Being locked in her room and unable to leave was certainly no greater trial to bear.

But she hadn't been locked in her room for any stretch of time since the very beginning. Mostly she'd been able to go to the common room or the kitchen whenever she wanted.

She'd gotten used to that freedom, and it was clawing at her to have lost some of it. That made it a very effective punishment all in all.

She wondered what the girls were doing. Had Alyssa calmed down? Was she ranting? Was she bringing reality to her threat to kill everyone in an effort to get out of there?

Gabby buried her face in her pillow and tried to block

it all out, but when she inhaled she could smell Jaime and something in her chest turned over.

Oh, Jaime. That was part of why this locked-up thing was harder to bear, too. She'd felt almost real for nearly twenty-four hours. She and Jaime had spent the night, and most of today, having sex and talking and enjoying each other's company. As though they lived in an outside world where they were themselves and not undercover agent and kidnapping victim.

It made it so much harder to be fully forced into what she really was. Victim. Captive. Not any closer to having any power than she'd been twenty-four hours ago.

Except she'd stolen a moment of it, and wasn't that something worth celebrating?

She heard someone unlocking her door from the outside and sat bolt upright in bed. Jaime hadn't been gone very long. If he was back already, it had to be bad news.

If it wasn't Jaime on the other side, so much the worse.

But it was the man she'd taken as a lover who stepped into her room, shutting the door behind him with more force than necessary. His face reminded her of that first day. Rodriguez. The mask, not the man.

"Do you have anything in here you'd want to take with you?" he demanded.

"What?" She couldn't follow him as he walked the perimeter of her room as if searching for something valuable.

"I don't have time to explain. I don't have time to do anything but get you out now."

"What happened?" she asked, jumping off the bed. His hand curled around her forearm, tight and without any of its usual kindness. "Is there anything you need to take?" he repeated, glaring at her.

"What's happened?" she pleaded with him. Her heart beat a heavy cadence against her chest and she couldn't think past the panic gripping her. "Is it Nattie? Is—"

He began pulling her to the door. "Your sister and the Ranger escaped."

"Escaped? Escaped!" Hope burst in her chest, bright and wonderful. "So we're…we're just running?"

He looked up and down the hallway. "You are. I'll get the other girls after."

That stopped Gabby in her tracks, no matter how he pulled on her arm. "What?" she demanded.

"Layne and Wallace are hurt. I can get one of you out now without raising any questions because you're supposed to be locked up, but I can't get you all out. Not right this second. I have to go with The Stallion to track down your sister. Which is good," he said before she could argue with him or ask him what the hell he was talking about. "Because I will obviously make sure that doesn't happen. I have—" he glanced at his watch "—maybe five seconds to contact my superiors to let them know to raid this place, and then to try to find one just like it in the south." He shoved her into the hallway, but she fought him.

"You can't take me and not them."

His gaze locked on hers. "Of course I can. And that's what we're doing."

"No. You can't. They'll fall apart without me."

"They won't. And they'll be saved in a day or two. Three tops."

"You really expect me to leave Tabitha and Jasmine

here with Alyssa? Alyssa will instigate something. You know she will. They'll all be dead before…" She didn't want to say it out loud, no matter how much he wasn't being careful himself.

He grabbed her by the shoulders and gave her a little shake, his eyes fierce and stubborn. "But you won't be."

It was her turn to look up and down the hallway. She didn't know where the girls were, where Wallace and Layne or The Stallion were milling about. Jaime was losing his mind and it was her… Well, it was her responsibility to make him find it.

"You have to get it together," she snapped in a low, quiet voice. "You have to be sensible about this, and you have to calm down."

He thrust his fingers into his hair, looking more than a little wild. "Gabby, I do not have time. You have to do what I say, and you have to do it now."

"Take Alyssa," she said, though it pained her to offer that. A stabbing pain of fear, but it was the only option.

"Wh-what?" he spluttered.

"Take Alyssa. I can handle more days here. Tabitha and Jasmine… We can hack it, but Alyssa cannot take another day. You know that. Take her. Get her out, we'll cover it up, and when the raid comes, you will come and get me."

"Have you lost your mind?"

"No! You've lost yours." Part of her wanted to push him, or reverse their positions and shake him, but the bigger part of her wanted to reach something in him. She curled her fingers into his shirt. "You know it isn't safe to take me out. Why are you risking everything?"

"Because I love you," he blurted, clearly antagonized into the admission.

She only stared up at him. It wasn't... She...

Love.

"I do not have time to argue," he said, low and fierce.

That, she was sure, was absolutely true. He didn't have time to argue. He didn't have time to think. But she knew the girls better than he did. She knew...

She reached her hands up and cupped his face. She drew strength from that. From him. From love. "If you love me," she said, low and in her own kind of fierce, "then understand that I know what they can handle. What they can't. I couldn't live with myself if I got out and they didn't. Not like this."

She wasn't sure what changed in him. There was still an inhuman tenseness to his muscles and yet some of that fierceness in him had dimmed.

"What am I supposed to do if something happens to you?" he asked, his voice pained and gravelly.

"I can take care of myself." She knew it wasn't totally true. A million things could go wrong, but she had to trust him to leave and save Nattie, and he needed to trust her to stay and keep the girls alive.

That she'd have a much easier time of doing if he took Alyssa. No matter that it made her want to cry. No matter that she wanted to be selfish and take the spot. But she couldn't imagine living the rest of her life if their deaths were on her head.

If there was a chance to get them *all* out, alive and safe, she had to take it. Not the one that only saved her. "You know I'm right."

He looked away from her, though his tight grip on

her shoulders never loosened. "You understand that I have to go. I don't have a choice."

"I want you to go. To save my sister."

His gaze returned to hers, flat and hard. "I'm not taking Alyssa."

"What? You have to." She gripped his shirt harder in an attempt to shake him. "If you can get one of us—"

"Gabby, I could get you out. Because you're supposed to be locked up, but more because I know you could do it. I could trust you to handle anything that came our way. I can't trust Alyssa. I can't trust her to keep her mouth shut when it counts. I can't trust her to get home. Like you said, she can't hack it. If I can't leave her here, then I can't take her, either."

"Then take one of the other girls!"

"You said it yourself. Alyssa would blab someone was missing. She'd… You can't trust her not to get you all killed. Don't you understand? It's you or no one."

"Why are you doing this?" she demanded, tears flooding her eyes. It wasn't fair. It wasn't right. He should take someone. Someone had to survive this.

"I'm not doing anything. I saw a chance for you—you, Gabby, to escape. If you won't take it, there's no substitute here. There is only you or nothing."

"Why are you trying to manipulate me into this? If you love me—"

"Why are you trying to manipulate my love? I know what the hell I'm doing, too. I have been trained for this. I have—"

"Gabby?"

Gabby and Jaime both jerked, looking down the hallway to Jasmine standing wide-eyed at the end of it. "What's going on?"

Jaime shook his head. "I can't do this. I don't have time to do this." Completely ignoring Jasmine, he got all up in Gabby's face, pulling her even closer, his dark eyes blazing into her. "I can save you *now*, but you have to come with me now. This is your last chance."

"It's your last chance to think reasonably," she retorted.

He looked to the ceiling and inhaled before crushing his mouth to hers, as though Jasmine wasn't standing right there. He seemed to pour all his frustration and all his fear into the kiss, and all Gabby could do was accept it.

"Goodbye, Gabby," he said on a ragged whisper, releasing her. "I love you, and I will get you safe."

She started to say his name as he walked away, but stopped herself as she looked at Jasmine. She couldn't say his real name. Even if she trusted Jasmine, she couldn't... This was all too dangerous now.

She wanted to tell him to save her sister. She wanted to tell him she loved him. She wanted to tell him he was being unfair and wrong, and yet none of those words poured out as he started to walk away. She wanted to tell him to be safe. That it would kill her if he was hurt.

But Jasmine was watching and she had to let him walk away. To save her sister. To save them all.

"What's happening?" Jasmine asked in a shaky voice. "I don't understand anything that I just saw."

Gabby slumped against the wall. "I don't know. I don't..."

"Yes, you do," Jasmine snapped, her voice sharp and uncompromising.

Gabby felt the tears spill unbidden down her cheeks. What was happening? She didn't understand any of it. But she knew she had to be strong. If they were going to be saved, she had to be strong.

She reached out for Jasmine, gratified when the girl offered support.

"We need to make a plan," Gabby said, sounding a lot stronger than she felt.

Jaime wasn't sure he could hide his dark mood if he tried. He was furious. Furious with Gabby for not coming with him. Furious at The Stallion for being the kind of fool who needed him to be there to do all the dirty work. Furious at the world for giving him something beautiful and then taking it all away.

Or are you just terrified?

He ground his teeth together and slid a look at The Stallion. The man sat in the passenger seat of the Jeep, typing on his laptop, swearing every time his Wi-Fi hotspot lost any kind of signal. He had a tricked-out assault rifle sitting precariously on his lap.

Jaime drove fueled on fear and anger. He'd had to leave the compound before he'd been able to be certain his message to his superiors had gone through. For all he knew, he could be out there alone with no backup. Gabby could be alone with no backup.

He wanted to rage. Instead he drove.

They were in the Guadalupe Mountains now, having driven through the night. Apparently, Gabby's sister and Ranger Cooper had run this way. Jaime was skeptical, considering how isolated it was. How would they be surviving?

But it didn't really matter. If they were on the wrong track, all the better.

What would actually be all the better would be reaching down to his side piece and ending this once and for all. It would put an end to two years of suffering. Eight for Gabby. Who knew how much suffering for everyone else.

But no matter how much anger and fury pumped through his veins, he knew he couldn't do it. Those same people who had been victims deserved answers and they deserved justice. In an operation like The Stallion's, so big, so vast, taking the big man out would produce perhaps a confused few days, but someone would quickly and easily usurp that power. Taking over as if The Stallion had never existed. It would create even more victims than already existed.

He couldn't overlook that. His duty was his duty. Intractable no matter how unfair it seemed. No matter what Gabby would think of it.

Gabby had implored him to trust her and, in the moment, he hadn't. He'd been too blinded by his fear and his anger that she wouldn't go with him.

In the quiet of driving through these deserted mountains, Jaime could only relive that moment. Over and over again. Regret slicing through him. He'd ended things so badly, and there was such a chance—

No. He wouldn't let himself think that way. There was no chance he wouldn't see Gabby again. No good chance they didn't escape this. He would find a way and so would she.

"Drive up there." The Stallion pointed at, what seemed to Jaime, a random mountain.

"There is no road."

The Stallion gave him a doleful look. "Drive to the top of that mountain," he repeated.

Jaime inclined his head. *"Sí, señor."* He drove, adrenaline pumping too hard as the Jeep skidded and halted up the rocky incline. He gripped the wheel, tapping the brakes, doing everything he could to remain in control of the vehicle.

Finally, The Stallion instructed him to stop. The man pulled out a pair of high-tech binoculars and began to search the horizon.

Jaime watched the man. He looked like any man, hunting or perhaps watching birds. He appeared completely sane and normal, and yet Jaime had seen him fondle dolls like they were real people.

"Señor, may I ask you a question?" It was a dangerous road to take. If The Stallion read anything suspicious into his questioning, Jaime could end up dead in the middle of this mountainous desert.

But The Stallion nodded regally as if granting an audience with the peasants.

"If you believe women are diseased, so you say, why do you keep so many of them?"

The Stallion seemed to ponder the line of questioning. Eventually he shrugged. "Waste not, want not."

Jaime didn't have to feign a language barrier for that to not make sense at all. "I… Come again?"

"Waste not, want not," The Stallion repeated. "I find them hideous creatures myself, as the perfect woman remains elusive. But some men, like yourself, require certain payments. Why should I waste the work they can do for the possible insurance they can offer me? It only makes sense to keep them. To use them. In fact, it's what women were really meant for. To be used. Perhaps the perfect woman is just a myth. And my mother was a dirty liar." The Stallion's fingers tightened on his gun, though he still held the binoculars with his other hand.

Jaime said nothing more. It was best if he stopped asking for motives and started focusing on what he was going to do if they found Natalie and Ranger Cooper. Focus on thwarting The Stallion's plans without tipping him off to it.

Or you could just kill him.

It was so tempting, Jaime found his hand drifting down to the piece on his left side without really thinking about it.

"There!" The Stallion shouted, pointing.

Jaime blinked down at the bright desert and mountain before them.

"I saw something down there. Get out of the Jeep. Remember, I don't care what happens to the Ranger, but I want the girl alive."

The Stallion jumped out of the Jeep, scrambling over the loose rock, his gun cocked, laptop and binoculars forgotten in the passenger seat.

Though Jaime wanted nothing to do with this, he also jumped out of the car. He had to make sure The Stallion did nothing to Ranger Cooper or Gabby's sister.

Jaime grabbed a gun for each hand. It was easy to catch up with The Stallion given Jaime's legs were longer. Since The Stallion had his gun raised to his shoulder, Jaime pretended to accidentally skid into him as he fired his weapon.

"Damn it, Rodriguez. I had a shot!" The Stallion bellowed.

Jaime surveyed the ground below. He could see two figures standing like sitting ducks in the middle of the desert. They were too far away to make a shot a sure thing, but why weren't they moving after that first shot?

Jaime raised his gun. "Allow me, *senor.*"

Jaime was surprised that his arm very nearly shook as he took aim. He'd used his guns plenty in the past two years, though usually to disarm someone or to scare them, not to kill them.

This was no different. He aimed as close as he could without risking any harm and fired.

"You idiot!"

"They are too far away. We have to be closer."

"Like hell." The Stallion raised his gun again and since Jaime couldn't run into him again, he did the only other thing he could think of. He sneezed, loudly.

Again, The Stallion's shot went wide. He snapped his furious gaze on Jaime, and as his head and body turned toward him, so did the gun.

Jaime held himself unnaturally still, doing everything he could to show no fear or reaction to that gun pointed in his direction. He couldn't clear his throat to speak, and he could barely hear his own thoughts over the beating of his heart.

"*Perdón, senor,* but we need to be closer," Jaime said as if a gun that could blow him to pieces wasn't very nearly trained on him at close range. "If you want to ensure the Ranger is dead and the girl is yours, we need to be closer." Jaime pointed out over the desert below, where the couple was now running.

With no warning, The Stallion jerked the gun their way and shot. The woman scrambled behind the outcropping, but Jaime watched as Ranger Cooper jerked. Jaime winced, but Cooper didn't fall. He kept running. Until he was behind the rock outcropping with Gabby's sister.

"Get in the Jeep," The Stallion ordered with calm and ruthless efficiency, making Jaime wonder if he was really crazy at all.

Jaime nodded, knowing he was on incredibly thin ice. The Stallion could shoot him at any time.

You could shoot him first.

He could. God, he could all but feel himself doing it, but Gabby was back in that compound, defenseless. And if the message hadn't gotten through to his superiors… Even if he shot The Stallion his cover would be blown. He'd have to take Ranger Cooper back, and the FBI would intercept all that. Then they'd make him follow their rules and regulations to get Gabby out.

As long as he remained Rodriguez, there was a chance to get Gabby, and the rest of the girls, out by any means necessary.

So he drove the Jeep like a madman down to where the couple had been hiding.

"They are gone by now," Jaime said, perhaps a little too hopefully.

"Keep driving. Find them." The Stallion clenched and unclenched his hand on the rifle.

Jaime did as he was told, driving around mountains until The Stallion told him to stop.

"Stay in the Jeep," The Stallion ordered. "Turn off the ignition. When I call for you, you run. Do you *comprende*?"

Jaime nodded and The Stallion got out of the Jeep, striding away. Jaime thought about staying put for all of five seconds and then he set out to follow his enemy.

Chapter 14

Gabby sat in the common room with Jasmine, Tabitha and Alyssa. They were huddled on the couch, pretending to work on a project The Stallion had given them a few days ago. Layne and Wallace were groaning and limping around the house. Both clearly very injured and yet not seeking any medical attention.

"They're vulnerable. We have to press our advantage now. We have to hit them where it hurts," Alyssa whispered fiercely, staring daggers at the men who were currently groaning about in the kitchen.

Jasmine looked down at her lap, pale and clearly not wanting any part of this powwow, but...

"Unfortunately she's right," Gabby said. "It's our only chance. They've had time to call for backup. The longer we wait...the more chance someone else comes."

She felt guilty for not telling them about the possibility of an FBI raid. They deserved to know the full truth, and they deserved to know what possibilities lay ahead, but Gabby knew they had to get Alyssa out of there before she got killed or got them all killed. They couldn't wait for the FBI to come. They couldn't wait for Jaime to magically fix everything.

No, they had to act.

"We have to time it exactly and precisely. Two of us against one, the other two against the other. Same time. Same attack. Same plan."

Gabby took stock of the two men grousing in the kitchen then of the three women huddled around her. Alyssa practically jumped out of her seat, completely ready to go, Tabitha looked grim and certain, but Jasmine looked pale and scared.

Gabby didn't want to draw attention to that. Not with Alyssa as…well, whatever Alyssa was. Without looking at her, Gabby reached over and gave Jasmine's hand a squeeze.

"I'm just not strong like you, Gabby," she whispered. "What if I mess up?"

Alyssa started to say something harsh but Gabby stopped her with a look. "That's why we're doing it in pairs. We're a team. Me and Jasmine. Alyssa and Tabitha. Right?"

Alyssa mostly just swore and Gabby watched her carefully. Jaime's words about trusting her rang through her head. Because how could she trust a woman who'd clearly lost her mind? Who'd just as soon kill them all as anything else?

But Jaime had been too cautious. Too afraid for her

safety. Gabby didn't have anyone's safety to be afraid for right now. She and the girls were getting to the now-or-never point. Alyssa was already there, and though Tabitha and Jasmine had been somewhat more resilient, they had to feel as she did. They had to be losing that perilous grip on who they were.

Jaime had given herself back to her. Hope, a possible future, but those women hadn't had that. So she had to get them free.

"We'll take Layne," Gabby said, nudging Jasmine with her shoulder. "You two will have Wallace."

"But he's the bigger one," Jasmine whispered.

"It'll be fine. He has a gunshot wound to the shoulder. Wallace has one to the leg. We're four healthy, capable women."

"B-but what do we do, exactly? After we attack them, what do we do? Run?" Tabitha asked, clearly forcing herself to be strong.

"Kill them. We want to kill them. They did this to us. They deserve to die," Alyssa all but chanted, a wild gleam to her eyes.

Gabby wasn't sure why she hesitated at that. She had indeed been stripped from her life by men like these two, and they surely deserved death. But she found she didn't want to be the one to give it to them.

"We're going to use their injuries to our advantage, hurt them, and then tie them up so we can get away without fear of being followed."

Alyssa scoffed. "I'm going to kill him."

Gabby reached over and grabbed Alyssa's hands, trying to catch her frenzied gaze. "Please. Understand. I don't want to be haunted by this for the rest of my life.

I want to leave here and leave it *behind*. No killing unless we absolutely have to. If we have a hope of getting out of here as unharmed as we are in *this* moment, we don't kill them. We incapacitate them."

"And then what? We're just going to run? Run where?"

"I have a vague notion of where we are, and that will help get us out. We've survived this, we can survive walking until we find a town."

Alyssa shook her head in disgust, but Gabby squeezed her hands tighter.

"I need you with me on this. We need to all be together and on the same page. Don't you want to be able to go home and go back to your old life and not have that on your conscience?"

"Who said I have a conscience?" Alyssa retorted, and for a very quick second Gabby believed her, believed that coldness. She'd seen nothing but cold for eight years.

Until Jaime.

That made Gabby fight so much harder. "The four of us are in this together. The four of us. They can't take that away from us. We have survived together, and when we get out, we will still be indelibly linked by that. We're like sisters. They can't make us turn on each other. You can't let them. As long as we work together, as long as we're linked, they can't hurt us."

Gabby wasn't certain that was true. They had guns and weapons, after all. But they were hurt. She had to believe it gave her and the girls an advantage.

Alyssa was looking at her strangely. "Sisters," she whispered. "I don't... No one's ever fought with me before."

"We will," Tabitha said, adding her hand to Gabby's on top of Alyssa's. Then Jasmine added her hand.

"We don't get out of this without each other," Gabby said, glancing back at Wallace and Layne. Wallace was still moaning, but Layne was glancing their way.

"We'll slowly make excuses to go to our rooms, but you'll all come to mine," she whispered as she pulled her hand from the girls.

Jasmine brought her sewing back to her lap and Tabitha pretended to examine the next package they were supposed to hide in the stuffing of a toy dog.

Gabby got to her feet, but Layne was there and, with his good arm, he shoved her back down.

Well, crap. This wasn't going to go well.

"Problem?" she asked sweetly, looking up at his suspicious gaze. She probably should avert her gaze and show some sort of deference to the man with a gun in his waistband and a nasty expression on his face.

"Aren't you supposed to be locked up?"

"I was just going back to my room when you shoved me back to the couch so rudely."

"I'd watch how you talk to me, little girl," Layne seethed, getting his face into hers.

Gabby bit her tongue because what she really wanted to do was tell *him* to be careful how he talked to her, and then punch him in his bloody bandage as hard and painfully as she could.

Instead she slowly got to her feet, unfolding to her full height. Though he was still much taller than she was, she affected her most condescending stare, never breaking eye contact with him as she stood there, shoulders back.

She was more than a little gratified by the way he seemed to wilt just a teeny tiny bit. As if he knew he couldn't break her.

"I'll just be going to my room now. Feel free to lock my door behind me."

"You little—" He lifted his meaty hand, she supposed to backhand her, and she probably should have let him hit her. She probably should let this all go, but whatever instincts to defend herself she'd tried to eradicate surged to life. She grabbed his hand before it could land across her face, and then put all her force behind shoving him, trying to make contact with his injury.

He stumbled back, though he didn't fall. He let out a hideous moan as, with his bad arm, he pulled the gun from his waistband and trained it on Gabby.

She was certain she was dead. She stood there, waiting for the firearm to go off. Waiting for the piercing pain of a bullet. Or maybe she wouldn't feel it at all. Maybe she would simply die.

But before another breath could be taken, Alyssa was in front of her, and then Tabitha and Jasmine at her sides.

"You'll have to get through us to shoot her, and if you shoot all of us?" Alyssa pretended to ponder that. "I doubt The Stallion would be too pleased with you."

"I'll kill all of you without breaking a sweat, you miserable—"

"Isn't it cute?" Alyssa said, looking back at Gabby. "He thinks *he's* in charge, not his exacting, demanding boss. Well, I guess it takes some balls to be that stupid."

Gabby closed her eyes, she didn't think goading him was really the road to take here, but he hadn't fired.

Yet.

There was a quiet standoff and Gabby tried to rein in the heavy overbeating of her heart. Jasmine's hand slid into hers and Tabitha's arm wound around her shoulders. Alyssa faced off with Layne as if she had no fear whatsoever.

Together, they couldn't be hurt. God, she very nearly believed it.

"If you aren't in your rooms in five seconds, I will shoot all of you," Layne said menacingly.

Gabby didn't believe him, but she didn't want to risk it, either. The girls in front of her hurried down the hall first, and Gabby tried to follow, but Layne grabbed her arm as she passed, digging his heavy fingers into her skin hard enough to leave bruises.

"Tonight you'll be screaming my name," he hissed.

Gabby smiled. It was either that or throw up. "Maybe you'll be screaming mine." She yanked her arm out of his grasp.

She was pretty sure the only thing that kept Layne from shooting her at this point was Wallace's sharp stand-down order.

When Gabby got to her room, she locked the door behind her. It wouldn't keep her safe from Layne since he undoubtedly had a key, but it at least gave her the illusion of safety.

When she turned back to face her room, the girls were all there, Tabitha and Jasmine on her bed, Alyssa pacing the room.

"And now we plan," Alyssa said, that dark glint in her eyes comforting for the first time.

Jaime stalked The Stallion. It wasn't easy to carefully follow a man who was carefully following another man, especially through a weirdly arid desert landscape dotted by mountains and rock outcroppings. But then, when had any of this been *easy*?

The Stallion stopped as though he'd seen something, and Jaime waited a beat. He realized The Stallion was peering around a swell of earth, and when The Stallion didn't move forward in the swiftly calculating pace he'd been employing, Jaime sucked in a breath.

On a hunch and a prayer, Jaime snuck around the other side of it. He kept his footsteps slow and quiet.

And then a shot rang out.

Jaime took off in a run, skidding to a halt when he saw The Stallion and Ranger Cooper standing off.

Jaime couldn't hear their conversation, but both men were unharmed and The Stallion didn't fire. Jaime dropped the small handguns he'd been carrying for ease of movement and unholstered his largest and most accurate weapon.

He trained it on The Stallion, only occasionally letting his gaze dart around to try to catch sight of the woman who remained hidden somewhere. The Stallion and Ranger Cooper spoke, back and forth, guns pointed at each other, lawman and madman in the strangest showdown Jaime had ever witnessed.

That gave Jaime the presence of mind to *breathe*. To watch and bide his time. Without knowing where Natalie Torres was, he couldn't act rashly. He—

Something in The Stallion's posture changed and Jaime sighted his gun, ready to shoot, ready to stop The Stallion before anything happened to Ranger Cooper. But before he could line up his shot and pull the trigger without accidentally hitting Cooper, Cooper fired.

The gun flew from The Stallion's hand and he howled with rage. Why the hell hadn't Cooper shot the bastard in the heart? Jaime was about to do just that, but the woman appeared from a crevice in one of the rocks, holding her own weapon up and trained on The Stallion.

She reminded him so much of Gabby it physically hurt. There wasn't an identical resemblance, but it was that determined glint in Natalie's dark eyes that had him thinking about Gabby. If she was safe. If any of them would make it through this in one piece.

He shook that thought away. They would. They all damn well would.

And then Natalie pulled the trigger. She missed, but before Jaime could step out from the outcropping, she'd fired again. Even from Jaime's distance he could see the red bloom on The Stallion's stomach.

"Rodriguez!" he screamed, followed by The Stallion's sad attempt at Spanish. Jaime sighed. He could only hope Cooper recognized him, or that they wouldn't shoot on sight. He could stay there, of course, but it would be worse if he waited for Ranger Cooper to find him.

He stepped out from behind the land swell and walked slowly and calmly toward his writhing fake boss.

Ranger Cooper watched him with the dawning realization of recognition, but Natalie clearly didn't have a clue as she kept her gun trained on him.

Jaime thought maybe, maybe, there was a chance he

could maintain his identity and get back to Gabby, so he nodded to Cooper. "Tell your woman to put down the gun," he said in Spanish.

Cooper looked over at the woman. "Put it down, Nat," he murmured, an interesting softness in the command. One Jaime thought he recognized.

Wasn't that odd?

"I won't let anyone kill us. Not now. Not when that man has my sister," Natalie said, her hands shaking, her dark eyes shiny with tears. The Torres women were truly a marvel.

The Stallion made a grab for Jaime's leg piece, but Jaime easily kicked him away. No, he wasn't Rodriguez anymore. He had to be the man he'd always been, and he had to do his duty.

He wasn't Rodriguez, a monster with a shady past. He was Jaime Alessandro, FBI agent, and regardless of *who* he was, he'd find a way to get Gabby to safety as soon as he got out of there.

"Ma'am, I need you to put your weapon down," Jaime said, steady and sure, making eye contact with Natalie. "I'm with the FBI. I've been working undercover for Callihan." Jaime ignored The Stallion's outraged cry, because he saw the way the information tumbled together in Natalie's head.

She didn't even have to ask about Gabby for him to know that's what she needed to hear. "I know where your sister is. She's…safe."

Natalie didn't just lower her gun, she dropped it. She sank to the rocky ground and Jaime had to raise an eyebrow at Ranger Cooper sinking with her.

He couldn't hear what they said to each other, but

it didn't matter. He turned to The Stallion. Victor Callihan. The man who'd made his life a living hell for two years.

He was still writhing on the ground, bloody and pale, shaking possibly with shock or with the loss of blood. He might make it. He might not. Jaime supposed it would depend on how quickly they worked.

Jaime slid into a crouch. "How does it feel, *senor*," Jaime mused aloud, "to be so completely outwitted by everyone around you?"

"You think this is over?" The Stallion rasped. "It'll never be over. As long as I *breathe*, you're mine, and it will never, *ever*, be over."

Jaime had been through too much for those words to have any impact. The Stallion thought he could intimidate him? Make him fear? Not in this lifetime or the next.

"There's already an FBI raid at all four of your compounds." He was gratified when the man's eyes bulged. "Oh, did you think I didn't put it together? The southern compound? You know who helped me figure out its location? Ah, no, I don't want to ruin the surprise. I'll let you worry about that. You'll have plenty of time to ruminate in a cell."

The Stallion lunged, but he was weakened and all Jaime had to do was rock back on his heels to avoid the man's grasp.

"Everyone should be out by the time I get back, and you know what my first order of business will be? Burning every last doll in that place," he whispered in the man's ear, before standing.

Jaime turned to Cooper who'd gotten Natalie to her

feet. He ignored The Stallion's sputtering and nodded in the direction of the Jeep. "I have rope in my vehicle. We'll tie him up and take him to the closest ranger station."

And then he'd find a way to get to Gabby.

Chapter 15

Gabby stood at the door to her room, Jasmine slightly in front of her. Alyssa and Tabitha had already gone back into the common room, plan in place.

Gabby felt sick, but she pushed it away. The girls were counting on her and so was… Well, she herself. She was the architect of this plan, the leader, and if she wanted them all to survive, she had to be calm and strong.

Jaime was out protecting her sister, and no matter how mad he might be at her for not leaving, she knew he'd do everything to keep Natalie safe.

And she hadn't even told him…

She forced it all away as Alyssa's cue blasted through the house. Gabby exchanged a look with Jasmine. Alyssa was supposed to yell at Tabitha, not scream obscenities at her.

As Gabby and Jasmine slid into the room, Alyssa attacked, stabbing one of her butter knives into Wallace's leg with a brutal force Gabby had to look away from.

Jasmine threw the cords they'd gathered at Tabitha. Wallace screamed in a kind of agony that made Gabby's blood run cold, but she couldn't think about that now. Layne was her target.

His eyes gleamed with an unholy bloodlust and his gun was in his grasp far too fast. But somehow everything seemed to move in slow motion. Before Gabby could even flinch, Jasmine was throwing her body at Layne's legs.

The impact surprised Layne enough that he fell forward, on top of Jasmine, who cried out, mixing with Wallace's screams.

Gabby scrambled forward, pushing Layne off Jasmine so he hit the hard floor on his injured shoulder. He howled in pain, but he didn't let go of the gun as Gabby grabbed it.

She jerked and pulled, but Layne didn't let go. He screamed, but she couldn't wrestle the weapon from his grasp.

Until Jasmine got to her feet and started stomping on his bad shoulder, a wholly different girl than the woman who'd, pale-faced and wide-eyed, told Gabby she wasn't strong enough. Gabby finally wrested the gun free of his hand, trying to think past the high-pitched keening from both men.

"Rope," she gasped then yelled louder. She glanced at Alyssa and Tabitha. Wallace thrashed, groaning in pain as he swung his hands out, but Tabitha had tied his legs tightly to the chair and Alyssa had already wrestled the gun out of his hands.

Alyssa kicked one of the cords Gabby's way and Gabby grabbed it as Layne tried to scuttle away from Jasmine, cursing and, Gabby thought, maybe even sobbing.

Jasmine stomped another time on his wound, which had now bled completely through his bandage and shirt. His face went white and his eyes rolled back in his head, and it was only then that Gabby realized Jasmine was crying and that Wallace had gone completely silent.

Feeling a sob rise in her throat, Gabby knelt next to Layne and jerked his arms behind his back, doing her best to tie the cord around his thick forearms and wrists. She pulled it as tightly as she possibly could and tied as many knots as the length of cord would allow.

She breathed through her mouth, because something about the smell of Layne—him or his wound—nearly made her woozy.

"I've got his legs," Tabitha said, moving to the end of Layne's lifeless body. Gabby could see the rise and fall of his chest, so he wasn't dead.

She almost wished he was, which was enough to get her to her feet. She glanced back at Alyssa who had ripped off half her shirt and tied it around Wallace's face like a gag. The man still wiggled, but the cords and knots were holding and if he tried to escape too much longer, he'd likely knock the whole chair over.

Alyssa held the gun far too close to Wallace's head.

Gabby crossed to her, holding her hand out for the gun. "Tabitha is going to guard them."

Alyssa didn't ~~spare Gabby~~ a glance. "My suggestion

of just killing them stands," she said, her hands tight on the gun, sweat dripping down her temple.

"I need your help to gather evidence."

"They can," Alyssa said, jerking her chin toward Jasmine, who stood with Layne's gun trained on his unmoving form and Tabitha finishing up the knots at his ankles. She never looked at them, just gestured toward them.

"No, I need you," Gabby said firmly.

Alyssa's gaze finally flickered to Gabby. "You need me?"

"Yes. You're the strongest next to me. We'll be able to break down the doors easiest and carry the most stuff. I need you."

Gabby didn't really know if Alyssa was stronger, but it was certainly the most plausible. Clearly it also got through to her since she'd looked away from Wallace.

Maybe it would be easier to kill the men, but Gabby... She didn't want to have to relive that for the rest of her life, and she didn't want the other girls to have to, either.

Alyssa waved the gun a bit. "We might need this to bust the lock off."

Gabby remained steadfast in holding her hand out, palm upward. "Give me the gun, Alyssa. We need to do this as a team."

The woman's mouth turned into a sneer and Gabby thought for sure she'd lost the battle. Any second now Alyssa would pull the trigger and—

She slapped the gun into Gabby's palm. "Let's go get those doors open," she muttered.

Gabby nodded, looking at Tabitha and Jasmine. Jasmine had Layne's gun and Tabitha had what looked to be a dagger of some kind that she must have taken off one of the men.

"Scream if you need anything," Gabby said sternly. "Once we have whatever evidence we can carry, we'll come get you and lock this place back up, and then we'll start out."

Jasmine and Tabitha nodded, and though they'd handled themselves like old pros, everyone seemed a little shaky now. Far too jumpy. She and Alyssa needed to hurry.

They raced down the hall to the door. "Give me one of those knives."

Alyssa pulled one out of her bra and if Gabby had time she might have marveled at it, but instead she used it to start picking the lock. Turned out Ricky and his ne'er-do-well friends *had* taught her something.

She got the locks free and pushed on the door. It creaked open only a fraction. Alyssa inspected the crack. "It's chained on the outside," she said flatly. "Give me the gun."

Gabby hesitated. "What if it ricochets?"

Alyssa raised an eyebrow. "It won't."

What choice did Gabby have? A butter knife wasn't cutting through chain any more than anything else, and Alyssa might be losing it, but she was sure. They had to be a team.

Gabby handed over the gun. Alyssa shoved the muzzle through the crack, barely managing to fit it, and then a loud shot rang out.

The chain clanked and then after another quick and overly loud shot, Alyssa was pushing the door open.

Both women stumbled into the bright light of day.

It very nearly burned, the bright sunshine, the intense blue overhead. Gabby tried to step forward, but only tripped and fell to her knees in the grass.

"Oh, God. Oh, God," Alyssa whispered.

Gabby couldn't see her. Her eyes couldn't seem to adjust to the bright light, and her heart just imploded.

She could smell the grass. She could feel it under her knees and hands. Hot from the midday sun. Rocky soil underneath. It was real. Real and true. The actual earth. Fresh air. The sun. God, the sun.

The one time they'd been let out it had been a cloudy day, and The Stallion hadn't allowed for any reaction. Just digging. But today...today the sun beat down on her face as if it hadn't been missing from her life for eight years.

Gabby tried to hold back the sobs, she had a job to do, after all. A mission, and leaving Tabitha and Jasmine alone with dangerous men no matter how injured or tied up wasn't fair. She had to act.

But all she could seem to do was suck in air and cry.

Then Alyssa's arms were pulling her to her feet. "We have to keep moving, Gabby. We've got time to cry later. Now, we have to move."

Gabby finally managed to blink her eyes open. Alyssa's jaw was set determinedly and she pointed to a fancy shed in the corner of the yard.

Gabby took a deep breath of air—fresh and sun-laden—and looked down at her hands. She'd grasped some grass and pulled it out, and now it fluttered to the patchy ground below.

The Stallion had kept her from this, *all of this*, for

eight long years. It was time to make sure it was his turn to not see daylight for a hell of a lot longer.

Jaime drove the Jeep toward where Cooper's map said there'd be a ranger station. Once they had access to a phone—The Stallion's laptop had been too encrypted to be of use—Jaime would call his superiors and Ranger Cooper's.

Things would be real soon enough, and he still wasn't back to Gabby.

Still, he answered Cooper's questions and only occasionally glanced at the woman sandwiched between him and the Texas Ranger.

She was slighter than Gabby, certainly softer, and yet she'd been the one to shoot The Stallion as though it had been nothing at all.

Jaime glanced at Cooper's crudely bandaged arm wound. It was bleeding through, though he'd looked over it himself and knew, at most, Cooper would need stitches.

There was an awkward silence between every one of Ranger Cooper's curt questions and every one of Jaime's succinct answers. Tension and stress seemed to stretch between all of them, no matter that The Stallion was apprehended in the back and would likely survive his injuries.

Unless Jaime slowed down. But it wasn't an option, not without news on Gabby and the raid. Too many unknowns, too many possibilities.

He finally found a road after driving through mountains and desert, and soon enough a ranger station came into view. Jaime brought the Jeep to a stop, trying to remember himself and his duty.

He pushed the Jeep into Park and looked at Cooper. "If you stay put, I'll have them call for an ambulance, as well as call your precinct. We'll see if there's any word on the raid to Callihan's house, where your sister was."

Ranger Cooper nodded stoically, putting his hand on his weapon, his glance falling to the back of the Jeep where Victor Callihan, The Stallion, Jaime's tormenter, lay still and tied up.

Bleeding.

Hopefully miserable.

Jaime glanced at Gabby's sister, but she only stared at him. She'd asked no questions about her sister. She'd said almost nothing at all. Jaime figured she was in shock.

"I don't know what to ask," she said, her voice weak and thready.

Jaime gave a sharp nod. "Let me see if I can go find out some basics." He left the Jeep and strode into the station.

A woman behind the counter squeaked, but Jaime held up his hands.

"I'm with the FBI and I need to use your phone." He realized he didn't have his badge, and he still had far too many weapons strapped to his body.

He needed to get his crap together and fast. He kept his hands raised and recited his FBI information. The woman shoved a phone at him, but she backed into a corner of her office and Jaime had no doubt she was radioing for help.

It didn't matter. He called through to his superior, trying to rein in his impatience.

"I'm in a ranger station in the Guadalupe Mountains National Park. I have Texas Ranger Vaughn Cooper and civilian Natalie Torres with me. The Stallion is hurt and disarmed. We need an ambulance for Callihan and Cooper, and I need an immediate debriefing on what's happening at The Stallion's compound in the west."

"Immediate," Agent Lucroy repeated, and though it had been years since Jaime had seen the man in charge of his undercover investigation, he could imagine clearly the man's raised eyebrow. "That's quite the demand."

"Sir," Jaime said, biting back a million things he wanted to yell. "There are four women in that compound, whom I left with armed and dangerous men. It is my duty and my utmost concern that they are safe."

There was a long silence on the line.

"Sir?" Jaime repeated, fearing the worst.

"The raid has been initiated per your message. Our agents are on the ground at the compound…"

"And Ga—the women?"

"Well… Let me get off the phone and contact the necessary authorities to get you out of there. We'll do a proper debriefing when you're back in San Antonio."

Jaime nearly doubled over, fear turning into a nauseating sickness in his gut. Oh, God, he hadn't saved her. She wasn't safe at all.

"What happened to the women?" he demanded. "One of the captives… Natalie Torres, the woman Ranger Cooper has been protecting, she's the sister of one of the captives. She deserves to know…" She deserved to know how horribly he'd failed.

Agent Lucroy sighed. "Let's just say there's a slight… situation at the El Paso compound."

Chapter 16

"Do you think we can carry a computer as far as we need to walk?" Gabby asked, looking dubiously down at the hard drive Alyssa was unhooking from a million monitors.

Alyssa shrugged. "We can get it as far as we need to. Then it's got just as much a chance of being found by whatever cops we can find as any Stallion idiots."

It was a good point. In fact, Alyssa had made quite a few. Though Gabby still didn't trust Alyssa not to go off and do something drastic or dangerous, the woman was very effective under pressure.

They hadn't found any bags or things they could haul evidence in, so they'd shoved any important-looking papers into their pockets. Gabby had come across a map with markings on it, and she thought with enough time she'd be able to figure it out. She'd taken a page out of Alyssa's book and shoved it into her bra.

Gabby went through a shelf of tech gadgets and picked up anything she thought might have memory on it. Anything that could make sure this was over for good.

It's not over until you're out of here.

She tried to ignore the panic beating in her chest and *focus.* "That should be good, don't you think?" When she turned to face Alyssa, the woman was staring at a shelf of dolls. They all looked like variations of the same. Dark hair, unseeing eyes, frilly dresses.

A heavy sense of unease settled over the adrenaline coursing through Gabby. She understood now, completely, why the dolls had weighed so heavily on Jaime. She tried to look away, but it felt as if the dolls were just…staring at—

The shot that rang out made Gabby scream, the doll's head exploding made her wince, but when she wildly looked over at Alyssa, the woman was simply holding the gun up, vaguely smiling.

"Think I have enough bullets to shoot all of them?" she asked conversationally.

"No," Gabby said emphatically. "Let's go. Let's get the hell out of here."

Alyssa nodded, grabbing the computer hard drive and hefting it underneath her arm. She kept the gun in her other hand, but before either of them could make another move, the door burst open.

Gabby dropped to the ground, trying to hide behind the desk that dominated the shed, but Alyssa only turned, gun aimed at the invasion of men.

Men in *uniform*.

"FBI. Put down your weapons," they yelled in chorus.

Gabby scrambled back to her feet, blinking a few times, just to make sure… But there it was in big bold letters.

FBI.

Oh, *God*. She searched the men's faces, but none of them was Jaime.

"Drop your weapon, ma'am," one of them intoned, his voice flat and commanding.

Alyssa stared at the man and most decidedly did *not* drop her weapon.

"Alyssa," Gabby hissed.

"I'm not going to be a prisoner for another second," Alyssa said, her voice deadly calm.

"It's the *FBI*. Look at his uniform, Alyssa. Do what he *says*." Gabby held up her hands, hoping that with her cooperating the men wouldn't shoot.

But Alyssa didn't move. She eyed the FBI agent, both with their weapons raised at each other.

"Ma'am, if you do not lower the weapon, I will be forced to shoot. You have to the count of three. One, two—"

"Ugh, fine," Alyssa relented, lowering her arm. She didn't drop the weapon and she stared at the men with nothing but a scowl.

"They're here to save us," Gabby said, feeling a bubble of hysteria try to break free. She wanted to cry. She wanted to throw herself at these men's feet. She wanted Jaime and to know for sure…

"It's over, isn't it?" she asked, a tear slipping down her cheek.

"Ma'am, you have to drop your weapon. We cannot escort you out of here until you do," he said to Alyssa, ignoring Gabby completely.

"There are two other women inside the house. Did you—?" Gabby had started to step forward, but one of the men held up his hand and she stopped on a dime.

"We will not be discussing anything until she drops her damn weapon," the man said through gritted teeth.

There were four of them, three with their weapons trained on Alyssa, a fourth one behind the three on a phone, maybe relaying information to someone.

Alyssa had her grip on the gun so tight her knuckles were white and Gabby didn't know how to fix this.

"What are you doing?" Gabby demanded. She wanted to go over and shake Alyssa till some sense got through that hard head of hers, but she was afraid to move. They were finally free and Alyssa was going to get them both killed.

That made her a different kind of angry. "Why are you treating us like the criminals?" she demanded of the four men, soldier-stiff and stoic.

"Why won't you drop your weapon?" the agent retorted.

Gabby didn't know how long they stood there. It seemed like forever. Alyssa neither dropped her weapon, nor did the men lower theirs. Seconds ticked on, dolls watching from above, and all Gabby could do was stand there.

Stand there in limbo between prison and freedom. Stand there with the threat of this woman who'd become an ally and a friend dying when they'd come this far.

"Please, Alyssa. Please," Gabby whispered after she

didn't know how long. Gabby had spent eight years trying to be strong. Beating any emotion out of herself, but all strength did in this moment was make this standoff continue.

She looked at Alyssa, letting the tears fall from her eyes, letting the emotion shake her voice. "Please, put down the gun," she whispered. "I want you safe when we get out of here. I don't want to have to watch you get hurt. Please, Alyssa, put down the gun."

Alyssa swallowed. She didn't drop the gun, though her grip loosened incrementally.

"We all want this to be over," Gabby said, pushing her advantage as hard as she could. "We all want to go home."

"I don't," Alyssa muttered, but she dropped the gun all the same.

Jaime supposed that someday in the future it would be a point of pride that he'd yelled at his superior over the phone and had to be restrained by three fellow agents, and still retained his job.

But when Agent Lucroy had explained there'd been a standoff—a *standoff*—with two women who had been *captives*, no matter how dangerous he'd felt Alyssa could be, Jaime had lost it.

He'd sworn at his boss. He'd thrown the phone across the ranger station. The only thing that had kept his temper on a leash as they'd waited for the ambulance was the fact that Natalie was Gabby's sister.

She didn't need to be as sick with fear and as stuck as he was.

The being restrained by three fellow agents had come

later. When they'd had to forcibly put him on a flight to the field office in San Antonio instead of to Austin with Ranger Cooper and Natalie.

There had been a *slight* altercation once getting off the plane when he'd demanded his car and been refused. In the end, a guy he'd once counted as a friend had had to pull a gun on him.

He'd gotten himself together after that. Mostly. He'd met with his boss and had agreed to go through the mandatory debriefing, psych eval and the like. Sure, maybe only after Agent Lucroy had threatened to have him admitted to a psych ward if he didn't comply.

Semantics.

He was held overnight in the hospital, being poked and prodded and mentally evaluated. When he'd been released, he was supposed to go home. He was supposed to meet his superiors at noon and inform them of everything.

Instead he'd gotten in his car and driven in the opposite direction. He very possibly was risking his job and he didn't give a damn. He should go see his parents, his sister. They were in California, but if he was really going to take a break with reality, shouldn't it be to have them in his sight?

When he'd spoken to Mom on the phone, she'd begged him to come home, and when he'd said he couldn't, she'd said she'd be heading to San Antonio as soon as she could. He'd begged her off. Work. Debriefing.

The truth was… He wasn't ready to be Jaime Alessandro quite yet. He'd neither cut his hair nor shaved his beard. He was neither FBI agent nor Stallion lackey, he was something in between, and no amount of FBI shrinks poking at him would give him the key to step back into his old life.

Not until he saw Gabby. So he drove to Austin. Thanks to Ranger Cooper apparently being unaware that he wasn't supposed to know, Jaime had the information that Gabby was still in the hospital and had yet to be reunited with her family.

When Ranger Cooper had relayed that information, Jaime may have broken a few traffic laws to get to the hospital.

All he needed was to see her, to maybe touch her. Then he could breathe again. Maybe then he could find himself again.

Maybe then he'd forgive her for not getting out when he'd wanted her to.

He did some fast talking, but either the hospital staff was exceptionally good or they'd been forewarned. No amount of flashing his badge or trying to sneak around corners worked.

Eventually security had been called. When one security guard appeared, Jaime laughed. Then another had appeared behind him and he figured they were probably serious.

He wasn't armed, but there were ways he could easily incapacitate these men. He could imagine breaking the one in front's nose, the one in back's arm. This middle-aged, not-in-the-best-of-shape security guard *and* his burly partner. Bam, bam, quick and easy.

It was that uncomfortable realization—that he was pushing too hard, pressing against people who didn't deserve it—that had him softening.

So, when the guards grabbed him by the arms, he

let them. He let them push him out the doors and into the waiting room.

"What the hell is your problem, man?" the one guy asked, clearly questioning the truth of his FBI claims.

That was a good enough question. He was acting like a lunatic. Not at all like the FBI agent who had been assigned and willfully taken on the deep undercover operation that had just aided in busting a crime organization that had been hurting the people of this state—and others—for over a decade.

"You come through these doors again, the police will be taking your ass to jail. FBI agent or not."

Jaime inclined his head, straightening his shoulders and then his shirt. "I apologize," he managed to rasp, turning away from the guards only to come face-to-face with two women frowning at him.

"Why are you trying to see my daughter?" the middle-aged woman demanded, her hands shaking, her eyes red as though she'd done nothing but cry for days.

If she was Gabby's mother, perhaps she had.

It was the thing that finally woke him up. Really and fully. Gabby's mother, and a woman who looked to be Gabby's grandmother. He'd assumed Natalie wasn't there, but then she walked in from the hallway carrying two paper cups of coffee.

"Agent Alessandro," she said, stopping short. "Did something hap—?"

"No, Ms. Torres. I merely came by to check on your sister, and I was informed, uh…" He glanced at the women who'd likely seen him get tossed out on his ass. "She wasn't seeing visitors."

Natalie handed off the drinks to the other two women,

offering a small and weak smile. "She's asked not to see anyone for a bit longer yet, from what the doctor told me."

"And her, uh, health? It's…"

"As good as can be expected. Maybe better. They've had a psychiatrist talking to her a bit. Are you here to question her? I'm not sure—"

"The case we're building against The Stallion will take time, but your sister's contributions… Well, we'll certainly work with her comfort as much as we can."

He looked at the three women who'd been through their own kind of hell. He didn't know them. Maybe they'd spent eight years certain Gabby was dead. Maybe they'd hoped for her return every night for however many nights she'd been gone.

Gabby would know. She'd be able to figure out the math in a heartbeat, or maybe it was her heartbeat, every second away from her family.

A family who had loved her and taken care of her for twenty years. A family who had far more claim to her than the man who'd spent a week with her and left her behind.

He straightened his shirt again, clearing his throat. He pulled out his wallet, a strange sight. It held his ID with his real name. His badge. Things that belonged to Jaime Alessandro, not Rodriguez.

He blinked for a few seconds, forgetting what he was doing.

"Do you want me to call some—?"

He thrust his business card at Natalie, effectively cutting off her too kind offer. "If you need anything, anything at all, any of you, please don't hesitate to contact me. I'll be back in San Antonio for at least another day or two, but it's an easy enough drive."

Natalie looked at him with big brown eyes that looked too much like Gabby's for his shaky control.

"I want all three of you to know how strong Gab— Gabriella was during this whole ordeal," he forced himself to say, feeling stronger and more sure with every word. FBI agent to the last. "She saved herself, and those women, and did an amazing amount of work in allowing us to confidently press charges against a very dangerous man."

She'd been a warrior, a goddess, an immeasurable asset and ally. She was a *survivor* in every iteration of the word, and he wasn't worthy of her. Not like this.

That meant he had to face his responsibilities and figure out how to come back as just that.

Worthy of Gabby.

Chapter 17

Gabby sat in a sterile hospital room dreading the seconds that ticked by. Every second brought her closer to something she didn't know how to face.

Life.

Her family was in the waiting room. She'd been cleared by both the doctor and the psychiatrist to see them. To be released from the hospital. There'd be plenty of therapy and police interviews in the future, but for the most part she could go home.

What did that even mean? Eight years she'd been missing. Eight years for her family to change. Daddy was gone. Who knew where Mom and Grandma lived. Surely, Natalie had her own life.

Gabby sat on the hospital bed and tried not to hold on to it for dear life when the nurse arrived. Gabby didn't want to leave this room. She didn't want to face whatever waited for her out there.

She'd rather go back to the compound.

It was that thought, and the shuddering denial that went through her, that reminded her... Well, this would be hard, of course it would be. It would be painful, and a struggle, but it was better. So much better than being a prisoner.

"Your family is waiting," the nurse said kindly. "I've got your copy of the discharge papers and the referrals from the psychiatrist. Is there anything you'd like me to relay to your family for you?"

Gabby shook her head, forcing herself to climb off the bed and onto her own two feet. Her own two feet, which had gotten her this far.

She took a shaky breath and followed the nurse out of the safety of her hospital room. The corridor was quiet save for machine beeps and squeaky shoes on linoleum floors. Gabby thought she might throw up, and then they'd probably take her back to a room and she could...

But they reached the doors and the nurse paused, offering a comforting smile. "Whenever you're ready, sweetheart."

Gabby straightened. She'd never be ready, so taking a second was only delaying the inevitable. "Let's go."

The nurse opened the doors and stepped out, Gabby following by some sheer force of will that had gotten her through eight years of hell.

The nurse walked toward three women sitting huddled together. None of them looked *familiar* and yet Gabby knew exactly who they were. Grandma, Mom, Natalie. Older and different and yet *them*.

Natalie got to her feet, her face white and her eyes wide as though she were looking at a ghost.

Gabby felt like one. Natalie reached out, but it was almost blindly, as if she didn't know what she was reaching for. As if Gabby were really a vision Natalie's hand would simply move through.

Her little sister. A woman in her own right. Eight years lost between them, and she was reaching out for a ghost. But Gabby was no ghost.

"Nattie." It was out of her mouth before Gabby'd even thought it. She grabbed Natalie's hand and squeezed it. Real. Alive. Her sister. Flesh and bone and *soul*. They weren't the same women anymore, but they were still sisters. No matter what separated them.

Natalie didn't say anything, just gaped at her. Mom and Grandma were still sitting, sobbing openly and loudly. Two women she'd barely ever seen cry. The Torres family kept their *sadness* on the down low or hidden in anger, but never...

Never this.

"Say something," Gabby whispered to Natalie, desperate for something to break this tight bubble of pain inside her.

"I don't know..." Natalie sucked in a deep breath, looking up at Gabby who remained an inch or two taller. "I'm so sorr—"

Gabby shook her head and cupped Natalie's face with her hands. She would fall apart with apologies from innocent bystanders. "No, none of that."

Natalie let out a sob and her entire body leaned into Gabby. A hug. Tears over her. Gabby didn't sob, but her own tears slid down her cheeks as she held her sister back.

Real. Not a dream. Nothing but *real*. She glanced over Natalie's head at her mother and grandmother. She held an arm out to them. "Mama, Grandma." Her voice was little more than a rasp, but she used as commanding a tone as she could muster. "Come here."

It only took a second before they were on their feet, wrapping their arms around her, holding on too tightly, struggling to breathe through tears and hugs.

Gabby shook, something echoing all the way through her body so violently she couldn't fight it off. It was relief. It was fear. It was her mother's arms wrapped tight around her.

"Are you all right?" Natalie asked, clearly concerned over Gabby's shaking. "Do you need a doctor? I'll go get the nu—"

But Gabby held her close. "I'm all right, baby sister. I just can't believe it's real. You're all here."

"They…told you about… Daddy?"

Gabby swallowed, her chin coming up, and she did her best to harden her heart. She'd deal with the softer side of that grief some other time. "The Stallion made sure I knew."

"But…"

Gabby shook her head. She shouldn't have mentioned that man, that evil. She was free, and she wasn't going back to that place. "No. Not today. Maybe not ever."

"One of us needs to get it together so we can drive home," Mama said, her hand shaking as she mopped up tears. Her other hand was a death grip around Gabby's elbow. Gabby didn't even try to escape it. It was like an anchor. A truth.

"I'm all right," Natalie assured them. "I'll drive. Right now. We're free to go. We're... Let's get out of here. And go home."

"Home," Gabby echoed. What was home? She supposed she'd find out soon enough. But as they turned to leave the waiting room, someone entered, blocking the way.

Gabby's heart felt as though it stopped beating for a good moment. She barely recognized him. He'd had a haircut and a shave and today looked every inch the FBI agent in his suit and sunglasses.

She stiffened, because she wasn't ready for this, because her first instinct was to throw herself at him.

Because an angry slash of hurt wound through her. He hadn't come to check on her, and no one had told her what had happened to him.

She'd been afraid to ask. Afraid he'd be dead. Afraid he'd been a figment of her imagination. So afraid of everything outside these walls.

Now he was just *here*, looking polished and perfect. Not Jaime, but the man he'd been before the compound. A man she didn't know and...

She didn't know how to do *all* of this today, so she threw her shoulders back and greeted him coolly, no matter how big a mess she must look from all the crying.

"Ms. Torres."

Even his voice was different, as though the man she'd known in the compound simply hadn't existed. That had been a beating fear inside her for days and now it was a reality.

She could only fight it with a strength she was faking.

His gaze took her in quickly then moved to her sister. "Ms.…well, Natalie, I've got a message for you."

Gabby's grip tightened on Natalie's arm, though she didn't dare show a hint of the fear beating against her chest.

"It's from the Texas Rangers' office."

It was Natalie's turn to grip, to stiffen. Jaime held out a piece of paper and Natalie frowned at it. "They couldn't have called me? Sent an email?" she muttered.

Jaime's gaze was on Gabby and she just…had to look away.

"Agent Alessandro, would you be able to escort Gabby and my family home while I see to this?"

Gabby whipped her head to her sister, whose expression was…angry, Gabby thought. She thought she recognized that stubborn anger on her sister's face.

"I'd love to be of service," Jaime said. "But I doubt your sister…"

He was trying to beg off because of *her*? Oh, no. Hell, no. "Oh, no, please escort us, Mr. *Alessandro. I* don't have a problem with it in the least," Gabby replied, linking arms with Mama and Grandma.

He didn't get to run away anymore.

Gabby saw the uncertainty on Natalie's face, but Gabby wanted to be done. Done with law enforcement and the past eight years. "Tie up loose ends, sissy. I want this over, once and for all," she said, not bothering to even look at Jaime.

"It will be," Natalie promised before she stalked past Jaime.

When Gabby finally looked at Jaime, his eyebrows

were drawn together, some emotion shuttered in his expression. She couldn't read it. She didn't want to.

He didn't want anything to do with her now. Couldn't even stand to be in her presence? Well, she'd prove that she didn't care about him at all, no matter that it was a lie.

Driving Gabby and her mother and grandmother home was very much not on Jaime's list of things to do today. It, in fact, went against everything he was *trying* to do.

The FBI psychiatrist he'd been forced to talk to had insisted that any relationship with Gabby had been born of the situation and not actual feeling.

Jaime didn't buy it. He was too seasoned an officer, had been in too many horrible situations. He knew for a fact Gabby was just *different*.

But the problem was that Gabby wasn't a seasoned officer. She was a woman who'd been a kidnapping victim for eight years, and no matter what he felt or what he was sure of, she had a whole slew of things to work through that had nothing to do with him.

He'd only meant to relay the message from Ranger Cooper to Natalie. Not…see Gabby. With her family. The same woman he'd shared a bed with only a few days ago, before the strange world they'd been living in imploded.

She'd been crying, it was clear. He'd had to stand there, forcing himself not to take another step, for fear he would grab her away from all of them.

He glanced over at her sitting in his passenger seat. She

was in his car. *His* car. In the daylight. Real and breathing next to him.

Her eyes were on the road, her profile to him, chin raised as though the road before them was a sea of admirers she was deigning to acknowledge.

He wanted to stop the car and demand she tell him everything, forget the fact her mother and grandmother were in the back.

But those women remained a good reminder of what had knocked him out of the raging idiot who'd nearly gotten himself fired and ruined the rest of his life. Women who'd truly suffered, nearly as much as Gabby, in the loss of her.

She deserved the time and space to rebuild with her family first. He didn't have any place in that. He would drive her home and...

He had to grip the wheel tighter because if he thought about leaving her at her house and just driving away...

But he'd made his decision. He'd made the *right* choice. He would keep his distance. He would give her time to heal. If she... Well, if she eventually came to him... He had to give her the space to make the first move.

You know that's stupid.

He ground his teeth together. No matter how stupid he *thought* it was, he was trying to do the right thing for Gabby. That's what was important.

"Natalie tells us you were undercover with the evil man?" Gabby's grandmother asked from the back seat.

"Yes." He turned onto the street Gabby's mother had named when they'd started. He didn't realize he'd slowed down to almost a crawl until someone honked from behind.

"It's the blue one on the corner," the grandmother supplied.

Jaime nodded and hit the accelerator. No matter that he didn't want to let Gabby out of the car, it was his duty. More, it was what she needed. Her family. Her life.

It would be a difficult transition for her, and he didn't need to make that any more complicated for her. It was the right thing to do.

No matter how completely wrong it felt.

He pulled his car into the driveway of a small, squat, one-story home. It looked well kept, if a little sagging around the edges.

Gabby blinked at it and it took every last ounce of control he had not to reach over and brush his mouth across the soft curve of her cheek. Not to touch her and comfort her.

She looked young and lost, and he wanted to protect her from all that swamp of emotion she'd be struggling with.

"I got written up," he blurted into the silence of the car.

What the hell are you doing?

He didn't know. He needed to stop.

"You..." Gabby blinked at him, cocking her head.

"I think they gave me a little leeway what with just being out of undercover and all, but they don't take kindly to ignoring orders."

Shut your mouth and let her go, idiot.

"You...ignored orders," she repeated, as though she didn't quite believe it.

"They told me not to come to the hospital. Or try to see you. I may have..." He cleared his throat and turned his attention to the house in front of them. "I may have caused a bit of a scene."

"He got kicked out by security guards that first morning you were in the hospital," Grandma offered from the back. "A little rougher around the edges that day."

Jaime flicked a silencing glance in the rearview at the grandma. She smiled sweetly. "Natalie said you must have spent some time together when you were both in that place. Did you take care of our Gabriella?"

Gabby stiffened.

"I tried," Jaime said, perhaps a little too much of his still simmering irritation bleeding through. *If* she had come with him, she wouldn't have been in that standoff with Alyssa. They would have had... They could have...

"Mama, Grandma, will you...give me a few minutes alone with Agent Alessandro?" Gabby asked, her voice soft if commanding.

"Gabriella..." Her mother reached over the seat and put a hand to Gabby's shoulder.

"Gabby, please. Only Gabby from now on," Gabby whispered, eyes wide and haunted and not looking back at her mother.

"Come inside, baby. We'll—"

"I just need a few minutes alone. I promise. Only a few." She looked back at her mother and offered a smile.

But he was supposed to be giving her space. Not... alone time. "You should go—"

Gabby sent him a glare that would have silenced pretty much anyone, Jaime was pretty sure.

"Come now, Rosa," the grandmother said, patting the mother's arm. "Let's let these two talk. We'll go make some tea for our Gabri—Gabby."

Gabby's mother brushed a hand over Gabby's hair, but reluctantly agreed. The two women slid out of the back of his car and walked up to the house with a few nervous glances back.

Gabby's gaze followed them, an unaccountable hurt languishing in her dark brown eyes. He kept his hands on the wheel so he wouldn't be tempted to touch her.

"So…" Jaime said when Gabby just stared at him for long, ticking seconds. "How are you feeling?"

She didn't answer, just kept staring at him with that hauntingly unreadable gaze.

"Well, I, uh, have things to do," he forced himself to say, wrenching his gaze from searching her face for signs of things that were none of his business.

"Take off your sunglasses," she said in return.

"Gabby—"

She reached over and yanked them off his face with absolutely no finesse. "Hey!"

"You look different," she stated matter-of-factly.

"A haircut and a shave will do that to a man," he returned, still not meeting her shrewd gaze. He had a mission. A job. A duty. Not for him, but for her. For *her*.

"You look *scared*."

"Scared?" he scoffed, despite the overhard beating of his heart. "I hardly think—"

"Then look at me."

Scared? No. He wasn't scared. He was strong and capable of doing his duty. He was a reliable and excellent FBI agent. He could face down a man with guns and evil, he could certainly face a woman—

Aw, hell, the second he looked at her he had to touch. He had to pull her into his arms despite the console between them. He had to fit his mouth to hers and *feel* as much as know she was there, she was alive, she was safe.

He brushed his hands over her hair, her cheeks, her arms, assuring himself she was real. Her fingers traced his clean-shaved jaw, over the bristled ends of his hair, as she kissed him back with a sweetness and fervency he wasn't supposed to allow.

"I'm not supposed to be doing this," he murmured against her lips, managing to take his mouth from hers only to find his lips trailing down her neck.

"Why not?" she asked breathlessly, her hands smoothing across his back.

"Space and…healing stuff."

"I don't want space. And if I'm going to go through all the shit of healing, I at least want you."

He focused on the edge of the console currently digging into his thigh, because if he focused on that instead of kissing her in daylight, real and free, he might survive.

He managed to find her shoulders, pull her back enough that her hands rested on his forearms.

Flushed and tumbled. From him.

"I'm supposed to give you space," he said firmly, a reminder to himself far more than a response to her.

"I don't want it," she said, her fingers curling around his arms. "And I think I deserve what I want for a bit."

She deserved *everything*. But he wanted to make sure giving it to her was…right. Safe. "I've had to see a psychiatrist, and there's some…mandatory psychological things I'll have to do before I'm reinstated to active duty. I'm sure the doctor suggested the same thing to you."

"Therapy, yes."

"There's a chance…" He cleared his throat and smoothed his hands down her arms, eventually taking her hands in his.

That wasn't fair because how did he say anything he needed to when he was touching her? "You shouldn't feel *obligated* to continue what happened in there. You should have the space to find out if it's what you really want."

She cocked her head, some mix of irritation and uncertainty in the move. "Do *you* feel obligated by what happened?" she asked.

"No, but—"

"Then shut up." Then her mouth was on his again, hot and maybe a little wild. But it didn't matter, did it?

He didn't want it to matter. He wanted her. This strong, resilient woman.

She pulled back a little, always his warrior, facing whatever hard things were in her way. "I want you. The Jaime I met in there. And I want to get to know this you," she said, running her finger down the lapel of his suit. "The thing is, awful things happened in there, but it was eight years of my life. I can't…erase it. It's there. Forever. An indelible part of me. I don't need to pretend it never existed to heal. I don't think that's *how* you heal."

"But I have this whole life to go back to, Gabby. I know you aren't starting over, but people knew I was coming back. I'm coming back to a job. It isn't the same space we're in. I don't want you to feel as though you need to make space for me. That…you need to love me or any of it."

She studied him for the longest time, and the marvelous thing about Gabby was that she thought about things. Thought them through, and gave everything the kind of weight it deserved.

Who was he to tell her she needed space? Who was he to tell her much of anything?

"I will tell you when I need space. You'll tell me when you need some. It's not complicated." She traced a fingertip along his hairline, as though studying this new facet to him. Eventually her eyes met his.

"And I do love you," she said quietly, weighted. "If that changes, I'd hardly feel obligated to keep giving you something I didn't have."

"Such a pragmatist," he managed to say, his voice rusty in the face of her confession. "I was trying to be very noble, you know."

Her mouth curved and he wondered how many things he would file away in his memories as *first in daylight*. The first time he'd kissed her with the sun shining into the car. The first smile under a blue sky.

He wanted them to outnumber his memories of a cramped room more than he wanted his next breath.

"I don't want noble. I want Jaime." She swallowed. "That is, as long as you want me."

"I practically lost my life's work for wanting you, and I'd do it a million times over, if that's what you wanted. I'd give up anything. I'd fight anything. I hope you know, I'd do *anything*."

She rubbed her hands up and down his cheeks as if to make sure he was real, and hers, though he undoubtedly was. Always.

"Come inside. I want to tell my mother and grandmother about the man who saved me."

"I didn't—"

"You did. I'd stopped counting the days. I'd stopped hoping. You came in and gave me both."

His chest ached, a warm bloom of emotion. Touched that anything he'd done had mattered. Moved beyond measure. "We saved each other." Because he'd been falling, losing all those pieces of himself, and she'd brought it all back.

"A mutual saving. I like that." She smiled that beautiful sun-drenched smile and then she got out of his car, and so did he. They walked up the path to her home with a bright blue sky above them, free and ready for a future.

Together.

* * * * *